THE DEAD FLORENTINES

THE DEAD FLORENTINES

Andrew Serra

ISBN 978-1-300-19555-9

Library of Congress cataloging-in-publication data available.

This is a work of fiction. All of the characters and events in this book are either products of the author's imagination or are used fictitiously. Any resemblance to actual persons or events, living or dead, is purely coincidental.

From the banks of the Arno, to Richmond Terrace,
throughout the ages, boys have idolized their fathers.
This book is dedicated to mine.

Acknowledgments

Great effort was taken to give the reader an authentic feel of sixteenth-century Florence. The book remains, however, a work of fiction. The depictions of historical figures contained herein are literary creations. Of the many writers who profoundly influenced my preparation of this book, I am particularly indebted to Edgcumbe Staley, whose monumental *The Guilds of Florence* was both informative and a pleasure to read. I also owe my gratitude to Dante Alighieri, who made me long to use our greatest medium, language, to chronicle the human condition; and to the dedicated professors of the Department of Romance Languages at Hunter College for introducing me to the wondrous beauty of Italian literature.

Last but not least, I would like to thank my greatest inspiration of all, my wife Teresa. From her reading and rereading early drafts, to her organizational talents in making the book a reality, her support has been indispensable. This book would not exist without her.

A.S.

Table of Contents

Prologus

The tall windows of the corridor magnified the bright summer sun. Throngs of visitors crowded the long hall. Each cluster of statues caused a logjam of people as tourists snapped photos and read captions from guidebooks. La Galleria degli Uffizi, the Uffizi Gallery, is Florence's most renowned museum, and a hot summer day makes for long lines. In the "Michelangelo and the Florentines" room, swarmed by visitors, a tall thin woman stood holding a three-foot-long wooden stick with a small orange flag tied to the end. She held the flag up above her head with her right hand. Her left hand slung a backpack over her shoulder. She wiped the sweat from her forehead with the back of her right hand, causing the flag to dip and knock the head of a man staring at a painting. The woman was young, in her midtwenties maybe, and pretty. Her hair was brown and curly. She wore it pulled back tight in a ponytail. She herded the people around her to a portrait hanging on the wall. When a sufficient number were crowded around, she spoke in German, slowly and with a French accent.

"Und hier, meine Damen und Herren, we see a work from one of the lesser-known Florentine artists of the sixteenth century, Francesco Granacci. Granacci trained with Michelangelo at the studio of Domenico Ghirlandaio and even helped Michelangelo with the Sistine Chapel." She struggled with her German. The crowd of people around her seemed more interested in moving on to Michelangelo's paintings than hearing about Granacci, so she quickly summed up the work.

"This here is a portrait Granacci was commissioned to paint for the Giotti family. The Giottis were a very rich and powerful family here in Florence in the mid to late fifteen hundreds. In this portrait we see a young Jacopo Giotti and his wife..."

LIBER PRIMUS

Pater noster

I

The sun peaked high above the Arno. The river was full from the recent rains and flowed hurriedly toward the bridge. The choppy water squeezed past the piers as if pausing to browse at the shops and vendors that had sprung up on the Ponte Vecchio, the old bridge. Once past the crossing, the river mellowed, though still ran with purpose. The water brought a breeze with it, giving a country scent to the dank city air.

Lorenzo sat on a rock and peacefully set pawns, rooks, and knights on the chessboard that lay at his feet. He removed the kings and queens from his satchel. He paused to replace the head of the dark king from its severed torso. A nail had been driven straight down into the glossy wood shaft, and Lorenzo guided the nail into the worn hole of the head's underside. He admired the result of his efforts and was thankful for the king's misfortunes. Had its previous owner not slammed it down in a fit of rage (after losing to his wife), the chess set would never have found its way to Lorenzo.

Simone Simoni, Lorenzo's father, worked for one of the oldest and wealthiest families in Florence, the Chilli family. Domenico Chilli had received the chess set from a wool dealer with contacts in the Turkish Empire, and soon fancied himself a master of the game. Unbeknown to Domenico, his wife, Adélaïde, became quite adept herself, never missing an opportunity to polish her skills against one of the servants, including Simone. One afternoon, during supper, Domenico and his younger brother, Francesco, were discussing chess strategy when Adélaïde (never one to keep quiet) corrected the two on some minor defense axiom. When Domenico asked what a woman would know about chess, Adélaïde issued a challenge. Though Adélaïde was hardly the quiet, obedient housewife, such an affront to her husband would not normally have been tolerated at a formal supper table. But since only his brother was dining with the family that day, Domenico paid little mind to the breach of etiquette and had a servant set up the board, eager to teach his wife a lesson.

The match went well into the night, with the children, the servants, and Francesco watching every move with nervous excitement. Adélaïde was aggressive and brilliant, showing a sharpness of mind that she had spent her adolescence acquiring and her adulthood underutilizing. Domenico was calculating and wise, for though he could be boorish at times, he was no fool. As the fire roared in the large dining hall and the candles fluttered with the winter wind that eased past the icy windowpanes, Adélaïde stared contemplatively at a seemingly hopeless situation. Just as she was about to waste a move to bide time, she noticed an opening that Domenico had failed to anticipate. She hurriedly picked up a bishop (of all pieces) and conquered Domenico's king. Domenico grabbed the king from her hand, smashed it down, and vowed to never play chess again. The next day he told Simone to get rid of the chess set.

Lorenzo set the king down and sat back, closing his eyes. The warm sun felt good on his face. He was small for his age. His fourteenth birthday was a month away. His days were fairly routine. He would wake with his father just before sunrise. (Lorenzo's mother had died during childbirth ten years earlier.) He would walk with his father to the gate of the Palazzo Chilli, then continue through the Piazza del Duomo and toward a little bakery behind Santa Maria del Fiore hoping to find work for the morning. If a delivery boy failed to show or if there were a lot of deliveries on a particular day, Lorenzo was allowed to help carry wide wheels of *pane toscano* to the wealthy houses in the city. His payment for a morning's work: a small (usually stale) loaf of bread. If his services were not needed, no loaf of bread. If the weather were nice, he would meet his father down on the bank of the river for the midday supper; otherwise, his father would return home to eat. After supper he might pick up an odd job at one of the little shops near their home, usually receiving some household ware or food as barter. Then he would return to their small apartment on the Via del Corso and wait for Simone to return.

He heard footsteps and opened his eyes without sitting up. The sun's glare blinded him, and he saw the upside-down silhouette of a man eclipsing his field of view from overhead.

"Is that a challenge I see?" Simone's voice was low and gruff and would have been intimidating had it not so often carried words of kindness.

"It's all ready, Papà!" Lorenzo stuck his legs straight out and raised them, then rocked forward to assist himself in recovering from his lounging position.

"I see. It'll have to be a quick one; I need to leave for Fiesole before too late."

"You're going to Fiesole today?"

"Yes, some urgent matter for Domenico." Simone patted the leather bag slung over his shoulder.

"Did he give you a horse?" Lorenzo muttered apprehensively, calculating the chances of his father making it home before dark.

"He's hunting wild boar in the morning with Francesco and the two boys; he said he wants all of the horses fresh for the hunt. Besides, a little stroll never hurt anyone."

"I have some bread." Lorenzo nodded his head in the direction of his satchel.

"It'll go nicely with this." Simone held up a small pot with a loop handle spanning the top and tilted it toward Lorenzo, showing the vegetable stew to the boy. Stew was to be the first course for the supper at the Chilli palace that day. The chef, as always, put a small pot aside for Simone. There was a never-ending network of favors among the household servants, each having something to offer the others. Simone saw to it that some of the wool cuttings and scraps from the storehouse found their way to the chef, whose wife had become quite skilled at stitching uneven patches of wool together as clothing for their children.

Simone sat beside Lorenzo and placed the pot between them. Lorenzo removed the bread from his satchel, tore off a piece, and handed the loaf to his father. The two took turns dipping hunks of bread in the stew and ate quietly for some minutes, Lorenzo staring peacefully out at the passing waters, Simone watching his son eat with a deep sense of love. After the death of his wife and newborn infant daughter, Simone had focused all of his attention, all of his love, all of his life on Lorenzo. It was Simone's dream to procure a good apprenticeship for Lorenzo. All economic activity in Florence was controlled by the guilds; each profession had its own. The only way to become a member was to be the son of a member or be apprenticed to a master of the guild. An apprentice worked and lived with the master for up to eight years. He then owed the master a fixed amount of time as an employee, before being accepted in the guild as a master himself. He was then guaranteed economic security and an active role in city life. A good apprenticeship was the ticket to a better life, and today was no ordinary day. Today was the day Simone had arranged what would be, for Lorenzo, the chance of a lifetime: an apprenticeship with a master of the Calimala guild.

Lorenzo was older than most new apprentices would have been, for two reasons. First, the procurement of this coveted apprenticeship was no easy task; it had required some maneuvering on Simone's part. Second, Simone was in no rush to see Lorenzo off. An apprentice would live with his master and work long hours. Simone just couldn't bear to let go of his son. He couldn't imagine not waking with his boy in the morning, not playing chess by the river, not coming home to a fire in the stove and an apple sliced up on the table waiting for him—along with a thousand questions about anything the boy could dream to be curious about. But now the time had come; if Lorenzo were to learn the Calimala, or foreign wool trade, he would have to start now.

Simone ripped off another chunk of the unsalted Tuscan bread. He tore the perfect mix of crust and center to form a scoop for the stew. He shoveled up stew and brought it slowly to his mouth, taking in the aroma of the Certaldo onions coated in olive oil, which gave off a sweet scent that would soon be oddly enhanced by the salty taste of the stew's juices. The stew was no longer hot and slid down easily to Simone's hungry stomach. He had a large frame and would have been a hulking figure if he had eaten as much as his appetite called for. But he always saw to it that Lorenzo had enough to eat first before devouring whatever was left. As he put another piece of bread into his mouth and chewed, he dipped his chin into the bend of his arm and wiped his dark, scruffy beard on his sleeve. He stifled a belch, turned toward Lorenzo, and placed his large hand on the boy's back and rubbed affectionately.

"I spoke with Coraggiosi!"

"What did he say?" Lorenzo didn't have to ask the subject of the conversation. Everybody knew that Giovanni Coraggiosi was taking on another apprentice, and everybody knew that that apprentice would be Jacopo Giotti, son of Lodovico Giotti. Lorenzo knew that his father wanted to see him apprenticed; Simone had always spoken about it. But the father of new apprentices was expected to pay the master for taking on his son, and Lorenzo could not imagine how his father would pay such a fee. Still, Simone was well liked by all and might have managed to borrow the fee through some kind of favor. Lorenzo was nervous. He knew an apprenticeship like this was a golden opportunity, but he dreaded leaving his father's house as much as Simone dreaded him leaving.

"You," Simone's eyes lit up with the excitement of delivering the news, "are to be his new apprentice!"

"But what about Jacopo Giotti?" Lorenzo was incredulous.

"Beh, Coraggiosi never did like Lodovico much...Besides, he was eager to take our offer instead."

"But what did *we* offer?"

"This little beauty!" Simone reached into a small pouch tied to the underside of his belt, which had been tucked into his pants. He pulled out a coin slightly larger than the end of his thumb, mostly round, and held it up for Lorenzo to see. It was gold and featured what looked like a king or emperor being crown by Christ. There was strange writing around the edge.

Lorenzo took the coin and laid it flat in the palm of his hand, gently touching the surface with the tip of his index finger. "What is it?"

"A bezant."

"What is that? What is this writing?"

"It's money from Constantinople before it fell to the Turks!" Simone was excited to show off his prize and to finally tell his son the story that went along with it, a story he had avoided telling him until now. "That's Greek written around the edges."

"How much is it worth?"

"Not sure really, but I think they're pretty rare nowadays...Coraggiosi took one look at it and offered to waive the first two years' fees for your apprenticeship. And from what I hear, Giotti offered him twenty florins a year to take Jacopo!"

"Woooh, but what will we do after two years? We don't have twenty florins to pay." Lorenzo was still mesmerized by the coin in his hand; he had never held gold before. He spoke to his father without looking up.

"You let me worry about that...Besides, Coraggiosi is in love with that coin; he may even give us a better deal yet." The sureness of Simone's words hid the fear in his heart that he would not be able to pay for the apprenticeship in two years. He tried not to think about it. He could rent out the apartment on Via del Corso and ask Domenico if he could sleep in the servants' quarters at the Palazzo Chilli. He had avoided doing this until now because he wanted to give his son a home of his own.

However, the rental income the apartment would earn would be very little. It wasn't an apartment so much as it was shed, attached to a larger storehouse, with a door that opened to a small alley just a few steps off the via itself. The room had been fitted with a small woodburning stove. There was a round wooden table in one corner, engraved with a beautiful design of flowers, and the elegance of the piece was out of place in the austere surroundings of the room. Adélaïde had given it to Simone after she had convinced her husband to redecorate one of the parlor rooms at the palace. There was only one chair. The three others had been broken up for firewood on different occasions over the years, when firewood was hard to come by. They were lucky to not have needed to burn the fourth chair that past winter. There was one mattress in a corner on which both Simone and Lorenzo slept. In the other corner was a bucket, which the two used to relieve themselves.

The shed had been the dowry given to Simone by his father-in-law upon his marriage to Lorenzo's mother. Though not very valuable, Simone had held on to the small apartment, and that made him a property owner, which was important. Only a property owner or the heir of a property owner could be apprenticed to a guild. Domenico paid his servants meager wages because room and board were considered part of the salary. Since Simone refused room and board, his salary had been begrudgingly raised, but not nearly high enough. If it had not been for Lorenzo's odd jobs and the secret deals with the chef at the palace, the two would have gone hungry more often than not. But now Lorenzo would be given room and board with the Coraggiosi family. Simone could live at the Chilli palace and perhaps earn some rent on the apartment.

"Why does he love it so much?" Lorenzo raised his gaze from the coin and looked his father in the eye.

"It's not so much the coin, though she is a beauty, as where it comes from. That's why he loves it!"

"Where does it come from?"

Simone swallowed his saliva and spoke deliberately. "It was given to me by Lorenzo de' Medici."

Lorenzo's eyes lit up, excited by the novelty of his own father having such a brush with fame. "You knew Lorenzo the Magnificent?"

"Lo conoscevo il Magnifico! I knew him!"

"When?" Lorenzo could not believe what he was hearing. Lorenzo de' Medici was the closest thing to royalty the Florentine Republic had ever known. Though there was no king of Tuscany, the Medici family had used its banking empire to gather more and more power over the years. Lorenzo de' Medici's grandfather, Cosimo, had become so powerful that he was recognized as the de facto head of state. By the time Lorenzo "the Magnificent" ascended to unofficial leader of the republic, the family was renowned throughout Europe as the keepers of the Florentine court. Lorenzo himself famously championed the arts, surrounding himself with poets and scholars, and had even given rise to a young Michelangelo. He was often seen walking the streets of Florence like any other citizen, and while he always had some political enemies among the old families and in the Signoria, he remained very popular with the people. His reign was the golden age of the Florentine Republic.

Simone had told Lorenzo about Lorenzo de' Medici many times, always when they were alone. The people of Florence remembered him well, of course, and he was always spoken of highly behind closed doors, but few praised any of the Medicis in public by the time Simone and Lorenzo were seated on the banks of the Arno. Lorenzo il Magnifico's arrogant son Piero had been forced to flee the city, and the fire-breathing Dominican friar Girolamo Savonarola had made it his life's mission to cast down the indulgent pleasures of this world (culminating in the famous Bonfire of the Vanities in the Piazza della Signoria, where countless books and works of art were burned). In sermon after sermon, Savonarola condemned everything Lorenzo's reign had stood for. Savonarola's fame was short-lived, however, and he himself was burned in the Piazza della Signoria after the friar irritated the pope with his criticism of corruption in the Church.

The Medici family was still in exile, and the Signoria ruled through a *gonfaloniere*, an appointed leader. Many enemies of the Medicis were in high places and suspicious of plots to return the Medicis to power. To avoid trouble, many people, including Lorenzo, simply avoided speaking about anything to do with the Medicis in public. For this reason Simone had never spoken of the coin or its origins to his son. He could not risk the innocent bragging of a child being construed as evidence of Simone's plotting with the Medicis.

"I saw him twice, once in the duomo…once at the Palazzo Chilli." Simone took the coin back from his son and held it with two hands, looking down at it while he spoke. "I was fourteen years old and had only been working for the Chillis a short time, Domenico's father, Francesco Senior, hired me. I used to deliver bread to the palace. Then one day Francesco asked me if I wanted a job at the palace. 'Doing what?' I asked. 'Little bit of everything,' he said. And that's why I never really had one steady job at the palace. Sometimes I take care of horses, sometimes I help dye wool, sometimes I deliver messages.

"Anyway…so one day Francesco asks me to go to a mass at the duomo with the family the next morning, not really sure why. Maybe he knew there might be trouble, but Domenico's a couple years older than me and could've handled it, but off to the duomo I went with them. We sat all the way up front with the other important families. I looked down the whole time, ashamed of my clothes and not wanting to be noticed by anyone. While I was looking down, I suddenly saw a hand with a knife in it reach between me and Domenico, real low so no one would notice it, but since I was looking down I saw the whole thing happen…real fast. The hand reached forward and stabbed the man in front of me. Then it pulled back and went to stab again. Without thinking, I grabbed the hand and pushed it straight up in the air. The man in front had yelled out already. Domenico turned and saw me pushing the hand up, and he grabbed the knife. A bunch of others around us grabbed the attacker, while Francesco Senior, Domenico, and a dozen others carried the stabbed man away. It was Lorenzo il Magnifico. He was hurt, but he lived. At the same time, Lorenzo's brother Giulio…not Giulio…wait…no, Giulio's father, Giuliano, was Lorenzo's brother…Sì, Giuliano was stabbed to death outside. It was the work of the Pazzi family; they tried to wipe out the Medicis that day. The people were so outraged that they threw the Pazzis out of the windows of the Palazzo della Signoria."

"Is that why we're not supposed to talk about the Pazzis anymore?"

"Who told you that?"

"You did, Papà, when we went to the fair at Santa Croce and Don Luciano said that the same man who built the dome at the duomo built the one at the Pazzi Chapel…and I asked who the Pazzi were and he didn't say anything and you told me not to ask about it."

"Sì, sì, now I remember…How do you remember these things?" Simone smiled at his boy, paused, and then resumed his story. "So one day, sometime later, while I was working alone at the palace in the big storehouse behind the courtyard, unloading rolls of wool from a cart, in walked Lorenzo de' Medici himself, alone...wanting to talk to me. He had come to see Francesco Senior and to thank him and Domenico. Then he asked them who I was, and when they told him, he asked to see me. I found out later, from the maid Antonella, that Francesco was going to have me sent for, but Lorenzo insisted on coming to find me! Can you imagine that...a Medici coming to me! He was taller than me, but then again I was shorter than I am now. He had perfect black hair down to his shoulders. He had a big hooked nose and a square jaw, but somehow he was handsome. His shoulders were broad, and he wore this cloak that was the brightest red I have ever seen in my life. But that was the only fancy thing I saw, no jewelry or anything like that. When he spoke to me, he addressed me as he would've addressed a visiting duke."

As always, Simone tried to educate his son while telling him a story. "Remember that...*he* addressed *me* like a duke! You don't need to knock others down to raise yourself up! He told me that he knew what I had done that day, and he wanted to thank me. He gave me the coin and said it was called a bezant and that his grandfather had given him a bunch when he was small, right after the Turks conquered Constantinople. He said this was the last one he had left, and he wanted me to have it. He could have just given me florins...not sure really why he gave me this instead! I've often thought about that. I think it's because I was young and he thought I might waste florins, whereas this I would keep, as I did. Or maybe I reminded him of himself when he was my age—though I don't see how—and he wanted to give me a piece of his childhood.

"Anyway, this is what he gave me, and I kept it all these years, had it buried in the dirt under the stove. I dug it up yesterday morning while you went out to dump the bucket. I wanted to show it to you now, because I was supposed to give it to Coraggiosi this afternoon. But I just saw Coraggiosi on my way here, and he was on his way out of the city. He said he just heard that part of the roof collapsed on his country villa, from all the rain. He said he had to go check on it. Even though I wanted to show it to you, I kind of wanted to give it to him today because I hate walking around with it, afraid I'll lose it. But he wouldn't take it today anyway; he said he was on his way out, and he didn't want to carry it through the country because he might be back after dark and the brigands on the road have been robbing travelers after dark again."

Lorenzo was awestruck. He had grown up idolizing his father. Simone's strength and jovial nature had made every day of Lorenzo's childhood seem like a fairy tale, where at the end of the day the hero makes it all better. But in adolescence the world becomes a smaller place, and fathers fall from god to human. Seeing his father scrubbing chamber pots or being yelled at by Domenico had, in Lorenzo's mind, leveled the relationship. Teenagers know all, and Lorenzo was no exception. At times he saw Simone as a friend more than a parent.

Simone, for his part, sensed this and did not discourage it. He was far too kindhearted to exert a possessive form of dominance over his child. He was also intelligent enough to allow the boy a certain sense of independence while still quietly protecting and nurturing him. Lorenzo had always loved his father, who was in every way the world to him. No matter how quickly he tried to grow up, he could never imagine a night not spent sitting next to the stove talking to his papà, which is why the thought of living with the Coraggiosis made him sad. But after hearing his father's story, all thoughts of growing up or of becoming an apprentice escaped him, and he was once again the little boy who idolized his father, the savior of il Magnifico.

"You going to make the first move?" Simone motioned toward the chess set at their feet.

Lorenzo didn't answer. His eyes welled up. He did not want to cry; he did not want to be a child. He didn't even know why he was crying. Was it happiness? Certainly he was happy to have a chance at joining the Calimala guild. Was it sadness? He didn't want to leave his father. Was it pride? Here was this amazing feat that his humble father had kept hidden all of these years. It was all of these things and something more. Everything would be different now. In an instant, all that had happened in the last thirteen years and eleven months had come crashing down over him like an unexpected rain. His heart suddenly ached to do something that he had not done in years, hug his father. He needed to feel his father's all-encompassing embrace one more time. In that instant he felt so incredibly lucky to have been raised by Simone that he thought his heart would burst. He also felt a profound sense of sadness at the same time, sadness for Simone and the way his life had turned out. Lorenzo could barely remember his mother, but he knew Simone still missed her desperately. He also knew that although Simone never complained about his job, it could be demeaning at times. His father deserved so much more. Tears ran down his cheeks, and still he said nothing.

Perhaps Simone read the boy's mind, or perhaps he acted on his own feelings, but he leaned over, wrapped his long arms around Lorenzo, and pulled him into his chest. Now it was Simone's turn to get teary eyed. A new stage of life was upon them; his son was growing up, moving on. He had done the best he could for his son. He had hid that gold coin all of these years. Had Lorenzo de' Medici lived, he might have asked the magnanimous ruler to help his son, a possibility he had thought of years ago when he named the boy Lorenzo, but alas, il Magnifico had died young and the gold bezant would be his benefaction from the grave.

As Simone held his son in his arms, the world was right. For one small moment there was perfection.

* *

From mid-span of the Ponte Vecchio, a dark, squat man shielded his eyes from the glare of the sun with a hand and squinted as he scanned the banks of the river. The bridge was crowded, and it was hard to stand in one place for long without being jostled around by the crowd.

"Son essi—it's them," he muttered to himself, stressing the *s* sound hard in his native Neapolitan style. He had spotted who he was looking for. He set off quickly to reach his target.

Throngs of people, from poor families with livestock in tow to rich men accompanied by a household retinue, jammed the bridge, which was lined with butcher shops, vegetable stands, and even a blacksmith shop. On any given day, most households in Florence needed something from the shops on the bridge, so it was always crowded. The traffic of shoppers had become so great that there was even talk among the Signoria of moving the butchers and grocers to a more open area and giving the shops on the bridge to clockmakers or jewelers. But there is always a great deal of politics that goes along with a plan of that sort, so few thought it would ever really happen.

The vendors would normally have been closed for midday break by now, but the crowd was so large they kept selling. People had let their stores of supplies dwindle during the rainstorms, and now it seemed all of Florence was out at the same time to stock up. The dark, squat man pushed his way through the crowd, frustratingly slowly. He mumbled curses in Neapolitan dialect, a dialect so rich in its description of the obscene that one could think *il dialetto* evolved solely for the purpose of turning mothers into whores.

* *

Lorenzo replaced the chess pieces in his satchel. One by one he picked each piece from the straight-line battle formation, two opposing armies standing down from a battle that was not to be. He had watched his father climb up the riverbank, cross the Lungarno, and disappear up a small street heading north toward Fiesole.

With so many out shopping on the bridge, Lorenzo thought, maybe he could find somebody who needed help carrying a purchase home; maybe he could earn a piece of fruit or some more bread. He would love to have an apple sliced up waiting for his father when he returned later that evening. Or maybe he could sneak under the gate adjacent their doorway in the alley and take a cup of wine from the jug that the workmen sometimes left in the yard. He was always careful to take only one cup so no one would notice. Then he would add the wine, some water, a pinch of the spice that Simone had managed to barter for (Lorenzo didn't know what it was called, but it went well with apples), and the apple peels and core to their one pot and heat it on top of the stove. His father would love a warm cup of cider after the long walk back and forth to Fiesole.

With his satchel slung over his shoulder Lorenzo headed down the Lungarno toward the old bridge. He was a few hundred steps away from the bridge but could see the throng of people at the foot trying to gain access. With an overhand motion, a short arm cloaked in a black sleeve parted the last few people as a swimmer parts the water ahead. Twisting out of the crowd was a short-statured man with a dark, Mediterranean complexion. He wore an angered expression that highlighted the fact that his eyebrows and hairline almost touched across his low forehead. He looked to be in his early thirties. As he approached Lorenzo, almost at a running pace, Lorenzo noticed that one sleeve of his cloak had remained rolled up his arm from the wade through the crowd. His forearm was muscular and hairy.

Lorenzo looked back over his shoulder to see if there was anyone behind him. Realizing there wasn't, and that the crazed man was running toward him, his heart sank. He would have liked to run toward a crowd, toward the bridge, but that would have only closed the distance between the man and himself. Thinking he could probably not outrun the man, especially carrying the somewhat bulky satchel (which he did not wish to leave behind), he made a quick decision to turn up a small alley and run toward the old city center, hoping a few tight turns might lose the man.

The alley was narrow and unpaved, and Lorenzo knew immediately that he had made a mistake. He made a right turn and saw that there was a dead end ahead. He frantically banged on a door and yelled up to a window that had its shutters open above him.

In an instant he felt himself entombed by hard, powerful arms. He squirmed and cried out for help. A hand quickly covered his mouth, and from behind he heard a forceful Neapolitan whisper: "Stai zitto! Shut up!"

II

Lucio was an ugly man, in both physical appearance and character, *bruttissimo*. He spoke the Bolognese dialect and made little effort to learn the Tuscan. He had hovered on the outskirts of the city for as long as anybody could remember. Nobody knew why he had left Bologna, but it wasn't hard to imagine him being hated enough to be in fear for his life, and no one knew his family name. He walked hunched over as if his body was physically manifesting a desire to repel human contact. If he hadn't been short to begin with, a lifetime of hunching had diminished his height permanently. His hair was thin, stringy, and gray. His nose hooked down like the beak of a bird, and his skin was blotchy and yellow. He rarely looked anyone directly in the eye, so it would be tough to say what color his eyes were. He had a cart that he pulled himself, and survived as would a scavenger in the wild, having a knack for profiting from others' misfortunes.

This was a time of relative peace in Tuscany, but the country roads (especially at night) were never entirely safe for travelers. There were still bands of brigands in the woods that harassed passersby. Instances were rare enough, however, that public outcry was far below what would have been needed for the Florentines to organize and hunt down these brigands. Besides, the decision makers of the city, the very wealthy, always traveled with a bodyguard. Of course, for a coin or two, Lucio would direct a traveler around the brigands (or toward them, as some suspected him of doing). Lucio himself would probably have been long dead if he were not useful on occasion to some local schemer.

The hour was late. The door to the Convent of San Marco was back away from the street, and little if any light reached the high arch and heavy timber doors. The bell tower loomed high over the courtyard, and light from the moon shone through the open windows of the bell chamber. The church itself was quiet and dark. Lucio approached the convent door with his cart in tow, raised the heavy iron ring of the knocker, and slammed it down three times. He waited. A small hatch opened in the center of the door.

A young quivering, voice rang out of the hatch. "Who calls at this hour?"

"Sono Lucio."

"Lucio…do you know what time it is?" The voice feigned annoyance but did little to conceal the fear the speaker had of Lucio. "What've you got there?"

"Un morto fiorentino—a dead Florentine!"

Immediately, slide bolts clicked open and key locks spun. The timber door creaked back, and a young friar, wrapped in a hastily tied brown robe, appeared at the crack in the door holding a candle. He stepped forward to see the cart and made out the human form underneath a blanket. He stepped back and motioned for Lucio to come inside. Lucio raised the handles of the cart and pulled it through the open portal. The young friar backed into the doorway, looked left, then right, then stepped back and closed the door.

The room was empty except for a small table with two large candles against a wall. Lucio stood next to his cart. The candlelight flickered behind him, and he stared at the large fresco that filled the back wall. The Virgin Mary knelt on a small wooden stool in a vaulted, columned room as the archangel Gabriel announced that she would be the mother of God. The archangel was young and effeminate with a golden halo and large wings. The expression on Mary's face was a mixture of serene acceptance and shock. The archangel folded his arms over his stomach and looked down. The corner of his mouth was curled up slightly, as if a disarming smirk had just been rendered. His eyes seemed to hide sadness.

The fresco had been painted some seventy years before by a friar at the convent named Fra Giovanni, who was now known as Fra

Angelico. Lucio was fixed on the archangel's eyes. Why were they sad? Was it sadness for the knowledge of the pain that Mary would experience on seeing her son crucified? Perhaps that was what the artist intended, but it was not what Lucio imagined the archangel to be ruing. Lucio thought of all that accompanied the coming of Christ, namely the hypocrisy that flourished in His name.

Lucio found the bodies of travelers on the country road and carted them back to town. He delivered them to the convent and was given a coin or two by the abbot. For this, he was reviled by all as a vulture. The abbot, on the other hand, would find out the identity of the body, notify the family involved, and then inform them of all the "donations" involved with a proper Christian burial. And for this the abbot was thanked for saving the immortal soul of the dead man. Surely the archangel Gabriel was aware of the hypocrisy he was "annunciating," and for this his eyes were sad.

The abbot entered the room accompanied by the young friar. He approached the cart, pulled up the blanket, and examined the body. As he pulled the blanket back farther, the arms of the corpse flopped out of the cart. The legs were already hanging out the back, as the frame of the man was large. The abbot noticed that the body had been stripped of anything of value. The shoes and belt were missing, there was no cloak, and there were no pockets or pouches attached to the pants or in the blouse.

"Clearly this is the work of brigands!" The abbot spoke to the friar as if Lucio were not in the room. He was in his sixties and bald except for patches of white hair on his temples. He matted the hair back behind his ears with his hands, yawned, and then looked down at his nightgown and remembered that he had been disturbed in his sleep. "Lay the body on a bed in the hospital room for tonight. Give a coin to our carter friend here. In the morning, have the brothers prepare the body; then go to the piazza and see if anybody has been reported to be missing." The abbot pulled the blanket back over the bearded face.

* *

Lorenzo stared into the fire. He didn't touch the plate of bread and cheese on the table next to him. He felt numb. Was all this really happening? For all the daily hardships in his life and the worrying about where the next meal would come from, he had been relatively shielded from major tragedy. He did not remember the death of his mother. It was so long ago and he had gotten so used to his routine that he could not imagine a life with a mother in it. He had heard of people he knew dying, but the only person he was really close to was his father, so none of these deaths were personal losses. In his young mind, life would always progress in the way that it had, with tragedies happening to other people and he hearing about them in the piazza.

But now he feared the worst. If something had happened to his father, how would he go on? This couldn't be what it felt like to be in the midst of a tragedy. Tragedies were heavy and final, and they had a certain order to them, in the way that history has a sense of finality when read from a book. But not this; this was chaotic, and delicate, so delicate. The slightest change of fortune or chance could alter his life forever, changes so slight as to seem randomly insignificant.

Tragedies were real. This was not real. This was a misunderstanding. Everything would be fine. The day had been full of terror and surprises, and had Lorenzo not been worried sick about his father, he would have been more shaken up over what had happened to him that day.

Lorenzo had struggled to free himself of the Neapolitan's grip. He tried to cry out, but the man was strong, and his bulging, hairy arms engulfed the boy while a strong hand cupped his mouth shut. The man spun Lorenzo around, still cupping his mouth shut and securely grasping his arm. The dark, burly man opened the distance between their two bodies and crouched to speak to the boy. It was then that Lorenzo noticed what he had failed to see before. It did not diminish the terror that he felt deep down in the pit of his stomach, but it brought a great cloud of confusion to his mind. There it was, unmistakable. Then, suddenly, a large club crashed down over the man, narrowly missing his head but landing squarely on his left shoulder. The man fell hard.

"I'll get the boy; you finish this one." The orders were given in an efficient, military style. There were two men standing opposite Lorenzo and the wounded Neapolitan on the floor. They wore baggy, brown wool hats and tattered gray and brown cloaks over dirty white blouses. They approached in a slow, methodical step. The nearer of the two, a thirty-something moustached man, threw the club he had swung to the ground and drew a dagger from his belt, behind his back. He grabbed Lorenzo by the blouse and lifted him slightly with one hand. Lorenzo was drained of all courage. He had no saliva, and his jaw was shaking and numb. He could not scream.

The second man rolled the Neapolitan over and raised a dagger in his hand high. He was about to stab it down hard when he stopped instantly, released his hold of the man, and stepped back hurriedly.

"Madonna!" he squeaked out from behind a hand that covered his frightened mouth. "Che facciamo? What are we doing?" The man tucked his dagger back in his belt, backing up slowly. Then he turned and ran out of the alley.

The other, still grasping Lorenzo by the blouse, spun to assess the situation. The Neapolitan rose to a knee, picked the club up off the ground, and stood. The moustached attacker released Lorenzo and shoved him toward the dead end of the alley. He readied himself for a fight, bending his knees slightly and holding the dagger out affront. He surveyed his opponent's stature and noticed at neck level what had so scared his partner. His eyes hardened, and he spoke.

"If you think I won't kill a priest, you're mistaken!"

"If *you* think you're getting your hands on this boy, it is *you* who are mistaken!" the priest answered calmly, in proper Tuscan, though the Neapolitan accent was thick. The two squared off. The moustached man crouched and charged, dagger leading the way.

The priest spun and sidestepped the stabbing thrust, then crashed the club down on the attacker's arm. The dagger dropped to the ground. The priest wasted no time, raising the club again and delivering a devastating blow to the head. There was a sickening thud. The man's body became limp, and he collapsed straight down. His body lay contorted as a rag doll. Lorenzo looked on in horror.

The priest dropped the club. He turned toward Lorenzo and took a second to catch his breath. When he had regained his composure, he spoke in a deep yet soft voice.

"I am Padre Vincenzo, parish priest of San Felice. I swear I will not harm you, but you and your father are in grave danger."

Father Vincenzo brought Lorenzo back to his own house. Very quickly, he explained to the boy that he had overheard a plot against Lorenzo and his father that afternoon and was determined to prevent it. He told his housemaid, Carla, to bring the boy some food. He told Lorenzo not to leave the house, as there could still be danger, and that he, Father Vincenzo, would borrow a horse and try to catch up with Simone. He hurried out the door.

It was now very late. After the sun had set, Carla had come and lit a fire. Lorenzo stared at the flames and worried.

* *

Father Vincenzo rode tiredly, the horse at a slow trot. He had ridden all the way to Fiesole, where nobody had seen Simone, then headed back, trying to check wooded areas, ditches, and side roads along the way. But the possibilities were far too numerous to have checked everywhere; and after the sun had set it was almost impossible to see anything more than the trodden road a few steps ahead lit weakly by the moonlight. A few hundred steps from the city gates, Father Vincenzo could make out a dark figure heading toward him, pulling a cart. From atop his horse he could now see a hooked nose and snarly expression.

"Buona sera!" Father Vincenzo waited for the man to return eye contact, but he would not. Instead, Lucio just nodded his head, grunted, "Anche a voi, Padre," and kept pulling his cart forward.

"Have you seen a tall fellow, wearing a beard, heading toward Fiesole?" Father Vincenzo added hurriedly, before Lucio was past him.

"Sì," replied Lucio simply, without stopping. He kept pulling his cart. He was now half a dozen steps or so away from the priest.

Father Vincenzo felt his blood begin to boil. His temper had always been a problem. It was one of the reasons he was forced to leave Naples. But he controlled himself; nothing was to be gained by losing his temper on this wretched creature. He reached into a pocket and pulled out a coin, then made a loud coughing sound as if to clear his throat.

"Might you be able to direct me to him?" He flipped the coin up in the air and caught it, over and over to let Lucio see.

Lucio turned, saw the coin, and dropped the handles of his empty cart. He retraced his steps and approached the mounted priest. Father Vincenzo tossed the coin toward the wicked old man.

"San Marco," Lucio exclaimed upon catching the coin. He then muttered something in Bolognese that Father Vincenzo did not understand.

"Speak clearly," spat the priest angrily.

Lucio grinned maliciously and walked back to his cart. Father Vincenzo was about to dismount when Lucio spoke again, in broken Tuscan, "You find him at San Marco."

LIBER SECUNDUS

Panem nostrum quotidianum

I

"Quis nomen tibi voco, O virgo pulchra, ego teneo non!"

Father Vincenzo listened attentively while Lorenzo read the Latin text with increasing confidence.

"And who is this fair virgin who visits Petrarca?" asked the priest with the smug air of one posing a trick question.

"La Madonna!" spat Lorenzo instinctively. He had taken the bait. For well over a millennium, literature in both Latin and the Italian dialects, or *volgare*, had been flooded with references to the Virgin Mary. But then humanism had arrived, and the return of classicism, and the yearning to think and write about something other than the divine will of God. The virgin that Petrarca wrote of was not the mother of Christ but a different type of deity altogether.

"Keep reading farther down…here." Father Vincenzo pointed at the page.

"Ea est verum ipsa quisnam orator nobis," Lorenzo paused, then stated unsurely, "So the virgin is truth."

"Exactly."

"But how can truth be a virgin?"

"It's a metaphor. The notion of truth is personified, the way the ancients personified the notions of love, war, even lightning in their gods."

"That's not what I mean…I mean, why would truth be represented as a virgin, of all things? To me, a virgin is pure, but truth…truth is never pure!"

Impressed, Father Vincenzo took in Lorenzo's comments and felt an upsurge of pride at seeing the young man use his mind so inquiringly. Far too often, young people simply accepted what was presented to them without challenging any of it. Lorenzo was different.

Father Vincenzo realized Lorenzo was waiting for a response. "And why would you call truth impure?"

"Take my father, for example. The truth, as everyone knows, as everyone believes, is that he was robbed and killed by brigands. But nobody asks why Coraggiosi had asked Domenico to send my father to Fiesole on a day when he knew Domenico would not allow him to take one of the horses out. Nobody asks why Coraggiosi suddenly had to go fix the roof on his country villa when he could have sent a servant to fix it. Nobody asks why two thieves tried to rob me on the same day my father was killed, and nobody looked into the plot you overheard. The truth is not pure; it hides many ugly things."

"Ah sì, but this is not truth that you speak of." The priest's thick Neapolitan accent camouflaged a deep erudition, for even when he spoke Latin or Tuscan, he spoke not with the graceful linguistics of the universities, but with the hard syllabic rhythm of the common people. "It is what Plato would have called the illusion of truth, an imperfect copy of truth. We may not find it in this life, but truth exists." He watched Lorenzo nod in comprehension, then added, "Your Latin has improved greatly!"

"I prefer Petrarca's *volgare*; I prefer reading about his love for Laura than his search for truth," Lorenzo answered rhetorically.

"That is because you are young. When you are my age you will seek answers."

"The answers I seek are not in Petrarca's *Secretum*."

* *

Lorenzo walked out of the small row house and into the Piazza San Felice. It was dark and clear, and the moon reflected brilliantly off of the wet paving stones along the Via Romana. He turned and saw the candlelit window on the ground floor of Father Vincenzo's row house go dark. The house was a three-story structure butted at a right angle against the front corner of San Felice Church itself, and in addition to Father Vincenzo and his maid, Carla, also housed the monks of Camaldolese order, who ran the church. While the monks lived an isolated existence, Father Vincenzo dealt with parish matters and gave the sacraments. He rarely interacted with the monks, whose living space in the rectory house was separate from Vincenzo's. The church was relatively humble looking as far as churches go, with brick sidewalls and a dark gray stone façade. The roof was a simple wood timber peak, and the front door was small with a rounded arch above. The windows were few and of clear glass.

Turning left out of the piazza, Lorenzo headed toward the Ponte Vecchio. The Palazzo Pitti was on his right, with its imposing three levels of rounded arches reminiscent of the great Roman aqueducts. The palace towered over the Piazza de' Pitti and loomed large over the Arno River to its immediate north. There were still some horses clattering around the glistening streets and a few stragglers walking. He crossed the bridge with its tables packed away and its shops shuttered. The autumn air was crisp but not cold.

He was walking home to the Palazzo Chilli, where he lived in a small room in the servants' quarters, facing the courtyard just opposite the stables. He had lived there for seven years, ever since he took over his father's old job at the palace. Lorenzo had been forced to sell the apartment on Via del Corso to pay the burial costs for his father. Domenico had bought it. Adélaïde had pleaded for him to simply pay the burial costs, but Domenico said that that would force him to pay the burial costs for all of his servants who died. In his business-oriented mind, buying the small apartment (which he did not need) at a fair price was charity enough.

Lorenzo didn't mind selling it. He didn't want to live there anymore without his father. It hurt too much to see the small room that had witnessed so many happy times. There had been, of course, no further talk of Lorenzo becoming an apprentice in the Calimala guild after his father's death. Without his father's income or even the gold bezant to pay Coraggiosi, Lorenzo was left with few options.

Father Vincenzo had offered to take Lorenzo in. The priest's dark, brutish features, thick accent, and quick temper disguised a charitable heart. He had been deeply moved by Lorenzo's loss and felt, after fighting two thugs and searching for Simone, as though he were involved in the boy's troubles. Lorenzo, however, chose to go live at the Chilli Palace. He did not yet know how important a part Father Vincenzo would play in his life and was reluctant to trust someone he had only just met, even if he was a priest who had saved his life. But there was another reason why Lorenzo had chosen to live at the Palazzo Chilli.

Shortly after Simone's death had been discovered, Adélaïde went to San Felice with a household servant and her daughter, Claudia. She had gone to see Father Vincenzo about the funeral arrangements. Father Vincenzo had made a charitable "donation" to the abbot at San Marco and brought Simone's body to San Felice. He performed the funeral at no charge to Lorenzo, but he had no control over the cemetery, which was run by a monastery outside the city walls and charged a standard, considerable burial fee. Father Vincenzo was far too honest a priest to have accumulated any personal wealth. Otherwise, he would have paid the fee himself.

Adélaïde knew that Lorenzo was still at the priest's house and asked to see the boy. The thirteen-year-old Claudia accompanied her mother. Lorenzo came down the steps to see the two seated at the table. He had known the Chillis had a daughter, but had never met her. Adélaïde stood immediately and embraced Lorenzo warmly, tears running down her cheeks.

Claudia stood but did not approach the boy. She just looked at him in awkward silence. Lorenzo accepted the hug noncommittally and gazed around Adélaïde's arm at Claudia. She was about Lorenzo's height and had a thin body. Her hair was below the shoulders and wavy, not pinned up like the rich adult women. It was brown and shiny and completely full of body as though it had just been brushed out. Her hair flowed down around her shoulders and lay softly on her cream-colored dress. A thick, white, embroidered liner was sewn around the neckline, and the dress puffed slightly at the shoulders before snugging the arms tightly down to the wrist. The dress followed a straight line down to the waist where it belled out subtly and fell to floor level.

Lorenzo looked at her face. Her skin looked soft and healthy and pink around the cheeks. Her nose was ever so slightly peaked and accentuated the sharpness of her girlish features. Her eyes were brown and deep and friendly. Lorenzo felt a new sensation overtake his grief-worn body, one he had never felt before. He felt as though he never wanted to look away; he could have stared at Claudia for hours.

The three sat down, and Adélaïde told Lorenzo that Domenico would give him Simone's job and that he could live in the servants' quarters. Claudia sat in silence. Lorenzo felt like he needed to be near her, to be wherever she was. He accepted the offer.

Lorenzo's days were spent the same way Simone's had been. He rose just before sunrise. Some days he saddled the horses; some days he yoked them to a carriage, some days a cart. Sometimes he unloaded bales of wool; sometimes he loaded finished fabric back onto carts. If the dyers needed help, he would roll up his sleeves and end up with arms the color purple from working the wool in and out of the dye barrels. If a message or errand needed running, off Lorenzo went.

His room and board were included in his salary. His pay was small, but he was able to eat well. If at the palazzo, he ate midday supper with the other servants. If out on an errand, he usually sat at an osteria and ate a hot plate of vegetable stew, or chicken roasted in olive oil and herbs, or if the *oste* was able to buy some, wild boar. It was always dark in the osteria, even on sunny days. Lorenzo would sit at a table, alone, and read the books that Father Vincenzo let him borrow. He never went down by the river to eat anymore; he had no desire to sit under the sun and stare at the ripples of the Arno.

Most nights Lorenzo visited Father Vincenzo. They would eat a light meal and discuss literature, politics, theology, or any other subject that crossed their thoughtful minds. This routine had started shortly after Lorenzo had moved into the Palazzo Chilli. Father Vincenzo had resolved to not only look after the boy but to educate him as well. Not many household servants could speak or read Latin. Though the ancient tongue of the Romans had long since evolved into the *volgare* as the language of the people, Latin was still the language of the Church and of the legal system. This left most people ignorant, and therefore dependent, in the ways of religion and the law. But with the reawakening of art, literature, and the wonders of the classical world that had begun in Florence over a century before, the artistry and beauty of the Latin language had reemerged, most notably in the writings of Francesco Petrarca and in the poetry shared in Lorenzo de' Medici's circle.

Lorenzo walked past the front gates of the Palazzo Chilli, which stood impressively on the Via dei Calzaiuoli and turned up a narrow alley that led to the courtyard gate in the rear of the palace. Next to the large double-door gate used for horses and carts was a small archway with an iron-bar gate. Lorenzo opened the gate with a key only slightly smaller than his hand, and then relocked it behind him. He passed the stables and entered the servants' quarters. The small entry room had a fireplace with only some coals and embers smoldering. Seated at the small table in the center of the room was the notary, Giovanni de Angelis, playing cards with Tommaso Orecchioni, another palace servant.

The two continued with their game without looking up, and Lorenzo went through the small doorway that led to the only other room of the quarters. The doorway had no door on it, and the room was barely larger than the mattress that lay on its floor. Lorenzo shared the bed with Tommaso. When the old stableman, Daniele, was still alive, the three had shared the bed.

Lorenzo set his satchel down on the bed and squinted through the darkness at a small table that stood beside the low mattress. He could see that the candle that stood in the black iron candlestick holder was burned to the base. He went back in the other room. There was just one candle lit in the room, set on the table.

"Do we have anymore candles?" he asked, wishing Giovanni were not there to hear the exchange.

"No…this is it," Tommaso replied regretfully.

"Had I known you were in need of candles," Giovanni added smugly, "I would have brought you some from my recent trip to Pisa. I find the candles from Pisa to be far superior to the Florentine variety. Of course, Venetian candles are the best. I shall have to remember to stock up on my next trip to Venice."

In his mind, Lorenzo added candles to the never-ending list of things that Giovanni was an expert on. He opened the door and walked out into the courtyard without responding. Giovanni and Tommaso went back to their card game. A minute later Lorenzo returned with two pieces of firewood. He squatted and stacked them carefully over the hot coals and blew three long bursts of air at the glowing red embers. He waited, then blew three more. On the third gust, the underside of one of the pieces of wood caught fire. Lorenzo stood and went in the other room. He returned with a book and sat on the floor, back to the wall, next to the fireplace. When he opened the book, there was just enough light from the fire to read.

Giovanni sat back in his chair pretending to contemplate the cards in his hand. His eyes, however, soon turned toward Lorenzo. "Learning to read…bravo, Lorenzo! I always say it would be a good thing if household servants could read an invoice or a receipt. I, for one, am tired of my clients asking me to attend simple transactions because their servants can't read basic inventory lists."

Lorenzo ignored him.

"He reads all the time, been doing it for years," answered Tommaso.

"How interesting," Giovanni replied surprised. "And what are you reading?"

Realizing he would now have to converse with Giovanni, Lorenzo muttered softly without looking up, "A poem."

"Let's hear it," Giovanni answered, anticipating some slow, stuttered recitation of a children's song.

Lorenzo did not want to indulge the notary. He wasn't the least bit interested in Giovanni's opinion of his reading ability or choice of material. He just wanted to read in peace. He knew this poem was Father Vincenzo's favorite, and he wanted to be well versed in it for the following evening's visit to the priest's house. He also knew that Giovanni would not stop pestering him until he read him something. What's more, Tommaso was looking on eagerly, and Lorenzo had no wish to be standoffish with his friend. He read aloud, "Nel mezzo del cammin di nostra vita, mi ritrovai per una selva oscura."

Giovanni finished the sentence: "Ché la diritta via era smaritta, sì, sì. Dante Alighieri, we read *La Commedia* my first year at the University of Bologna. It was not part of the curriculum, of course; no dialect poet will ever rank among the classics. My professor showed it to us during our study of Virgilio's *Aeneid*. He used it as an example of the decline of modern language. He hated *La Commedia*, but the students loved it. It does seem to be very popular among the common folk; they love to have it read to them. Who could blame them? I suppose if I had never read Virgilio or Ovidio or any Latin at all, I would think it a lovely poem."

Lorenzo did not respond. He didn't bother to tell Giovanni that he had read Virgil and Ovid and that he could read Latin. He was happy to let Giovanni go on thinking himself superior. He did not want to say anything to him that would prolong the conversation even a little. Giovanni went back to his cards and Lorenzo, his book.

"Better make this the last round," Giovanni said to Tommaso. "Coraggiosi is coming early tomorrow with some new wool."

Lorenzo stayed focused on his descent into hell with Dante, ignoring Giovanni's bragging about how important he was to be attending this transaction.

"I hope he leaves the Giotti boy at home. Since Jacopo's almost done with his apprenticeship, his father's been sticking his nose in a lot of Coraggiosi's deals. I can't stand that old crank Lodovico. I know us notaries ought stick together, but there is just nothing to like about that man. And since his son will soon be a Calimala merchant, Lodovico has been absolutely intolerable lately."

Lorenzo cleared his throat and went on reading, hoping Giovanni would take the hint.

"The only good thing about this meeting will be seeing Claudia!" added the notary.

Lorenzo stopped reading but did not look up.

"What I wouldn't give for a night with her," Giovanni lamented.

"Like you'd have a chance," Tommaso spat back, "and why is she coming to see you?"

"Coraggiosi is bringing some new fabrics from India or something. Adélaïde and Claudia are picking out patterns for new dresses. The way those two spend Domenico's money, I'm sure the meeting will last all morning."

Lorenzo listened attentively but kept on pretending to read. His mind drifted to visions of long brown hair, wavy and resting gently on perfect shoulders. He thought of an elegant neck with soft, smooth skin. He envisioned the slight peak of her nose and her deep brown eyes. He remembered the smile she'd given him as they awkwardly sidestepped each other in a hallway once. He thought of the way she smelled, like flowers and summer air. He didn't see Claudia every day. The times he did see her were brief, and he could only remember speaking to her on two occasions. Between Adélaïde's tutoring and Domenico's efforts to keep all young men away from her, there was little opportunity for Lorenzo to see her.

Giovanni shuffled and dealt the cards again, his need to finish early having been merely an excuse to brag. Lorenzo closed his book. He stared at the fire and thought of ways he could happen upon this meeting the next morning.

II

It was a beautiful October morning, sunny and warm. The courtyard at the Palazzo Chilli was full of activity. Coraggiosi's cart stood center of the yard with a mule still bridled into it. Giovanni Coraggiosi and Domenico walked slowly around the cart and spoke in low, short sentences. Coraggiosi's sentences were short from nervousness,

Domenico's from impatience. Domenico, who had spent a lifetime in the wool trade, was not the least bit interested in these new patterns. He simply wanted his wife to pick out what she liked.

The Chillis were not part of the Calimala, or foreign, wool guild. For generations, Domenico's ancestors had been of the regular, or local, wool guild, L'Arte della Lana. A member of the guild by birthright, he had served a shorter apprenticeship than others and had his entrance fees waived. The Chillis' operation was so well established and profitable that Domenico rarely dealt hands-on with the material. He still exerted great political influence in the guild, of course, and therefore great influence in Florence itself. But the Chillis had grown so powerful and wealthy that Domenico was far removed from the purple-stained forearms of his forefathers. He spent his time making large deals and left most of the nitty-gritty to smaller merchants and producers in the guild. Trading in a more exotic material, the Calimala was ostensibly a more prestigious guild, but few families in Florence had more prestige than La famiglia Chilli, and Coraggiosi spoke reverently to Domenico.

"We've moved a dozen bales already this week, which is nothing compared with the volume of your business, Don Domenico."

"Well, let the women of the house pick out their favorites, and I'll take a couple more off of your hands," answered Domenico as he walked away. He retired to the house, leaving the rest of the deal to his wife and servants.

"You're better off without him here." Lodovico spoke at a whisper aside to Coraggiosi. "He's thrifty with his money. His wife, on the other hand, is easily persuaded to spend."

"I brought you here as my notary. I do not need advice on how to sell my wool!" answered the Calimala master, annoyed.

"This is beautiful," exclaimed Adélaïde as she held up a piece of red cashmere. She turned to ask her daughter's opinion: "Que penses-tu de ça?" Though she had lived in Florence since the age of nine and spoke perfect Tuscan, she always spoke to her daughter in French. It was her way of teaching her daughter the language, and she felt like it was a special bond between them.

"C'est bien, Maman. It's nice," Claudia replied.

Lorenzo walked through the open courtyard gate. He had practically run to and from the old market. The delivery could have occupied his entire morning; now Domenico was sure to find some other work for him to do, but he didn't care. He had returned in time to catch a glimpse of Claudia, and that was all that mattered. Lorenzo stood at the gate. He removed his floppy wool cap and brushed his dark, sweaty hair back with his fingers. He stuffed the cap in his brown leather satchel. He wished he were wearing nicer clothes.

Claudia browsed fabric samples with her mother, her figure a model of simple beauty. She wore a plain brown shawl, and her hair was pinned back behind her head. Lorenzo felt faint quivers in his stomach. Looking at Claudia was like a tonic to him, of which he could not drink enough.

Talking to the two women from behind was Jacopo Giotti. He explained the finer details of the cashmere. Adélaïde asked questions; Claudia listened quietly. Decked in the garb of the Calimala, Jacopo had the awkward air of a boy in man's clothes. He was handsome and tall. At twenty years old (a year younger than Lorenzo), he was a full head taller than his father. Jacopo, however, was everything Lodovico was not. He was friendly, even to servants and strangers. He was shy, especially around women. As he rambled on about thread counts and dye, he avoided looking directly at Claudia, talking nervously to Adélaïde instead.

Lorenzo stood still at the gate watching the whole scene. As he daydreamed about holding Claudia in his arms and kissing her lips, an apple core hit him in the chest and fell to the ground at his feet.

"You going to stand there all day, or are you going to get back to work, Simoni?"

Lorenzo turned to the far side of the courtyard where the apple core came from. Pierfrancesco Chilli, the eldest son of Domenico and Adélaïde, sat on a block and yelled again across the courtyard.

"Mi senti? Do you hear me?" he repeated.

Lorenzo bowed his head and crossed the courtyard toward the palazzo, thankful that nobody else in the yard seemed to notice him being reprimanded. He entered the house through an open set of double doors under an arched portico.

* *

Lodovico and Jacopo walked at a slow pace behind the cart. A driver negotiated the mule and cart through the tight street. Coraggiosi sat next to him.

"She would make a fine wife, don't you think?" Lodovico asked his son. Jacopo said nothing, just stared at the rickety rear wheels wobbling over the paving stones.

"The dowry alone would make you rich, not to mention the new business your father-in-law would bring to you." Lodovico was excited at the prospect, but his son seemed hesitant, and this annoyed him. "You must think of the future of this family," he added curtly.

There were times when Jacopo really hated his father.

III

From 1305 to 1378, the seat of the Roman Catholic Church was in Avignon, France. Seven popes ruled in this period. In the year 1378, Saint Catherine of Siena, among others, convinced Pope Gregory XI to move the papacy back to Rome. Controversy followed. The French cardinals elected their own pope, and for a period of about forty years there were two popes ruling simultaneously, one in Rome, the other in France. Clement VII and Benedict XIII were the two French popes in this time, now known as the time of the antipopes.

By 1417 there were numerous claims to the successor of Saint Peter, and the Church convened the Council of Constance to elect one official pope. Benedict XIII had long since been forced to flee the palace at Avignon. The palace became papal property again in the 1430s, when legates from Rome took command.

Le Palais des Papes, the Papal Palace at Avignon, is a beautiful and spacious castle. Pointed arches and sleek towers camouflage the functional turrets and archer slits. One of the towers, the Saint-Jean tower, houses two chapels. The Saint-Martial and the Saint-Jean chapels were frescoed in the 1340s by Matteo Giovanetti. By the year 1475, however, there were no popes at Avignon to patronize Italian artists. The city was home, however, to a young archbishop named Giuliano della Rovere. His uncle, Pope Sixtus IV, had appointed him bishop of Avignon the year before. Sixtus then made Avignon an archdiocese in 1475, thereby elevating his nephew. The city was once again taking a prominent position in Church politics, with Archbishop della Rovere leading the charge. The renewed interest in Avignon, and by extension the Papal Palace, brought many visitors from Rome to the chapels of the Saint-Jean tower to both worship in the former papal chapels and admire the Giovanetti frescoes. This gave the chapels' resident priest, Father Pierre Jean Laroche, the opportunity to make many influential connections.

By 1475, Father Pierre was in his midfifties. He was soft-spoken and highly intelligent. His Latin treatises on Church doctrine had been read in Rome. He was of average height and had a full head of gray, a handsome face with sharp features, and deep brown eyes that seemed to always be contemplating. He lived in a small suite at the palace with his housekeeper, Adèle, and his young niece, Adélaïde.

Early one morning, as sunlight poured in the high, narrow windows of the Saint-Martial chapel and enlivened Giovanetti's deep blue tones on the vaulted ceiling, Father Pierre knelt alone at a dark oak pew. He followed the light up toward heaven. Above the pointed arch window, he noticed the four angels from the *Funeral Procession of Saint Martial* scene of the fresco. The first angel appeared to be singing, the second praying, and the final two stood with arms crossed in apparent annoyance: one looking at the viewer, the other looking away. Father Pierre tried to regain his thoughts.

"Sicut et nos dimittimus debitoribus nostris, et ne nos inducas in tentationem, sed libera nos a malo. Amen," he mouthed rhythmically while still focusing on the last two peeved angels. From behind, he heard footsteps. He turned and was surprised.

"Votre Èminence," he said and dipped his head. Archbishop Giuliano della Rovere stood a few feet away.

"You are very talented and pious. It has not gone unnoticed in Rome," the archbishop said quickly, wasting no time on a formal greeting.

"Merci, Votre Èminence. I live to serve God's Church."

"And serve it you will. But I come here today with a warning."

"Am I in danger, Votre Èminence?"

"You are, my son," he answered, although Father Pierre was older than he.

"I fear no enemy. The almighty Father is my protector."

"Indeed. But, my son, I'm afraid your enemies are within the Church."

Father Pierre did not answer. He could not imagine who in the Church could wish him harm. He had always tried to lead a holy life. He could not think of any in the Church he had wronged.

"Rumors have been circulated, my son, terrible rumors. I, of course, have complete faith in you. But a talented theologian as yourself is bound to make lesser men jealous. Somebody has said that the girl you raise is not your niece, but your daughter."

Still Pierre said nothing. There was nothing to say. He was guilty. He could not lie to the archbishop. He had fathered a child with his housekeeper, Adèle. He loved the Church and believed he had been called upon by God to be a priest. He had lived with Adèle for many years before giving in to temptation. They were not lovers anymore. Father Pierre had confessed his sin and had determined to not repeat it. The outside world accepted Adélaïde as his niece. Many priests had "nieces" or "nephews." He felt he needed to say something, but the archbishop spoke again before he could.

"I wish to protect you, my son. You must leave this place before such gossip destroys you."

"Where will I go, Votre Èminence?"

"I have written His Holiness, and he has directed me to send you to Florence. Archbishop Orsini needs a secretary, and the Holy Father thinks your talents will serve the archbishop well."

"Merci, Votre Èminence." He had no wish to leave the chapels of the Saint-Jean tower, or Avignon, but what choice did he have? He couldn't imagine who was stirring up trouble over Adélaïde. "I will leave at once."

"Dominus tecum, the Lord be with you," answered the archbishop.

* *

"Are you sure the archbishop will have room for all of us? Suppose he says you no longer have need for a housekeeper; what will we do then?" Adèle was nervous. Her position was very precarious. As the priest's orphaned niece, Adélaïde, of course, would not be turned away, but the archbishop of Florence could easily object to a secretary needing a housekeeper in his quarters, especially when the archbishop's palace was fully staffed.

"Then we shall find an apartment outside the palace. Do not worry! I shall not let anyone separate you from Adélaïde." Father Pierre was reassuring. He knew that Archbishop Orsini could very well turn Adèle away. He would simply have to find her an apartment. She and Adélaïde could live together, and he would visit whenever possible. He would have to accept a room at the archbishop's palace, of course; he could not justify refusing the room to live with a woman. He had some money stashed away; he had come from a wealthy family before entering the priesthood and received a substantial inheritance. He would find a place for Adèle and Adélaïde if needed.

"Will I like Florence, Oncle?" asked the young girl standing in the doorway. She was nine years old with big brown eyes, and she was scared.

"Adélaïde, come here, ma chére," answered the priest as he stopped packing items in a large trunk and sat at a nearby chair. He patted his lap, and Adélaïde climbed up on it. "Florence is a beautiful city. Did I ever tell you about the time I went to Florence?"

The girl shook her head no.

"Their cathedral has a dome, the biggest dome I've ever seen, and it hovers magically over the giant cathedral with no supports."

"But what if it falls?" she asked.

"It was built many years ago by a genius. He figured out every angle, weight, and distance in perfect proportion. It is a thing of wondrous beauty. Would you like me to show it to you?"

She nodded.

"Good." He kissed her forehead. "We're going to be very happy in Florence."

Adélaïde was a happy child. She knew Adèle was her mother, but she called her Adèle, as she had been taught to as a baby. She did not know that Pierre was her father. She called him *oncle*, uncle, and that was what she believed. Pierre intended to tell her the truth when she was older and could understand better the subtleties of divulging such information in front of others. He could have told others that Adélaïde was simply Adèle's daughter from a man who had abandoned her, and that he had taken them both in out of charity. Adèle and Pierre had agreed, however, that Adélaïde would fair far better in life as the orphaned niece of a priest than as the bastard daughter of a housekeeper. As Father Pierre's niece, she would be educated and have every opportunity that the daughter of an upper-class household would have had. Most importantly, Adélaïde was being raised by two loving parents.

It was dark in their suite. The weather had turned in the twenty-four hours since Archbishop della Rovere had come to see Father Pierre. It was an overcast day, and little sunlight came through the window. There was a knock at the door.

Pierre picked Adélaïde up off of his lap and placed her gently on her feet next to him. He stood and opened the door to see Archbishop Giuliano della Rovere.

"Votre Èminence, won't you come in?"

"Bonjour, my son," the archbishop answered reflexively as he entered the room and sat. Adèle and Adélaïde stood off to the side and said nothing. The archbishop nodded as he made eye contact with the housekeeper and patted Adélaïde on the head as he leaned back to sit."

"Can I offer you anything, Votre Èminence?"

"I'm afraid I am in a hurry. I just received an urgent letter from His Holiness. It seems there have been some dangerous plots afoot against the Holy Father. My uncle fears that Lorenzo de' Medici has been making allies against him. As you may know, Archbishop Orsini is a relative of Lorenzo's wife. It is of utmost importance that you keep your eyes and ears open for anything that may be useful to the Holy Father."

"But, Votre Èminence, I will be but a secretary. What will the archbishop tell me?" Pierre asked tentatively, nervous about being asked to spy on an archbishop.

"You would be surprised at how much those around an archbishop know, even the most closely kept secrets. Besides, the slightest bits of information could protect His Holiness. You do believe that the pope is Christ's vicar on earth and should be protected at all costs, don't you?"

"Of course, Votre Èminence."

"Good, then I will write the Holy Father at once and tell him he has a trusted friend in you; it will be of great relief to him." The archbishop stood and stepped toward the door. He opened the door, turned, and faced the three. "Dominus vobiscum." He left.

Father Pierre began packing again. He said nothing to Adèle or Adélaïde. He had a sick feeling in the pit of his stomach. He realized then that he had been set up. Della Rovere and his uncle, Pope Sixtus, had conspired to blackmail Pierre into being their spy in Florence.

* *

Father Pierre sat in a cushioned chair and sipped a metal goblet of red wine. In the last three years, he had grown used to the Tuscan cooking. He was quite fond of the variety of stews and enjoyed the *cinghiale*, wild boar, very much. But he missed his French wine. The warm and comforting reds from the Tuscan hills were enjoyable, but the refreshing rosé from Provençe was engrained in his soul.

"She's growing into a beautiful young woman, your niece," Francesco Chilli commented as he, too, took a sip of wine. "How old is she now?"

"Twelve." Father Pierre took another sip of wine and placed the goblet down on a small table beside the chair. The studio at the Palazzo Chilli was a large room off the main entrance hall. There was a large fireplace on the outer wall, but it was not lit. Books lined shelves on the other walls, and the ceiling had a bright fresco of angels and clouds. "They grow so quickly. How old are your boys now?"

"Domenico is twenty, and Francesco is seventeen. You know, Padre, you could have paid your bill the next time you saw me instead of coming here on a Saturday night. I'm glad your niece likes my wool, and she seems to have outgrown her clothes every other month. I don't handle many special orders, you know. Most of my business is in bulk. So if I sell you some cuts of wool special, it means that I trust you to pay me…whenever!"

"Oh, of course, I know you are a patient man Don Francesco, but I hate to owe."

"Nonsense. You have something else to say. Well, let's hear it. What did you really come here to talk about, Padre?"

"Well, Signore, I have this…this feeling. I can't say exactly how or why, but I fear something terrible is about to happen."

"Go on," urged Francesco, his interest piqued.

"I've received strange inquiries from Rome. They ask me small details about the routine of Lorenzo de' Medici. I am not to speak of these inquiries, you understand. And Archbishop Orsini has been called to Rome; the timing seems strange. I have a terrible feeling that something will happen tomorrow, at the duomo." Father Pierre was speaking very low. His voice was trembling.

"Have you told this to Signor Lorenzo?" Francesco did not sound dismissive; he believed the priest was telling the truth, but he could not see why he was telling this to him.

"No, he does not trust me. The archbishop knows I was sent here as a spy. He never discusses anything with me except archdiocese business. He must have told Lorenzo. Lorenzo never receives me at his palazzo, even when I bring messages from the archbishop. He has a servant bring me his replies."

"Would you have me bring him the message myself?" asked Francesco genuinely.

"No, he would ask where it came from, and I have no proof except my own intuition. I was asked about where Lorenzo sat during mass and with whom. You must believe, Don Francesco, that I was forced into my dubious role as a papal spy, and that I never transmitted information I considered vital. Over the past months, as questions came in about Lorenzo's church habits, I thought they were futile attempts at gathering evidence for another excommunication or something of that sort. I offered these small details, figuring they would be of no help to Sixtus. But now I fear an attack is being planned for tomorrow. They cannot get to Lorenzo at his palace, so they have chosen a place where everyone's guard will be down."

Francesco sat in amazement. He had known Father Pierre for three years and respected him. He knew nothing of the priest's activities at the archdiocese, only that he held an important position. He was surprised to learn that he had been sent by Rome to act as a spy, and that the pope even felt he needed a spy. Still, he was not sure how he fit into this whole thing. "And how can I help you, Padre?"

"You must protect Lorenzo de' Medici. You sit up front with the important families; be on guard…and bring help, anyone you can, to protect the lord of this beautiful city."

Pierre's appeal to Florentine beauty was superfluous. Francesco had already made up his mind to help. He believed that Father Pierre was a good man in a difficult position. He believed the priest was genuinely looking to avert bloodshed. But most of all, Francesco believed that it was the duty of all Florentines to protect their city from the attacks of outsiders, even if that outsider was a pope. He would have his two sons with him at mass, of course, but that would not be enough. He would bring the stableman Daniele and station him at the main door, on the lookout for anyone who might be bringing weapons into the cathedral. He would position his household staff around the church with instructions to warn him if anything looked out of place. And close by his own side, he would bring a strapping teenage servant who had just begun working at the Palazzo Chilli, Simone.

* *

A month had passed, and now it was time for Francesco Chilli to pay Father Pierre a visit. The two walked along the Via dei Calzaiuoli, where Father Pierre was often seen shopping for the niece he doted on.

"And Jacopo de' Pazzi, thrown out of a window, dragged through the streets naked, and dumped in the river," Father Pierre lamented. "I honestly thought I could avert bloodshed, but the carnage I witnessed...Is there anything more savage than a mob seeking revenge?"

"I know, Padre, seeing Archbishop Salviati hanging lifeless on the walls of the Palazzo della Signoria was a horrible sight. What I am surprised at, however, is the lack of outrage toward Rome. All I hear is the Pazzi name in all this; I hear nothing of Sixtus." Francesco was somber, yet agitated. He wanted his fellow citizens to see their true enemies for themselves.

"The pope has powerful allies, and all concerned are willing to let the Pazzi take the fall, even Lorenzo il Magnifico. He knows who was truly behind the plot, but his position, and that of his city, is precarious. He will make peace with Sixtus somehow, you'll see."

"Well, what lies in store for our city may be uncertain," Francesco replied, "but one thing is not: my gratitude to you. Lorenzo himself has personally thanked me. My family and my business are now among the most favored in Florence. I owe all of this to you."

"What I did, I did in the name of peace. I want no credit for this savagery!" Father Pierre's eyes were watery.

"All the same, I feel I owe you. Certainly there is something I can do for you, Padre."

"There is." Pierre was quick and to the point now.

"Good, well what is it?"

"My niece, you've seen her. She is beautiful. She has been educated and refined; she comes from a good French family, my own. She is a most pleasant young woman."

"I agree with you in all of those things, Padre, and I take it now you wish to see her married well."

"I do, of course. I am old. I am a priest, but one far removed from the pious service I love. I hold a position perched between one ostensible master and one secret, yet I enjoy the confidence of neither. Anything can happen to a man in my position."

Francesco listened without commitment. He was grateful to the priest, for sure, but he was not about to promise one of his sons to marry a girl from a family with no political clout in the city. Marriages were an opportunity to acquire power that should not be squandered.

"She is, of course, still quite young, so a wedding would have to wait at least two years. But I was hoping to see her engaged. I am seeking to secure her future. It would not be charity at all. You may not know this, Don Francesco, but I am quite wealthy. I received a substantial inheritance and still own some property in Provençe. I intend to give a dowry of fifteen thousand florins."

Francesco was shocked. His attitude changed instantly. Fifteen thousand florins would place his son among the richest young men in Florence. It would also bring the Chilli business to a new plateau. He was now genuinely interested in a proposed marriage.

"I would, of course, be willing to give part of that dowry in advance," Pierre added, "upon agreement of the terms of marriage."

Francesco had made up his mind.

IV

Lorenzo sat alone at a table in the dark osteria. He twirled a fork in the bowl of *pici*, thick pasta noodles, bathed in olive oil and salt. He ate heartily and read from his borrowed copy of Dante's *Commedia*: "Nessun maggior dolore che ricordarsi del tempo felice ne la miseria." He thought of the words he had just read: There's no greater pain than remembering happy times while in misery. They were the lamentations of Francesca da Rimini, Dante's condemned lover, executed for adultery. He thought of the words' meaning. He remembered sitting by the river with his father, playing chess. He remembered falling asleep crouched on the floor by the stove, his father carrying him over to the bed. He felt sad. He also thought of something else. Francesca had loved her brother-in-law, Paolo. Political alliances had forced her to marry, but they had not been able to make her love. She had loved Paolo, and for this love she died.

"Pierfrancesco is a fool."

Lorenzo turned to identify the voice behind him. It was Jacopo Giotti. "Scusa?" he asked.

"I saw what he did. He's a brute."

"It was nothing." Lorenzo returned to his reading, thinking the exchange concluded. He was not about to defame the eldest son of his master, especially in a crowded osteria to someone he did not know.

"Coraggiosi has as many servants as Chilli, and two apprentices also; he never throws food across a courtyard or yells like that." Jacopo sat at Lorenzo's table and motioned for the *oste* to bring him some food and wine. "Why doesn't Chilli have any apprentices?" he asked.

Lorenzo closed his book. He normally ate alone and read at the osteria. Nobody had ever tried to join him before. It didn't bother him, though. Jacopo seemed genuinely friendly. "I never really thought about it," he answered. "He apprenticed Pierfrancesco into the guild, but that doesn't count. He only had to be an apprentice for a couple of years because he's the son of a master. Maybe Domenico figured that was enough. Besides, Domenico doesn't do much production, only once in a while some dyeing. He's more into buying and selling."

"Have you worked there long?" inquired Jacopo. He wasn't usually this curious about people. For the past seven years he had been Coraggiosi's apprentice. He spent most of his time working at the Bottega Coraggiosi on the Via Calimala, and had little time for friends.

"Ever since my father died," Lorenzo stated without showing emotion. "That was seven years ago."

"Did you love him? Your father, I mean," Jacopo asked reflexively, quickly wishing he could take the question back—not because he thought it inappropriate, but because he was worried he might be asked the same question in return.

Lorenzo said nothing. He thought it a stupid question. Who could not love their father?

Jacopo contemplated the silence. Was Lorenzo having trouble answering? Love for a father could be complicated. To clear the awkwardness he spoke again. "What are you reading?"

"*La Commedia* di Dante."

"I've heard of it, is it good?"

"I think so. Padre Vincenzo thinks he's the finest poet Italy has ever produced, better even than the ancients!"

"Your priest lets you read poetry?"

"He reads it with me. He's the smartest person I know. He taught me to read, in Tuscan and Latin. He also teaches me how to really know what the poets are saying, more so than just what's on the page."

"I wish I could read poetry. All I ever have time for is wool."

"Aren't you almost done with your apprenticeship?"

"Just a few more months. Then I have to pay the entrance fee to the guild, and I become a full-fledged member. I still have to work for Coraggiosi for about a year, though, before they'll make me a master."

"They don't ever let you out?" Lorenzo felt sorry for Jacopo. It could have been him in those shoes. He said nothing of it to Jacopo, but he thought of how close he had come to being apprenticed to Coraggiosi. Jacopo would be wealthy some day, but Lorenzo liked his life now. At times it was hard, but at others he had a degree of freedom—running errands across the city with no one looking over his shoulder. He spent his evenings with Father Vincenzo. His mind was opened up to the wonder of books and learning. He caught glimpses of Claudia from time to time.

"I get out more now than I used to," Jacopo said cheerfully. "Since my apprenticeship is coming to an end, Coraggiosi gives me more leeway. Besides, I think he's tired of my father coming around the bottega, so he sends me off on errands to keep him away."

"Well, if you can get out tonight after sunset, you can come with me to Padre Vincenzo's. We'll be reading Dante." Lorenzo hoped Jacopo would accept the invitation. The only other boy his age he was friendly with was Tommaso Orecchioni. Tomasso was pleasant enough to talk to, but he was the type to laugh at Lorenzo when Pierfrancesco berated him. Jacopo, on the other hand, had come over to sympathize.

"I would love to," Jacopo began shoveling the bowl of *pici* the *oste* had brought over into his mouth. "I better get back soon then, so I can finish all of my work before sunset," he added with a mouth full of pasta. He smiled at Lorenzo with a noodle hanging out from between his teeth.

Lorenzo smiled back.

* *

In the center of the city, between the Via Calimala and the Via dei Calzaiuoli, was a small district called Or San Michele. In the heart of this district sat a compound of interconnected palaces and workshops, all property of the local wool guild. In the palazzi lived the consuls, or leaders of the wool guild. A narrow street wrapped around the Or San Michele, and many merchants of the guild had their botteghe, or workshops, along this tight alley. There were also countless sheds and yards for the subsidiary trades of the guild, such as the dyers, fullers, shearers, spinners, combers, and washers, to name a few. These workers were under the laws of the guild but not considered masters. They were usually employed by a master, but their wages were set by the guild. A large set of wooden doors faced the street, restricting access to the consuls' palazzi. In the stone wall next to the doors was a carved insignia. The Agnus Dei, Lamb of God, stood proudly holding a flag with his hoof. The flag had a cross on it. Above the Lamb was a wool comber's rake above four lilies. Under the insignia was carved L'ARTE E UNIVERSITA DELLA LANA, the official name of the wool guild. Domenico Chilli raised the heavy iron knocker and banged it down three times on the tall wood doors.

The door opened. A short man with powerful forearms stood at the opening. He wore tight pants with brown felt boots. His white blouse was tucked in, and the sleeves were rolled above the elbows. Muscles bulged to the wrist.

"Buona sera, Don Domenico," he muttered and stepped aside.

Domenico entered the Hall of Audience, a large, open space with a lavishly decorated ceiling, marble pillars, and numerous frescoes along the walls. Unaccompanied, he crossed the room to a long table at the other side.

Seated at the table were five of the guild's eight consuls. They were the highest authority in the guild and responsible for setting and enforcing all of the guild's rules, which included at that time not only professional conduct, but also moral and criminal conduct of all guild members and associates. They were talking among themselves and writing.

Seated opposite the consuls were two notaries. Notaries performed a wide range of legal and clerical functions and were required by the laws of the *comune*, as well as agreements between the notaries guild and all other guilds, to be present at all official proceedings and document signings. The proceeding took no pause for Domenico's entrance. Noticing his arrival, however, one of the consuls rose and met Domenico a few steps before the long table.

"Benvenuto, Signor Chilli," started the consul, putting forth two hands to accept one of Domenico's. He shook the hands warmly and dipped his head slightly.

Domenico was a *sensale* of the guild. He oversaw the business practices of other merchants. He made sure their quality was excellent and their weights and measures beyond reproach. Any infraction was brought to the attention of the consuls immediately, who dealt out fines and penalties. *Sensali* often spent a lot of time checking on others. As a result, they were not usually directly involved in the production process. Most were, as Domenico, middlemen, buying and selling large quantities from smaller merchants and shipping them to foreign markets. Domenico kept only one small bottega that had been in the family for generations.

Though a *sensale* was an agent of, and therefore subordinate to, the consuls, Domenico's wealth and political influence attracted respect. "Grazie for coming so quickly," added the consul.

"Di niente," responded Domenico.

"As you can see, the consuls are hard at work. We're trying to reach out to the new king of England. Do you know of him?" The consul, Luigi Spigliati, was in his sixties and had white hair and a poorly trimmed beard.

"I've heard he is young—seventeen, I believe, when he was crowned two years ago," Domenico answered, unsure.

"Sì. Henry he is, like his father. He's the eighth Henry of England, I believe. Well, as you know, his father was not very favorable to our business. His tariffs and prohibitions against his subjects dealing with us hurt us substantially."

"I know," replied Domenico, slightly annoyed at being told something he knew all too well. "My father bought fleeces from English shepherds for years, and he made a fortune selling finished fabric to English merchants. The old king's ban killed our English dealings."

"Well, from what we hear, the new king is far more interested in hunting, jousting, and chasing the women of his court than trade policies. The advisers to whom he leaves such decisions have been overturning many of his father's trade prohibitions. We are dispatching an emissary to plead our case."

"Well you can count on me for anything that is necessary."

"We know that, of course, Signor Chilli." He paused. "There is something else."

"Dimmi, Tell me."

"The dyers have made a complaint. They say you have a servant boy dyeing wool. They want to know why a dyer of the guild is not being used."

Domenico's blood began to boil. The trades of the guild were, of course, fiercely protected. A spinner would not dream of cutting in on a fuller's work, and vice versa. Domenico's bottega was small. He usually only stored a dozen or so bales. He kept them on hand for special orders, and set aside a certain amount of finished fabrics. There were dye pots in the bottega, and Domenico employed a guild dyer, who had an apprentice. A couple of weeks before, the dyer's apprentice had been bedridden with a fever. Domenico wanted to get an order filled, so he sent Lorenzo over to help the dyer. While he did not specifically tell Lorenzo to do some of the dye work, he did not really care either, as long as the work got done.

Domenico had employed this dyer for years; he never caused trouble. The dyers, like all of the subsidiary tradesmen, were good workers but could be incited to strike or rebel from time to time. The question in Domenico's mind was who was inciting the dyers this time. "I sent one of my house servants to help my dyer one day. I did not tell him to dye. He was supposed to have just helped with the lifting."

"You know how these things go, Signor Chilli. The truth gets lost in the allegation."

"Is that why I am here? What is the fine now? Fifty lire?"

"There'll be no fine. None of us want to see a sensale stand under the judgment of the consuls; it looks bad for the guild. Just keep the boy's arms out of the dye pots; don't give anybody a reason for complaint."

Domenico nodded in agreement and crossed his arms pensively.

V

"D'un peccato medesmo al mondo lerci. By the same sin they were marked to the world."

"But what was this sin?" Jacopo asked.

"Well, it depends on how you read the lines," answered Father Vincenzo. "There are some who say the sin was sexual immorality with another man." The priest's tone was somber. The thought of being condemned for loving a man troubled him.

Lorenzo reached across the table and slid the wooden cutting board closer. He cut a corner off of the wedge of cheese and bit down into the sharp, grainy *formaggio*.

"Read on," Vincenzo asked, pointing to a line farther down. Jacopo read aloud, clearly and with great feeling.

"Dove lasciò li mal protesi nervi. Where he left his insides stretched from sin."

"But isn't this the circle of hell where Dante puts those who committed sins of violence?" Lorenzo asked, confused. It was clear from the canto that Dante respected Brunetto Latini, and it did not seem like Brunetto had hurt anybody.

"If you look back throughout history," Father Vincenzo sat back in his chair, expecting to talk for a while, "sodomy has been considered an especially heinous sin, a sin of violence against nature, therefore violence against God. In the ancient world, however—"

"But," Jacopo broke in, "my father says that sodomy was practiced openly in Florence before Savonarola came. He says that even Lorenzo il Magnifico had male lovers, and that Savonarola came and changed the city's ways. He says he saved the city, saved its soul."

"The friar had a profound effect on the soul of this city," Vincenzo lamented, "but I would not say he saved it."

"Were you here, Padre, when Savonarola came?" Lorenzo asked, unsure if he had already asked the priest this question.

"No, I arrived shortly after they burned him alive in the Piazza della Signoria."

"Why did they burn him?" Jacopo inquired, never having been told this part of the story.

"They were acting on the pope's orders. Savonarola spoke out loudly against the corruption of the Church. He was right in that respect, but the pope branded him a heretic, and an angry mob burned him to curry favor with Rome. The true shame for Florence is that the friar had convinced the people to burn the very beauty that the city is famous for, the art, the books, all of it up in flames. I've heard that even Botticelli threw dozens of his own paintings on the bonfire."

"But why?" asked Jacopo.

"Savonarola had convinced the people that art which glorified humanity instead of God was sinful. After a century of creativity that rivals the ancient world, he sent Florence back to the days when a painter could only paint a crucifix or la Madonna."

"Why are men so ignorant sometimes?" asked Lorenzo.

"It's the great paradox of humanity…People can at once create wonders of art and beauty and at the same time destroy the same with fear and ignorance," Father Vincenzo added.

"But I, too, would be afraid if a priest told me that a painting I made was sinful," Jacopo interjected.

"That is why I believe priests should be careful of what they tell people. They should stick to Christ's words and avoid the passions of men," retorted the priest. "Do you like Dante?" he asked.

"Tantissimo, Padre! Very much!" Jacopo's excitement was visible.

"Well, you're welcome to join us anytime you'd like." Father Vincenzo was happy to extend the invitation. Jacopo was a delightful young man, and he thought it would be good for Lorenzo to have a friend his own age.

"Grazie, Padre, I will." Jacopo looked at Lorenzo and smiled. Lorenzo smiled back. Father Vincenzo's house was always a welcoming place for Lorenzo, and now he was glad to share that feeling with somebody else.

* *

Lorenzo and Jacopo walked down the Via Calimala. It was dark and cool. There was no moon to illuminate the way. Just past a small piazza was the Coraggiosi bottega. The shop was closed up with wooden shutters.

"Is this where you sleep?" asked Lorenzo.

"No, the guild does not allow the masters to keep shops in their residences. Coraggiosi has a palazzo around the corner. It's not as big as the Palazzo Chilli, and there's no courtyard, just a stable in the back."

"I'm going back to Padre Vincenzo's tomorrow night, if you'd like to come," offered Lorenzo.

"I'll try to get my work done early. Don't know if Coraggiosi will let me out two nights in a row, though he said nothing when I left before. If I can get out I'll meet you there." Jacopo smiled and walked away. He turned off the Via Calimala up a narrow street and disappeared in the darkness.

Lorenzo hoped to see him again the following night. He turned down the Via degli Speziali and walked toward the Via dei Calzaiouli and the Palazzo Chilli. It was not that late, but peacefully quiet. He passed the front gates on the via and turned up the alley toward the courtyard entrance. It was dark, but he knew the steps by heart. From the shadow in front of him, he saw a quick movement and felt a powerful, devastating blow crash across the bridge of his nose. He smelled blood and felt warm liquid running down his face. He could taste the salty blood that ran over his lips. He was dizzy. He heard nothing.

Suddenly he felt another blow to the back of his legs; his feet were swept out from under him, and he fell back hard. He hit his head on the ground and felt sharp pain from the back of his skull. Through the tears that watered his eyes and clouded his vision he could make out two faint figures towering above him. He could just about make out the shapes of their arms being raised. He saw both figures swing at once, with clubs raining down on him. He felt pain everywhere. Their arms went up again and crashed down. The world went black and silent.

VI

In the center of Naples was a religious complex called Santa Chiara, which included the Church of Santa Chiara, a monastery, and tombs. The church was built in the Gothic style in the fourteenth century. The bell tower, which took over a hundred years to complete, loomed over the courtyard of the complex. On a sunny spring afternoon in 1498, two men sat on a bench in the shadow of Santa Chiara's façade.

"As dean of the College of Cardinals, you'll hold great influence in the next conclave," said the younger of the two. He was in his midfifties and wore a short salt-and-pepper beard. He held a red cap in his hands and wore a red shawl over a white blouse, which was unbuttoned at the neck because of the warm weather. His name was Cardinal Giuliano della Rovere.

"You'll remember that I supported you in the last conclave," answered the second man.

"Sì, but only after your own candidacy was thwarted, and from what I remember you would have supported anyone over Rodrigo Borgia."

"But alas, Alexander is the pope we have, and he shows no signs of slowing down, Giuliano, so what is all this for anyway?" The man was bald save a small strip of gray hair above his ears. He coughed, holding a fist to his mouth. Cardinal Oliviero Carafa had been born to a wealthy Neapolitan family and held numerous titles and bishoprics in the Church; he was an important ally for an aspiring pope.

"It is never too early to make allies. The future is always uncertain." Della Rovere was driven and spoke to the point. "I want there to be no question as to the outcome of the next conclave."

"Who could ever predict such a thing?" Carafa retorted. "Besides, Piccolomini has many supporters, and you…you have enemies."

"Basta, enough. I will win them over. But for now I have another favor to ask."

"What is it?" Carafa replied.

"As you may know, I have a niece, Felice. She lives at my estate in Ostia."

"Sua nipote! Your niece!" Carafa stifled a small laugh and added, "I've heard."

"She is fifteen now, and I do not want to see her married just yet."

"Meaning you want to wait till an alliance that brings you the papacy or more can be struck."

"Meaning I wish to wait till the time is right," della Rovere answered "Instead I wish to find her a tutor."

"And how is this any concern of mine?" Carafa was becoming impatient; he was due for his midday nap.

"I would like to arrange for the poet Jacopo Sannazaro to go to Ostia, to be my niece's tutor."

Carafa laughed heartily. "And what will he teach her, *Nnapulitan?*" the cardinal added sarcastically, exaggerating his Neapolitan accent.

"I'm more interested in his Latin, his Latin poems are brilliant."

"And who better to teach your *niece*," he paused for effect, "than the personal poet to the king of Naples. I knew you thought highly of yourself, Cardinale, but this is one trophy you can't have. He lives at court; the king would never let him go. What does a girl need to know Latin for anyway?"

"I want her to help me with my dispatches. She is the only person I fully trust."

"Get a notary or a young priest for your dispatches, like everyone else."

"I only trust blood." Giuliano was resolute.

"There's a novice at the monastery here at Santa Chiara. He's very good; he can teach her. I'll talk to the abbot. He'll let you take him."

* *

"So you're just going to leave!"

"What choice do I have? The abbot was going to throw me out of the order anyway. He suspects what we've been doing, he never would have let me take my final vows," the novice monk answered. He looked around his small chamber, there was little to pack. He slipped his brown robe up over his head and threw it over the back of a chair. He now stood in a dirty, white dressing gown that ran to his mid calves.

"Se' pazzo Matteo! You're crazy! He suspects nothing."

"And how could I stay? I could not take my vows. I could not go on living a sinful life after swearing before God! There would be too many difficulties." Matteo was young, twenty maybe. He was very handsome. He had dark wavy hair, which was cropped very short in the monastic style. His eyes were a greenish blue, his skin olive. He was thin but muscular; the lean diet at the monastery had not yet made him boney.

"And what now? You will walk away from the order anyway!"

"No. The abbot said I can take my vows tomorrow and leave as a member of the order. Then, when I am finished tutoring the cardinal's niece, I can return here, he said, or maybe even be summoned to Rome by the cardinal...I must do this."

"Quit now! I will quit, too; we can run off together. We can go to Sicily and tell everyone we are brothers so no one will question us living together."

"And how will we eat? The Church is all I know; it is my life." Matteo spoke tenderly now. "Vincenzo." He grabbed his lover's hands and pulled them to his chest. "This could never last, you know that. We could never be together the way we want. The world will not allow it. You should know this...You're five years older than me, and you're training to be a priest; you must have seen what the Church does to men like us."

"I don't care about that," Vincenzo answered angrily. "We are happy together. All the sneaking around, the secret meetings, are worth it. When I hold you in my arms, I feel a happiness I've never known before. I cannot believe that that is sinful!" Tears ran down his cheeks.

Matteo pulled Vincenzo close to him. He wrapped his arms around Vincenzo's squat, powerful frame and hugged him. He turned his head and pressed his lips against Vincenzo's scruffy cheek and held the kiss a while.

* *

The following afternoon, Vincenzo walked the bustling streets of Naples in a depressed daze. He could think of little else to live for; his love was leaving. He perused the carts of the *fruttivendoli* that lined the street, selling fruits and vegetables. He wore a black robe with a wooden cross on a string around his neck. Nothing looked worth buying; he wasn't hungry. The sun was setting over the rooftops. Vincenzo stepped in and out of shadows as damp clothes, draped over ropes that crossed the street high from window to window, rippled in the soft breeze and blocked the sun in swaying patches. There was a commotion at the end of the street coming toward him.

"Via, via! Make way! Make way for the cardinale!" yelled a man in the entourage.

The crowd grew closer. People in the street squeezed themselves close to the buildings and vendor carts, but still there was little room for the crowd to pass through. Vincenzo stepped closer to the crowd and approached the man shouting, "Via."

"Which cardinal is he?" Vincenzo asked.

The man put a hand on Vincenzo's shoulder and made to push him aside before noticing his robe and cross; he loosened his grip and lowered his voice.

"Il Cardinale della Rovere, Padre."

Vincenzo felt his stomach tighten. His fists clenched, and he could actually feel his own blood pumping hard through his veins. All rational thought abandoned him. Della Rovere was the cause of his misery, and he was just a few steps away. As the cardinal slowly made his way through the crowd, red hat sitting high on his head, Vincenzo's anger boiled over, and he lunged at him. Della Rovere was caught by surprise. Vincenzo wrapped his strong hands forcefully around the cardinal's throat and squeezed violently. Giuliano della Rovere was terrified. He could not shake Vincenzo's grip.

Dozens of hands ripped Vincenzo away from the cardinal, and chaos ensued. The mob swayed back and forth as a single body. Fists began to fly in all directions. Vincenzo was shoved to the ground and stepped on by countless feet as the crowd continued to shuffle down the tight street, pushing the rumblers forward. When the density of bodies on him thinned slightly, Vincenzo was pulled to his feet swiftly. He recognized the man at once.

"Pastore!" he cried out, surprised.

"We have to get out of here at once," said the older priest. He dragged Vincenzo between two vendor carts and waited a few seconds for the crowd to shuffle on. He moved and grabbed Vincenzo by the collar and yanked him around the back of the carts. They squeezed between the carts and the building for twenty steps or so. The older priest stood and raised Vincenzo up and dusted him off. He looked around guiltily but kept his composure.

"Are you two all right, Padre?" asked a shopkeeper who had not been able to see the cause of the ruckus.

"Sì, grazie. What is the best way out of here?" asked the old priest.

The shopkeeper motioned for them to follow and led them to a narrow space between his shop and the next building. Most buildings on the street touched each other, and the space between these two building was so narrow that it would have been easy to miss if one looked quickly.

"This lets out on the next street over."

"Grazie!" replied the priest, echoed by Vincenzo.

* *

By the spring of 1504, Father Vincenzo had been at the Church of San Felice in Florence for six years. He had been sent to see Father Egidio Struzzo shortly after the incident with Cardinal della Rovere. Vincenzo's *pastore*, Father Guglielmo, sent him with a letter of introduction to his old friend at San Felice. The letter stated that Vincenzo de Marco was a brilliant young priest's apprentice and asked that he, Father Egidio, allow him to complete his training in Florence. Egidio trusted Guglielmo and took on the apprentice.

Father Egidio had died in the winter of 1502, and Father Vincenzo, ordained only a year and a half prior, became the sole priest at San Felice. It was a small, poor parish, comprised mostly of tradesmen of the guilds and the Camaldolese monks.

One spring afternoon, the first sunny day after a long period of rain, Father Vincenzo walked about the city, shopping and paying visits to people. As he crossed the Piazza del Duomo between the huge cathedral of Santa Maria del Fiore and the ancient baptistery, he fixed his eyes on the Campanile, the colossal bell tower built by Giotto di Bondone in the fourteenth century. He suddenly had the urge to climb the tower. It was the first sunny day in a while, and he felt like looking out on the city from up high. The small door that gained access to the tower was in the rear, and Vincenzo walked over to it. A young man in tattered clothes was leaving the tower.

"Are you the keeper?" Vincenzo asked.

"Sì, Padre, I was just about to head home." He quipped, "Pranzo—lunch."

"Would it be all right if I walked up to the top? I like the view."

"Go right ahead. Just don't ring the bell; they'll get mad at me."

Father Vincenzo laughed and entered. He climbed the endless steps that wrapped around the interior of the square tower. For a man who preached for a living and spent his spare time in books, he was fit and strong, and the steep climb did not tire him. When he reached the top level, the view was breathtaking. From one side the giant red dome of the duomo filled the view panel. The marble lantern that crowned the dome was massive. The mystery of this gigantic vault inspired awe in him. Looking out the other direction, he saw a sea of terracotta roofs, and the Arno and the hills in the distance. It was in every way beautiful. Vincenzo stared out and felt peaceful.

After a while, he headed down the steps. He descended one level, then heard voices below him. He was about to make some kind of noise to alert them of his presence but decided not to. He stopped and listened. The voices were talking in forceful yet hushed tones, as if guarding against eavesdroppers. Father Vincenzo quietly descended another level until he was just above the speakers. He could see them through work-holes in the floor. He stepped back, leaned against a wall to remain hidden, and listened.

"I told you, the boy leaves at the same time every day; we have the place to ourselves."

"Are you sure it's all taken care of?"

"I already told you it would be." This voice sounded annoyed, as if impatient with the other's cautiousness. "Are you sure he has it with him?"

"Sì, I saw him this morning."

"And you're getting him out of the city?"

As Vincenzo listened intently, a pigeon flew into the tower suddenly and startled him. He jumped and knocked over a broom leaning on the wall next to him. The two voices stopped. A few seconds later, a head slowly crept up the stairway.

The man looked carefully. He saw the broom laying on the floor and the pigeon pecking around next to it. The head descended back down, and the conversation resumed.

Father Vincenzo clung to the stone wall of the staircase he had hastily ascended to avoid being seen. He was sweating. He could tell the conversation had resumed, but he was now two levels above and could not make out the words.

* *

"Sì. I told Chilli that I had to go to my country villa to fix the roof, and I was taking my servants with me. I said I needed a letter brought to Fiesole and paid him to send his servant for me."

"What is your fascination with this coin?"

"It's a remnant of the great Eastern Empire, destroyed by Saracens. And it belonged to Lorenzo de' Medici."

"That godless tyrant!"

"Nonsense! Besides, you want the man out of your way also. What difference does it make to you if I end up with the coin?"

Vincenzo tiptoed down the stairs, being extra careful. He moved one step at a time. He still could not make out the words.

"I only need him out of my way because *you* agreed to take his little *bastardo* as an apprentice."

"Well…he has something I want, but this arrangement works out better! Whom did you send?"

"People who owe me, they're dependable. And as insurance I sent a couple of bravi to fetch the boy. They'll hold him until it's done, just in case we have any problems. We can use the boy to scare Simone into forgetting the whole matter."

"Lodovico," the voice was a combination of angry and frightened, "I never agreed to hurt the boy."

"We shouldn't have to hurt him."

"This is too much. I let you talk me into this."

"Why don't you live up to the name of your ancestors, Coraggiosi, and show some fortitude? Do you see where we are? My ancestor Giotto built this tower...higher than anybody said he could. Ingenuity is in my blood, and my plan will work."

"I don't believe you, not about your ancestry or your plan!"

"It is the only way. Chilli heard you promise the apprenticeship to Simone's boy. He has no heart, but he hates to see people cheated in business deals. He'd have caused all kinds of trouble with the guild if you'd reneged. This way, we both get what we want. I get my son apprenticed, and you get the coin and the full fee paid by me."

Vincenzo gently eased into the position he had been in before, having taken great pains not to creak the wooden floor. He could now hear the conversation fully again.

"They better not hurt that boy. I never agreed to hurting the boy," Coraggiosi spoke to assuage his own guilt.

"I was very clear to them. I've been watching Simone; he and the boy meet down by the river, between the Ponte Vecchio and the mill. They eat and play chess. I told them to wait till Simone leaves and to quietly take the boy. There's an abandoned shed along the river just before the mill. They're going to hold him there until told to let him go, after Simone is dead."

The voices stopped talking. Father Vincenzo heard the two men descending the stairs. He waited until he thought they were out of the tower and then descended.

He ran to the Ponte Vecchio, fighting the crowd to reach center span, and scanned the riverbanks. He was not sure from what he had overheard which direction the boy and his father would be. Passersby bumped him, but he was determined to find them. He shielded his eyes and looked up and down the river line. Finally, he found who he was looking for. "Son essi," he muttered in thick Neapolitan.

VII

Lorenzo saw blackness and felt his head throb. He cracked his eyes open and saw a bright blur. He had no idea where he was. Slowly the room came into focus. The windows were tall and had their curtains drawn, flooding the room with sunlight. He was lying in a bed, the softest bed he had ever been in. The room was not long or wide, but the ceilings were high, making the room feel spacious. Seated in a chair next to the bed was an angel.

"Can you speak?" asked the angel. Her voice was soft and comforting. She smelled amazing, like a garden of flowers after a sun-shower.

"I think so," Lorenzo muttered. His entire face hurt when he spoke. His eyes gained focus, and he turned his head slightly to see the sunlight raining down over Claudia's wavy brown hair. The window was large, and the light poured around her outline. She reached out and grabbed his hand. Her skin was warm and soft like a rose petal. Underneath the physical hurt, he felt happiness. Could he really be holding Claudia's hand?

"You need to rest," she said.

"Where am I? What happened to me?"

"You're in one of our guest rooms. They found you lying in the street outside the gate; nobody saw what happened."

Lorenzo tried to sit up. His ribs hurt, his back was sore, and both legs felt like dead weight, covered in bruises. Claudia pushed him back down.

"Maman says you need to rest, at least a week. She made Papà have them bring you here."

The thought of a week of lying in bed with Claudia holding his hand was heaven to Lorenzo. "Beh, if she thinks it's necessary!"

"Don't worry, Lorenzo, Maman is very good at making people better. When I was in bed for a week with a fever, she is the only person who made me feel better. Not even the doctors Papà sent for made me feel better."

It was the first time Lorenzo had ever heard her say his name, and he thought his heart would burst. It is one of life's wonders that beautiful moments can poke their way through terrible times, like the way he had felt when he first saw Claudia, right after his father had died.

Adélaïde entered the room carrying a bowl of water.

"Apportes-moi la petite table, ma chére!" she told her daughter as she walked in, "Oh, Lorenzo, mon cher, you're awake…I am so glad. How do you feel?"

"I feel terrible. I don't know what happened. I was walking, and then I just remember being hit. Was I robbed? Where is my satchel?"

"It's with your clothes over there." Adélaïde motioned with her head to the corner of the room where Lorenzo's clothes and satchel hung on hooks. "You must try to relax, mon cher."

Lorenzo had another thought. He was wearing a dressing gown that was not his. How had he gotten it on? Had Claudia seen him naked? He was embarrassed, but also excited by the thought.

"Il est beau, non? Handsome, isn't he?" Adélaïde asked Claudia. The girl giggled and blushed. Lorenzo smiled ignorantly. Tuscan, of course, he spoke, and Latin he was able to learn (many of the words sounded the same), but French sounded like one long word to him. He liked the way it sounded, however, and he liked seeing Claudia blush.

Claudia stood, and Adélaïde took the seat. Claudia slid a small table from the corner to her mother's side. Adélaïde placed the bowl on the table, pulled a white rag out of it, and wrung out the excess water. She folded the rag and pressed it to Lorenzo's face, dabbing the bruises that covered it. The wet rag was cold and felt nice. Lorenzo looked over at Claudia, her brown eyes filled with emotion.

I could get used to this, he thought.

* *

"Sei sicuro? Are you sure?"

Jacopo nodded. "Absolutely, Padre. I didn't see or hear anybody else. The streets were desolate."

"Can you think of anyone who would want to hurt him?" Father Vincenzo was persistent but not unfriendly.

"No, but I only just met him a few days ago. I don't know any of his friends, or enemies."

"Well, if you hear anything, anything at all, Jacopo, that sounds suspicious, you let me know right away."

"I will." Jacopo pushed a long, bright red roll of fine fabric back and forth on the *banco*, counter. He rolled it from one hand to the other nervously. He was glad Coraggiosi was out of the bottega on business. He would not have wanted to have this conversation in front of his master. He had been upset and anxious ever since he'd heard about the attack on Lorenzo. He could not imagine what had brought on such violence. On one hand he felt lucky to have left before the attack; on the other he felt incredibly guilty about not being there. He liked Lorenzo; he was the first person he considered a friend. Even if they had just met, Lorenzo was one of the few people in his life with whom his interaction didn't revolve around wool. Most of all, he felt sad.

Father Vincenzo walked out of the Bottega Coraggiosi and down the Via Calimala toward the Palazzo Chilli. He was determined to get to the bottom of this. It was a cool autumn morning. The citizens of Florence went about their business, the merchants and tradesmen walking to and from their botteghe. He turned down the Via degli Speziali and then onto the Via dei Calzaiouli. The front doors of the Palazzo Chilli faced the wide via. There were two doors that met and arched up high above Vincenzo's head, each door with a large iron ring as a knocker. The thick, dark wood of the doors was weathered. A coat of arms, made of wood, was affixed to the door on the right. It was a red shield. Inside the shield was a spear with the head painted gold, representing the bronze-headed spear of Achilles. The name Chilli was an ancient derivative of the name Achilles, and for generations the Chilli family crest had born the spear of the Greek hero. Father Vincenzo knocked three times.

A servant opened the door and stepped aside to allow the priest to enter. He said nothing; he had seen the priest so many times that week that his presence was expected daily.

"Signor Chilli?" Vincenzo asked.

The servant nodded toward the study and then walked away from the priest. The study door was open. Inside, Domenico sat at a desk writing in a ledger. Father Vincenzo gazed up at the bright frescoes on the ceiling. Clouds and angels circled the room, the sky a bright *azzurro*. He knocked on the doorframe.

"Buon giorno, Padre, come sit down," answered Domenico without looking up. He kept writing. "Have you any news?"

Vincenzo crossed the room and sat opposite the desk. "No, it seems the attackers came from nowhere and disappeared after. Nobody knows who they were or why they did it."

Domenico placed the writing quill in its holder and looked up. He had hoped that the priest would have some information for him. He wanted to hear that Lorenzo had owed someone a gambling debt and they had come looking to collect. He wanted to hear any reason at all except the one he knew to be true. He was reasonably sure that the dyers had roughed him up to teach him, and maybe even Domenico, a lesson. His dyer, Michele, had worked for him for years. Domenico had always sent Simone, and now Lorenzo, to give him a hand when needed. It wasn't even a question of money; Domenico could have easily afforded a day's wages for an extra guild dyer on busy days. It was the hassle of going over to Or San Michele and finding an available dyer on short notice for a few hours' work that he hated. It was easier to just send Lorenzo over. It was only once in a while, and Michele never complained.

Now, somebody among the dyers was complaining. After taking their case to the consuls and not being satisfied with the outcome, they had taken matters into their own hands. Domenico told none of this to Father Vincenzo. He had no problem with the priest, but he was not sure how this situation was going to play out and wanted to play his cards close. "Maybe it was robbers who got scared off," he said, after thinking for a moment.

"I think they would have grabbed the boy's satchel, or something!" Father Vincenzo was not going to let the matter go. "I'm sure something will turn up."

"I'm sure you are right, Padre. I can't have my workers being attacked, and right outside my gate! If I find anything, I'll let you know."

"Grazie, Signor Chilli. Would it be all right if I looked in on the boy again?"

"Prego! Be my guest. You know the way," Domenico nodded, picked up his quill, and began writing again.

The door to the guest quarters was open, and Vincenzo peeked his head in slowly. Lorenzo was sleeping. Vincenzo sat beside the bed. Lorenzo's face was covered in black and blues. His eyes were swollen, his nose crooked. He did not look comfortable in his sleep; he kept twisting his body and moving his head.

Father Vincenzo was a bright man and well versed in all of the Church's teachings. But when it came to death, violence, and tragedy in general, he did not subscribe to the Church's doctrine of divine will. He could not believe that God would have intended this for

Lorenzo. The boy had suffered enough. He was a kind and thoughtful young man, and his life had been filled with tragedy. Vincenzo strongly believed that men followed their own will and appealed to God when it suited them. The evil he had seen perpetrated in the name of God's will sickened him, and he decided a long time ago to simply show kindness to others, as Christ would have. That was Father Vincenzo's sole interpretation to God's will. He had struggled, personally, with what it meant to live according to the will of God, and he was determined to not put others through the same. He read. He read for knowledge. He read to teach himself patience. His temper had been a problem for him in his youth, but he worked on it by reading and praying.

He took the cross he had strung around his neck up over his head and held it in both hands. He leaned forward with his elbows on his knees and whispered prayers. He liked prayer. He felt it was a private conversation with God that could not be corrupted by men.

* *

Claudia stood in the doorway. She had come to check on Lorenzo but now did not want to disturb the praying priest. She just watched. She was glad that Father Vincenzo was so concerned for Lorenzo. She didn't know why, but she was very concerned also.

VIII

"The boy shows no initiative. How can I secure him a good marriage if he does nothing to help himself?"

"Lodovico, per favore! He's just finishing his apprenticeship. He's known nothing but rolls of wool for the last seven years. What do you expect? Most of the well off young men in Florence don't even think of marriage until they're thirty." Maria was torn between protecting her son and helping her husband advance the boy's prospects.

"In case you haven't noticed, we're not that well off," answered Lodovico, "and his apprenticeship hasn't been cheap; he'll need to pay an entrance fee soon to join the guild."

"I still don't understand why he couldn't apprentice as a notary," Maria lamented.

"And he would be like me, a witness to the deeds of greater men. If our family is ever to return among the great names of Florence, he must be his own man, make his own fortune…and the Calimala trade is the way to get there!"

"But how on earth will you convince Chilli to give his daughter to Jacopo? What would he gain by doing so?" Maria rarely had faith in Lodovico's schemes. She stood from the table and started clearing the dishes. The table sat in a moderate-sized hall with a small kitchen and a small bedroom branching off. Lodovico owned the two-story house; he and Maria slept upstairs. Jacopo was their only remaining child. Another son and a daughter had both gotten sick and died as young children. Maria, grief-stricken after the death of their young daughter, miscarried. That was her last pregnancy.

"The marriage will be mutually beneficial." Lodovico said no more. His wife would not understand what needed to be done. No great family was ever made without decisive action. Lodovico would leave nothing to chance.

* *

Lodovico walked the tight alleys of Or San Michele hurriedly. The fewer people who spotted him there, the better. He spotted the bottega he was looking for and entered. The dye pots stood almost rim to rim. Large wooden forks leaned against the rims and dripped dye onto a dirt floor. Young men busied themselves. Some stirred soaked lumps of wool around the pots; others carried in rolls of wiry, grayish-white fabric.

A man with a serious face entered the bottega from the back door. He was short and powerful, and looked to be in his late thirties. His bare arms were stained purplish-red, and his thick, curly hair was wet. He was about to bark out orders at the younger dyers when he noticed Lodovico. He had been expecting another visit from the notary. He motioned with his head and eyes for the notary to join him in the back room. Lodovico followed.

IX

Claudia stared at the board pensively. She had only learned how to play chess a few months before. After Domenico's outburst,

Adélaïde had lost interest in the game, only recently rediscovering both her passion and talent as she taught her daughter.

Lorenzo could smell Claudia's hair from his bed; the scent was heavenly. He was not sure if she was more beautiful when concentrating or when smiling. Of course, her laughter was angelic. There was really no expression her face could wear that would not cause him to fall instantly in love with her over and over again.

Her delicate hand slid a pawn forward intently, and she smirked at Lorenzo, then blushed. Lorenzo returned a smile. The undaunted sunlight cut through the crisp autumn air and flooded the high-ceilinged room. Claudia's hair shined in its rays. The room was warm, but Lorenzo remained under a blanket, though he sat up in the bed. A small table held the chessboard, and Claudia sat opposite Lorenzo on a stool.

Lorenzo lifted his knight and slid it two spaces forward and one to the right, capturing one of Claudia's rooks.

"You play very well," Claudia said.

"I haven't played in a long time," he answered awkwardly.

"I remember that when your father was here, he used to play with Maman. Did you used to play with him?"

Lorenzo nodded his head affirmatively.

"I'm sorry. Do you miss him?" Claudia was sympathetic and curious. She remembered when her grandmother had died, but she had not been very close with her. She didn't know how it felt to miss someone you loved.

"Very much," he answered thoughtfully, suddenly aware of how different his life would have been if his father had lived.

Claudia reached across the board and placed her hand on top of Lorenzo's. She looked him in the eyes with great kindness. She had never felt so completely conscious of someone else's pain. Lorenzo felt euphoric. His only thought now was Claudia's touch. Her leaning forward made the heavenly scent of her hair stronger. It smelled flowery and silky. He gazed into her eyes. He knew he was in love.

Adélaïde entered the room, and Claudia snapped her hand back and sat up. She and Lorenzo exchanged smiles.

"Vas-tu preparer pour le déjeuner, ma chère ?" asked Adélaïde. Claudia rose and lifted the chessboard, setting it in the corner without upsetting the pieces.

"Perhaps we can finish later," she said to Lorenzo, intending to gauge her mother's reaction to the statement.

"You can visit him later and finish if you'd like," responded Adélaïde. Claudia left without saying anything else.

Adélaïde placed a bowl of soup on the table. The steam wafted across to Lorenzo; he could smell the onions and the herbs. "How do you feel today, mon cher?"

"Benissimo, grazie!"

"You are looking much better. The swelling on your face is gone."

Lorenzo was glad to be feeling better but sorry to be healing. He did not want this treatment to end. He was able to sleep whenever he wanted, eat three good meals, read, and most importantly, spend time with Claudia.

"Well, eat up; it will help you with your strength." For a wealthy housewife with household servants doing most of the actual housework, Adélaïde could be very nurturing. Lorenzo wasn't sure if she had made the soup herself or had had it made, but he liked it. He liked the kindness that came with it as well.

Adélaïde combed the boy's hair with her fingers, patted him on the head and left. Lorenzo scooped up a spoonful of soup and placed it gingerly against his lips. It was too hot. He set the spoon down and reached under the bed for Father Vincenzo's copy of Dante's *Commedia*. He found the page he had marked and read.

> E io senti' chiavar l'uscio di sotto
> a l'orribile torre; ond'io guardai
> nel viso a' mie' figliuoli sanza far motto.

> *And I heard them close off the door from below*
> *that horrible tower, and I looked*
> *into my sons' faces without moving.*

Lorenzo absorbed Count Ugolino's account of being locked in a tower with his sons. Father and sons starved to death, with Ugolino, blind and delirious from starvation, resorting to cannibalism. Ugolino had been condemned to such a fate by the treachery of an archbishop. The count had conspired with the archbishop to betray his own faction, but the archbishop betrayed him and had him and his sons killed. Ugolino's actions not only sealed the fate of his children; they damned his soul. Dante places him in the circle of the treacherous, in hell. Lorenzo read the lines again. "Io guardai nel viso a' mie' figliuoli." I looked into my son's faces. The children paid a heavy price for their father's actions, Lorenzo thought.

* *

Claudia walked a few steps ahead of her family. She was eager to be outside although the air was cool and damp, the sun hidden in a grayish haze. Sunday morning mass at the duomo was a social event as much as a religious one. All of the powerful families of Florence attended the service at Santa Maria del Fiore. The working class of the city usually stayed in their neighborhood parishes, but the wealthy, regardless of where they lived, trekked to the cathedral to see and be seen.

The massive front entrance doors were held open, and Claudia stepped out to the Piazza di Battistero, opposite the ancient baptistery of Saint John. Just outside the central doorway stood Lodovico Giotti, conversing with someone and waiting on a chance encounter with Domenico Chilli. Off to his side stood Jacopo, talking to no one. Claudia made eye contact and stepped toward him.

"How is Lorenzo?" he asked.

"He is doing much better. Papà said he will return to work tomorrow." Claudia relayed the news without expressing her own apprehensions. She and Adélaïde both thought that Lorenzo could use a few more days to recover.

"Do you think I could pay him a visit later today?" asked Jacopo.

"I'm sure he would like that," she answered, and smiled.

Jacopo now noticed how beautiful Claudia was. When they had met at the Palazzo Chilli that day, he had been too nervous to look her directly in the eyes; he spoke only to Adélaïde. He stared into Claudia's kind, brown eyes and felt very drawn to her. After a moment, he spoke nervously, "A più tardi, allora! Till later, then." He bowed his head slightly and stepped back.

Claudia smiled. Jacopo looked handsome and important in his Calimala garb. He wore a long reddish-brown robe with vertical pleats, cinched at the waist with a decorative rope. A full merchant of the guild would have also worn a floppy, pleated hat to match. As an apprentice who had almost completed his training, however, Coraggiosi had given Jacopo just the robe to wear to Sunday mass.

It made him look older than he really was, but he spoke kindly and disarmingly. Claudia liked him.

She turned to find her family. A few steps away, Pierfrancesco and his younger brother, Giambattista, exchanged lewd comments about the young girls exiting the Duomo. Adélaïde stood apart contently, and Domenico was speaking with Lodovico.

X

"You are in no position to negotiate, Ambasciatore. I expect the emperor's support." The pope was arrogant in his certainty; he gripped his long gray beard in his right fist and twirled it around his palm. His rounded red hat sat bunched on his knee, and he slouched in the large wooden chair. The chair was not really a throne of any sort, just a piece of an oversized desk and chair set standing on its own. That did not stop this pope from taking a regal air as he gave the Holy Roman Emperor's emissary an audience.

"Through the treachery and incompetence of those I trusted, my army has lost ground all across the Romagna. It is time to restore God's kingdom on earth to its rightful ruler. I blessed Maximilian as emperor because I trusted him to uphold the will of God, to restore the rightful possessions of the Church. As we have seen in the past, rulers who fail to uphold the will of God bring excommunication on them and their subjects…and who could want such a thing for a *Holy* Roman Emperor!"

"Certainly, Vostra Santità, my master serves God, and his vicar on earth." The ambassador spoke the Milanese dialect, learned at the court of the Sforza family, with a thick German accent. It was difficult for the pope to understand him and he knew it, so he spoke slowly. "We hear that King Louis will send his nephew, Gaston de Foix, to take command of the French troops in Italy."

"He is young and inexperienced. Cardona's Spaniards should handle him easily, and if not, our forces will move down from Ravenna and annihilate him."

"Of course, Vostra Santità. The sooner the French are driven from Lombardy and Romagna, the better."

"The emperor will need to send reinforcements to Ravenna at once. After we have dealt with Gaston de Foix, then we will discuss your master's Venetian problems!"

"Capito. Understood," replied the emissary. The pope's secretary handed him some documents to bring back to the emperor, then motioned him toward the door. The two men exited the papal chamber.

"Julius is losing his mind, Matteo. First he allies with the French against the Venetians. And now, when we need his help against the Venetians, he moves against the French. The French would not be in Italy if it were not for him!" The ambassador was polite but incensed. Although the door had shut behind them, he kept his voice hushed to keep the conversation private.

"Getting the French out of Italy is in all of our interests," responded Matteo patiently. He was still quite young, early thirties, but was well respected for his political astuteness. He had come a long way in the Church. He'd started as a novice monk, then became a tutor to the illegitimate daughter of a powerful cardinal, and was now the private secretary to the pope himself. The pope was Julius II, the former Cardinal Giuliano della Rovere. Della Rovere might have failed to secure an ally in his meeting with Carafa (the cardinal being one of only three who voted against della Rovere in conclave), but he did secure a trusted aid, Matteo.

Matteo taught Felice (who was by now widely known to be the pope's daughter, not niece) Latin grammar and basic arithmetic. Felice did, in fact, become what her father had intended, his personal secretary. She sat in on his meetings and wrote most of his correspondences. Had she been born a boy, she would have been made a cardinal, as Julius had done with all of his nephews. Her papal employment, however, came to an end when a marriage was arranged with a member of the powerful Roman family Orsini. Julius's alignment with the Orsinis helped tip the scale of power in Italy toward the pope. After Felice's instruction had been completed, Matteo was given a clerical position in the Vatican. He was once again plucked from obscurity, however, when Felice recommended him as her successor. Julius trusted him, though there were some dealings he was kept out of.

The more ambitious il Papa guerriero, the Warrior Pope, became with his military adventures, the more meetings Matteo was kept out of. With so many of Julius's family members in powerful Church positions and so many mercenary generals visiting the Pontiff, Matteo was happy to be kept out of the court intrigue. He contented himself to writing out treaties to be signed, answering foreign dispatches, and escorting diplomats to and from their papal audience. He wore the brown robe of the Franciscans, still being a monk officially, but he performed no religious function.

"He blesses Maximilian as emperor, yet delays crowning him as such here in Rome!" The ambassador's tone remained tense.

"Circumstances change quickly here in Italy, Vostra Eccellenza. The emperor may not wait long to be in the Santo Padre's favor once again. I think the generals here underestimate Gaston de Foix. The French soldiers love him; they will fight for him. The mercenaries on our side have little loyalty." Matteo was convincing, and the ambassador's demeanor became instantly friendlier.

"Perhaps you are right," he replied with his thick accent, as he placed a hand on Matteo's shoulder and smiled.

"If the French are victorious, the pope will need the emperor's help more than ever," Matteo added. "Will the emperor call another Reichstag?"

"I think not. He is still fighting to implement the reforms of the 1495 Reichstag. He will be meeting with some of the dukes in Worms next month. I am going to meet him there."

"Buon viaggio, Vostra Eccellenza!" Matteo dipped his head.

"Danke…mmm…grazie…I will return with the emperor's reply." The ambassador took his leave.

Matteo had a small desk in the antechamber, where he sat and shuffled through some papers.

XI

Weeks went by, and Lorenzo returned to his routine. He worked in the courtyard and ran errands across the city. Occasionally he would see Claudia at the palazzo, but now instead of going about seemingly lost in her own world, she would stop to smile at Lorenzo or exchange a few kind words. He always looked forward to these moments.

Things were not going as well for L'Arte della Lana, the local wool guild. The ministers of King Henry VIII's court had indeed opened up trade again with Italian merchants. The wool guild of Siena had also sent a delegation to London. The Sienese wool trade had been in decline for decades. Political factions fought bitterly for control of the city, and Siena's guilds suffered for it; all of its trades were in decline. A number of wealthy wool merchants were able to agree on a delegation, however, and now it was rumored that Siena would host a major wool fair that next spring, with a large number of English and Flemish merchants making the journey. Such a fair would be a huge boost to the city's economy. Wool merchants, innkeepers, butchers, bakers, and nearly all other city tradesmen would benefit (even prostitutes). The fair would also give the merchants a chance to make connections for future business deals. The wool guild of Florence was determined to sway the decision of an English delegation en route to Siena. The consuls entrusted this important task to Domenico Chilli.

Few in Florence spoke English, but most educated Englishmen spoke French. Accordingly, Domenico brought Adélaïde along as a translator. He also brought his notary, Giovanni de Angelis, in case Latin was to be spoken. Adélaïde convinced Domenico to allow Claudia to come along, wishing to show her daughter the great cathedral of Siena. Pierfrancesco and Giambattista were left behind to watch over affairs in Florence.

To Lorenzo's delight, Domenico brought him along to take care of the horses during the journey. A carriage and driver were hired for Adélaïde, Claudia, and the luggage. The others rode on horseback. Two bodyguards were also hired to accompany the family. Brigands and thieves were always a threat on country roads. It was a full day's ride to Siena from Florence, weather permitting. It was now early December.

The roads were wet, and the going was slow. As darkness fell, they decided to spend the night in an osteria in the walled city of Monteriggioni. Domenico had been forced to bribe the guards into opening the city gate so they could enter after dark. Lorenzo and the carriage driver led the horses and carriage around to the back of the inn. The two bodyguards rode their horses around. They dismounted and unstrapped their large, heavy swords from the saddles, along with some small saddlebags. Lorenzo unbridled the horses and handed them off to the stableboy.

"If Domenico needs us, we'll be at a table downstairs," said the younger of the two bodyguards. They had ridden just ahead of the party and kept to themselves. They looked alike; perhaps they were related, both with curly black hair and scruffy cheeks. They were both burly and looked as if they knew how to handle a sword. Though quiet, they did not seem unfriendly. They walked around front and entered the osteria.

Facing the stable was a back door with a set of stairs that went straight up to the second floor. Lorenzo ascended and knocked on the first door at the top landing. Adélaïde answered. She opened the door halfway and smiled.

"The horses are stabled. The bodyguards, the driver, and I will be downstairs," he informed her.

"Merci, mon cher," she answered politely and shut the door.

The osteria had two rooms upstairs, but Domenico would not pay for both. The bodyguards, the driver, Lorenzo, and Giovanni would sleep downstairs, either on tables or the floor, after the patrons had left. The *oste* charged a minimal fee for this. At least they would be in front of the fire. Food would be brought upstairs for Domenico, Adélaïde, and Claudia. The others would eat downstairs with the inn patrons.

The osteria was small, just four tables. The tables were about the length of a man and only slightly wider. Benches were strewn around the sides. Each side of the room had two tables, and a stone fireplace jetted out from the back wall and split the room in equal halves. A wooden door, propped open, separated the main room from the kitchen, built behind the house itself. The only way upstairs was to go through the kitchen, out to the rear yard and in the door that faced the back.

Lorenzo sat alone and ate his stew—thick, stringy, hunks of wild boar bathed in a heavy broth of onions, carrots, and soggy cubes of stale bread. He blew on each scoop to cool it and sipped it off of the spoon. The room was loud. The bodyguards and driver played cards with two other men, and the five drank and laughed heartily. Giovanni sat next to a woman in her late thirties. She had long, brown hair, which was tied in a ponytail by a red kerchief, but then flowed down and draped over her right shoulder. She looked somewhat weathered, though superficially made-up. She laughed at Giovanni's stories and rubbed his forearm often.

The *oste* came out of the kitchen and circled the room refilling wine glasses. When he reached Lorenzo he spoke quietly. "You are Lorenzo?"

"Sì."

"Signor Chilli requires your presence upstairs."

Lorenzo took another spoonful of stew and rose from the table. As he went out through the kitchen, he turned to see if anyone had noticed his getting up. It didn't seem so. He went out the back door and through the door with the stairs, and climbed. In the dark upstairs hallway, a candle flickered. The candlestick was on the floor. Next to it was a chessboard with all pieces in place. Behind the board, Claudia sat on the floor with her legs crossed in front of her.

Lorenzo was surprised. His heart beat faster. "Your father called for me?"

"I told the *oste* that Papà was asking for you. My parents are both asleep." Claudia was whispering.

Lorenzo sat down opposite her. In the soft, subtle candlelight her eyes reflected tiny flames. Her skin was radiant. Without speaking she slid a pawn one square forward. Lorenzo stared for a moment and then slid the opposite pawn forward one square.

"You seem completely healed," she muttered as she contemplated her next move. Lorenzo had thought her to be shy at first, but after sneaking out of her parents' room and lying to the *oste*, she seemed to have more of Adélaïde's audacity in her than first appeared.

"I'm feeling much better…grazie to you." He smiled nervously.

"Maman did all of the work, I just looked in on you."

"You were both very kind. Other than Padre Vincenzo, and my own Papà, no one has ever been that nice to me."

"He cares about you very much, Padre Vincenzo."

"He does." Lorenzo paused to think about the statement. Father Vincenzo had been a steady presence in his life since his father died; he was a teacher, parent, and friend all at once. He had never said this before, but now it felt natural: "He's my only family."

Claudia gazed across the chessboard, feeling sympathy for Lorenzo, but more than that she was impressed. Not many boys Lorenzo's age gave careful thought to those close to them. Most, like her brother Pierfrancesco, for example, thought only of hunting or impressing others in the piazza. Of course, only the wealthier young men acted this way, and Lorenzo was the first person from another social class that she had ever known beyond an acquaintance. She was all the more drawn to him. "Do you think you'll always work for Papà?"

Lorenzo shrugged. "I never really thought about it."

"You never thought about the future?"

"There are so many things beyond my control that I never thought there was much point in planning a future. I'm just happy to have a roof over my head and to eat every day…and to spend my nights with Padre Vincenzo."

"What do you do with him?"

"Talk…We read together. He explains to me what the authors really mean."

"What do you read?"

"Everything. Virgilio, Petrarca, Dante!"

"Maman read Dante to me. She read me lots of poems, in French and in Tuscan."

"Do you remember any of the French poems?" Lorenzo knew that he would not understand a word of it, but would love to hear her speak French.

She sat up, closed her eyes, and spoke.

> Dictes moy ou n'en quel pays
> Est Flora le belle Romaine
> Archipiades, ne Thaïs,
> Qui fut sa cousine germaine,
> Echo parlant quant ruyt ou maire
> Dessus riviere ou sus estan,
> Que beaultè ot trop plus qu'humaine.
> Mais ou sont les neiges d'antan?

Lorenzo listened attentively. The rhythm of her soft voice gave emotion to every syllable. He hadn't thought Claudia could ever be more beautiful, until now. "That was amazing. What does it mean?"

"He speaks of famous women, long dead. He wonders where they are now. He says that beauty fades like an echo over a lake, and he wonders where are the snows of years gone by."

"Who wrote it?"

"His name is François Villon."

"I've never heard of him."

"He's not very famous. Maman says he was in prison when he wrote it. She said that he gave a copy of his collection of poems to her *oncle* and that he used to read them to her when she was a girl."

"Well, he writes beautiful poems."

"I always liked that one. It makes me think about our lives here in Florence. We are important people in the city, but will anyone even care when we are gone? People respect Papà, but centuries from now what will it matter? People tell me that I am beautiful, but five hundred years from now, who will know that I was beautiful?"

"I will always know." Lorenzo spoke before he could think. The words just came out. He wished he could take them back, not because he did not mean them but because he was afraid he was being too forward with Claudia.

Claudia reached over the chessboard and placed the palm of her hand on Lorenzo's cheek. The flickering candle gave the scene a dreamlike quality. Her touch gave Lorenzo butterflies in his stomach. She leaned forward and pulled him toward her. Several chess pieces were knocked over. Lorenzo gently brushed his fingers around Claudia's ears and into her silky hair. Their faces drew nearer. Her brown eyes were an ocean of feelings from which he was unable to look away.

Their mouths touched. Lorenzo closed his eyes and felt her soft lips against his. He held it for a moment, then pressed in harder and locked his tongue against hers. It was warm, wet, and soft. This lasted a few seconds, and then they puckered their lips and held them against each other a second or two longer. They pulled their heads apart. He breathed in her heavenly scent and opened his eyes. Her hand was still on his cheek.

"I've never kissed anyone before," she said, looking him in the eyes and smiling.

"Me neither."

Claudia leaned back. She replaced the toppled chess pieces. Lorenzo stared at her. He wanted to kiss her again. He was in love.

"I wish we could see each other more at the palazzo," he added.

"Me too." She very much wanted to see him more, but it would be almost impossible at the palazzo. Even if her father were not around, there would be plenty of other eyes looking for the slightest bit of gossip. Any time Claudia spent with any man would be closely observed. Anything more than a greeting or some kind of order given to Lorenzo would raise eyebrows. She did not tell Lorenzo this, but he already knew it. And they both knew the mere thought of Lorenzo formally courting Claudia was laughable. Domenico would not even entertain such thought. No man in his position would.

Lorenzo switched thoughts to the present. He could not believe that he had just kissed Claudia. It was everything he had always imagined. He thought of her as a girl, in Father Vincenzo's kitchen, the first time he ever saw her. He thought of all the times he had seen her at the palazzo and admired her youthful beauty.

From inside the Chillis' room, the floor creaked. Claudia looked at Lorenzo, startled. She handed him a felt bag.

"Aprila, per piacere. Open it, please," she whispered.

Lorenzo held the bag open, and she dumped the chess pieces in and slid the board in on top. She leaned in again and kissed Lorenzo quickly on the lips. She blew out the candle and rose to her feet, holding the bag and candlestick in one hand, behind her back. She motioned to Lorenzo with her hand to go away, then opened the door and entered the room. She closed the door behind her, subtly dropping the bag and candle to the floor. In the darkness, she kicked them under a chair.

"L'eau est sur la commode, ma chère." Adélaïde's voice carried through the blackness.

"What's going on?" asked Domenico in a groggy voice.

"Claudia just got up to get a drink of water, mon cher, go back to sleep."

Claudia found her bed in the dark and lay down on top of the covers, appreciative of her mother.

* *

Lorenzo made his way back downstairs. The patrons had all left. The *oste* had retired to his own room. The fire was smoldering down. The two bodyguards each lay sleeping on a table, using their cloaks as mattresses and their saddlebags as pillows. The carriage driver slept seated at a table with his head resting on his folded arms, near a bodyguard's legs. Giovanni de Angelis was sprawled out on a table also. His boots on the floor below, he lay fully clothed with a folded rag of some sort as a pillow. He was on his side facing Lorenzo, and his eyes were closed.

The bodyguards snored loudly. Lorenzo took off his boots and his cloak. He climbed up on the table, folded one boot, and put it behind his head as a pillow. Pulling the cloak over himself as a blanket, he closed his eyes and thought of kissing Claudia.

Giovanni opened his eyes for a second and looked at Lorenzo, then closed them.

XII

The winter winds whipped across the Arno and through the Piazza de' Pitti. Few were out of doors on this Saturday evening. The little

Piazza San Felice was poorly lit. A dim glow from the small windows of the church gave the tiny inlet its only illumination.

Inside the church, the lighting was not much better. Two tall candles flanking the altar lit the front of the small nave. A grouping of prayer candles, burned nearly to the bottom, lit the rear. The wind rattled the wooden doors. In the back of the church were two smaller doors. Father Vincenzo sat in the cramped closet, facing a hole in the wall covered with a curtain. From beyond the curtain came a voice.

"Mi perdona, Padre. I have sinned."

"Dimmi, figlio mio. Tell me, my son," he answered.

"I was with a woman…not my wife. One of the women on the street, and we did it in the alley, behind a barrel. I gave her two lire."

"Go on, my son."

"And I beat a man. Three of us from the guild, we found him late at night and beat him with sticks."

Father Vincenzo's interest was piqued, but he maintained his apparent disinterest. "And when was this, my son?"

"The other night. We heard he was making sandals and clogs and selling them to a master of the guild. The master was reported to the consuls."

"L'Arte de' Calzolai punished the master, I take it."

"Sì, Padre. They fined him one hundred lire. But the clog maker is not a member of the guild, so the consuls told us to handle him ourselves. They said he was taking food out of our children's mouths, we guild shoemakers. It made sense at the time. But after we started beating him, he begged us to stop. I can't stop thinking about him now."

Though Vincenzo knew this was not Lorenzo's attacker, it gave him a new avenue for investigation. His mind started to wander before he reminded himself of the man behind the curtain. "Guilt is God's way of keeping us from making the same mistake twice. I want you to think of how you feel now, the next time you are tempted by the passions of others to commit violence."

"I will, Padre."

"And I want you to be true to your wife. A promise made before God is a promise to be kept."

"I will, Padre."

"I want you to say the Pater Noster. Do you know the words?" This question was obligatory in a parish made up of mostly illiterate, non-Latin speakers.

"Sì, Padre, I do."

"Good. Say it when you leave here and resolve yourself to not commit these sins again."

"Grazie, Padre."

"Te absolvo in nomine Patris et Filii et Spiritus Sancti."

* *

"I asked around the Or San Michele. I spoke with a lot of dyers. None of them know anything, or so they claim." Vincenzo sighed. "But it is the only explanation that makes sense to me. You weren't robbed; it was obviously a message. When was the last time Domenico had you doing any dye work?"

Lorenzo shook his head. "A couple of weeks before I was attacked."

"That makes sense, then. You have to be careful. Domenico does not care…He'll use you for anything he needs done to get his orders filled, but it's you who will catch a beating." Father Vincenzo was frustrated that he could not do more for Lorenzo. He knew the realities of his relationship with his employer, and it made him angry to see the wealthy show little regard for those who depended on them.

"I'll be careful." Lorenzo knew there was no arguing this point with the priest, and figured it was best to simply make this small promise. He also knew that Domenico would not exactly entertain complaints.

Vincenzo stood from the table to retrieve a carafe of wine and three cups from the cupboard. He brought them back to the table and sat again. "Allora, how did the trip to Siena go?"

Lorenzo was excited and a little embarrassed. He smiled reflexively. "Benissimo, Padre."

"So Domenico was able to persuade the English to hold the fair here next spring?"

"I don't think so. I didn't go to their meeting. Once we were in Siena, we stayed at the Palazzo Martino. I looked after the horses and stayed with the servants, I didn't see much of the Chillis….But Domenico seemed angrier than usual on the way back. He made Giovanni, the bodyguards, and me ride ahead of the carriage."

"Then I'm confused. What exactly about the trip went very well?" Father Vincenzo asked sarcastically.

Lorenzo smirked. He felt an overwhelming desire to tell somebody the news, to make it real. He knew the dangers of such a story circulating, but he trusted Vincenzo more than anyone in the world. And though it was not the typical topic for conversation with a priest, Lorenzo had come to know Father Vincenzo as family. "I kissed Claudia," he blurted out.

"I see." Vincenzo was happy for Lorenzo. He was much more accepting of people showing their affections than other priests, perhaps because of the way he had been forced to suppress his own. At the same time, he worried about the young man. "She is very pretty, and kind. She cares about you, I can tell." The priest's smile was as big as Lorenzo's. He reached across the table and squeezed Lorenzo's shoulder in a congratulatory gesture.

"I wish I could marry her, Padre. I've never regretted being a servant, but had I become a guildsman, Domenico might have accepted me as a husband for Claudia."

"The rules of our society take little notice of love," Vincenzo answered, more retrospectively than Lorenzo could have known.

"Claudia asked if I ever thought about the future. To be honest, I've never given much thought to it. I usually think about my day's work at the palazzo and look forward to coming here at night. When I read the books you give me, I think about what life means sometimes, but I've never really asked where I fit into this world. But everything has changed now. I love her. How can I go on working, day after day, without building the life I want to build, my life with her?"

"Be patient, my boy. Life has a way of presenting us with opportunities. Things do not have to go on forever with your life the way it is now." Vincenzo was being sincere, though he was thinking that Lorenzo might end up falling in love with another woman who he could marry and be happy with. He didn't really think that circumstances would change in a way in which Lorenzo and Claudia could be together.

There was a knock at the door.

Lorenzo got up and opened the door. Outside stood Jacopo, bundled up in a thick cloak. He ushered his friend inside and hung his cloak on a hook by the door. The two took their seats opposite Father Vincenzo, and the priest poured another cup of wine for the new arrival.

"It's good to see you again, Jacopo. How have you been?"

"Good, Padre, it's good to see you," Jacopo answered.

"Lorenzo tells me you are finishing your apprenticeship soon."

"Sì, this spring."

"That's quite an achievement; you must be very excited. What will you do next?"

"Well, I still have to work for Coraggiossi for a year, but as an employee not an apprentice. Then, the guild will make me a full master."

"Maestro Giotti!" Lorenzo interjected. Jacopo and Lorenzo laughed.

"What will we be reading tonight?" Jacopo was eager to delve back into the *Inferno*.

"I thought we'd skip a little ahead to the twenty-seventh canto. Dante has some interesting thoughts that still hold truth in our times." Vincenzo slid the bulky book across the table and opened it for the boys to see. "Guido da Montefeltro asks Dante for news of his homeland, the Romagna, and here is how Dante answers…Start here."

Since the book was closer to Lorenzo, he read first.

> Romagna tua non è, e non fu mai,
> sanza guerra ne' cuor de' suoi tiranni;
> ma'n palese nessuna or vi lasciai.

> *Your Romagna is not, and never was,*
> *without war in the heart of its tyrants;*
> *but none was evident when I left there.*

"So even in Dante's time there was war in the Romagna?" asked Jacopo.

"Exactly," the priest answered.

"What were they fighting for?" asked Lorenzo.

"Well, pretty much the same as they are today. There were those who thought the pope should be the temporal ruler of the land and those who thought otherwise. In Dante's time it was the emperor who wanted to control all of Italy. Today it is the king of France."

"But if the pope is like a priest, the most important priest, then why does he want to be like a king? Isn't a pope more important than a king, in the eyes of God?" Jacopo was confused.

"Popes have long maintained that their authority extends not only to religious matters but to all aspects of power. There was supposedly a letter signed by the Emperor Constantine that gives power over the territories of the West to the pope, after Constantine moved his capital to Constantinople. The pope was to rule the West from Rome." Father Vincenzo was happy that the boys were taking an interest in the subject.

"He was the first Christian emperor, Constantine, wasn't he? So it makes sense for him to give power to the pope," Lorenzo added.

"I doubt an emperor would give power to anybody but himself. He also persecuted many Christians before converting, Constantine. Look a little farther down at what Dante tells us." Vincenzo pointed to the page.

Lorenzo read again.

> Ma come Costantin chiese Silvestro
> d'entro Siratti a guerir de la lebbre,
> così mi chiese questi per maestro.

> *But just as Constantine asked Sylvester*
> *on Mount Soracte to cure his leprosy,*
> *so this one asked me to be his master.*

"There is a legend that God had stricken Constantine with leprosy because of his persecution of Christians. Saints Peter and Paul visited him in a dream and told him to visit Pope Sylvester on Mount Soracte, and it was there that Constantine was baptized…thus curing his leprosy," explained Vincenzo.

"So leprosy represents the stain of the persecutions on Constantine's soul," Lorenzo remarked unsurely.

"Sì, and what do we call that?"

"Una metafora, Padre," Lorenzo answered.

"A metaphor, exactly."

"Constantine was the first emperor in Constantinople?" asked Jacopo.

"Sì, and there were emperors there until just fifty years ago, when the Turks conquered the city," the priest replied.

"My Papà had a gold coin from Constantinople!" Lorenzo announced.

"Is that the coin you told me about? The one that was taken when he was killed?" Vincenzo asked.

"Sì, it's called a bezant. It was given to him by Lorenzo il Magnifico!"

"Your father knew Lorenzo de' Medici?" Jacopo asked.

"He did. Papà saved his life when the Pazzis tried to kill him in the duomo, and Lorenzo himself went to the Palazzo Chilli and gave my father the coin." Lorenzo left out the part about his father saving the coin to use as payment for Lorenzo's apprenticeship. He had never told Jacopo that he was supposed to be apprenticed to Coraggiosi. It didn't feel right, discussing the matter with him. Jacopo had become the apprentice; there was no point in looking back. He had told Father Vincenzo about it, years ago, but they had never discussed it since. Did Vincenzo even remember?

Jacopo was impressed with Lorenzo's father's heroics. He wished he could feel the same pride for his own father. Nobody spoke ill of Lodovico in front of Jacopo, but there was always a sense that few, if any, liked the man. Coraggiosi couldn't stand to be around him, that much was obvious. It was as if the sight of Lodovico brought up some bad memory. The feelings of others aside, Jacopo's only memories of growing up with the man were of Lodovico's criticisms. Lodovico was convinced that it was Jacopo's destiny to restore the Giotti name to the greatness of their ancestor Giotto di Bondone, the great Florentine artist. "Why did Constantine persecute the Christians, Padre?" he asked.

"Well, many of the emperors persecuted Christians. They saw the new religion as a threat to their own gods. They believed that their gods protected the empire and felt that the Christians worshiping just one true God would anger their many gods."

"So God helped Constantine set his own path, instead of following that of his ancestors!" Jacopo stated thoughtfully.

"Well, in a manner of speaking, sì." Vincenzo agreed.

Jacopo liked the thought.

* *

Claudia stared into the mirror peacefully. She always loved having her mother brush her hair. It brought her back to her childhood.

Adélaïde stood behind her and worked the silver-handled brush smoothly through her daughter's long, soft hair. Claudia's bedchamber was small, compared to her parents' room, but cozy.

The walls were stone, but the crackling fire warmed the room nicely. It was dark outside, and the fire lit the room dimly.

"Tu sembles heureuse récemment, ma chère! You seem happy lately," said Adélaïde.

"Oui, Maman." Claudia smiled at her mother in the mirror. She had never felt happier. Although she had not been alone with Lorenzo since that night at the osteria, she had seen him almost daily. She found reasons to go out in the courtyard or come downstairs if she heard his voice, and they would exchange smiles.

"Il est très beau! Very handsome," Adélaïde whispered in her ear.

Claudia blushed. "How did you know?"

"I see how you look at him."

"Do you think that Papà knows?"

"No, ma chère, it is our secret."

Claudia smiled. Her mother always understood her. "I wish I could marry him Maman."

Adélaïde rubbed her daughter's shoulder affectionately. Her eyes watered up a bit, but she maintained her composure. She knew such a thing could never happen. "Je sais, ma chère, I know!"

Claudia was now twenty. Most girls her age were already married. Wealthy men in Florence tended to marry later, in their late twenties, even thirty. Women, however, were usually married in their teens, to older men. Marriage was a contract between two families, mutually beneficial if possible. They both knew that it was only a matter of time before Domenico found a husband for his daughter.

"Well, he will always be my love," proclaimed Claudia boldly.

Adélaïde smiled warmly at the girl, again holding back tears. Pierre had been very good to her, but he had given her hand to a man she did not love. He had been looking out for his daughter's security, and he married her off well. Adélaïde knew how it felt to love someone she could not be with, and the thought of her daughter sharing the same fate made her sad. But outwardly she smiled. Her daughter was in love. This, at least, made her happy.

XIII

Just north of the Piazza della Signoria and a few blocks east of the Or San Michele ran the Via de' Pandolfini. Along the via stood a modest but dignified palazzo. It served as the residence for the consuls of the Arte de' Giudici e Notai, the guild of judges and notaries. It might not have been as large or ornate as the palace of the consuls of the wool or Calimala guilds, but its inhabitants wielded great power in the city.

Above the main entrance of the palazzo was an inverted oval with a pointed bottom, blue in color. Inside the oval were four gold stars. This so-called Stemma dell'Arte de' Giudici e Notai was the symbol of the guild that conducted no commerce itself, but was integral to the function of all other guilds and to Florence as a whole.

Lodovico Giotti and Giovanni de Angelis sat in an antechamber inside the palazzo. Guild members often called on the consuls to discuss any number of matters. One half of an oversized wooden double door swung in and an elderly yet scholarly-looking man came through. He closed the door behind him and began to cross the antechamber. Just before exiting, he recognized one of the two men seated.

"What are you doing here, Giotti? Stirring up more trouble, I gather," spat the man with disgust.

"Messer Altoviti, it is always a pleasure," replied Lodovico smugly.

The man nodded at Giovanni and exited the antechamber. Lodovico and Giovanni were again alone, waiting.

"He sure doesn't like you!" Giovanni said after a moment.

"The feeling is mutual."

Giovanni asked no more about it.

* *

Lodovico had attended the University of Bologna, the oldest and most prestigious institute for legal studies, just like his father before him. Upon completion of his studies, he joined the guild of judges and notaries. Entrance to this guild varied from the merchant guilds. There was an apprenticeship, but it was much shorter. The new member was then examined by the consuls and upon successful completion of this exam, he became a full member. All legal and commercial proceedings had to be witnessed by a notary. Accordingly, a notary could expect a prosperous life.

Apprentices must have come from respectable families, with no public debt. Many wealthy families sent sons (other than the firstborn) to study and train as notaries. This allowed the family to have the necessary counsel on hand for all its transactions. Other families with large operations hired notaries for their businesses. All government officials had notaries assigned to their office, and every guild had dedicated notaries.

After the death of Lorenzo de' Medici, the exile of his son Piero, and the brief, ill-fated reign of Friar Girolamo Savonarola, the leaders of the Florence, or Signoria, agreed on a *gonfaloniere di giustizia* to lead the city. The man they chose was Piero Soderini. To avoid favoritism, he was given the position for life. Soderini quickly gained a reputation for being a fair and just ruler, often acting against his own interests for the public good. The seat of government in Florence was in the Palazzo della Signoria, also known as the Palazzo Vecchio, the Old Palace. Gonfaloniere Soderini's office was inside, along with most other civil offices of the city. The Pazzi conspirators had been hanged from its walls. Fra Girolamo Savonarola had been burned alive in the piazza in front of the palazzo. Numerous notaries worked in the Palazzo Vecchio, including the young Lodovico Giotti.

The guild of judges and notaries differed from other guilds in that they produced nothing. Their bylaws were not set up to regulate a commercial activity, but in a sense to give a structure to the city as a whole. While the consuls of the other guilds sat in judgment of its own members when it came to matters of their business dealings and even at times their private conduct, the consuls of the Arte de' Giudici e Notai were actual judges. They not only judged their own, but all citizens when it came to crimes against the Florentine state. The notaries worked for merchants of other guilds; they even worked directly for other guilds. They certified legal documents, supervised commercial transactions, and gave legal advice of all kinds.

Lodovico Giotti had worked mostly for the *comune*, or city government, since finishing his studies in Bologna. His father, called Iacopo (and later in life Jacopo, in the style of the times) had spent his career much the same way. Iacopo worked at the Palazzo Vecchio when Lorenzo de' Medici's father, Piero, called Piero the Gouty because of his illness, lead the city. While Lodovico was making a good living as an average guild notary, Niccolò Altoviti was a senior *giudice* and consul of the guild. He held great power in both the guild and the city at large.

On a hot August day in 1502, Lodovico stood before three consuls in the grand chamber of the palazzo on the Via de'

Pandolfini. Sweat dripped down his face; his hair was completely damp. Because of the heat, he did not wear the customary gray robe of the notaries; he wore only a baggy white blouse, tucked into tight woolen pants with high *calze*, or stockings. He had a decorative money purse attached to his belt, like all respectable merchants and legal professionals. The consuls, too, wore only loose-fitting blouses as they sat in the stuffy chamber. The windows were open high, but no breeze blew in.

"So I hear you've become quite close to the gonfaloniere, Giotti!" Altoviti spoke with thinly veiled contempt.

"Sì, Messere, I am not one of his personal notaries, but I am in the palazzo. I feel I have done a good job for him, and he trusts me," Lodovico answered. He had worked at the *comune* for some years now and gained a reputation as a competent and loyal civil servant. He had always done his duty faithfully. He was one of many notaries working under the *gonfaloniere*, but Soderini recognized talent.

"He trusts you enough to ask your opinion of other members of this guild?" Altoviti wasted little time in getting to the heart of the matter.

"He did so just the one time, Messere."

Two other consuls flanked Altoviti, with five empty chairs on their sides. They said nothing. Altoviti continued, "And what was your answer?"

"I told him that Gianluigi Bastone was a brilliant and honest judge who would make an excellent judge of appeals," Lodovico confessed.

"Yet you knew that my son was in line for that position!" accused the consul.

"Messere, your son is a good man, but Bastone is older and more accomplished. He has an unmatched knowledge of the law. I gave my honest answer for the good of the city."

Altoviti paused. He looked at the consul to his right, then laughed ironically. "Well, I was not aware we had such an honest man in our ranks...I must commend you, Notaio!"

Lodovico knew better than to respond. His blouse stuck to his sweaty body, and he wiped his forehead uncomfortably.

"Clearly, we could use such an honest man's talents more effectively. I am having you sent to the apothecaries' guild; they could use an *honest* man to help them count bags of herbs. I spoke with the captain of the guards at the Palazzo Vecchio; you are no longer allowed to enter the building," Altoviti was condescending and harsh in tone.

Lodovico was incensed. He felt powerless; there was nothing he could do. He had done his duty honorably, and this was his reward. The consuls of the guild were always judges, and the notaries often felt looked down upon by their supposed brothers. This was just another example of the judges feeling superior to the notaries and taking out their petty revenges. Wanting to be out of their presence as soon as possible, he asked, "Will that be all, Messere?"

"I understand that you, too, have a son, Giotti."

"Sì, he's just a boy, ten years old."

"Well good luck getting him admitted to this guild," Altoviti concluded as he motioned at the door for Lodovico to leave.

* *

Lodovico and Giovanni de Angelis now stood in the same grand chamber. There was just one consul seated at the long table. He was old, with a well-trimmed white beard. He sat back comfortably in his chair and spoke warmly. "How can I help you, old friend?"

"Messere, I was wondering if the notary position for the ambassador to Rome has been filled yet," said Lodovico respectfully.

"No, we only found out about Dottor Buonocuore's death a few days ago. We've not yet discussed who to send."

"Might I recommend young Giovanni de Angelis here…È molto bravo—very good.

"I'm sure we could accommodate you, Giotti. I have not heard much interest from the other consuls in naming someone to the post. It shouldn't be a problem."

"Grazie, Messere!"

"Di niente, Dottor Giotti."

Lodovico and Giovanni walked along the Via de' Pandolfini. They spoke quietly, though the street was quite desolate at the moment.

"Grazie, Lodovico," whispered Giovanni.

"I am a man of my word."

"Do you think the dyers will cause enough trouble for Domenico?"

"I told you never to speak of that!"

"Mi scusa," Giovanni replied contritely. "I just thought that your plan was brilliant, and I wanted to know how it worked out. Working at the emissary in Rome, I suppose I will need to be cunning if I hope to do well…I wanted to learn from you." The young notary was reverent and admiring.

Never one to be outsmarted, Lodovico saw through Giovanni's sycophantic excuse. But just as a rabbit inches closer to the bait, ignoring the signs of a trap, Lodovico let down his guard in the face of a compliment. He so seldom received any. He had been disgraced years before and had been bitter ever since. His bitterness, in turn, made others dislike him, which then made him even bitterer. "The plan was well conceived, but there was one factor I had not foreseen," he admitted calmly.

Smugly aware that his tactic had succeeded, Giovanni fought the urge to smirk. Instead, he gave all the outward appearance of an admiring student while in fact eager for more gossip. "Ch'è successo, what happened?" he asked.

"Well, since you had mentioned to me in the past that the Simoni boy sometimes does dye work, I thought I could conjure up some anger among the guild dyers. First, I laid the groundwork. While certifying a contract in the Or San Michele, I let it slip out that some merchants were underpricing competitors by hiring out-of-guild tradesmen. Nobody would believe such a thing, of course, not just hearing it once. So I also hired two boys from Lucca, who were in Florence delivering something for their master. I met them in the mercato and paid them twenty lire to go to the osteria on the Via dei Calzaiuoli and brag to the oste that they had come to town for a couple of days to do dye work at Chilli's bottega. You'd be surprised how fast news of that sort travels around the tradesmen."

Giovanni switched from curious to impressed. "I never would have thought of that!"

Lodovico liked the feeling of being admired. "The next time you told me about the Simoni boy doing dye work, I went and told a dyer I thought to be particularly vocal in his anger."

"And that's when they beat Lorenzo?" asked Giovanni.

"No, first they went to the Guild with the complaint. There was plenty of evidence; the consuls should have brought Chilli to trial…at least, that's what I had hoped would happen. But of course, as with any plan, there is the unknown. As events unfolded, the guild became entangled negotiating with England for trading rights. The consuls were consumed with the negotiations, and I think they had already decided to send Chilli to Siena on their behalf. The last thing they wanted was to put one of their sensali on trial, least of all one they had chosen to send as a delegate. They let him off with a warning. The dyers were furious and took matters into their own hands."

"But what good would it have done *you* if they had put Domenico on trial?" Giovanni could not make the connection.

"One of the consuls of the wool guild is indebted to me. As preparations for a trial moved forward, I would have offered Chilli my assistance in making the case go away. He faced being removed as a sensale, as well as an embarrassing public trial and fine; he would have been eager for my help."

"But one consul alone could not have dismissed the charges!" Giovanni knew enough about guild procedure to be confused at Lodovico's assumptions.

"È vero, that's true, but I took other precautions. The ringleader of the dyers, whom I had been meeting regularly to feed information, was to be bought off. He would recant his allegation. My friend the consul would then move for a dismissal. It should have worked well. But as I said, outside events changed the equation."

"You are truly a genius, Lodovico. And what would you have asked for in return from Domenico?"

"His daughter's hand, of course, for my son."

Giovanni laughed heartily, then stopped himself, realizing that Lodovico was being serious. "Do you think he would agree to such a thing? He is enormously rich; would he not have simply tried to buy his way out of the mess without giving away his daughter?"

Lodovico, slightly annoyed at being laughed at, was determined to show the merits of his plan. "Not exactly. He could not offer such bribes himself. If allegations of bribery came forth, he could be expelled from the guild. My plan would keep him out of the dirty end of the deal. But there is more. Jacopo will soon be a Calimala master. Chilli, of course, is forbidden from dealing in foreign wool, as a member of the local wool guild. But as you know, foreign wool has become much more profitable. With new trade deals for raw wool sheared from sheep abroad, the lines between what is foreign and local have been blurred. With a son-in-law in the Calimala guild, he could move to corner whole new markets of importing. I could have offered him a solution to two problems at once, I think he would have gone for it."

As soon as he had finished speaking, Lodovico regretted telling Giovanni so much. He had been charmed into opening up, and then eager to prove himself right. He was now especially glad that Giovanni would be going to Rome. "This is all between us, you understand. If these details came to light, you would be guilty of conspiring for your own appointment and thrown out of the guild!"

"Of course, Dottore, that goes without saying," Giovanni took notice of the fact that he now had something over Lodovico, but he was outwardly reassuring: "It is our secret. It's a shame that the negotiations with England got in the way!"

"Indeed. Some things are out of our control."

"You might had been too late anyway," Giovanni added.

"How so?"

"Well, on the trip to Siena, Domenico's daughter seemed to take a liking to Lorenzo. They sneaked off together…The girl could be pregnant now for all we know. Who'd want to marry her then?" As always, Giovanni took delight in being the bearer of salacious news.

"I see." Lodovico was astonished. He had not anticipated such a turn of events. "So perhaps it was for the best anyway." He soon had another thought as the two men turned onto the Via del Proconsolo, but he kept this plan to himself.

LIBER TERTIUS

Dimitte nobis debita nostra

I

SPRING 1512

In a valley, between distant hills, mobs of infantryman fought with long lances and swords. From a distance, no distinguishable army could be discerned; it looked like a free-for-all. The mass of clashing bodies seemed to move as one across the plain. As far as the eye could see lay the dead and wounded, men and horses. Shouting voices echoed many languages. Screams of agony came from all directions. It was chaos.

A haze of smoke lingered across the landscape. The tall, thick city walls of Ravenna stood off in the distance, obscured through the fog-like residue of cannon barrages. The smoke rose slowly in the warm air, and above its billowy form hung a clear, blue sky. Cannon fire still roared in the distance as separate pockets of fighting raged all across the countryside outside the city.

From under a dead body came a groan. The dead body rolled aside, and from under it a monk struggled to free himself. He stood, adjusted his robe, and dusted himself off. *How did I get myself into this?* he thought. He hated war. At that moment, he felt further away from his original calling than he had ever felt before.

He had nearly been killed. He began the day at what was the rear of the papal army's lines, but the French forces pushed forward far into their ranks, and then there was no longer a front; there was only chaos. A cavalry charge came out of nowhere and seemed to slaughter everything in sight. The monk was knocked to the ground and nearly trampled.

As he stood wondering how he was still alive, a team of horsemen now returned to the hilltop and surrounded him. Last to arrive was a tall, young man with a regal air. His hair was light and curly, and he wore a well-trimmed beard. The horse's reins were wrapped tightly around his left hand, and his right hand wielded a long silver sword. He was handsome and rode his white horse very well.

If the great painters of Florence were to brush the perfect warrior, a living god, and the form of male beauty, he would be their model. He had a breastplate of high-shined tin and chain mail underneath. His determined eyes seemed at odds with an adolescent face, cheekbones and nose in perfect proportion.

He tugged the leather reigns sharply and the horse bucked slightly and let out a huff. "Qui est-il?" the horseman asked sharply, addressing one of the other cavalrymen in polished French.

The second horseman turned to the monk. "He wants to know who you are," he said.

"Fra Matteo di Napoli, of the Franciscan Order, secretary to Pope Julius."

"Il est Matheu, un moine et le secrétaire au Pape Jule!" said the horseman to his leader.

The handsome rider spun the horse directly toward Matteo and spoke: "Savez-vous qui je suis?"

"Do you know who he is?" said the other.

"Gaston de Foix, I presume." Though he had never met de Foix, Matteo was quite certain.

"Oui," replied the young general as he dismounted the white warhorse. He approached Matteo and sat on a rock, next to the dead body that had pinned the friar. He nodded to another horseman and clapped his hand. The horseman pulled an apple out of his satchel and tossed it to de Foix. The general held it out to Matteo, who accepted and sat on the ground opposite de Foix.

The horseman tossed his commander another apple and Gaston took a large bite. "You must forgive…if my Italian is not…uhhh, perfect." The combination of food in his mouth and his French accent made it difficult to understand him, but Matteo was able to follow.

Matteo bit down on the greenish, yellow apple. He had arrived that morning, just before the first cannon barrages, and had not eaten breakfast. The skin was crisp and the fruit juicy and cool. He found it very refreshing in his dry mouth. His hands were still shaking from the cavalry charge, and the chewing calmed him. He took a second bite without speaking. Cannons still roared in the distance.

"You understand...what happening today?" de Foix asked.

"Sì," Matteo replied as he chewed slowly and stared at the dead body in front of him.

"I want that you go to the pape...I want you to tell him about this. Look around. His men either die, or flee. Roi Louis has won a great victory here today!"

"*You* have won a great victory today!" Matteo added.

"The two things are the same."

"You are famous in Rome. The scourge of Italy. First Bologna, then Brescia, now Ravenna."

"Italy needs no scourge. She is the source of all her own problems. I merely have capitalized on the...dèsunion."

"What city will you capitalize on next?"

De Foix laughed. He took a last bite of the apple and tossed the core to the ground. "My king's rightful possessions...I defend them; I seek nothing else."

It was clear to Matteo that de Foix was not going to harm him, and this emboldened him. "From what I hear, you cannot press any further. Most of your army will be recalled to France to fight the invading English."

"You hear a lot, then, Fra Matteo." De Foix smiled charmingly. "And it is true. You may tell your master that if it is peace he desires, now...the time is, uhh...bien. Roi Louis will be eager to settle matters in Italy...with Henry's troops on his doorstep."

"And it is peace that *you* desire, Monsieur Gaston?"

"Oui. I have done what I came to do." De Foix rose and mounted his horse. He wrapped the reigns tightly around his left hand and drew his sword with his right. "My breath is uhh...gaspillèe...wasted. Pape Jule does not want peace; he wants victory."

"I will pray for peace," Matteo responded.

"And will you say a prayer for me on this Easter Sunday, Frère?"

"I will."

"Adieu!" De Foix bucked his horse high and pointed his sword toward the fighting. The horse galloped hard, and de Foix's men followed.

Matteo watched as the band rode hard at a retreating Spanish regiment. The Spaniards were scattering, some running down to the

Ronco River, others for a patch of woods over a small hill. De Foix led the charge. He rode magnificently. He was daring and bold. His armor shone in the sunlight. He rode as if the timeless glory of the conquering general lay just at the foot of the river and he was determined to seize it.

As a pack of Spanish infantrymen reached the woods, a dozen or so men with crossbows stepped out from behind the trees. They paused as their countrymen passed them into safety and lowered their bows in aim. All of them fired at once. The entire front rank of de Foix's charge was hit. Gaston slumped forward at first and then slid off of his horse. He fell to the ground dead.

* *

Matteo rode slowly. The road to Florence was winding, but the views were breathtaking. Cypress trees lined the dusty path, and rolling green hills basked in the spring sun. Every few miles a vineyard or farm saddled the roadway. The Apennine Mountains seemed to cut up into the horizon in all directions.

He rode alone. He had traveled to Ravenna with another papal emissary but had been unable to find him after the battle. The horse bounced rhythmically, and Matteo stared ahead in a trance. He had never seen war before. He hated it and now detested the men who brought war into this world. He could understand defending oneself, but that was it. The wars being fought across Europe now had nothing to do with self-defense; they were about egos and glory. Julius had kept him out of most of his meetings with generals and mercenaries, and it was difficult to know what to believe from papal announcements and court gossip around Rome. But Matteo had now come to believe that his master was nothing more than a glory-seeking warmonger. Thousands of men had been slaughtered, most of them far from home, for a cause that would have had little effect on their lives had they stayed home. What was the point? The battle was fought to make either the pope or the king of France the nominal ruler of Ravenna, to redraw a line on a map. The people of Ravenna would go on being Ravennese, of course. They weren't now suddenly French because of the outcome of the armies' actions, but their governor spoke Français.

Matteo rode and thought. He thought about the path his life had taken. Julius had sent Matteo to meet with Ramòn de Cardona at

Ravenna. He was to deliver a letter and a personal message. He did not know the contents of the letter, but the personal message was to instruct Cardona to move toward Florence after taking Ravenna. A garrison was to be left at Ravenna while the bulk of Cardona's coalition of Spanish troops, papal guards and mercenaries encircled Florence and awaited further orders. For some reason, Julius had felt the need to choose Matteo as messenger. He was instructed to tell no one but Cardona these instructions. Perhaps Julius did not have full faith in any one general and felt only Matteo, having been kept ignorant of much of the planning, could be trusted now.

Of course, Julius would not utter the notion of a possible defeat at Ravenna, but he did ensure that Matteo understood that the plans were to be carried out in any event. Matteo was to instruct Cardona to march on Florence at battle's end with no regard to setbacks.

Matteo arrived the morning of the battle and met Cardona hastily in his tent. He delivered the message and waited while Cardona read the letter and wrote out two responses. The general sealed both envelopes and told Matteo to bring the first to Cardinal Giovanni de' Medici in Florence and the second back to the pope in Rome.

"Cardinale de' Medici! When will I see him in Florence?" Matteo asked Cardona.

"When you leave here. El Santo Padre has given me my instructions, and I am to give you yours." Cardona opened the tent flap and called in an aide. He slipped a tin breastplate over his head, and the aide began fastening the laces while the general stood with his arms outstretched. He was slightly shorter than Matteo, but his commanding demeanor gave him greater stature. "You are to go to the baptistery in Florence, on the third day from now. At noon a man will meet you there and take you to the cardinale. Adiós, Monje!"

Matteo now approached Florence wearily. He had no wish to be Julius's messenger. Whatever machinations were being put in place, he was sure there would be more bloodshed.

* *

Lorenzo and Father Vincenzo stood in front of the Palazzo Vecchio. In front of the imposing palazzo stood a seventeen-foot-high statue of a nude male figure. The white Carrara marble was perfectly chiseled, and the flawless muscle tone portrayed strength. The young warrior held a stone in his right hand and draped a slingshot over his shoulder with his left. The boyish face stared off in the distance, determined, yet unsure. Vincenzo and Lorenzo were walking together but had stopped in front of the statue to admire its beauty.

"So tell me, who do you agree with…those who say he has just slain Goliath, or those who say he is just about to?" asked the priest.

"I thought David had already slain the giant; that's why he's holding the slingshot that way…That's why he's being sculpted, because he's already famous for killing Goliath," answered Lorenzo.

"That could be the case. I like to think not, though. I like to think that he is about to face the giant. After all, he is still holding the stone! I like to think he is looking out to his future, where all will be different. Someday he will be king, and he will fall from grace. But now, at this moment, he is at the crossroad where his old life is ending and his new one beginning. He is about to reach the pinnacle of fame and glory…and at this moment all is good. There is no corruption, there are no detractors, there is only glory. It is temporary; glory always is. But the purest glory is often found in the quest, not the achievement." Father Vincenzo shielded his eyes as he spoke, to lessen the glare of the midday sun on the shiny marble. Passersby took no notice of their conversation, though the piazza was crowded.

"I never knew you could see so much in a statue," replied Lorenzo, genuinely impressed with a new sense of appreciation for the work.

"Michelangelo Buonarroti is a master of portraying human emotion in marble…but in the end, it is not what the artist feels that makes a work of art remarkable; it is what the work makes you feel!" Vincenzo put an arm around Lorenzo's shoulder and pointed up to the statue's face to guide his gaze. He continued, "All that I just described to you is what that face makes *me* feel. It is not important what Buonarroti was actually trying to portray when he carved it. Look at it; what does it make you feel?"

Lorenzo was used to being put on the spot by Father Vincenzo and did not hesitate to open his mind and offer his emotions. He looked at the defined cheeks, the innocent eyes, the wavy hair, the anticipation, the nervousness, and the resolve…It was all there in polished stone. "I see a boy about to become a man!"

"And how will that happen?"

"By his determination, by his action. He knows what he has to do. He knows what is right. Others may doubt his ability, but he knows he is ready. He can no longer hide behind his youth. It is time for him to act like a man."

"Bravo, Lorenzo."

The two started to cross the piazza.

"Vincenzo?" muttered an unsure voice from a few steps away.

They both turned to see who was calling. Looking at them was a monk, handsome, but with a worn look on his face. His greenish blue eyes were fixed on Vincenzo's eyes. His brown, hooded robe was dusty, and the knotted rope that stood for a belt was frayed and askew, but as Vincenzo looked the man in the eyes, his heart dropped. He felt slightly weak in the knees and had to swallow before he could speak.

"Sei tu? Is that you?" he asked in a low voice.

Matteo nodded and smiled.

Vincenzo was completely shocked. For most of the last fourteen years, barely a day went by where he didn't think about Matteo. He often wondered where he was and what he was doing. He wondered what life would be like if they had been able to stay together. He longed to embrace him, to hold him, to feel his touch and smell the scent of his olive skin, to hear his voice say his name, *Vincenzo*, in his warm Neapolitan accent. For years Vincenzo had hardly turned a corner without expecting to see Matteo's face around the bend. Without thinking, he looked for him in crowds. He lived with a subconscious expectation of finding his love again. The expectation was a double-edged sword; it both warmed and stabbed the heart simultaneously.

But as the years went on, the pain lessened. Recently, he had hardly thought of Matteo at all; and on this beautiful, sunny day, talking with Lorenzo in the piazza, he was the last thing on his mind. But here he was. In an instant, Vincenzo was right back to where he was fourteen years ago, the longing returned.

"Non ci credo! I don't believe it!" Matteo exclaimed as he rushed toward Vincenzo and outstretched his arms. Vincenzo opened his as well, and the two embraced. It was with muted affection, of course; the two were all too aware that they were in public. But in the few seconds where their shoulders touched and their arms wrapped and squeezed and their cheeks rubbed together, they shared the unspoken joy of reuniting.

"What are you doing here?" Vincenzo asked.

"Delivering a letter. And you? Is this where you live?"

"Sì. I left Naples just after you did and came here. I am the parish priest of San Felice. It is a small church on the other side of the Arno. And what about you? Did you go back to the monastery after working for della Rovere?"

"Actually, I never stopped working for him. I am secretary for il Papa."

"*Io* non ci credo! Secretary to the pope!" Vincenzo was flabbergasted.

"Well, it is a long way from the pious service I set out to give our Lord," Matteo replied sullenly.

Lorenzo stood off to the side silently, not sure of what to do with himself. Father Vincenzo soon remembered him and called him over.

"Lorenzo, come here. This is an old friend of mine from Naples, Matteo." Vincenzo was a bit nervous. It showed.

Lorenzo bowed his head. "Piacere, Frate!"

"The pleasure is mine, my boy. Vincenzo, can I call on you for dinner this evening?"

"Of course, old friend, I look forward to it."

Matteo was excited by the idea. "Excellent. I am very sorry but I must not miss my appointment. A più tardi!"

"A più tardi!" Vincenzo replied.

Matteo smiled and stepped back. He looked at Lorenzo and bowed his head. "Will I see you there, Lorenzo?"

"Sì, Lorenzo usually has dinner with me," replied Vincenzo.

"No, Padre, tonight I will be working late," Lorenzo interjected.

"Peccato, pity," said Matteo. "Well, I will be in town a couple of days; perhaps I will see you again."

"I look forward to it," Lorenzo added genuinely.

Matteo turned and walked away.

"I didn't know you were working late. He does not have you working with the dyers again, does he? I told you how dangerous that could be." Vincenzo kept his Neapolitan temper in check, but was clearly worried.

"Relax, Padre, I am not working tonight. I just thought you should have some time to catch up with your friend. I do not want to be in the way."

"You are family to me, Lorenzo. You are never in the way"

"I know. But even family members need time alone with friends. Besides, I may be meeting up with Claudia later."

"I see. Well, like I told you before, be careful. Watchful eyes are all around."

"I will be, Padre. Was Matteo a good friend of yours in Naples?"

"We were very close."

Lorenzo had discussed love with Vincenzo, but only as it pertained to himself. It had never occurred to Lorenzo to ask the priest about his past loves or sexuality. Did priests even experience such things? Lorenzo had believed that priests were graced by God to be above such earthly emotions. He still did not make such a connection in regards to Vincenzo and Matteo, but he did sense something greater than ordinary friendship between them. He, Lorenzo, had a special relationship with the priest, but it was a paternal type of love he received. It did not seem the same with Matteo, but Lorenzo did not know why. He had never seen the priest act so nervous before. Above all, he was happy Vincenzo had found his old friend. "Have a good dinner. Perhaps we can all eat together tomorrow night, if he is still in town."

"It sounded like he will be. I will see you tomorrow."

"A domani, Padre, till tomorrow." Lorenzo walked off toward the *mercato* to buy some hemp rope for the stable.

Vincenzo watched him leave. He walked back toward the statue of David and sat with his back against the base. His hands trembled, and he breathed a bit uneasily. He had not felt this way in a long time.

II

"Fra Matteo?" asked a handsome young priest.

Matteo turned his attention away from the brilliant bronze relief carvings of Ghiberti's baptistery doors. "Si," he replied.

"If you'll follow me, Signore, the cardinal is expecting you."

Matteo turned and took in one last view of the heavenly scenes. He looked upward to the top left panel, the scene of Adam and Eve where Adam is raised from the ground by an elderly, fatherly God, while Eve is lowered by four winged angels. In the background a serpent tempts the naked couple, and on the bottom right of the panel, Eden is transformed. Matteo thought about paradise. He thought of how the decisions we make transform our world around us. He wished he had made a different decision many years before.

The two men crossed the spacious piazza, passed the massive duomo, and arrived at a small palazzo facing the Via dei Servi. Inside the door, a long table sat in the main entrance hall. Seated on either side were what appeared to be mercenary generals, or *condottieri*. At the head of the table sat a portly, round-faced, youthful-looking cardinal, Giovanni de' Medici. He was chewing, and he placed a chicken drumstick down on a plate, wiped his mouth on his plush, red sleeve, took a swig of wine, and spoke in a loud, friendly voice. "Sedete vi, Frate, sit," he said as he motioned toward an empty chair.

Matteo sat, his dusty, plain brown robe at odds with the grandeur of the other's wardrobe.

"So I hear you've come straight from the battle at Ravenna!" The cardinal was boisterous.

"It is true, Vostra Eminenza. I bear a letter from Signor Cardona."

"Tell me, Frate, what was the battle like?"

The two *condottieri* looked on eagerly, for though they both made a great show of military prowess, neither had actually fought in a battle. They had led armies, stood in battle formation, and brokered treaties on numerous occasions, but Italian *condottieri* were notorious for delaying, bargaining, and even on occasion switching loyalties on the battlefield itself. The generals were hired from time to time by the many republics, duchies, and principalities of the disunited Italian peninsula, none of which kept a standing professional army to speak of. In the never-ending game of Italian politics, various alliances and hostilities broke out, and both sides hired mercenaries. All of this, of course, left the countryside ripe for foreign invaders, be they France, Spain, or the Holy Roman Empire.

"It was horrible, Vostra Eminenza. It was chaos. The screams of the dying haunt me still. I cannot see how any man could intentionally bring war upon us." Matteo's hands trembled under the table.

"And Gaston de Foix…is he as gallant and as fearless as they say?" The cardinal was undaunted by the somber tone of Matteo's account.

"He was indeed a magnificent sight, gallant indeed. He was soft-spoken and bold. But even he was not immune to the senseless horror. When he fell, he died no differently than the miserable, unarmored peasants who make up the front lines."

"Gaston de Foix is dead!" De' Medici was shocked. "This is good news! I had heard that Cardona had been turned back. I thought it was a total defeat. But with de Foix dead, the French advance is finished. With England poised to invade, the French will have to leave Italy."

Matteo sat silently; he had nothing else to add. He presented the cardinal with Cardona's letter. De' Medici broke the wax seal and unfolded the thick parchment. He began to read and then stopped.

"Spagnolo! Spanish!" barked the Cardinal as he handed the letter to the *condottiere* on his left. "We cannot even use our own *language* to fight a war!"

"Mi Ilustre Señor Cardenal," began the *condottiere*, his Spanish accent thick, "it is my intention to move, with the blessing of our Santo Padre in Rome, upon the city of Florence. I will restore upon the city of your birth the rightful rule of your most illustrious house. My army will march, victorious from Ravenna, in one week's time."

"Let's hope his less-than-victorious showing in Ravenna doesn't slow his move." De' Medici leaned over and slapped the *condottiere* on the shoulder, "I told you the pope would keep his word." The news was the highlight of the cardinal's clandestine trip to his native city.

III

Matteo and Vincenzo sat opposite each other at the cozy table. They had finished eating and were completely caught up on each other's history of the last fourteen years.

"Lorenzo seems a fine young man," Matteo stated sheepishly, afraid to finish the question.

"I have practically raised him. He was orphaned not too long after I arrived here in Florence, and I've looked after him ever since. He is like a son to me."

Relieved, Matteo added, "You always had a charitable heart. What will the boy do now?"

"He works for a wealthy wool merchant, Domenico Chilli. It is a living, but barely more than that."

"Why not apprentice him as a priest with you? The Church is a good life, if you manage to stay away from Rome."

"He is a very smart and thoughtful young man, but I think his heart lies elsewhere—he is in love!"

"And love and the Church do not mix," Matteo cut in. He reached across the table and rested his open palm on top of Vincenzo's closed fist. "I'm glad I found you." He looked nervously into Vincenzo's eyes before turning his gaze down to the table.

"Anch'io son contento. I'm happy, too," Vincenzo answered.

"You have a Florentine accent now." Matteo smiled.

"Well, everyone here says that I sound Neapolitan!"

"Of course they do. They are Tuscan. To a fellow Neapolitan, you sound Florentine, to a Tuscan, you sound *Nnapulitan.*"

Vincenzo laughed.

"Do you still think about the day I left, and how you said we could go to Sicily together?" Matteo's face became solemn.

"I used to a lot, but as the years went by, the thoughts faded, like a wound that scabs, then scars, then fades… until you only notice the faded skin and hardly ever think of the original wound."

"Would you go now?" Matteo asked apprehensively.

Vincenzo was stunned. Butterflies turned in his stomach. "Now…after all of these years?"

"Sì, now." Matteo looked him in the eyes; he was serious.

"Non è possibile. I have a life here; my parish needs me. Lorenzo needs me."

"You said yourself, the boy is in love. Soon he will marry and have his own family. Where will that leave you?"

"He will not marry his love; it cannot be."

"Surely someday he will marry. You have done a world of good for the boy. It is time you do something for yourself."

"And you? You will walk away from the Church, from the pope?"

"I can no longer serve il Papa guerriero. I wanted to serve God, not a general. I can no longer serve a man who would bring war upon this land."

"Matteo," Vincenzo was now sad, the old heartbreak having returned, "we are not kids anymore. I wasn't thinking when I spoke all those years ago. How could we run off together? How could we get there? How could we support ourselves? The world would be very suspicious of us, even if we said we were brothers. No one would hire us; they would take us for criminals on the run. It would be impossible."

Matteo could not argue with any of these points. He stood and pulled Vincenzo into his arms. They embraced in silence. After a moment, Matteo said softly, "I can't believe you choked Pope Julius!"

Vincenzo laughed with teary eyes. Then as their laughter stopped, they tightened their embrace. They touched lips and kissed forcefully. Years of longing were worked into every locking of their mouths. The future did not matter. All they had in the world was this kiss.

* *

Domenico opened one-half of the double doors that faced the courtyard. He looked at Lorenzo, standing at the door holding a wooden crate filled with candles. "What is it?" he asked curtly.

Lorenzo, surprised to find the master of the house answering the door, cleared a lump in his throat and spoke. "Signora asked me to change the candles in the entrance hall."

"*Now?* That's crazy! Do it in the morning." Domenico was now perturbed.

Lorenzo was about to turn and go back to his quarters when he heard Adélaïde's voice echo from deep within the palazzo. "I don't want to feel my way up those stairs one more night. Let him do it now."

In no mood to argue, Domenico walked away, leaving Lorenzo to enter and close the door behind him, shutting out the darkened courtyard. In the entrance hall, he set the crate of candles down and fetched a rickety, wooden stepladder from the kitchen. He climbed and pulled the melted wax stubs out of the chandelier over the main hall. Domenico and Adélaïde had both gone upstairs, leaving the first floor empty, other than for Lorenzo. He worked slowly, not wanting to finish quickly. He climbed up and down the shaky ladder repeatedly, carrying no more than one candle at a time.

Sometime later, Claudia descended the dark, stone steps. She wore a long white nightgown. Her hair hung loose over her shoulders, and she guided herself down the dark stairs with a hand on the wall. Lorenzo stood atop the ladder and watched with nervous excitement. This was a risky encounter, schemed up by Claudia with her mother's help.

He stepped down off the ladder and looked around for assurance of their solitude. Claudia reached the ground floor, and the two embraced. They exchanged youthful smiles before kissing passionately for a few short seconds. Lorenzo reluctantly released her, and she sat down on the bottom step. Lorenzo sat on the lower rung of the stepladder.

"Are they asleep?" he whispered.

"I think so."

"Why is your mother so good to me?"

"She likes you; she always has."

"Lo so, I know. I wish I could thank her somehow."

"Maybe someday we both can!" Claudia reached for Lorenzo's hand. The soft warmth of her fingers caressed his calloused palm.

"Have you ever stopped to look at the David in the piazza?" he asked.

"Once, with Maman, but Papà made us keep walking, I think he was uncomfortable about his wife and daughter pointing and staring at a nude man."

"Padre Vincenzo brought me there today. I never realized just how beautiful it is."

"He is extraordinary, Michelangelo Buonarroti. I hear he is also painting a giant ceiling in a church in Rome. It is supposed to be the greatest painting ever made. Some men where speaking of it in the duomo a few months ago."

"What kind of painting?"

"Non lo so, I don't know, but it is supposed to be amazing."

"Let's run off to Rome together, you and I, and go see it," he said with a smile.

"I'll go up and pack...You bring the horse and carriage around front!" Claudia laughed as she played along.

"Shall we stay a month, or all summer, Signorina?"

"Who said we're coming back!"

"Excellent choice, Signorina. Shall we purchase a palazzo or rent a villa in the countryside for now?"

"You mean to tell me that you would not build your love a castle?"

Lorenzo tried to keep his laughter hushed. "Brick by brick, Signorina!"

IV

On the Via dei Calzaiuoli just north of Or San Michele was a tiny, dark osteria. The *oste*, Luca di Bartolomeo, filled his rooms with visitors attending to guild business in Or San Michele, along with feeding local tradesmen. The ground floor shop had stable doors, which were kept open in hot weather for air and light to enter the small inn. One side of the doors was now closed, giving the room a dimly lit, quiet air.

Across the narrow via, opposite the osteria, stood two men. The older of the two handed the other a small bag of coins. The second looked inside quickly, then slid the bag into his satchel.

"This is the place," said the older man softly, nodding toward the osteria. "Remember...catch him alone. On Mondays, he usually heads out shortly after *pranzo*. He'll walk from his palazzo to the guildhall here in Or San Michele. You remember where the palazzo is?"

"Sì."

"Bene. And say exactly what I told you, nothing more, and then get out of Florence."

"I was leaving today anyway. You won't see me again."

"Bene."

V

Matteo wandered the city streets deep in thought. He knew Vincenzo was right; it would be almost impossible to run off to Sicily together. The sun was arching away from the city, and people were beginning to reappear on the streets after their midday meal. He had spent the night at Vincenzo's house; it was perhaps one of the happiest nights of his life. Vincenzo's housekeeper, Carla, had retired early, and nobody else knew that Matteo was even there. He would spend tonight with Vincenzo also before heading back to Rome early in the morning.

He stepped aside for a priest, sharply dressed in a clean black robe. The priest was followed by a laborer pulling a small handcart. The priest was speaking to the laborer in what appeared to be concise sentences. Matteo was then struck by a thought.

It would have been necessary, all those years ago, to run far away together to escape the monastery and Cardinal della Rovere.

But now things were different. Vincenzo was established here in Florence, and because San Felice was so small, nobody watched over him. Matteo, on the other hand, needed a clean break. As a Franciscan monk, he could not simply transfer to Florence. He would then have to live at the monastery, and spending nights out of the monastery walls would surely raise suspicions. Moreover, he was now disillusioned with the Church. It was time for him to break free. He could send Ramòn de Cardona's and Cardinal de' Medici's letters back to the pope via messenger, along with a letter from himself stating that he had fallen gravely ill in his travels. He would never be heard from in Rome again. The only people who knew him here in Florence were Giovanni de' Medici and the other three men at the meeting the day before; surely he would never see any of them again. He could change his name.

What if he lived at San Felice? Most old churches had a room in the basement for a keeper of some kind. He could be a laborer at San Felice. He could be close to Vincenzo. Excited by the idea, he immediately headed back toward San Felice. He wanted to tell Vincenzo right away.

* *

Domenico Chilli exited the front palace gates of the Palazzo Chilli. The heavy wooden door swung closed behind him, and he began walking down the Via dei Calzaiuoli toward Or San Michele. A tanned, skinny young man with dusty clothes approached.

"Scusa…Signor Chilli?" he asked as he removed the floppy wool cap from his head and twirled it in his hands.

"Sono io, that's me," Domenico answered curtly.

"I heard you were hiring a new household hand and wondered if I might have the job, Signore."

"I am afraid you heard wrong," Domenico answered gruffly as he kept walking. The young man walked with him. "Where did you hear such a thing?"

"At the osteria down the via here. The *oste* said you were forced to fire the previous boy and that I might find work." The young man was timid and convincing.

Confused, Domenico stopped walking and looked the man straight in the eye, "Did he happen to say why I fired him?"

The young man became very fidgety. "Signore, perhaps I was mistaken, forgive me." He looked down at the ground and said no more.

"Did he?" Domenico was now losing his patience. "Tell me!"

Without looking up, the young man said in a low voice, "Signore, he said the boy had taken your daughter's virtue."

Domenico's blood boiled. He turned and stormed down the Via dei Calzaiuoli in the direction of the osteria. The young man picked his head up and watched Domenico stomp down the via in a fury. He smirked and turned, then left Florence immediately.

One-half of the stable doors to the osteria was still propped open, and Domenico ran in. There were now quite a few patrons in the inn, some travelers, some locals. Domenico recognized the *oste* and grabbed him, forcing him to drop a pitcher of wine he'd been carrying.

"Di Bartolomeo!" Domenico snarled as he clinched his powerful hand around the *oste*'s throat and pushed him up against a wall. Most people in the osteria recognized Domenico immediately. All conversations ceased. All eyes were on the action.

"Don D-D-Domenico," squeaked the terrified innkeeper.

"So you've been telling travelers about my daughter losing her honor!" Domenico was shouting with no regard for the patrons.

"I d-d-d-did not," Luca choked out. "I s-swear it!"

"You didn't tell this boy I fired a servant for stealing my daughter's honor?"

"W-w-w-what boy?"

Domenico turned his head and realized that the young man was no longer with him. He was also aware that he had been shouting in a room full of people. Many of the patrons got up and left, afraid to witness what might come next. Domenico let go of the man's throat.

"Signor Chilli, I swear on the Virgin Mary, I said no such thing." The *oste* had tears running down his cheeks, but he was not sobbing. He looked Domenico square in the eye, and Domenico believed him.

He sat and leaned back in the chair. He looked straight ahead and spoke without looking at the *oste*. "I apologize, Luca. Would you be so kind as to bring a bottle of wine and two cups?" When Luca returned and began to fill one cup for Domenico, Domenico slid the other toward an empty seat and looked up at Luca. He motioned toward the empty chair. "Per favore."

Luca sat and poured himself a cup.

Domenico thought about the situation. Perhaps it was the culmination of many little clues, clues he had chosen to ignore over the last few months, but his mind began to piece together a situation in which Claudia and Lorenzo were indeed secret lovers. He believed the young traveler had lied about where he had heard it, but he did not at all suspect that the man had fabricated the entire story. "So where would this traveler have heard such a thing?" he lamented.

"Perhaps he thought that by telling you such a thing, you would fire the boy and then you would hire him," Luca replied between sips of wine.

"Perhaps," Domenico answered, his demeanor the complete opposite now from when he had stormed in, "but then where is he now?

"Maybe the boy heard it someplace else and was afraid to say where!" added an anonymous voice from the dark rear corner of the inn. A man stood from a table with just one chair and approached. As he stepped out of the shadow, Domenico recognized him. It was Lodovico Giotti. He pulled a chair over and joined them without asking. Domenico was in too contrite a state to notice Lodovico's presumption.

"I hear all kinds of gossip, especially gossip about sex and wealthy families, Signor Chilli, and I never heard even a whisper of such about your daughter. Perhaps it is all a lie." Luca was consoling.

It was not grief over hearing such news that had tempered Domenico, however. If such a scandal were to surface, he would handle it privately within his own household. Domenico's melancholy sprang instead from the realization that he himself, in his rage, had done more to spread the salacious gossip than a thousand whispers in an inn. He had shouted it in a room full of drunken tradesmen and travelers; the cat was out of the bag. Lodovico would affirm this dilemma right off.

"Lie or not, Don Domenico, you know that news of this will spread now!" Lodovico did his best to sound sympathetic. Domenico was prone to be suspicious of the surly notary from past dealings, but his guard was now down and he welcomed kind words. "She is matured, I know. Have you already arranged a marriage for her?" Lodovico asked convincingly.

"No…I was waiting. The right offer has not yet come along." Domenico was paying more attention to his wine than to Lodovico.

He took full swigs and held them in his mouth, savoring the pungent fruitiness of the grapes. His answers were uncharacteristically candid. "I have worked hard to advance my family name and want a marriage for my daughter that brings the same."

"Then I suggest you act quickly, Signore. Do not wait for rumors to take hold, or worse!" Lodovico was grave in his tone.

"What do you mean, worse?"

"Forgive my frankness, Don Domenico, but if there is any truth to the story, then your daughter must marry before any pregnancy can be noticed."

Just an hour before, Domenico would not have entertained such conversation with someone beneath him, but he was now desperate to salvage the situation. What's more, he actually felt lucky that Lodovico happened to be in the osteria that day. He needed someone who could scheme his way through a problem. "Marry whom?" he asked

"My son Jacopo!"

Domenico was silent. Lodovico had no idea what he was thinking. He continued, "I was in the process of arranging a marriage for him, but nothing has been set. I, of course, would be honored if you'd consider my son for your daughter. My name may not be what you hoped for, but I am descended from Giotto di Bondone. My son will soon be a Calimala master and will provide quite well for her, perhaps even being of assistance to your own business…Foreign importers could combine their Florentine wool orders with foreign wool from Jacopo; you may find more customers."

Domenico thought about the business aspect. The respective guilds had very strict rules about dealing in the other guild's wool, but having a son-in-law do it for you might be a way around such rules. He did have another question, however: "And if the situation is…urgent…as you say?"

"Signore…" Lodovico paused. His voice cracked, and his eyes became teary. He was not acting anymore. "My family has served this city faithfully for generations. We may not be as grand now as in years gone by, but the honor of joining our two households together would erase the past. As for what may have happened with your daughter and this servant…I say, let us act now! Let them marry this week, and only God will know the answer to your question!"

Domenico nodded silently. Lodovico still could not tell what he was thinking.

Luca di Bartolomeo drank his wine in silence. This had been a very strange hour indeed.

VI

Father Vincenzo refilled all four cups with the dark red wine. Though Matteo was new to the group, the conversation flowed freely. Embers faintly crackled in the fireplace; nobody had tended to the fire in some time. A cool spring breeze blew in the open window from the small piazza in front of San Felice. None of the four were in the habit of getting drunk, but the jovial atmosphere of the evening had made them all lose count of how many cups they had downed.

Jacopo was happy indeed, his apprenticeship having officially ended. Lorenzo was happy for his friend, and also happy to be spending time with an old friend of Father Vincenzo. Vincenzo was happy to have his friends with him and to be reunited with Matteo. Matteo, most of all, was happy to have made a decision. A burden had been lifted from him; his life would start anew. He had not yet told Vincenzo, however. He had not had the chance to that afternoon, and now there was company. He would tell him later after Lorenzo and Jacopo had left.

"So Vincenzo hears the footsteps before I do and sits up perfectly straight," Matteo recounted boisterously, "and then he notices the look of sheer terror on my face I cleared my throat and said, 'Buona sera, Abate!'"

Vincenzo grinned with embarrassment. Lorenzo and Jacopo smiled and hung on every word.

Matteo went on, "So Vincenzo, without turning his head, says in a loud and deep voice, 'I am sure you are not in the habit of interrupting confessions, Abate!' The abbot stopped dead in his tracks and said, 'O, mi scusa, Padre!' He turned around and left the cloister without saying a word. He didn't notice that Vincenzo was not yet a priest!" Matteo laughed heartily, and the other three followed, Lorenzo hardest of all. He knew Vincenzo to be caring and at the same time serious and dedicated; he had never known him to have a rebellious side.

"What were you doing there?" asked Jacopo innocently.

Matteo and Vincenzo exchanged glances. Matteo smiled and lied. "Reading," he said.

"Even then Father Vincenzo was crazy for his books," Lorenzo observed.

"Well, I for one am glad…If it were not for you, Padre, I would never have read Dante," Jacopo said.

"You have read the *La Commedia*?" Matteo asked the two young men.

"We finished the *Inferno* a couple of months ago, and now we've been reading *Purgatorio*," Lorenzo answered.

"Is that how the three of you spend your time? You read Dante?" Matteo replied.

"Quite often, sì," Vincenzo answered. "We were going to read the sixteenth canto tonight…It is one of my favorites."

"Well by all means go on. I would love to hear it. I have never read the *La Commedia*." Matteo was excited by the idea.

"It is late…Do you boys want to read a little?" Vincenzo asked.

Both shook their heads affirmatively with no hesitation.

"We'll just read part of the canto. There is one passage in particular I'd like you boys to read." Vincenzo retrieved the book from a shelf over the cupboard. He found the page he wanted, and without handing the book off as usual, he began reading it himself, without sitting back down.

> Voi che vivete ogni cagion recate,
> pur suso al cielo, pur come se tutto,
> movesse seco di necessitate.
>
> *You who are living ascribe every cause,*
> *up to heaven, as if all,*
> *were moving with itself of necessity.*

"They are the words of Marco Lombardo, with whom Dante discusses the difference between the will of God and the free will of men," added Vincenzo.

"But isn't God more powerful than any man?" asked Jacopo.

"Exactly," Vincenzo replied, "and therein lies the dilemma for Dante."

"But doesn't God know what path we will choose?" Lorenzo was now perplexed by the same dilemma.

"In a manner of speaking, sì," Matteo jumped in, "but He puts us here on earth to make our own mistakes."

"Ascoltiamo a Dante—let's listen to Dante," answered Father Vincenzo. "Marco goes on to say:

> Se così fosse, in voi fora distrutto,
> libero arbitrio, e non fora giustizia,
> per ben letizia, e per male aver lutto.

> *If it were this way, in you would be destroyed,*
> *free will, and there would be no justice,*
> *having joy for good, or mourning for evil.*

"You can see here the central theme of this canto: the source of good and evil in this world is man himself. If not...if it is as some believe, that our actions are dictated by the heavens, then where would be the justice of heaven or hell? How can a man be rewarded or punished for an action not of his own free will? It is clear to Dante that God has given us the power to choose our own destiny!" Vincenzo was excited to interpret this canto. Perhaps it was because of Matteo's presence, but he was eager to give what he felt to be the answer here, instead of working the answers out of Lorenzo and Jacopo as he usually did.

"Do you really believe that, Padre?" asked Lorenzo in a somber voice at odds with the previously upbeat tone of the evenings conversation.

Sensing Lorenzo's sadness and having a pretty good idea of its source, Vincenzo answered, "Sì, certo! Our lives are what we make of them, Lorenzo. We may not always get the results we desire, but we always have the ability to make a change...to take a chance. There will always be disappointments, but even our worst days can bring unforeseen blessings."

Lorenzo thought of the day his father had been killed, the day he had met Father Vincenzo. He thought of the beating he had received in the via; it had brought him closer to Claudia. The priest was right. But did he, Lorenzo, really possess the power to have the life *he* wanted? He knew what he wanted now.

"I like this canto!" said Jacopo, drawn to its theme.

"Anch'io, me too," Matteo added, certain Vincenzo was speaking about their own future and how he, Vincenzo, was going to carve out his own path in life, one that led him to Matteo.

* *

Lorenzo and Jacopo walked slowly in the fresh evening air. The streets were not crowded, and the clopping of horseshoes was distant. As they crossed the Ponte Vecchio, they could hear the soft ruffles of the Arno's waters easing under the bridge.

"Do you ever think about getting married?" Lorenzo asked out of nowhere.

Jacopo shrugged. "Not sure...I guess. I was so worried about getting through my apprenticeship that I hadn't thought much about it. But now that I'm finished, I guess I should start thinking about it more."

"Who would you like to marry?"

"Well my father wants me to..."

"What?"

"Umm...get married soon." Jacopo suspected that Lorenzo had strong feelings for Claudia and thought it better not to tell him that Lodovico had mentioned what a good match Claudia would make for Jacopo. "Do you think you'll get married soon?"

"If there were only some way of marrying Claudia!"

Jacopo had never heard Lorenzo speak in such strong terms before. He thought about Claudia, how beautiful she had looked in her Sunday dress outside the duomo that day. For the first time, he was conscious of the attraction he also felt for Claudia. He thought of her soft skin, the gentle upturn of her nose, her flowing hair. He was soon conscious of something else: Lorenzo's love for the girl. He felt guilty. "Does she want to marry you?"

"I think so. I never told you, but we kissed."

Jacopo was stunned and a little jealous. He had never kissed anyone. He instantly imagined himself kissing Claudia.

Lorenzo had only told Father Vincenzo, and he knew the dangers of such news getting out, but he trusted Jacopo and was dying to tell him.

"What was it like?" Jacopo needed to know.

"It was like...like heaven." Lorenzo smiled.

Jacopo smiled, too. He was happy for his friend. He put aside any envious feelings, slapped Lorenzo on the shoulder, and smiled.

They parted ways at the Piazza della Signoria. Jacopo no longer lived with Coraggiosi; he was going home to Lodovico's house. Lorenzo walked up the Via dei Calzaiuoli, past the Via degli Speziali, and up the ally behind the Palazzo Chilli. He entered the rear gate and saw that the first floor of the palazzo was fully illuminated. He could hear a gathering of people conversing and laughing. He had no idea what the occasion was.

He went into the servants' quarters off the courtyard and found it empty. Tommaso Orecchioni was not there. He filled the chamber pot in the corner and then went outside to empty it. Lying down on the mattress in the small bedroom, he fell asleep.

* *

Jacopo walked through the door to find his mother still awake, sitting at the table.

"Your father was looking for you."

"I was with my friend."

"He went to the Palazzo Chilli; he wanted you to go with him."

"Why?"

"To announce your betrothal!"

"My what?"

His mother beamed. "Domenica sposerai!"

"I'm getting married Sunday? To whom?"

"Claudia Chilli." Maria was nervously happy. It was a good marriage for her son, but how had Lodovico managed it?

"Claudia Chi…" Jacopo could barely speak. He was taken completely by surprise. Fathers arranged marriages for their children all the time, and he found nothing odd with this, but Claudia? How? Was it true? And then as if a bucket of ice cold water had been dumped over his head, he had another thought. What about Lorenzo? "How did this happen?"

"Your father arranged it with Domenico Chilli today." Maria stood and kissed her son on the forehead. "Everything will be good, figlio mio!" She went upstairs.

Jacopo sat at the table stunned. He couldn't marry Claudia; it would devastate Lorenzo. Would Claudia even love him? It seemed like she loved Lorenzo. Was love important? He knew that he himself loved her; he was certain of that now.

He sat and thought for a long time about the right thing to do. He felt it would be right to let Lorenzo marry Claudia, but that could never happen, Domenico would never agree to such a thing. So why then should he not marry Claudia, if Lorenzo could not anyway? But that would hurt his friend dearly. But why? He, Jacopo, would be happy for Lorenzo if it were the other way around, so why shouldn't Lorenzo be happy for him?

But Claudia loved Lorenzo. Could she not also learn to love him? And what about himself? he thought. He had done what his father had told him his whole life. He had completed his apprenticeship. So finally his father had set a path that actually pleased him; why should he not follow now?

* *

Vincenzo sat at the table thinking. He was taken by surprise at Matteo's plan. In theory, it could work. There was a small cellar room that could be a servant's quarters. Few would raise an eyebrow at a foreigner taking up residence at the parish and doing odd jobs for the church. Vincenzo had performed most of the maintenance on the church himself, and Carla kept the rectory house. "There's no money to pay for a servant," Vincenzo stated, without communicating any feeling on any other aspects of the plan.

"I am a Franciscan, I have nothing and need nothing…a roof over my head and food would suffice." Matteo had thought of all contingencies.

Vincenzo envisioned a life of happiness, shared with his one true love. He would have the best of both worlds. He would still be a priest, still work in his parish. He would still be near Lorenzo, and he would have Matteo with him. But he was haunted by another thought: the memory of the confession he had heard from the shoemaker. "A promise made before God is a promise to be kept," he had told the penitent guildsman. He had sworn his loyalty to the Church and had promised to remain chaste. Many priests broke this vow. Vincenzo thought about what the vow meant to him and to God. The God Vincenzo loved, the God he prayed to, was a forgiving God. God would forgive a moment of giving in to passion, a moment like what Matteo and Vincenzo had shared the night before. But living together with a man, choosing to permanently ignore his vow, would be hypocrisy. He had told the shoemaker to live by his vow; how could he now choose to live outside of his own.

Vincenzo became very emotional, but kept his composure to speak clearly: "Non posso, I cannot."

Matteo was surprised. He had thought Vincenzo would jump at this. "But it was you, all those years ago, who wanted to run off together!"

"I was young, and I had not yet taken my vows." Vincenzo's eyes teared up. "We have now gone on different paths."

"I was happy to have made up my mind, to be leaving the Church. I cannot go back now!"

Vincenzo did not like seeing Matteo get upset. "You must choose your own path, caro. As I said before to Lorenzo, we all have the power to shape our destinies, to make our own decisions. You must choose the path that is right for you. I believe that God wants us to find the place in this world that is right for each of us…and if you've found that you are not in that place, you must act."

"And you, why is your vow unbreakable and mine something I should disregard?"

"Because yours has lost all meaning to you. The Church you pledged yourself to is not the Church in which you now find yourself. I, on the other hand, find meaning in my work. The words of the vow are not what count; it is their meaning to me. I could not live with you, in that way, and live within the meaning of my vows. I could not choose to be a hypocrite."

"Do you think our love is a sin?" Matteo was less interested in his vows than in what Vincenzo meant to him.

"I think about that every day. I don't know."

"I see men spending their lives with wives they do not love. I see them chasing courtesans and prostitutes because they do not love their wives. Is this not sinful? Our Lord Jesus preached love over hate, over violence. If two men love each other, and they hurt no one…where is the sin? I see only love." Matteo was heartbroken and spoke now to assuage his own grief.

Vincenzo turned his head and stared at the glowing embers of the dying fire. As the years had gone by, this same conflict within him had only grown.

* *

In a darkened, stone-walled chamber in the Palazzo Chilli, Claudia lay in her bed sleeping. She was facing the wall and cuddled a blanket in her arms. The tears that had run down her cheeks had not yet dried.

To her back, seated on the bed, was Adélaïde. She rubbed her daughter's shoulder and cried.

VII

Lorenzo woke. It was still mostly dark outside, but hints of light could be seen rising up from the eastern horizon. He sat up; Tommaso was passed out next to him on the mattress. He slipped his feet into his boots and went in the other room without waking Tommaso. He filled the chamber pot in the corner and went outside to empty it.

After dumping the pot in the courtyard, he noticed Pierfrancesco walking toward him. It appeared that he was coming to give Lorenzo instructions of some kind, and Lorenzo figured he would tell him which horse to saddle or something of the sort.

Without saying a word, Pierfrancesco slapped the chamber pot out of Lorenzo's hand and shoved him to the ground.

"Get your stuff and get out of here...capito?" Pierfrancesco was furious.

"What do you mean?" Lorenzo was completely surprised; he had no idea what was going on.

"You're no longer welcome here...and if you show your face in our palazzo again I'll kill you. You're lucky my father doesn't have you dumped in the Arno as it is!"

"But I—"

Pierfrancesco kicked him so hard that his thigh-length leather riding boot slid down partially off his foot, and he stumbled slightly before recovering.

Lorenzo cringed in pain; the kick had crushed his lower back and kidney area.

"Get out of here now!" Pierfrancesco turned and went back in the palazzo.

Lorenzo walked slowly down the Via dei Calzaiuoli, his side still hurting from the kick. Over his shoulder was his leather satchel containing everything he owned. He carried his only wool cloak over his arm. Depression had set in. How could Jacopo and Claudia be getting married? If only he could talk to Claudia, but it was impossible. If he was seen anywhere near the Palazzo Chilli, he would end up floating facedown in the Arno. He felt like he could cry. What would he do? Working for the Chillis had been the only job he'd ever had, and now it was gone. Tommaso had filled him in on all the details.

Apparently, Domenico came looking for Lorenzo last evening while he was at Father Vincenzo's. He then told Pierfrancesco in the courtyard that he'd better never see Lorenzo at the palazzo again. Domenico then gathered the family to announce Claudia's engagement, and guests started arriving.

Lorenzo stumbled in a daze, turning left and right down winding alleys. He knew where he needed to go first. He had to know if it was true. Before he could even get there, he turned a corner and found who he'd been looking for.

"Salve," he muttered without emotion.

"Buon giorno," Jacopo answered.

"I needed…"

"Lorenzo…look, before you say anything, I had nothing to do with this. My father and Domenico arranged it. I couldn't have refused even if I'd wanted to."

"But you don't want to?"

"Lorenzo…I know you love her, but I love her too."

Lorenzo was shocked; he'd had no idea. "You hardly know her!" he spat back.

"That's not true. I know her and I love her."

"So it is your choice then! Don't say you had no choice; you always have a choice!"

"Why are you so upset? You know you could have never married her. If you are my friend, you should want me to find a wife I love."

Hearing Jacopo repeat that he loved Claudia was salt on Lorenzo's wounds. His depression was now total. He turned and walked away. When he was no longer facing Jacopo, his eyes watered.

"Lorenzo! Aspetta, Lorenzo!"

Jacopo's calls went unanswered; his stomach was turning.

VIII

Father Vincenzo opened the door and was surprised to see Adélaïde Laroche Chilli standing alone. She had wrapped herself in a long gray shawl and was only recognizable after lowering the cloth from her head. Vincenzo stepped back and lifted his arm welcomingly.

"Prego, Signora Chilli."

"Grazie, Padre," she answered and glanced in both directions before entering.

Vincenzo took her shawl and hung it on a hook by the door. Adélaïde sat down. Also seated at the table was Matteo, who had half stood when she entered before slouching back down.

"Forgive me, Padre, I did not mean to disturb you," she said politely.

"You did not, Signora. This friar here is an old friend of mine."

"Piacere, Frate." Adélaïde tipped her head toward Matteo.

"The pleasure is mine, Signora," Matteo answered respectfully.

"May I offer you anything, Signora?" asked Vincenzo.

"No, grazie, Padre. I've come to see how the boy is doing, I figured he'd be here."

"He is. He is upstairs sleeping."

Adélaïde felt a twinge in her heart for Lorenzo. She knew how upset he must have been. She could feel his pain and her daughter's; she knew that same pain. It also pained her to think of her husband's and son's anger toward the boy. She hated to see Lorenzo lose his job and wanted to do something about it.

"Is he hurt?" she asked, wanting to hug the boy there in that room just like she had so many years ago.

"He is bruised, but he will be all right…in body anyway." Vincenzo did not blame Adélaïde for Lorenzo's troubles; he knew that she had always cared for him greatly, and his voice was kind to her now. "It is good of you to come here."

Adélaïde's eyes teared. She took a moment to respond. "I think I will trouble you for a cup of wine."

Vincenzo nodded toward Matteo, and the friar left the table to fetch a carafe of wine and three ceramic cups from the cupboard. He poured, and all three took a sip in silence.

"I was fourteen years old when I married my husband, did you know that, Padre?"

"Non lo sapevo, I didn't," said the priest although it was not at all an uncommon age for a girl to be married.

"It was arranged by my uncle, Padre Pierre Jean Laroche, who was really my father. Did you know that, Padre?"

Vincenzo shook his head affirmatively.

"I was a child who did not know any better, and I did what I was told. Domenico has provided for me well; we are among the richest families in Florence. He is a strong man, and though he often loses his temper, he has never hurt me. But in all the years we have been married, I cannot remember one word of kindness, not one loving embrace.

"But there was also a strong man in my life whose kindness filled my life with joy. He was not much older than I, and from the moment I laid eyes upon him I was in love. He worked for my husband and was often in our house. You must understand, Padre, there was never a sinful moment between us; he was entirely devoted to his wife. And when she died giving birth, I saw a piece of him die, too, and his devotion and his sadness made me love him all the more. I would find all sorts of excuses to find him some free time in the house where we could play chess and talk. He understood me in a way my husband never has." Adélaïde was now very emotional; tears ran down her cheek. "When he died, a piece of me died. I still cry for him."

Vincenzo listened with quiet compassion. Matteo took in the story without making the leap that the priest had already made.

"He was Simone Simoni, Lorenzo's father," she added with her eyes closed. She was silent for a moment to gain her composure. "I spent my life crying for the man I loved while being married to a man I didn't. I won't see my daughter suffer the same fate."

"What are you saying?" asked Vincenzo.

"I'm saying that Claudia and Lorenzo belong together, and I think I know a way to make that happen."

Vincenzo looked at Matteo. "I a svegliàr o' ragazz'! Go wake the boy," he said in his thick Neapolitan dialect.

IX

The spring air was unusually hot in Rome as the massive reconstruction project of Saint Peter's Basilica ground on. Pope Julius II was determined to leave his stamp on history, and building the largest church in Christendom was a key component. Hundreds of laborers toiled day after day on the already six-year-old project. A few yards away, in the chapel named for Julius's uncle, Pope Sixtus IV, a recluse genius was putting the finishing touches on the frescoed ceiling that would ensure his place among the greatest artists who ever lived.

Inside the papal palace, in a large, stifling, unadorned antechamber, Pope Julius II slouched in his oversized timber throne. A page presented three sealed letters to the pontiff and then proceeded to read aloud the day's appointments. After hearing two or three items, the pope picked up a small bell resting on the arm of his seat and rang it delicately but with purpose.

The page knew this meant to be quiet. Julius had done this many times, to servants, ambassadors, generals, and princes. The pope was driven to great deeds and had little time for distraction. The bell kept his callers on point.

"Qualcos'altro, Vostra Santità? Anything else?" asked the page.

Julius examined the letters and did not answer. The page understood the unspoken negative and withdrew. Julius recognized the first two seals as being those of Cardinal Giovanni de' Medici and Ramòn de Cardona. The seal on the third letter was that of the pope. The letter was from Fra Matteo; he cracked the seal and opened the letter.

"Vostra Santità, please forgive my sending these dispatches by messenger, but I have fallen gravely ill in my travels and am presently bed-bound in Florence. Please pray, my santissimo Padre, for me, your humble servant, Matteo di Napoli Francescano."

The pope discarded the letter from Matteo and broke the seals and read the other two letters. With no thought of his Franciscan aide, he rang the bell again, and the page returned.

"Take a letter for me," he said gruffly, sounding more ancient than his actual years. He had had a long year militarily and had even grown a beard for a time, vowing not to shave it until the papal lands were restored to their former grandeur. With de Foix's death and France's retreat from Italy, his luck had changed. He was clean-shaven now, but the removal of the beard revealed an older face than the one it had hidden. He was now frequently sick, but no less ambitious. The page retrieved a sheet of paper.

"Illustrissimo Cardinale de' Medici, move to the north of Florence at once and take command of all papal forces moving on Florence. When in position to enter the city, inform me of events and await my instructions."

* *

Claudia followed her mother as the two walked briskly across the Ponte Vecchio. The last couple of days at the Palazzo Chilli had been a never-ending parade of dressmakers, musicians, jewelers, and priests. All were milling about the palazzo in preparation for Sunday's wedding ceremony. Claudia had never been measured and poked at so many times in her life.

As the two women squeezed through the throng of people, their way was blocked by four men. All wore black robes trimmed with red lining and had long, sullen faces. They gathered in front of a small *banco*, a table set up by a vendor. It was not immediately clear to Claudia and Adélaïde what business the vendor was engaged in, but he was pleading with the four men.

"L'avrò stasera…I'll have it this evening!" he pleaded.

"You have had your chance, Signetto. You know the penalty for not paying your debts," answered one of the four, indistinguishable from the others. "Il suo banco sarà rotto—your table will be broken!"

"Bancorotto, bancorotto!" repeated the other three in unison: "Bankrupt, bankrupt!"

One of the three raised an oversized wooden mallet over his head and crashed it down on the *banco*, splitting it in two. The four men then hauled the dejected vendor off to debtors' prison.

Adélaïde grabbed her daughter's arm and squeezed their way through the commotion. Having crossed the Arno, the two followed the curved via that lead to the Piazza de' Pitti and passed the majestic Palazzo Pitti. After the piazza, the two made a sharp right turn into a tiny *piazzetta* in front of a humble gray stone church. They approached the narrow, three-story house to the left of the church itself, and Adélaïde knocked.

Claudia wondered where they were and what was going on. She assumed it had something to do with the wedding, and she followed her mother with resignation. She had cried so often over the last few days that she was emotionally drained and had no will to fight the inevitable. Her mother, on the other hand, had been acting strangely. She had been out of the house for long periods of time and spoke little to anyone, even Claudia, except for a couple of kisses and reassurances that everything would be all right. Adélaïde did not even show much interest in planning the reception feast at the palazzo. She answered the questions of the servants, of course, on decisions being made, but showed little of the initiative she normally had in organizing such events.

The door opened, and there, to Claudia's surprise, stood Father Vincenzo. He stepped back, and the two women entered. At the table sat Lorenzo, who immediately stood up, tipping the chair over behind him.

Claudia saw him and cried out, "Lorenzo!" as tears poured down her cheeks. She ran to him, and the two hugged with all the strength they had.

Lorenzo fought back tears as he buried his nose in the flowery paradise of her hair. They held together a long moment before backing apart. Lorenzo stood in a white woolen blouse that belonged to Father Vincenzo and hung loosely off of his slender frame. Claudia wore a plain but elegant, long maroon dress, her soaked eyes deep with released emotion.

"Are you all right?" she asked.

"I am. I've been staying here," he replied.

"Oh, Lorenzo, this was not what I wanted, I swear it. It is you I love."

"I know it's true, and it is *you* that I love." Lorenzo was not in the least embarrassed by the presence of Vincenzo, Matteo, and Adélaïde. "Please sit, we have something to tell you."

Claudia sat, not knowing what to expect. Vincenzo, Adélaïde, and Lorenzo sat also. After picking up the knocked-over chair from the floor and sliding it back toward Lorenzo, Matteo stood, leaning on the shelf of the cupboard. Adélaïde spoke first.

"Do you remember, ma chére, that my family owns estates in France?"

"Oui, Maman," she answered apprehensively.

"They belonged to Oncle Pierre, and after he died I inherited them."

Claudia looked on, saying nothing.

"Just outside Salon-de-Provençe, there is a villa and small farm. The caretaker's name is Jean; he is a distant cousin of mine. I will write to him that you will be moving into the villa with your new husband."

Claudia's eyes watered, and she sighed in disappointment. "But I don't want to marry Jacopo Giotti."

"Écoutes-moi, ma chére fille…I will not see you marry a man you do not love, not while there *is* a man you love so much. It is Lorenzo you will marry!" Adélaïde rubbed her daughter's shoulder and smiled with misty eyes.

Claudia was shocked with excitement, her spirits lifting instantly, without a thought to the question of how. Tears now flowed freely down her cheeks. She reached for Lorenzo's hand and squeezed it tight. Then after a few quick seconds of euphoria, reality descended on her. "Mais comment? But how?"

"Fra Matteo here will escort you to Salon-de-Provençe. You will go straight to the Château de l'Empéri. In the Chapel Saint Michel, you will find Père Claude. My family has supported the chapel for years, and I will write to him requesting that he marry Lorenzo and yourself at once."

"Et Papà?" asked Claudia.

"He knows nothing of this, and he will not know until after you are married, and then there will be nothing he can do!" Adélaïde was only telling half the truth. True, there would be little chance of Domenico pursuing his daughter in France, but there would be plenty he could do here in Florence. He could denounce Adélaïde in a court of law for her disobedience of her husband, even have her thrown in prison. At the time this was actually seen as a means for a disgraced husband to regain his family honor. There was also the possibility that Domenico would go to the archbishop to have Claudia and Lorenzo's marriage annulled. Adélaïde had resolved to deal with the consequences to herself here in Florence. As for the marriage, she was working on a plan that just might induce Domenico to let the marriage of Lorenzo and Claudia stand.

Claudia was speechless. For a moment nobody spoke. Lorenzo took Claudia's hand. He was no longer shy around Father Vincenzo, Adélaïde, or Claudia. The past few days had matured him and filled him with a self-confidence he had not known before. He knew he loved Claudia and was prepared to act.

"What do you think?" he asked.

"I think...I think it is a wonderful idea! When will we leave?" Claudia had never been so happy in all her life.

"Tonight, ma chére," answered Adélaïde. "After dark, when everyone is asleep, we will sneak you out of the palazzo. Fra Matteo will meet you by the courtyard entrance. You will dress like a nun, and the two of you will hide here at San Felice. The constables won't hassle a friar and a nun walking the streets at night. Before sunrise, the three of you will set out for Pisa. You will be able to sail to France from there. I will give the friar the money necessary for lodging and passage."

"It is very kind of you to escort us, Frate," Claudia told Matteo.

"It is my pleasure, Signorina," answered Matteo, "but I am not simply escorting you both to Provençe. I will be staying as a servant at your villa. I have decided to give up my Franciscan's robe." Matteo smiled, then looked at Vincenzo and said nothing more.

"See, ma chére, we have made all of the plans," Adélaïde reassured her daughter, unnecessarily.

"All plans but one, Mademoiselle," Vincenzo added, butchering the French with his Neapolitan tongue.

"What would that be, Padre?" asked Adélaïde.

"Your family has supported the Chapel Saint Michel for years, you have said?"

"Oui."

"And you are now, undoubtedly, on a friendly basis with the archbishop here in Florence?"

Lorenzo, Claudia, and Matteo exchanged glances ignorantly.

"Oui, of course, Padre we see him every Sunday." Adélaïde, too, was unsure of Vincenzo's questioning.

"Might it be at all unusual for you to ask the archbishop to see to it that the pastor of a small parish church would be sent to the favored chapel of your family in Provençe?"

"I do not see why not; after all it was my uncle who recommended Père Claude for his position. I am certain he would accept anybody we recommend. What did you have in mind?" Adélaïde already knew the answer to this question before she was done asking it.

"I was thinking of moving to Provençe as well," Vincenzo stated unceremoniously. "I would like to start again at Saint Michel, not as pastor, of course, but a simple priest. The work would be rewarding, and I could be close to those I love.

Lorenzo's heart filled with joy, for he knew Vincenzo was speaking about him. The priest had been Lorenzo's only family since the death of his father, and the thought of leaving him behind saddened him. But now, they would be together in an exciting new place.

Matteo's heart also filled with joy, for he was certain Vincenzo was speaking about him. Maybe they could never truly share their lives together the way they would like, but they could live near each other, spend time together, grow old together. "You would give up being pastor here, to be just another parish priest, in a foreign land?" he asked his love.

"My life is with the people in this room," answered the priest. "I go where they go!"

* *

Adélaïde and Claudia exited the house into the small *piazzetta* in front of San Felice. Claudia held her mother's hand and rested her head on her mother's shoulder as they walked. She could barely contain her excitement. As the daughter of one of the wealthiest men in Florence, she had always had certain expectations placed upon her. She had lived the life that others had planned for her. She had only known brief moments when she had felt totally alive, her moments with Lorenzo. Now she would be spending the rest of her life with him, away from the expectations of other, and the thought was almost too exhilarating to bear. She had her mother to thank for it, and she knew it. She loved her mother with all her heart.

Adélaïde was filled with satisfaction. She was giving a new life to her daughter. She loved her sons, of course, but they were brought up in their father's way and were destined to follow his path. Claudia, however, was special. She was brilliant in the way Adélaïde knew herself to be brilliant, and Adélaïde did not want to see this brilliance snuffed out the way her own had been. The consequences of these actions here in Florence would be severe, she knew, but this was not her biggest worry. The plan hinged on whether or not Domenico could be convinced to not have the marriage annulled.

Firstly, the newlyweds would have to consummate the marriage immediately. An unconsummated marriage was easily annulled. Secondly, Domenico must be made to see the marriage as beneficial. Perhaps a long-lost relative of Lorenzo could write to Domenico to congratulate the father of the bride. And being that this long-lost relative was a man of business, perhaps he would be eager to associate himself with his newfound extended family by marriage. Perhaps he would even place an advanced order for hundreds of bales of wool, sending thousands of florins as down payment. There was a chance such a plan could work, if thousands of florins could be found, perhaps from estates in France, without her husband's knowledge. These thoughts occupied Adélaïde's mind greatly as the two strolled leisurely past the Palazzo Pitti.

* *

A handsome young man, replete in his little-worn Calimala robe, sat at the base of the steps in front of the Palazzo Pitti. He had set out to visit his friend, to make amends, only to be startled by the sight of his fiancée and her mother leaving the house where his friend was staying. The sight made his knees weak, and he rushed to sit on the steps. He sat there unnoticed and brewed. The initial tingle in his stomach slowly turned to jealous rage. He said nothing as the two women who caused his dismay fluttered by, oblivious to his existence. Their lack of notice made him angrier. He wanted to be noticed by Claudia; he wanted to be loved by her.

X

Lodovico lifted the heavy iron knocker and slammed it three times. The response was not immediate. Jacopo turned to his father nervously.

"This is a mistake," he said and readied himself for a harsh reply from his father, but instead he was surprised.

"Figlio mio," Lodovico started with a tenderness his son had never heard before, "I have tried all my life to give you more than what I was given, and we are here on the verge of raising our family to a level of fortune never seen before. I have been tough with you, I know, but it is because I believe you are capable of great things, and I never wanted to see you settle for less. I know you don't always approve of the way I go about things, but injustices done against me have made my methods necessary. Anyone can be virtuous when fortune is to his favor, but some of us have to find our own fortune. That is what I have done for you, and trust me, it is no more than Chilli would do for his children. It has all been arranged, you will see, and if what you saw was correct, removing this obstacle from the path of your destiny is what we as a family must do…It is what I as your father *will* do!"

It was the nicest thing Lodovico had ever said to his son, and it served to strengthen Jacopo's resolve to take this drastic action.

One-half of the double doors swung back, and a slight, unfriendly servant surveyed the two men before his master's doorway.

"If you would be so kind as to inform Signor Chilli that Messeri Lodovico and Jacopo Giotti wish to call on him?" Lodovico asked with an air of superiority.

The servant closed the door, saying nothing. In a moment he returned and led the two to the study off of the main entrance hall. Lodovico and his son sat staring at the soft clouds of the frescoed ceiling. After some time, Domenico entered.

"What is it, Giotti? We are very busy here making preparations, as you can see." Domenico motioned to them to remain seated as he passed them and sat at his desk.

"I'm afraid they may be in vain, Signor Chilli, if immediate action is not taken," answered the ever-wily notary.

"Dimmi, tell me," retorted Domenico.

"Well, I fear the boy who is the cause of so much trouble is plotting some bold action to interfere with this wedding."

Jacopo sat silently looking down at his feet. He was partly ashamed to be coming to Domenico with salacious gossip, but he was also filled partly with anger. If Lorenzo were truly *his* friend, why would he interfere with Jacopo's wedding?

"And you say this because…?" Domenico was now interested.

"The boy has been staying at San Felice, with Padre Vincenzo de Marco. My son here witnessed this morning your wife and daughter paying him a visit."

"Davvero? Truly?" asked Domenico with a tone of annoyance.

Jacopo shook his head affirmatively as the other two looked at him for confirmation.

"Don Domenico," Lodovico went on, "the boy has disrespected your house on more than one occasion. He has clearly broken the trust between servant and master, and as you know, the Signoria discourages such behavior in servants. It should be fairly easy for a man of your stature to have the boy arrested, given his behavior, at least until after the wedding."

Domenico nodded and sat pensively for a long, uncomfortable moment. "Ci penso io—I'll take care of it," he said at last.

Wishing to press his luck no further, Lodovico stood and pulled Jacopo to his feet as well. "In that case, Signore, we will see you at the chapel in the morning."

Domenico sensed that Lodovico also wished to ask him about the dowry, but he had no wish to put the notary's mind at ease. He would hand over the dowry after the ceremony as agreed upon. He nodded a good-bye. Father and son respectfully backed out.

Domenico leaned back in his chair and yelled for the servant.

"Send in my wife and oldest son," he barked when the servant appeared at the doorway.

XI

Pierfrancesco Chilli was often angry. He was the eldest son of one of the wealthiest men in Florence. He was a child of privilege, and he knew it, and everybody he came into contact with knew it. The only way he knew to be taken seriously, to not be dismissed as a pampered accident of fortune, was to be serious, which for him meant be angry. He often yelled at servants and associates and just about anybody he considered beneath him.

Domenico had a quick temper, for sure, but only when provoked. Indeed, the elder Chilli was wise enough to know the importance of well-placed courtesy. Pierfrancesco, on the other hand, felt anger was the appropriate response to most problems. His father knew this about his son, and Domenico had been angered, too, by recent events. When Lodovico Giotti delivered a warning about an insolent former servant of his plotting to interfere with the very non-ideal wedding the servant himself had made necessary, Domenico decided to turn his son's anger loose on the situation. It did not take much provocation.

Pierfrancesco stomped his thigh-high leather riding boots angrily across the Ponte Vecchio, two constables at his side. He wore an embroidered red tunic of fine linen. His amber hair flared around his broad shoulders, and what he lacked in height he made up for in posture, holding his chest out in front of himself and never seeming at ease. His peaked nose was more pronounced than that of his fair younger sister, adding to his stern appearance.

The three arrived at the three-story rectory house next to San Felice, and Pierfrancesco pounded on the door. Father Vincenzo opened the door.

"Salve, Padre, we have come for the Simoni boy," the defender of Chilli honor spat quickly.

"I see...Come in, won't you, and I will have him brought downstairs," Vincenzo stepped back and motioned the three in with his open arm. "The good frate here will go up and fetch the boy!"

"Nothing funny, just bring him down, capisce?" answered Pierfrancesco without stepping through the doorway.

"I'm afraid he does not understand your Florentine tongue, Signore. He is from a small village south of Naples and speaks only his native vernacular." Vincenzo turned to Matteo and said in the thickest dialect he could muster, as quickly as his words could leave his lips, "Pigliate o' uaglione fori ra' finest!"

Matteo bowed his head and went up the stairs.

"Prego," Vincenzo said as he motioned again. This time the three men entered and Vincenzo closed the door. Nothing was said among them for a minute, and Pierfrancesco became impatient.

"Andiamo, Frate, let's go!" he shouted up the stairs. There was no reply, and he ascended quickly and kicked open a door at the top of the steps. He turned into the room and approached the open window to see a sight that made his blood boil. On the shadowed cobblestones of the Piazzetta San Felice, a young man with a brown leather satchel over his shoulder and a brown-robed Franciscan were running fast under the darkening sky. "Merda!" he shouted. "Shit!"

* *

Matteo and Lorenzo ran hard. The friar struggled against the ankle he had twisted jumping down from the second story and the tearing he felt of the leather strap of one of his sandals, and hoped he would not lose the shoe altogether. After turning into the Piazza de' Pitti, the two ducked down a narrow ally and crouched behind a wooden cask. In was only a few seconds before they heard Pierfrancesco and the two constables running by. Matteo peeked his head up and could see them running down toward the Ponte Vecchio.

"We must stay hidden until later tonight. If our plan is still intact, la Signora Chilli will sneak her daughter out of the palazzo after the others are asleep," said Matteo.

Lorenzo did not respond. He hoped the plan was still intact.

* *

It was a cold and rainy day, so cold and rainy that there was little business being attended to outside of the palazzo's walls. Domenico Chilli, not long before having succeeded his departed father, was away on business, and there was little for Simone to do with the weather as such. On a work table in the palace kitchen sat a chessboard, and Adélaïde sat across from the tall, bearded, kindhearted servant with whom she so loved to while away the time in conversation.

The memory of those times, now, seemed like a dream to Adélaïde, a dream she often revisited. That cold and rainy day stood out particularly in her memory. Simone, whose warmth of spirit vanquished the wear his not yet thirty years had put on his face, smiled as he slid a rook forward with deliberate sureness.

"You miss your wife, I know it, and it saddens me," she said bluntly.

Simone looked taken back, but then, they had never known such intimate conversation. "Sì, sempre, yes, always," he answered, sounding neither sad nor offended.

"Do you think you will marry again?"

"I do not."

"You are certain."

"Of only one thing I am certain," he started, looking her dead in the eye in a manner heedless of his station. "My son, my Lorenzo, is my life. Never has a father been so blessed with such a son. He wakes with me, and we ready ourselves together. He accompanies me out the door and finds a way of occupying his small hands for a day's bread. He eagerly waits for me by the river at midday, and at day's end I return to find him slicing me an apple. It is the light of my otherwise dark life to spend my evenings with my boy at my side. I pray for him a better life, and I work toward that end every year. That is my end, of that I am certain."

Adélaïde listened in heartbroken silence. Her heart broke, of course, for the man she secretly loved. It broke for not being his, and it broke for the break of his own heart. But more than that, her heart broke for her own lot. She wished for the simplicity of Simone's life; she wished for a life in which her children basked in the paternal love afforded by such simplicity. Her own husband was but a wall to her children, a mere buffer between them and the outside world, affording no warmth of its own accord and often keeping out much light. She tried to counter her husband's manner, but with boys such a thing was hard in a society not yet free of medieval chivalric notions of manhood. Domenico would have his boys riding on a hunt over learning anything their mother could teach them. Only young Claudia was left to her mother's direct care, and for this Adélaïde was grateful. Oh, how different her life would be if Simone were the father of her children! None of these thoughts were befitting a signora, of course, and she quickly came back to point. "You will give him a better life, I am certain of it."

"Mi preoccupo." He shook his head. "I worry."

"You are strong and work hard. Why should you fail?"

"I am all he has. Only I can protect him in this world. What if he were to lose me?" Simone was somber, his smile having evaporated. He upturned a hand and rubbed his young-man's beard thoughtfully. His eyes were deeper and stiller than any lake she had ever seen.

"Such talk! You are young and will protect him many years to come."

There was a silence, where play resumed to mask the discomfort of lost conversation. Each swapped two moves before Simone broke the pause.

"I wish to ask something I've no right to ask, Signora."

"Mais bien sûr, of course."

"Look after my son, should misfortune strike again!"

Adélaïde's eyes swelled, and she felt a rush of emotion to her head that threatened to take her consciousness. To combat this she stood quickly, knocking the stool back with her legs.

"Perdona mi, forgive me, Signora," Simone said quickly. "I forget my place. After bowing his head, he looked up and in her eyes.

"I pray to never have occasion, but your request will be happily granted," she said very lowly.

* *

The young man Giambattista and his daydreaming mother walked two steps behind the impatient Domenico. Adélaïde heard Simone's voice over and over in her head: "Look after my son, should misfortune strike again!" In her memories of that beautiful man, she found courage.

Domenico had decided that on the eve of such an important day for their family, the three of them should go and light a candle in the duomo. He needed a reason to keep his wife close to him and away from the house. He had left his only daughter under close guard, so as to ensure her rest on such a momentous eve, of course.

* *

On three stools at the foot of the small stone staircase that led to Claudia's bed-chamber sat the unfriendly servant of the house, Paolo; a wiry, drunken, unkempt constable who looked anonymously like every other constable; and Father Antonio del Prato. Padre Antonio was set to perform the marriage the next morning and eagerly anticipated a "donation" befitting such an illustrious family. He knew not why Domenico Chilli had asked him to sit outside his daughter's door that night, but he was determined to ensure the marriage took place.

Claudia sat and stared at herself in the mirror. She had heard the rest of her family go out, but she knew not where. The ever-unfriendly Paolo told her it was her father's wish that she remain in her room, which angered her, the fact that this wretched creature was the vessel of her father's instruction, that in a sense he, the servant, was more in her father's confidence than she, his daughter. She resented the restriction of her own will, a continuation of the resentment she felt at being forced to marry Jacopo. She wanted to get out of the situation. Her mother was supposed to get her out, but Domenico had taken her away somewhere. She went over to the window and gazed out onto the darkened courtyard. The window was high off the ground; escape was impossible. Despair set in. She looked down and in her desperation thought of the only option left to her.

* *

Adélaïde knelt at the offering candles in front of the altar of Santa Maria del Fiore, the duomo. She prayed for the strength to keep her promise to Simone. She asked God for the wisdom to find a way through this crisis and for God to allow her husband's heart to soften for his daughter's sake.

She looked up into the cupola of Brunelleschi's famous dome and marveled at the space. The width and height were incomprehensible. She remembered when Pierre had kept his

promise and brought her to see it for the first time as a young girl—
how it had seemed to bring her eyes straight up into heaven. The
whiteness of the walls gave purity to its destination. There was talk
of the Signoria commissioning a fresco on the underside of the
dome, but she had mixed feelings about the idea. While she loved
the color and beauty of frescoed ceilings, it was the dome's massive,
peaceful whiteness, the infinity of its ascent, that amazed her the
most.

Domenico sat in a wooden chair among a long row of empty
wooden chairs. Workers had lined up a few rows of wooden chairs
for the Sunday mass the next day. Important families sat in rows of
chairs up front, while the rest of the congregation stood behind.
After mass, the chairs were collected up again and stored in the
basement, leaving the spacious marble floor open for the week.
Domenico thought of how he had sat in almost the same spot when
he and Simone had wrestled the assassin who tried to kill Lorenzo il
Magnifico. That had been a fortuitous moment in his life. The
goodwill of il Magnifico had greatly advanced his family's fortunes;
the incident even indirectly resulted in his marriage to Adélaïde,
whose dowry also greatly advanced his wealth. He was about to pay
out a dowry himself, and it was the source of great annoyance to him.
He had hoped to purchase great advancement for his family with that
dowry, and he knew the marriage to Jacopo Giotti was not
guaranteed to bring such advancement at all. Indeed he considered it
a second-rate marriage for his daughter, but was determined to see it
through.

Giambattista stood in the rear of the church, some hundreds of
steps away from his parents, and Adélaïde sat next to her husband,
emboldened to speak more frankly to him than she ever had.
Without turning her head toward him she spoke.

"For what end do you press this marriage, my husband? If the
boy's family were wealthy or influential, I would see the appeal to
you...but the Giottis are neither. If your daughter loved the boy,
I would see that more...yet she does not."

To Adélaïde's surprise he did not cut her off, but listened with
the reverence of his memories.

"The boy will be a Calimala master. Our families together will
amass great business."

"But the guilds will never allow you to deal in foreign wool, you
know that." She knew more about the business of her husband than

he thought and now felt confident to speak in these matters. She was not going to back down without speaking her mind.

He responded, "The guilds are dying…in Florence, in Siena, all across Italy. The Spanish, the French, and the pope all take more and more control of our cities, and they appoint their dukes, who care little for the politics of guilds and guild councils. As we speak, Giovanni de' Medici gathers an army set to invade Florence, to restore his family's rule with the blessing of the pope. When he comes, he will remember our service to his family, and we will certainly be in a favored position. Being firmly established in both the wool and the Calimala guilds will put us in a position to import and export all over Europe and even with the New World."

"And for this you give your daughter away?"

"She must marry now!" he answered with less patience.

"Perché?"

"Because I will not see her with the Simoni boy."

"But they love each other."

"I know it…and I know you loved the boy's father. I always knew it. I saw how you spoke to him, I saw how you made excuses to be around him, and I saw how you wept for his death. You should have loved me, your husband. I won't give my daughter over to the man's son."

Adélaïde felt a queasy rumble in her stomach, her courage drained. She had been certain that nobody knew of her feelings for Simone. She was not afraid; Domenico, uncharacteristically, was not the least bit intimidating in his admission. Far from it, he seemed pathetic.

"Marito mio, my husband," she began, "it was my weakness to put another before you, I know that. But do not punish our daughter because of my actions."

"I do not punish her. She would not marry a servant regardless. If it had not been the Giotti boy, then it would have been someone else."

Adélaïde looked ahead at the offering candles, discouraged. She could not change her husband's mind. The only way to prevent Claudia marrying Jacopo Giotti was to get Claudia away, far away. But how? Her husband seemed to suspect something. How would they get Claudia out?

* *

Paolo and the constable played cards while Father del Prato slept upright on his stool with his back against the wall. Suddenly, Paolo sat up straight and sniffed his nose around.

"Do you smell that?" the servant asked.

"Smell what?" was the constable's reply.

"Smoke. It's getting stronger!"

A haze of smoke lifted slowly up the stairs at the end of the corridor. As it hit the ceiling and banked down, it started pushing harder and harder. The hallway was quickly filled with black smoke.

"Incendio! Fire!" Paolo yelled. The other two jumped to their feet and ran down the stairs, regardless of any other soul in the palace or the fact that the smoke was coming from downstairs. Paolo ascended the narrow steps that led to Claudia's room and banged frantically on the door.

"Signorina…Signorina! Incendio…incendio!" he yelled without receiving any response. He shook the knob feverishly, but the privacy latch was locked. He shouldered the door hard, and it swung open fast, throwing him into the room. Smoke filled in the doorway around his short frame. He looked in the room, horrified.

"O Dio mio!" he gasped.

XII

Lorenzo and Matteo made their way toward the Palazzo Chilli painstakingly slowly. They stayed off of the main thoroughfares and did not cross the Ponte Vecchio, but walked west along the Arno to the next bridge. Matteo was limping.

The merchants of the Mercato Vecchio were closing shop. The widened via bustled with late shoppers and small wagons being packed with banchi, collapsible wooden tables used by transient merchants, and whatever wares they might have sold. Overhead, second-story porticos reached out over the via, and at various intervals, red canopies stretched across the via covering the pavement below. The towering aurora dome of the duomo was barely visible above the porticos, a few hundred steps behind the mercato, with the last traces of sunlight weakly reaching out from the distant west.

A constable climbed a stool to light a lamp that swung out over the via, and Lorenzo and Matteo avoided eye contact with him.

"Lorenzo, Lorenzo," a voice shouted excitedly, "non ti vedo più! I don't see you anymore!"

Lorenzo's shoulders cringed up nervously at being recognized, but he relaxed when he turned to see the merchant who called him.

"I've been out of town, but now I am back, Michele. Will I see you here Monday?" Lorenzo was eager to keep moving.

"Sì, Lorenzo, certo!" the merchant replied.

"Ciao."

Lorenzo took a few steps before stopping. "Actually, Michele, la signora has been having headaches. Might you have anything for her?"

"Certo! Come in and I will show you," Michele motioned toward his bottega. He was taller than Lorenzo, by at least a foot. He was skinny and acted older than his age, which could not have been thirty. Belonging to the Arte dei Medici e Speziali, the doctors' and apothecaries' guild, he stocked hundreds of herbs that were mixed, ingested, or rubbed on for almost any ailment.

"What are you doing?" Matteo whispered in Lorenzo's ear as they approached the bottega.

"We need to stay hidden for a while," he mumbled back.

* *

In an instant, the house servant Paolo no longer feared the flames raging somewhere in the palazzo below. He stood paralyzed in the doorway and stared into Claudia's chamber. The silk blankets on the bed were undisturbed. The chair in front of the table and mirror, empty. The window shutters flapped open, and the evening air blew in softly, even as smoke gathered behind him. He had been given an important task, to guard Claudia, and she was gone. Had she jumped to her death? What would come of him? Certainly he would end up thrown out of the house, maybe thrown in prison, maybe worse.

He ran to the window to look down into the courtyard. Flames and smoke rose out of the window directly below, but beyond that he saw nothing. No corpse of a young girl sprawled out on the ground below, nothing. He stepped back and noticed that one of the drapes that flanked the large window had been pulled off and was missing. He looked around the room and did not see it. Had Claudia used this to somehow climb down? He was in a state of panic. He ran out of the room and descended into the plume of smoke. The room was still and filling with smoke.

After a few seconds, the silk trimming around the base of the bed was raised up by a soft, young hand. Claudia slid herself out from under the bed and pulled the case off of a pillow. She filled it with a light wool shawl, a dress from her armoir, and some personal effects from atop the table. The smoke started to thin out, as she knew it would. She had been quite certain that when she ripped the drapery down, lit the end of it on fire with the burning candle on the table, and swung the drape down into the open window below that it would ignite the drapes below, which would burn for a few minutes before fizzling out in the otherwise empty, stone-walled room. The room normally housed wooden tables and chairs, which had been carried out into the courtyard for the wedding.

With her guards out in the courtyard panicking, Claudia walked out the front door of the palazzo.

XIII

Lorenzo and Matteo moved carefully from doorway to doorway. They avoided the front entrance of the Palazzo Chilli on the Via dei Calzaiuoli, working their way up the side alleys and trying to get as close as possible to the rear courtyard entrance. It was now fully dark. Neither of the two was sure what time it was, but they had spent as much time as they could in the Mercato Vecchio and thought it now best to try and rendezvous with Claudia behind the palazzo. At least, that had been the plan before Pierfrancesco came looking for Lorenzo.

Opposite the rear gate, across the narrow alley, a pushcart was backed into a tiny inlet. Lorenzo and Matteo climbed behind the cart and sat on the ground, hidden. They waited. The evening spring air was warm.

It was quiet behind the courtyard, but activity could be heard from inside the palazzo.

"Can you hear what's going on?" Matteo asked as the two spied on the illuminated palazzo windows.

"No, can you?"

"No."

Suddenly there was some jostling above their head, and something dropped into the cart they were crouched behind.

"If you two don't keep quiet, what's going on in there will be going on out here!" a young girl exclaimed in a hushed voice before dropping herself from the ledge of a stone wall into the cart. She picked up the stuffed pillowcase she had dropped and quickly climbed down next to the other two.

"Claudia!" Lorenzo let slip, louder than he would have liked. He hugged her quickly but did not linger in the embrace.

"Frate," she said with a greeting smile toward the friar.

"Buona sera, cara," he answered.

"How are we going to get out of here?" she asked.

"We were hoping you could tell us," Lorenzo replied.

"What were your mother's instructions?" Matteo added.

"I don't know…They all went out before sunset. My father left a guard at my door, and my parents and brothers went out. I don't know where." She sounded more confused than nervous.

"Well, we can tell you where your brother went. He came to arrest me," Lorenzo replied.

"Pierfrancesco?"

"Sì."

"My father knows…He must! He sent Pierfrancesco after you. That is why he put me in my room with a guard. That is why he took my mother and Giambattista out. He knows what we are up to, and he's trying to stop us!"

"Then we must get out of here now," Lorenzo answered.

"It will be tougher now, with Pierfrancesco and the constables out looking for us," said Matteo.

"We've got to stay out of sight," replied Claudia.

"I've got an idea," said Matteo as he untied the rope around his waist and pulled his robe up over his head. "Lorenzo, give me your trousers and blouse."

* *

A young constable leaned a small stool up against a lamppost and climbed up to light the oil-soaked wick inside the glass cage, which swung precariously over the via. He liked the predictable rhythm of his nightly routine. There was no system of street lighting per se. Most of the streets of Florence were completely dark at night, but the constables had strung up a few lanterns to mark off their sectors.

There was no hereditary constable of the city, in the way there were for some kingdoms or duchies. Instead, the Signoria hired a small band of men to roam the streets at night and keep the peace.

The constable had a certain number of lanterns to light and a certain area of the city to patrol. He knew who should be on the streets after dark and who shouldn't. He worked for the *comune*, or city government of Florence. Supposedly, he worked for the people. Inevitably, however, constables did the bidding of the rich, and he resented being told to be on the lookout for a friar traveling with a boy and young girl. *Let the rich keep their own in line*, he thought, *and let me light my lanterns and keep drunkards from bothering the citizens.*

He climbed down off the stool and picked it up to walk to the next lantern. Down the via, coming toward him, a merchant pushed a cart. It was late to be closing up for the day, but merchants did sometimes return late, after stopping at an osteria for some wine. The merchant was in his thirties and handsome. He looked strong, but walked with a limp. He wore a loose, white blouse and brown trousers, like many merchants, but he wore leather sandals instead of the felt, ankle-high boots of the tradesmen. The contents of his cart were covered with a brown cloth.

The merchant slowed his pace and made eye contact with the constable while bowing his head slightly. "Buona notte, conestabile," he said warmly.

"Notte!" returned the constable without stopping the man. He watched as the cart was pushed further down the via.

A shadowy figure, obscured from view, leaned back into a doorway and watched the transaction. The constable stood, stool and lantern in hand, and regarded the merchant and cart as they wobbled away. He then turned and marched swiftly down the via, toward lanterns already lit.

The shadowy figure let him pass, then worked his way from doorway to doorway, remaining hidden. His pace was slightly faster than the merchant and cart, and he gradually closed the distance. He softly stepped out onto the stone path and tapped the merchant on the shoulder, knowing he would startle him.

Matteo spun in fright and almost cried out before restraining himself. "Vincenzo!"

"I see you've gotten far! I thought you'd be halfway to Pisa by now," Vincenzo jested.

"Mannaggia 'a pressa, dicette 'a maruzza!" Matteo exclaimed the ancient Neapolitan proverb. "Damn the haste, said the snail!" He hugged Vincenzo quickly and then regained his composure.

Lorenzo and Claudia both popped their heads out from under the brown cloth and looked up smiling at Vincenzo.

"Buona sera, ragazzi," greeted the priest, "We must get off the streets for the night. We'll never get out of the city gates tonight. In the morning, when carts are coming and going through the gates, we'll slip out."

"What do you suggest, Padre?" asked Lorenzo.

"There is a monastery not far from here; perhaps they will put us up for the night," replied Vincenzo, not at all sure.

Lorenzo and Claudia ducked back down under the brown friar's robe. Vincenzo and Matteo pushed the cart hastily. In the distance, horseshoes echoed from paving stones at a trotting pace, closer and closer. The two men pushed harder. The bell tower of a monastery could be seen in the distance, and they needed to get there quickly. The clopping horseshoes was getting louder.

Under the brown robe, Lorenzo and Claudia lay on their sides, cradling each other. Claudia's back was to Lorenzo, and he wrapped his arms around her as the cart wobbled on the uneven stones. He wore no trousers, having given them to Matteo, and had on only the thigh-length white under gown Matteo had given him in return. Holding her tightly in his arms, with the exotic smell of her hair in his face, filled him with excitement. He fought to keep his mind distracted, to hide this excitement, out of embarrassment and also out of respect for the danger of the situation. Still, it was the most intimate moment of his life.

He then thought of something else. How, very often at the worst times in his life, brief moments with Claudia had always lifted his spirits. After the death of his father, he fell in love with her instantly in Vincenzo's house. After he was beaten in the street, she held his hand by his bed. And now, fleeing from Florence, the only home he had ever known, he lay half-naked with Claudia in his arms. Neither spoke. Claudia rested her head on Lorenzo's bicep and closed her eyes. Their hands were locked together in front of her.

Lorenzo could hear the trotting horse approach. The animal snorted as it halted. Claudia and Lorenzo both held their breath and lay very still. For a brief, long, second there was complete silence. Then the horseman yelled.

"Maledetti bastardi!" shouted Pierfrancesco Chilli.

Human footsteps now flooded the scene, three or four pairs. The two lay motionless, still holding their breath. From outside the brown robe, once again there was silence. It was still and dark under the robe. Lorenzo could feel his heart beat in his chest.

Then, in one swift motion, the robe was ripped away, leaving a dismounted Pierfrancesco standing over the sight of his sister cuddled up against a pant-less Lorenzo. This sent the eldest Chilli son into a rage. He ripped Lorenzo out of the cart and slammed him down on the hard paving stones in one swift motion, before the boy could react. Vincenzo stepped forward to intervene and was quickly tackled by two constables. Matteo did not even have a chance to move before being clobbered across the back of the head by the long wooden lance of a constable. His legs gave out and he hit the ground.

Pierfrancesco beat Lorenzo savagely, bloodying his face profusely. Lorenzo, however, kept his senses and was able to get a hand around a wheel spoke of the cart. He used the upswing of Pierfrancesco's hand to kick him hard in the shin, stunning the aggressor. Lorenzo pulled himself up, bloody faced but determined not to lie down as he had in the courtyard. Pierfrancesco rushed. Lorenzo landed a hard punch on Pierfrancesco's cheek, causing sudden and sharp pain. This only heightened Pierfrancesco's rage, and he pulled a dagger out of his belt. He stepped toward Lorenzo.

"No!" cried Claudia as she threw herself across her brother's back.

Instinctively, Pierfrancesco spun and smacked Claudia hard across the face, knocking her down to the ground.

Lorenzo charged and buried his shoulder in the small of Pierfrancesco's back, driving him into the cart. He then reached up and landed another blow to the head. As Lorenzo stood upright, a wooden lance landed heavily across the back of his legs, sweeping his feet out from under him. He crashed to the stone roadway, and the lance came down again on his head. The wood clank on his skull echoed in the via. Lorenzo was in terrible pain. He held his hands up to protect his head, but they were grabbed by strong hands and spun behind him. His hands were tied painfully tight behind his back, and he lay on the ground facedown, in agony. Claudia held her cheek and sobbed.

Pierfrancesco tucked the dagger in his belt. "Bring the boy to the Stinche!" he told the constables.

"No!" yelled Vincenzo. "By what right?"

"Kidnapping! He intended to take my sister away from a legally contracted marriage. And you should be careful, Padre; it could seem like you were aiding him, if I didn't know any better."

"You don't scare me," Vincenzo snarled, his Neapolitan accent thick and furious.

"Mi scusa, Padre, but that was never my intention," Pierfrancesco answered smugly. "Take the other one away also," he directed the constables.

"That man is a Franciscan friar!" Vincenzo shouted with yet more rage, the two constables struggling to restrain him.

"He is not dressed like a friar. He looks like a common merchant, one who was giving aid to this kidnapper here."

"He is secretary to the pope in Rome!" Vincenzo shot back, Matteo still too stunned to speak.

"Huh," Pierfrancesco laughed sarcastically. "I think he was lying at your house, when he donned a friar's robe, and perhaps he has deceived you, too, Padre."

"His robe is there. A small pocket is sewn inside. In it you will find the papal seal. You will see the proof of who this man is!"

Pierfrancesco approached the cart and rifled through the brown robe. He then walked away from the robe and mounted his horse. "There is no seal in the pocket. Take them both to the Stinche!"

"Bugiardo—liar!" shouted Vincenzo.

A constable punched the priest hard in the stomach, taking his wind. He hunched forward. Another constable stood Claudia up, and Pierfrancesco pulled her up onto his horse. She did not resist. She saw Lorenzo writhing in pain, bound, and her heart was broken, her will drained. The constables dragged the two prisoners away. Pierfrancesco and Claudia rode down the via, and soon it was quiet.

Vincenzo placed a hand on the rail of the cart and at last stood upright, his breath still constricted. He gritted his teeth. His anger was getting the better of him.

XIV

Quinci comprender puoi ch'esser convene,
amor sementa in voi d'ogne virtute,
e d'ogne operazion che merta pene.

Therefore you can understand that it must be,
love is the seed in you of every virtue,
and of every action that merits penalty.

Father Vincenzo de Marco sat back in his chair and slid Dante's *Commedia* in on the table a little. He thought about the words. *Love is the seed of virtue and sin.* He thought about his own life. He loved Lorenzo like a son; he was his only family. He loved Matteo, deeply. The two people he loved the most in the world were at that very moment wasting away in cells at the Stinche, the forebodingly square monstrosity of a prison on the Via Ghibellina. They had been there a month. Vincenzo had tried in vain to gain access to them, had spoken to every civil and church official in Florence. Nobody would help. The Chillis were one of the most powerful families in the city, and no one dared cross them.

His love for the two condemned and the despair he felt for the situation was the seed of a powerful sin, rage. He had struggled his whole life to control his temper, and he almost never let it get the better of him. But now, alone at his table, he fought an urge he knew he must suppress, the urge to kill Pierfrancesco Chilli.

Vincenzo sat and read. Carla had gone to the market, and he was alone. He read to calm himself. He read to pass the time while he waited for the messenger to return.

* *

Lodovico ripped a piece of bread off in his mouth and sat back to chew. He washed it down with a healthy gulp of wine and felt satisfied. The vegetable stew was tasty. They had meat—rabbit, which was always a treat. He had eaten his full, and he sat at the head of the table of his expanding family. After decades of struggle, the Giotti family was on the rise again.

His son Jacopo sat opposite him, equally full, but less satisfied. He had been married to Claudia for a month now, and he was happy about that, but Claudia did not love him; he felt it. She showed no disrespect to him. She was learning from Maria how to be a wife. She learned to cook and to sew and launder Jacopo's clothes, all foreign concepts to the daughter of Domenico Chilli. Lodovico had announced that after the construction was complete (and paid off), they would hire a household servant befitting their newfound status. He had used the dowry to purchase the adjoining house (also of two stories) and the small yard behind it. Work then began at combining the two modest houses into the beginnings of a Palazzo Giotti. It would still be modest, of course, but in time, as their wealth grew, it could be expanded even more. For the time being, Jacopo and Claudia slept in the small bedroom off the entrance hall, next to the kitchen.

Jacopo enjoyed the respect his father now showed him. For the first time in his life, he felt loved by the man instead of merely being groomed. He, too, was happy about the construction. He was happy about his wife, if only she would warm up to him.

Claudia, for her part, struggled to mask the depression that had settled in the moment Lorenzo had been bound in the street. Any chance she had had at happiness was now dead; *she* was dead. She went through the motions of life. She did not hate cooking and sewing; it gave her some sense of independence, no longer relying on others to take care of her, but she found no joy in her new married life. She gave herself to her husband, as a good wife should. She put all thought of her true love out of her head and surrendered, body and soul. She cried the first time, not for the pain, but for the loss of herself; she had nothing left to give in this life. The times afterward had become more and more mechanical for her, with no emotion at all.

At any chance she had, she asked her mother for word of Lorenzo. Little news was forthcoming. He was imprisoned, indefinitely. She hated what her brother had become and wondered if her father was truly the same way. Was that how all rich men behaved?

She thought she had noticed Jacopo eavesdropping, the Sunday before, when she had asked Adélaïde for news of Lorenzo, and this, too, made her wonder. Did her husband think about the fate of his friend at all?

Claudia helped her mother-in-law clear the table, but her mind was someplace else.

* *

Pierfrancesco strutted down the Via dei Calzaiuoli. His high brown leather riding boots were rolled down to just above the knee.

The brown stockings underneath, moistened with sweat on this hot, sunny day, stuck to his legs. The white sleeves of his blouse were rolled up above the elbow, and his red tunic was perfectly tailored with gold trim. There was no breeze to ruffle his long, wavy hair, and he walked with his peaked nose turned up a bit at the people who crowded the via.

He put his hand into the money pouch tied to his belt and pulled out a small, rounded silver object with a tiny wooden handle on the back of it. He admired it for a second and thought of ways of turning it into money in his hand. He didn't really need the money, but he needed the object even less. Besides, it excited him a little, profiting from the previous owner's misfortune.

He then remembered that a business acquaintance had once shown him his collection of small objects that had once belonged to famous people. Surely he would pay for this object. Where did he live again? He thought of his brother-in-law; he would know where. He turned and went to find Jacopo.

Lodovico answered the door at the Giotti house. "Buon giorno, Signore, please come in. We have just finished eating, but my wife can make you a plate," said Lodovico.

"No, grazie, I only come to call upon my sister's husband." Pierfrancesco was polite but gave off an air of superiority. "Hello, sister, it is good to see you well," he said to Claudia when she entered the hall. He stepped forward and kissed her cheek.

Claudia stood motionless with an uneasy feeling in her stomach. After a moment she responded, "Good to see you, brother."

"Jacopo, I was wondering if you could help me. I need to call upon your master. He should still be home for pranzo; will you bring me to him?" Pierfrancesco asked, but all in the room knew it was not really a question.

"I will." Jacopo kissed his mother's cheek and then his wife's, who accepted it stiffly. "Papà, I will see you tonight."

Lodovico beamed with pride. All of his plans had come to fruition; his son was important now.

Jacopo and Pierfrancesco went out. Jacopo led the way to the Palazzo Coraggiosi, down the Via Calimala and then down an alley. The pranzo, or midday meal, had just ended at the Coraggiosi residence and Giovanni Coraggiosi received them in the main entrance hall warmly.

"Signor Chilli, to what do I owe this pleasure?" he greeted the two as he made eye contact with his former apprentice and bowed his head slightly.

"Maestro Coraggiosi, I remember you once showed me a sword, very old, that was used to fight the Saracens," Pierfrancesco started.

"Si, certo. It belonged to my ancestor, who earned our family name in the Crusades."

"I remember, and you showed me a book, handwritten."

"Of course, that is a manuscript of the *Decameron*, in Boccaccio's own hand. My father bought it; he never told me from whom."

"Well seeing that you have such a passion for famous objects, I was wondering if you might buy something from me?"

Coraggiosi was intrigued. "Come into my study, prego." He motioned to a door off of the main hall.

The study was a large, high-ceilinged room with bookshelves on two walls, a fireplace on one, and a portrait and a sword hung on the other. There was just one small window, with iron bars across it, and little natural light came in. The host lit two candles on the desk and sat. "What is it that you have, Signore?"

Pierfrancesco reached into his money pouch and pulled out the object. It was a letter seal, silver and round, with a small wooden handle. He handed it over, and Coraggiosi read the backward Latin inscription on the stamp.

"È vero? Is it real?" he asked, dumbfounded.

"It is. It is the official papal seal. It belonged to Pope Julius, and I'll say no more of how it came to be mine."

Coraggiosi was amazed and excited. Pierfrancesco sat, and the two men discussed price. Jacopo stood off to the side, disinterested. He knew nothing about what Pierfrancesco had and did not care. He looked at the objects carefully arranged on the shelves: books, some looking very old; wine goblets; a small stone statue of a mounted knight. He paced in front of the objects and was about to turn away when something caught his eye. In a wooden case, with a silk lining, sat a gold coin. It was small, not much bigger than the tip of his thumb. On it was pictured what looked like a king or an emperor being crowned by someone else. Around the edge was Greek writing.

"What is this?" asked Jacopo, pointing to the coin, mindless of having interrupted the others.

Coraggiosi looked up. "It's a bezant. It came from Constantinople, before the Turks invaded." He looked to Pierfrancesco, who showed no interest whatsoever. He turned back to Jacopo and added, "And it belonged to Lorenzo il Magnifico!"

Jacopo stood motionless. A sick feeling turned in the pit of his stomach.

* *

There was a knock at the door, and Vincenzo closed the *Commedia* and rose to answer. It was the messenger he had expected.

"Salve, Padre, I came to you straight from the road," he said in exasperation, seeking sympathy and perhaps an extra coin or two. He was scrawny, and his clothes were full of dust from days of hard riding.

"Vi ringrazio, I thank you," answered the priest in formal tone. "What news do you bring?"

"I was granted access to a page, who took the letter. He gave me no assurances of its delivery to the pope. I returned the next day to ask the page if it was delivered and was turned away by the guards. Mi dispiace, sorry," he added.

Vincenzo crossed the room and came back with a few coins, which were happily received. The messenger bowed his head and left without speaking. Vincenzo closed the door and sat. He rested his thought-heavy forehead on his two hands on the table and came to one sole conclusion. He must go to see Julius himself.

Fourteen years had passed since he had attacked the then Cardinal della Rovere in the streets of Naples. Would the man, now an aged pope, remember Vincenzo's face? He had seen the enraged Neapolitan for but a brief few seconds, many years ago. He could not possibly remember.

XV

Il Carcere delle Stinche, situated on the Via Ghibellina, sat in an open piazza, with high walls. It was a square-shaped building and was set apart from any surrounding structures, earning it the nickname L'isola delle Stinche, the island of the Stinche. Its only point of entrance or egress was a disproportionately small doorway. Above it was the Latin inscription "Oportet misereri," mercy is necessary, but the people of Florence dubbed it the "Porta della miseria," the gate of misery.

Prisoners were isolated, and their treatment depended on their wealth. Prisoners with money were often given many comforts while those without money suffered greatly. In a dark, windowless cell, one such *povero* sat on the floor with his back to the wall. There was little light, and the stone floor was coated in a thick layer of dirt. He was given scraps of hard bread and cups of water in unpredictable and infrequent intervals. His face was now bearded, but the hair was not thick and grew in uneven patches. He leaned his head back against the hard stone wall and remembered the sound of a sweet voice:

> *Dessus riviere ou sus estan,*
> *Que beaultè ot trop plus qu'humaine.*
> *Mais ou sont les neiges d'antan?*

He could hear Claudia's voice. He was not really sure what the words meant, but he could recite them perfectly. He remembered the last line: "Where are the snows of years gone by?" It had been written by a man in prison, wondering if he would be remembered at all by the outside world.

Would he, Lorenzo, be remembered at all? What was happening in the world outside? What was Father Vincenzo doing? A guard had told him that Claudia had married Jacopo, and the news sank Lorenzo into the worst depression of his life. Claudia was his one hope. He had used that hope to overcome the loss of his father, but now, with that hope gone, even the wound of Simone's death seemed to be freshly opened. He was left alone with this pain, alone with his thoughts.

* *

In another cell sat a prisoner who was hardly left alone. He was visited frequently. His fate was the topic of much discussion among the officials at the prison and at the Signoria. Even the *gonfaloniere* Piero Soderini had been briefed on the situation: a papal spy had donned the robe of a Franciscan monk to gather intelligence on Florence's defenses, and was only apprehended by chance while trying to escape in the company of a kidnapper. The matter had been debated among the city leaders. The prisoner did not deny having worked for the pope, but swore that he was, in fact, a Franciscan friar and was traveling on church business, not spying. The Signoria all agreed that the prisoner must be examined in greater detail.

Four of them came, nameless, faceless. There was no introduction. The prisoner was dragged from his cell down to the cellar. His hands were tied tightly with thick rope behind his back. Another rope was then passed through the one that bound his wrists, and it was hung from the ceiling with a pulley. Without warning, the prisoner was raised swiftly eight feet off the ground by nothing but his arms, bound behind his back. He screamed in agony. He was held for a few seconds before being allowed to drop four feet, then yanked to a halt. The prisoner let out a gut-wrenching scream. He was lowered to the ground, where he fell to his knees sobbing in agony.

A voice from behind him spoke. "Who are you really?"

"Matteo di Napoli, Order of San Francesco," squeaked the prisoner between sobs.

"And you work for the pope?"

"I am his secretary."

"What brings you to Florence?"

"I delivered a letter to Ramon de Cardona at Ravenna. I was on my way back to Rome."

"But first you stopped to spy out our city's defenses!"

"I did no such thing."

The man nodded, and Matteo was again hoisted in the air. The friar dangled slightly forward as he writhed in pain and screamed. None of the four men in the room had any sympathy. If the prisoner were telling the truth, God would protect him. They looked on with the sense of self-righteous superiority which a torturer, by definition, holds over his victim. Again he was dropped and stopped. He passed out from the pain.

A bucket of cold water was dumped over his head to revive him. There were still more questions to answer.

"Why did Julius send you here?"

"I told you...to deliver a letter. I am a friar; I know nothing of defenses even if I wanted to spy." Matteo was again kneeling; he rested his head on the ground. His arms and shoulders felt as though they were lit afire. He could think of nothing else but the pain.

He had no other concern in life but to make it stop. His words were slow, but his voice was raised.

"Tell me about this letter," the inquisitor asked with macabre politeness.

XVI

Adélaïde spoke little at the supper table. She did not have Claudia to converse with, and Domenico and Pierfrancesco spoke only about the politics of Florence and the rivalries among the powerful families and the inner workings of the Signoria and the guilds. She had little interest in their conversation.

Giambattista rarely interjected either, though not for lack of interest. He was deeply interested but intimidated by his father and older brother. He was a thoughtful boy without any of his brother's brutishness, though at times he would go along with Pierfrancesco out of self-consciousness. Adélaïde often tried to engage the boy the way she had Claudia, but this only led him to further introversion. As children, Pierfrancesco had made fun of him for speaking French to his mother, so he never did so again. He now sat quietly and listened to his father and brother.

"What the Signoria has feared for months is now true. Giovanni de' Medici is leading an army of Spaniards to march on the city. It has been confirmed," stated Domenico with a mouth full of food.

"Confirmed how?" asked the elder son.

"The spy you turned over...he's been questioned. They expect the army to move south from Bologna and attack Prato first, before marching here."

"Will our army be able to stop them?"

Domenico let out a sarcastic laugh. "Despite what Messer Machiavelli will have the Council of Ten believe, our citizen-army doesn't stand a chance."

"What will happen?" Pierfrancesco followed.

"The Medicis will be restored to power." Domenico was serious and calm.

"E per noi? And us?"

"We have always shared a good relationship with the Medicis. Our service to il Magnifico will not be forgotten. Giovanni de' Medici and his troops will enter the city; it is inevitable. By then, all the leading families will be vying for favor. It is important that we beat them to it. You must go to Prato, in secret, and speak to Cardinale Giovanni."

"Io? Me?" asked Pierfrancesco with equal excitement and apprehension.

"It must be you. I cannot go; my absence would be noticed, and we must keep up appearances in case the Florentine army does repel the attack. You must set out, quietly, and avoid being seen along the main roads and in the osterie."

Adélaïde was full of fear. Her son was heading out to meet an invading army. Her husband was gambling the family's fortune and indeed their very lives on the Medicis' return. "You will send our son alone to face such danger?" she asked, to her husband's annoyance.

"No," Domenico spat back, "he will go as well." He nodded toward Giambattista.

Adélaïde's heart dropped.

XVII

Father Vincenzo looked over his things one last time. The satchel was packed; he would carry a cloak in case of rain and to use as a blanket. He checked the small purse he kept tied to his belt; not as much money as he would have liked, but it would have to do.

Carla watched in nervous silence; she did not think this was a good idea. Vincenzo had taken her in while she was still a teenager, so she had grown up with him and grown to love him. For his part, Vincenzo was always kind to her and appreciative of the housework she performed, though he never felt the strong paternal ties for her as he did with Lorenzo. Perhaps he was ignorant of the filial love she garnered, as one so often misses things right in front of one's eyes, but he was a kind and generous protector to the girl nonetheless. He was therefore ignorant also of the anguish Carla felt in watching him risk so much to help the ones he loved. She knew the history, and she knew the danger. She worried in silence.

There was a knock at the door.

Vincenzo pulled the door open and felt a surge of anger at the sight before him. Jacopo Giotti stood still and humbly, clutching a felt cap in his hands. Nothing was said by either for a few uncomfortable seconds.

"Buon giorno, Padre, may I speak with you?" Jacopo was contrite in tone, disarming the priest's rage.

"Entra," answered Vincenzo, once again in control of his emotions.

Jacopo entered and sat at the chair Vincenzo cleared off for him. The priest sat across the table. Jacopo looked around.

"Are you going away?"

"Sì. I am leaving for Rome this morning. I intend to plead for Lorenzo and Matteo to the pope himself."

The reminder of Lorenzo's state stung, and Jacopo swallowed a lump in his throat. "I wanted to talk to you about Lorenzo," he offered, finally making eye contact with Vincenzo.

Vincenzo reminded himself that he had once liked Jacopo, and he motioned to the boy to go on, keeping his emotions in check.

"I know who killed his father," Jacopo stated timidly, taking Vincenzo completely by surprise.

Vincenzo's attention was immediately focused on this new development. "Chi?" he asked. "Who?"

"Giovanni Coraggiosi!"

The name hung in the room like a feather caught by a breeze.

Vincenzo thought back to the conversation he had overheard in the Campanile. It now made sense that one of the voices he heard had been that of Coraggiosi; after all, he had asked Domenico to send Simone to Fiesole. The pieces all fit except one: who was the other voice in the Campanile?

"How can you be so sure?" the priest asked.

"The bezant, the coin Lorenzo told us about...Coraggiosi has it. He even admitted that it once belonged to Lorenzo il Magnifico, just like Lorenzo said."

Interessante, Vincenzo thought silently, leaving Jacopo to sit awkwardly. Coraggiosi had gained the coin, but what about the other voice; what gain was there for him? "So what will you do with this information?"

"I will denounce Coraggiosi to the guild!" Jacopo was confident.

"Unwise." Vincenzo paused, unsure why he felt the need to give Jacopo advice; he was still angry with the boy. "You are his former apprentice; he is still your master. He holds a lot more influence in the guild than you. Besides, his having the coin, even if you managed to get it to the guild, is not proof he killed Simone."

"Lorenzo can swear it belonged to his father."

"He is a prisoner; his oath would mean nothing."

"So what should I do?"

"Find out who else was involved. Coraggiosi would not have done this alone. Look into the matter; leave no stone unturned."

"I want to help Lorenzo, Padre, I swear I do."

"And suppose this quest of yours costs you your admittance to the guild, what then? Will you still pursue it for Lorenzo's sake?"

"Perhaps if I confront Coraggiosi with what I know, maybe I can convince him to work toward Lorenzo's release. He is popular among the Calimala masters; he may hold some influence among the Signoria. He may be able to convince them to release him."

"Or he may have you expelled from the guild or imprisoned yourself for trying to blackmail him." Vincenzo doubted Jacopo's resolve.

Jacopo paused a second, closed his eyes, and replied calmly, "Then that is a chance I will take." He was conflicted to his core. He knew he had hurt Lorenzo, but only because he, too, loved Claudia and because Lorenzo could never marry her anyway. But the murder of Lorenzo's father was different, and Jacopo still felt drawn to his friend; he had to get him out of prison.

Vincenzo was somewhat moved by Jacopo's answer. "Tell Coraggiosi that you also have a witness to his conversation in the Campanile. He'll know what you mean. That should convince him to help."

* *

Adélaïde sat at the table in the hall of the Giotti house. Claudia served her and Jacopo a sliced apple and some diluted wine. Maria had left to buy vegetables for supper. After Claudia filled the cups, Jacopo placed his hand on hers and spoke kindly.

"Siedi ti, cara, sit," he told her.

He had always spoken to her with warmth, but though she was always polite, she never returned the warmth in her own voice. She sat and looked at her mother; neither woman knew why Jacopo had wanted to speak with them.

"I know who killed Lorenzo's father," he announced.

A jolt of electricity shot through Adélaïde's veins. Her hands trembled, and she placed them on her lap to keep them hidden.

"Chi?" asked Claudia.

"It was Giovanni Coraggiosi," he answered as the door swung in. Lodovico entered.

"Why would Coraggiosi kill Simone?" asked Adélaïde.

Lodovico froze. He surveyed the three, saying nothing, and awaited the answer to the question.

Jacopo looked to his father for a reaction; sensing no objection he continued, "Because he wanted a gold coin that Simone owned, a bezant, it is called, and it was given to Simone by Lorenzo de' Medici. I saw the coin in Coraggiosi's study."

"A coin in his study is not proof of a murder," replied Lodovico dismissively.

"I know it was him…Even Padre Vincenzo agrees. He says he knows of a witness to Coraggiosi's conversation in the Campanile, whatever that means. But he, too, believes Coraggiosi is guilty."

Lodovico's face turned pale. Who was this witness? Was it the priest himself? Why had he never mentioned it before? Did Jacopo know about Lodovico's role in the murder? It did not seem so. Lodovico regained his composure and listened.

"Why do you tell us this?" inquired Adélaïde.

"I think we can use this information to get Lorenzo out of prison," Jacopo replied.

Claudia's eyes teared. She looked at her husband for a few seconds and then spoke, without the politeness she usually showed him: "*Now* you want to help him!" Her voice was shaky and hinted of suppressed anger. All eyes in the room turned to Jacopo.

"Sì, adesso, now," he answered. "He does not belong in prison, and if that bastardo Coraggiosi killed his father, maybe he can help us get Lorenzo out."

"Now you care about your friend?" Claudia replied coldly.

Jacopo was angered slightly. Claudia was *his* wife; it was he she should be loyal to. His anger, however, quickly dissipated into self-doubt, and he answered only, "He doesn't belong in prison."

Claudia was silent, her anger softened.

Adélaïde listened in silence, the pain of Simone's death renewed.

"And how do you plan on helping him, figlio mio?" asked Lodovico.

"I will confront Coraggiosi with what I know and demand that he use his influence to get Lorenzo released. If he speaks to the Calimala consuls, he may be able to do it."

"He may also have you thrown out of the guild, your apprenticeship wasted," answered Lodovico.

Jacopo did not answer.

"My husband would fight Lorenzo's release. I don't think Coraggiosi will be able to arrange such a thing without my husband's approval," added Adélaïde.

"Perhaps I can persuade Signor Chilli that the boy is no longer a threat," answered Lodovico. "After all, it was my child's marriage that was jeopardized as well. I will speak to him, and perhaps I can soften his heart. I will be the one to speak with Coraggiosi as well. Your status in the guild must be protected, my son. I will confront him and show him how it is in his best interests to help us."

Jacopo was surprised by his father's willingness to get involved.

"And what about Fra Matteo? Who will act on his behalf?" asked Claudia.

"Father Vincenzo is on his way to Rome to petition the pope," Jacopo answered. "Certainly the pope will order the release of his own secretary. It is only Lorenzo's release that is in doubt; that is why we must act."

Lodovico took in this last bit of information and plotted.

XVIII

Pope Julius II slouched in his chair. The seat was made of wood and rounded like a bowl, with high armrests. It sat so high that a stool was needed to mount it, and had the back been taller it would have been a throne.

Julius coughed forcefully into his fist. His health had been waning; he was no longer the vibrant Warrior Pope who led military expeditions. He now spent all of his time inside the Vatican.

"Who is next?" he asked a page, grumpily.

"A Florentine priest has brought news of Fra Matteo, Vostra Santità," answered the scrawny page with his head bowed.

"I suppose he is dead and they have come to recoup his burial costs. Send him in."

Vincenzo entered the suite and stood some twenty feet before the seated, elevated pope. He avoided eye contact and concentrated on being as unrecognizable as he could be.

"What news do you have of my secretary?" Julius inquired without introduction.

"He is imprisoned, Vostra Santità, in the Stinche. They do not believe he is a friar, or that he works for you. They believe him to be a spy. They arrested him and an innocent boy as well, under dubious charges."

"A spy! For whom?"

"For you, Vostra Santità. They think he spies in advance of an invasion of Florence by the papal forces."

Julius coughed in a fit for half a minute. Visibly annoyed, he inquired further, "And when will this supposed invasion take place?"

"I do not know, Santo Padre, I come only as a priest, to bring a shepherd news of one of his flock."

Julius sat silently for a moment, in contemplation. "Your tongue, it is not Florentine."

Knowing that lying about the nature of his accent would be useless, Vincenzo answered in half-truth. "I moved to Florence from Naples, as a young boy, Vostra Santità."

Julius stared at the priest in front of him. Something seemed familiar, but he could not figure what it was. He ordered the page to go find the resident *condottiere*; there would be military matters to discuss. He then turned back toward Vincenzo. "I will need you to stay here, Padre, as our guest, of course, while I respond to these developments. I can't have you arriving back in Florence with any news of my reply until after our troops have entered the city."

With no regard to his place, Vincenzo replied in shock, "You *are* invading Florence?"

"Invade, no. I will assist your magnificent city in restoring its legitimate rulers, the Medicis. I thank you, my son, for warning us of the Florentines' intelligence."

"I did no such thing!" Vincenzo was losing his patience. "I came to beg your intercession on behalf of your servant and an innocent boy!"

The pope showed little alarm at the rise in Vincenzo's voice; he liked heated discussions. "I see…a mission of Christian virtue then! God will reward such virtue, my son, in the next life! For now, enjoy what Rome has to offer, as our guest. Dominus tecum."

Julius stood and stepped down off of the stool with his back to Vincenzo. His sickly body slowly crept toward the door, and Vincenzo realized his audience was concluded.

"You will not help them then?" cried Vincenzo in Neapolitan rage.

Now angered himself at having to explain himself to a priest, and at the lack of reverence being shown to him, the pope turned as he answered, "My plans have already been made. I will not alter them." He looked Vincenzo in the eye and was startled.

Vincenzo's eyes bulged with anger. He clenched his fists at his sides and breathed in heavy rhythms. He knew his anger was taking over, and that it would only make things worse, but he was powerless to control it. Here was this man, a so-called holy man, who had already altered Vincenzo's life in immeasurable ways. He was launching an invasion against the city Vincenzo loved, and he was refusing to act in even the simplest of ways to save the two people Vincenzo loved most in the world. There it was again, as Dante had written: the seed of all good and bad in the world, love. Vincenzo's love for Lorenzo and Matteo was the cause of his hatred for Julius. It was the seed of his anger, which now boiled on the verge of spilling over. He wanted to wring the man's neck again, but he fought the urge with every fiber of his being. His eyes, however, were a truly frightening sight.

Julius looked into the priest's savage eyes. The fear he felt was one he had known before, many years ago, for only a few seconds. Instantly, he placed the face. It was the same face that had grabbed hold of him in the streets of Naples.

Julius's fear turned into anger as well. "Guardia! Entrate!" he yelled.

XIX

Pierfrancesco banged forcefully on the doors of Santo Stefano, the Duomo di Prato. The centuries-old, midsized, Romanesque cathedral was partially finished in a black-and-white horizontal striped façade. To the right of the main nave, a bell tower stood high above the roofline.

The city of Prato was in a frenzy. Spanish troops, under the papal banner and led by Cardinal Giovanni de' Medici, were outside the city walls and poised to sack the quiet Tuscan town. People scrambled to get indoors. Wealthy citizens hid their money, jewelry, and silver in spaces in the walls or in buckets dropped in wells, or in hastily dug ditches in courtyards. Then they either fled the city, if possible, or sought shelter in churches. The poor of the city sheltered indoors with their families. No semblance of a city government could be found; there were no representatives of the city to negotiate. It was every man for himself.

Pierfrancesco banged still harder, but the massive timber doors had been barricaded from the inside. Nobody inside dared open them. Giambattista stood behind his brother. Two bodyguards sat mounted, each holding the reins of Pierfrancesco's and Giambattista's horses. All four men grew more anxious by the second.

They had hoped to arrive at Prato sooner, well in advance of de' Medici's army. Pierfrancesco was to introduce himself to the bishop and seek refuge until such time as the arriving cardinal presented himself to the head of the diocese, as he would surely do after entering the city. Pierfrancesco would then introduce himself and his younger brother and welcome the cardinal on his return. From such a welcome would spring the beginnings of a new era of favor for the Chilli family under the restored princes of Florence. But alas, there had been numerous delays in their journey, and now it was too late to find the bishop. They would have to find whatever shelter they could; the city walls were not adequate to repel any worthwhile attack, and the troops would be inside the city shortly.

From all around and from no direction in particular, bestial screams roared to life. Wood cracked loudly, and horseshoes clapped down ubiquitously. Women screamed and men cried out. The sound was terrifying, and still the four on the church steps saw nothing. The narrow vias that filed into the piazza in front of the cathedral were curved and hid from view the carnage that closed in on the four.

One of the bodyguards grabbed the handle of his sword and made to unsheathe it. The other, wisely, stopped him. "We've no chance at charging this mob; we must get out of here now!" he said. "Boys…on your mounts, now!"

Pierfrancesco did not even protest being given an order by a bodyguard; he jumped up on his horse quickly, scared for his life. The four rode around to the back of the church, but an iron gate sealed off the work yard in the rear. Each surveyed in different directions for a place to hide.

Dozens of soldiers stormed the piazza. Small doors were kicked in. Men were dragged out of doors, as their wives tugged at the soldiers' arms, and slaughtered in the street. Women were thrown on the ground and raped, by two and three men, then run through with a sword as the last pulled up his pants. Children screamed as their parents were butchered in front of their eyes, and were often hacked to pieces to have their screams silenced. Anything of value was carried off.

The four rode hard down a narrow alley as the soldiers poured into street after street, alley after alley, by the thousands. Spanish cavalry stampeded any living thing in its path. A dead-end alley closed the four in, and they turned back to the sight of four armored Spanish horsemen. The cavalrymen charged as the bodyguards drew their swords. Pierfrancesco dismounted and drew a dagger from his saddle, shielding himself behind his horse. Giambattista froze in fear. Horses collided and swords clanged loudly. A man screamed, and so did a horse. Pierfrancesco heard cursing, and cries of agony. A Spanish horseman was thrown from his mount and hit the paving stones at the Chilli heir's feet.

Pierfrancesco wasted no time in slashing the soldier's throat, and thick blood spouted up on his own tunic. Another Spaniard lay dead not far away, and a riderless horse and a mounted Spaniard rode off down the alley. One bodyguard slumped over, dead, on his horse, which turned and bucked nervously. The other bodyguard lay motionless and bloody on the ground. Pierfrancesco looked down at himself, amazed to be uninjured, covered in the blood of the Spaniard.

"Did you see how I slit that barbarian's throat?" he asked his brother excitedly.

There was no reply, and Pierfrancesco turned toward Giambattista, slightly annoyed that his younger brother was too timid to answer. He spun and froze.

Giambattista lay dead on the ground with multiple stab wounds.

Pierfrancesco's hands shook. He did not know how to feel. Did he want to weep? Tears would not come. Would his father blame him for not protecting his younger brother? What should he do? The bodyguards were dead, and he was still in great danger. Instinctively, he picked up his brother and draped him over the back of his horse. He stripped a dead soldier of his gold tunic, breastplate and helmet, and hastily dressed himself. He mounted the Spaniard's horse and led Giambattista's horse out of the alley.

LIBER QUARTUS

Sicut et nos dimittimus debitoribus nostris

I

AUTUMN 1512

Francesco Granacci was by now a well-respected Florentine artist. Like his friend Michelangelo, he had studied painting under the great Domenico Ghirlandaio, and then sculpting in the garden of Lorenzo de' Medici. After serving as an assistant for Michelangelo during his painting of the Sistine Chapel in Rome, Granacci had returned to Florence and made a nice living fulfilling commissions, both public and private. He painted everything from large murals for convents and churches to portraits for wealthy citizens.

As part of a wedding gift for his daughter, Domenico Chilli had arranged to have Granacci paint a portrait of the newlywed couple. It wasn't until early fall, however, that the painter was available to do the work.

In his early forties, Granacci was at the height of his craft. Straightforward portraits provided little challenge. He usually spoke with his subjects ahead of time and asked about what type of pose and background they preferred. He then painted the background and bodies of the subjects in his studio, using assistants as models. Then he set up his easel in the subjects' home and had them stand in similar poses while he painted their faces and filled in details of clothing or scenery.

Jacopo and Claudia stood in the entrance hall of the Palazzo Chilli. The grand staircase rose behind them. Jacopo wore his formal Calimala garb, the long pleats of the reddish-brown robe neatly pressed. On his head was the floppy beret-type cap with similar, albeit smaller, pleats. A gold-colored rope was decoratively tied around his waist. He stood proudly with his shoulders back. His right arm was bent in front and clasped his wife's hand over his left arm.

Claudia stood alongside her husband. She stared ahead, her thoughts someplace else, neither smiling nor frowning. Her dress was a light, aurora-colored linen. The neckline was cut square and low on the bosom, where it was finely detailed in a crisscross pattern. The sleeves were tied to the shoulders with thick bows. Around her neck was a chain of gold squares and red rubies. Long curls of her soft brown hair framed her face on either side, with the rest of her hair pinned up behind her head and confined with a thin, crescent-shaped headdress. The dress was not form fitting below the breast and shoulder area, hiding the swollen belly that the painter would have brushed away anyway.

Granacci steadied his hand with a wooden stick as he delicately hovered the brush over the canvas-Claudia's eyes. He had been working on her eyes for over an hour. He kept adding light and shadow, contrast and shading. He was intrigued by her eyes, by the depth of feeling he saw in them, and he wanted them to be perfect. Whereas Jacopo's face in the portrait seemed slightly rounder than in real life (in Granacci's style), Claudia's face, figure, features, and most importantly her eyes seemed to be in perfect proportion and alive.

The painter balanced his wiry frame on a stool. He alternated his glance between subject and canvas, trying not to be seen as staring at the beauty that so captivated him. He had painted beautiful woman before, but this one was different. Her eyes told a story, and he needed to hear it.

In the sitting room off of the entrance hall sat Adélaïde. A book sat open, facedown in her lap, and she stared ahead. She could not formulate a train of thought in her head. It would have been a struggle to remember how she had gotten out of bed, dressed herself, and ended up on the cushioned chair. She did not live. She merely existed, one activity at a time. If she tried to think ahead, grief would overwhelm her. At times, breathing overwhelmed her. It hurt to draw air. She had no interest in eating. She just wanted to die, but even the thought of dying seemed to be too complicated a thought to process. There were days where she did not get out of bed. She missed her son. She hurt for all the things she wished she had told him. She hurt for not having fought harder for him. She hurt because outside the door, for everyone else, life went on. She measured her own life in two parts: everything that came before the death of her son, and every day since.

It was cool and overcast outside; autumn was upon them. Adélaïde sat still while drops of rain beat an irregular rhythm on the sill of the window.

* *

Domenico, his brother Francesco, and his son Pierfrancesco stood shoulder to shoulder in the Hall of Audience of L'Arte della Lana, the wool guild. Around the edge of the room, between the marble pillars, were clusters of other guild members sporadically glancing at the Chillis and whispering. Some shook their heads after looking; some let out small giggles. The guild consul, Luigi Spigliati, approached the three.

"Buon giorno, Signori," he began, coolly but respectfully, "grazie for having come so quickly."

"Di niente," Domenico responded quickly.

"I will get right to the point, as I know you are a busy man," the consul went on. "The consuls have decided to strip you, Signor Chilli, of your title of sensale. You remain, however, a master of this guild with all rights, privileges, and duties thereof."

Domenico had known it might come to this, but hearing the news still angered him. Though the consul spoke softly, all in the room knew what was being said. Domenico looked around the room at all of the gossiping eyes waiting for a reaction. He refused to give them satisfaction.

"Grazie, Don Spigliati, addio!" Domenico turned toward the door.

Pierfrancesco started to speak but was cut off before a word could leave his lips.

"Stai zitto! Shut up!" his father whispered and pulled his son's sleeve.

As the three walked out onto the tight via in Or San Michele, the sky opened up. Rain fell hard in thick, impenetrable sheets, drops the size of *fagiolini* beans. They were instantly soaked. Domenico thought of going back in the guildhall but was too angry to spend another minute there. It was petty politics, pure and simple. The leading masters and consuls were angry that

Domenico and Giovanni Coraggiosi were collaborating in a deal with an English vendor to import both raw and finished wool. Domenico would take the raw wool to process in his bottega (making it local wool), and Coraggiosi would take the finished wool to sell it (as foreign wool).

Domenico had proposed the deal to Coraggiosi through his son-in-law, Jacopo. Jacopo could not buy the wool himself because he was not yet a full master. Domenico had met the English vendor on his trip to Siena. Importing both quantities in one shipment made it possible to negotiate a much better price. It also was dangerously close to violating both the wool guild's and the Calimala's ban on dealing in the other's wool. Retail prices in Florence were set by the guilds, so the cheaper purchase cost of the materials to Domenico and Coraggiosi gave both a huge advantage over other guild merchants. The consuls, however, felt powerless to stop the deal.

When Cardinal Giovanni de' Medici had heard that Giambattista Chilli died at Prato while coming out to welcome the cardinal, he had instantly ingratiated himself to the Chilli family. After hearing about the two days of slaughter, rape, and pillage at Prato, in which thousands of citizens were killed, the Signoria in Florence thought it best to ask the *gonfaloniere*, Piero Soderini, to leave the city, and to surrender to the papal forces. The Medicis were reinstated at once as the ruling family. Cardinal de' Medici was by now back in Rome, and his brother, Giuliano, was left to rule Florence. The Chilli family once again enjoyed the favor of the ruling family of Florence. Ironically, Domenico's plan to have his sons meet Giovanni de' Medici was paying off more than he could have imagined. The consuls of the guild did not have the political power to prevent Domenico's English deal. They could, however, strip him of the title of *sensale*. The *sensali* kept other guild masters in check. It was considered an honor.

The rain fell hard and Domenico, Francesco, and Pierfrancesco cowered under their cloaks and moved quickly toward the Palazzo Chilli. As they turned onto the Via dei Calzaiuoli, Francesco shouted through the sound of the rain.

"Tre generazioni," he yelled, "three generations of sensali...out the window. Figli di puttane—sons of whores!"

"They'll get theirs!" Pierfrancesco joined in, as he shielded his squinting eyes with his hand.

Domenico stopped and stood upright, disregarding the barrage of rain. "Basta, enough!" he stated forcefully. "You two are missing the point. Those bastardi acted pettily but predictably. This was necessary. We can no longer concern ourselves with monitoring scales and measuring the bales of other merchants. We are above that now. We are among the most favored families in the city!" The wind was blowing his hair aside, and the rain seemed to fall sideways. "The guilds are not what they used to be...you will see. All the cities of Italy will be shuffled among foreign powers like a deck of cards. The politics of years gone by are meaningless. We must think ahead and make our alliances accordingly, as I have done with the Medicis."

Pierfrancesco waited for his father to finish and then pulled his arm to move him along. They were soon back at the palazzo and stood dripping in the entrance hall where Jacopo and Claudia were posing for Francesco Granacci. Painter and subjects turned toward the door; none spoke. The house servant, Paolo, helped Domenico remove his wet cloak, and the elder Chilli began shivering. A chill took over his body.

"Signore," began Paolo, "go up and undress, and I will light a fire in your chamber and have some warm milk brought up."

Domenico slipped his wet, shined leather boots off and climbed the stairs shivering, his arms crossed. Adélaïde remained sitting in the other room; she did not get up to greet her husband.

II

Jacopo had not yet discussed the bezant, or Lorenzo, with Coraggiosi. Lodovico had said he would take care of it. Many weeks had passed, and it seemed odd to Jacopo, that had his father indeed approached Coraggiosi, the Calimala master would not have mentioned it or taken any meaningful steps toward freeing Lorenzo. Twice he had asked his father about it, and both times Lodovico assured his son that plans were in motion for the outcome he desired.

Lodovico was right in that approaching his master was dangerous for Jacopo. He was no longer an apprentice, but he was bound to work for his master for the time being, and his acceptance as a full master depended heavily on Coraggiosi's recommendation. Alienating his master could mean expulsion from the guild. Moreover, at this moment Coraggiosi was very pleased with his former apprentice. The deal that Jacopo had brokered between him and the Chilli family stood to make him a lot of money. This goodwill between master and apprentice was a valuable asset for Jacopo, and he did not want to squander it.

After the wedding, Lodovico had begun acting very kindly toward his son. But now, since the conversation about the bezant, Lodovico was back to his old demeanor. He was dismissive of his son's inquiries and quick to remind Jacopo about the importance of protecting his future. Jacopo was back to resenting the man.

Claudia sat on the bed in her nightgown. She leaned back against the headboard, with pillows propped up behind her back and rested two hands on her belly. She contemplated the child growing inside her. She rubbed the small mound now protruding and wondered about motherhood. Jacopo changed into his night robe and sat beside his wife. She made no acknowledgement of his arrival.

"I don't think my father approached Coraggiosi," he stated as a matter of fact, with no emotion.

Claudia stopped rubbing her belly and turned toward her husband. "And now what?" she asked.

"He is not telling me something, I know it."

Claudia had never heard Jacopo discuss his father before. She sensed tension in him after dealings with Lodovico, but he never spoke about it with her. As time went by, she hated Jacopo less. She began to see him as much as a pawn of his father's will as she had been of her father's. In addition, she knew that he did, in fact, love her. She did not love him, however, and she still resented her situation greatly. "Do you see any way we can convince Coraggiosi to help Lorenzo?" she asked.

Jacopo had never heard Claudia refer to him and her as "we" before, and he liked it. "Maybe, but your mother was right. Your father, or your brother can easily stop any release from the Stinche that Coraggiosi might arrange."

"He is pleased with you right now, Coraggiosi, and he is about to make a lot of money on this deal with the English wool; he won't want to jeopardize it by harming you in any way. If you threaten him, I think he will go along," Claudia told him.

Jacopo was surprised to hear such a thought-out plan from Claudia. He knew her to be smart, but she hardly showed this side of herself to him.

"If you can convince him to have the Calimala consuls petition for a pardon," she went on, "I will confront my father and my brother. I think I can convince them to let the pardon stand."

"Do you really think this will work?" Jacopo was sincere in his quest for his wife's opinion.

Claudia was warmed by his tone. He was defensive when he felt judged, but usually he was kind. He was one of only three people in the world (her mother and Lorenzo being the others) who did not dismiss her opinions as the mindless whims of a young girl. "It is our only hope," she answered. "Maman says that Padre Vincenzo has not been heard from. If he had been able to talk to the pope, we would have heard by now. We must use the leverage we have."

"I will confront Coraggiosi then."

"And I, my father and brother."

"Buona notte, cara mia, good night," he added warmly as he turned his head and closed his eyes.

"Buona notte," she answered in a whisper. She put her hands back on her belly and sat up thinking for quite a while. She closed her eyes and envisioned a scared and lonely young man in a dark cell. She wondered what he was doing at that moment. Was he thinking of her?

* *

Through the damp, quiet darkness, Lorenzo reached toward the empty space between himself and the open cell door. Brilliant beams of light poured into the blackness like the Arno overflowing its banks, like hope filling the void of hopelessness. He was dazed and heard nothing but the harmonic song of angels. In the doorway stood a figure, femininely divine, a shadow whose features were obscured by the rays of light surrounding it. The beautiful shadow spoke, her voice heartbreakingly soothing:

> Guardaci ben! Ben son, ben son Beatrice.
> Come degnasti d'accedere al monte?
> Non sapei tu che qui è l'uom felice?

> *Look well at me! I am, I am Beatrice.*
> *How did you deign to climb the mountain?*
> *Did you know not that here man is happy?*

The words were familiar. Beatrice spoke them to Dante as she met him in Purgatory. It was the moment when Dante's guide, his conscience, Virgil, must leave (as the pagan could ascend no further toward heaven) and Beatrice, the love of Dante's life, appeared to shepherd the pilgrim toward the kingdom of God. For Dante, Beatrice was the embodiment of spiritual love (for there was never a physical love between them). She had died young and remained, for the rest of Dante's life, the vessel that would bring the poet toward God. His love for her was a divine love, a love of humanity, a love that saves the soul that is lost and shows it the way home.

The figure stepped forward and illuminated the cell. The angelic song became louder as the white silkiness of her dress hugged the feminine curves of the divine figure. She knelt down in front of Lorenzo and placed a loving hand on his cheek. The face became clear. It was Claudia. Her deep, brown eyes locked onto his, and her beautiful voice whispered:

> Dante, perché Virgilio se ne vada,
> non pianger anco, non piangere ancora;
> ché pianger ti conven per altra spada.

> *Dante, just because Virgil goes away,*
> *do not cry yet, do not cry yet;*
> *for crying will come to you through another sword.*

She held his cheek and his tears wet her palm. He shook and felt a sharp pain in his back and reached behind. It was a cramp. The cold hardness of the cell floor woke him, and he opened his eyes to darkness, his eyes still teary. He was, once again, alone in his cell.

III

"Carissimo Messer Giotti," the letter began, "I have made inquiries into the matter to which you have requested and found that the man in question is at the present time a prisoner at the Castel Sant'Angelo. His offense is not known, but it appears he is being held on the orders of Pope Julius himself. As to the money you sent to use in my gathering of information, it was necessary that I go into my own purse for an additional ten florins. If you would be so kind as to reimburse me this hardship. Your servant, Giovanni de Angelis."

Lodovico crumpled the letter and tossed it into the fire. He sat back and contemplated this new development. If Father Vincenzo were indeed the witness in the Campanile, then having him locked away in Rome was to Lodovico's advantage. There was, however, somebody else who knew Lodovico's secret. What to do with him? For the time being he would wait, but if he needed it taken care of, whom could he turn to? He thought for a while and decided he would turn to an old acquaintance, somebody he hadn't used in many years.

IV

Claudia sat at the table in the main room of the old section of the Giotti house. She pushed a needle and thread through the seam of a white men's blouse that had separated. Maria had taught her to sew, and she now enjoyed the repetitive serenity of the craft. Her mother-in-law had left some garments in need of stitching while she went out shopping for vegetables. While she worked the needle Claudia mouthed the lyrics of a French children's song her mother had sung to her.

Jacopo entered and hastily sat beside her without taking off his cloak. Claudia put the blouse and sewing kit on the table and waited attentively for the news she knew her husband to be bringing.

"È fatto! It's done," he said.

Needing much more information, Claudia prompted him, "Dai, go on!"

"I told him that I knew the bezant belonged to Simone Simoni…and that I knew of a witness to his conversation in the Campanile. He was quiet. He seemed very nervous at first. He did not talk about the guild or my apprenticeship at all. I was confused."

"He did not threaten you at all?"

"No, that is what is so confusing. It seemed as if he thought I was holding something back, as if I knew something else. I told him that I thought the least he could do was to ask the consuls of the Calimala guild to petition the giudici for Lorenzo's release."

"And what did he say?"

"He said that that might not be necessary. He said that he had heard that all the political prisoners in the Stinche were set to be freed by the orders of Giuliano de' Medici. He wasn't sure if Lorenzo was considered a political prisoner, but that it would not be hard to bribe the guards into releasing him with all of the others. They are making room in the cells for enemies of the Medicis; enemies of the old republic will be released."

"So Fra Matteo should be released! But how can we be sure Lorenzo will be as well?" Claudia asked nervously.

"He said he would make sure of it; he would go talk to the guards himself and pay them whatever he had to," Jacopo replied.

Claudia was surprised at Coraggiosi's eagerness to get involved. She had expected a volley of threats back and forth between master and apprentice and hoped that the former would fold to the bluff. She knew they had little real leverage against him. But he seemed to have given in very easily. Did he feel guilty for Simone's death? Was he protecting somebody else? Was he plotting something?

"There's something else," added Jacopo. "My suspicion was right. My father never confronted him. This was the first he was hearing of it, I can tell—but why would my father lie?"

"Non lo so, I don't know," Claudia replied. Lodovico always made her nervous.

* *

Domenico coughed forcefully into a handkerchief. Green mucus filled the fine linen cloth, and the coughing caused a sharp, compressive pain in his chest. He pulled his blanket up to his chin in an effort to combat the chills that had overtaken his body. He was nauseous and had a high fever.

Paolo took a wet cloth out of a bucket, wrung it, then placed it neatly folded on his master's forehead. Adélaïde had stayed away from Domenico's chamber since he had fallen ill the week before. She had visited him once, early on, and then saw to it that Paolo took care of her husband. She now slept in the antechamber and passed most days in the sitting room downstairs, staring out into nothing.

Pierfrancesco entered the palazzo, the large timber door shutting loudly behind him. He surveyed the first floor. His mother was in the sitting room alone. No servant came to greet him at the door; everyone was busy someplace else. With an air of annoyance, he hung his own cloak on a hook near the door and went to the kitchen. He returned to the hall, biting into an apple, and went to sit across from Adélaïde. She took note of his arrival, saying nothing.

He ate in big bites, chewing with his mouth open, not at all discomforted by his mother's silence.

"We are opening a new bottega in Or San Michele, to comb and dye the English wool," he announced proudly.

"Très agréable, very nice," she answered in polite, emotionless French, without turning her eyes away from the window she stared at.

He said no more. He had thought that some good news might put his mother in better spirits. Now, he didn't know what to say. Her behavior was a mystery to him.

After a few moments, the chef entered the sitting room and announced, "A tavola, Signori," with a smile. The midday supper was ready.

The silver clanking on ceramic made by Pierfrancesco's spoon echoed in the spacious dining hall. The head seat was empty, along with all but two places at the long table. Adélaïde watched Paolo carry a bowl of soup and a piece of bread from the kitchen, through the dining hall, and toward the stairs, to Domenico. She then focused again on the table. She sat at the right of the head seat, across from her son, who mindlessly shoveled steamed onions and small, hand-rolled half spheres of pasta into his slurping mouth. As was customary, a large ceramic baseplate and set of silver were set neatly in front of every seat. Adélaïde looked at the empty head seat, then to her right where Claudia once sat, and then across the table to Pierfrancesco's left. She stared numbly at Giambattista's empty seat. The profound emptiness of the red velvet padding seemed infinite, as did that of her heart.

Claudia then entered the hall, alone, and sat in her usual seat without greeting. Her brother took little note as he raised the bowl and drank the remaining broth. She raised her mother's hand and kissed it, then held it in her lap. "Bonjour, Maman," she said softly.

Adélaïde held her hand up to her daughter's cheek and rubbed it with her thumb. With glassy eyes she answered, "Bonjour, ma chère."

The chef entered and placed an oval, silver platter of lamb shank in the table center. Juices coated the pan bottom, and the bone of the shank stood straight up proudly. Green leaves surrounded the sliced meat stacked around the pan's border, and the hall filled with the scent of tender roasted meat. The chef collected Pierfrancesco's empty bowl and paused over Adélaïde's shoulder. "Signora?" he asked politely, and the lady of the house waved a hand over the untouched bowl of soup, giving him permission to take it.

"Something for you, Signora Claudia?" he asked with hands full.

"No, grazie," she replied quickly.

The chef returned to the kitchen, and Pierfrancesco tore into the lamb.

"Maman," started Claudia, "I heard that Giuliano de' Medici has announced that all political prisoners will be released.

Pierfrancesco set down the boned shank he had been stripping of meat and alternated glances between his mother and sister, waiting to hear more. Adélaïde signaled with her eyes for her daughter to continue.

"They will surely release Fra Matteo, but Lorenzo may not be," she added.

Pierfrancesco let out a loud, sarcastic sigh and recommenced eating.

Adélaïde thought for a moment and through the fog of grief formulated the first lucid thought she had had in weeks. "We must ensure it!" she said surely.

Pierfrancesco felt annoyed at the supposition that the two women could interfere with the politics of crime and punishment in the city. "Lasciatelo stare! Let it be!" he retorted condescendingly.

Claudia's temper was as foreign to Tuscany as her mother's tongue, especially in the Chilli household where Domenico and his eldest son were quick to anger, often lashing out violently at the source of their ire with little provocation. Claudia's temper, on the other hand, was that of her mother's. It was cool and slow cooking, patient, Provençal, and once brought to a boil, impossible to cool down. She grabbed a cup of water from in front of her mother and tossed it into the face of her smug, chewing brother, much to his astonishment.

He jumped to his feet, knocking his chair back, and stood for a second with water dripping from his face. He breathed heavily and charged his sister violently. Adélaïde was practically knocked over as he crashed into Claudia and made to grab her throat. Claudia put a hand up to his face and scratched the skin of his cheek, causing the now irate Pierfrancesco to raise his right hand back in preparation of a hard blow. Adélaïde threw her body on top of her son's. Ceramic plates and silver spoons and knives and food and water and wine flew across the room and crashed and splashed everywhere. The chef ran out to see what the commotion was and cried out obscenities of disbelief as he tried to separate the three.

"The baby, the baby…you'll hurt the baby!" screamed Adélaïde.

The chef managed to pull Pierfrancesco away. Pierfrancesco looked his angry mother in the eye. His temper was cooled by the shame his mother's look brought upon him. He left the dining hall without helping his sister up.

"Ma chère," cried Adélaïde as she kneeled next to her daughter, "es-tu bien? Are you all right?"

"Oui, Maman, help me up, si il te plait," she replied.

Claudia stood and reflexively rubbed her pregnant belly. All seemed fine. Adélaïde was embarrassed and horrified at her son's actions.

They heard the large front door slam and knew Pierfrancesco had gone out.

"Come, ma chère, sit with me and we will figure this out," said Adélaïde.

V

Lorenzo crouched on the floor against the wall and crossed his arms tightly against his chest for warmth. There was a small fireplace in the cell, but being September, no one had lit it yet, and he wondered what month there would be a fire. His bones hurt, and he felt weak. He had grown so used to feeling hungry that he no longer noticed it. His mind played tricks on him, and only the routine of the guards from the other side of the door gave hint to the passage of hours or days.

There had been some commotion in the corridor the past few days. He heard a lot of voices and foot traffic and cell doors slamming. He even thought he heard cheers from outside the thick walls, but he was not sure. He hoped he had been wrong about the cheers for, to him, it could only mean one thing, executions. He'd heard the man in the adjoining cell being taken out the night before, and he had not yet come back. Had he been executed?

Lorenzo had seen groups of prisoners being killed before; most people in Florence had. Every so often, six or ten men would be taken out to the piazza in front of the Stinche or to the Piazza della

Signoria and beheaded on a wooden platform. Crowds always gathered to watch, to jeer at the condemned, to cheer at the fall of the hatchet, and feel good about themselves for not being under it.

Though the damp air and the thick walls dampened the sound, Lorenzo heard, once again, a crowd cheer outside. This time he was certain. Like a bolt of lightning, a shot of fear struck through his chest and seemed to grip his spine. He did not know why, but he knew they would be coming for him soon. It was an intuition he could not explain, the kind of certainty of his future that sprung from the vacuum of hope that was a solitary prison cell. He waited and he fretted.

What surprised him the most was the fact that he did not want to die. He had spent most of the last few months in prison wishing he were dead. The news of Claudia's marriage had drained him of all hope. He had missed his father terribly and once again wept for his loss. He did not think he could feel any lower, and no relief ever came. Finally, time lost all meaning. His mind became an endless chain of noncontiguous fragments, memories, and impulses. But now, with the specter of guards coming for him next, dragging him down to the platform, he felt focused for the first time in months. He was certain that he wanted to live.

He was right. They did come for him next, two of them. He heard the rattle of keys being jostled around a ring and the metallic snap of an interior locking latch being spun. The cell door swung in fast, and light poured over him and pained his sensitive eyes. A rat scurried out the open door, and two burly, humorless guards squeezed in. Lorenzo's weak legs lost any strength they had left.

"Alza ti. Get up," one said. His words were foreboding.

Lorenzo was terrified. "Where are you taking me?" he asked.

"No questions" was his only answer as they each grabbed hold of an arm and pulled him forcefully to his feet. His legs were cramped, and he had trouble straightening them and nearly fell. The guards pulled up hard again to steady him, and their grip hurt his upper arms.

They dragged him out of the cell and down the corridor. Lorenzo did not know what to do. He was too weak to fight. He felt sick with a horrible sadness in the pit of his stomach. It was a black misery that completely overtook him. He wished he could see Claudia just one more time. He thought of Simone. Would he be with his father soon? That thought felt comforting, but how could he be sure? He felt regret, deep regret. If he had been stronger, or cleverer, he would not be in this position. He felt hatred for Pierfrancesco, but he was too weak to hold on to this hatred and he let it go. He felt shame, shame for disappointing Father Vincenzo, who had had so much hope for Lorenzo's future. He felt like a child again, and he wanted to be embraced by his father's strong arms. It hurt his legs to keep up with the quick pace of the guards.

* *

Jacopo sat at the table thinking. He chewed on a piece of bread and washed it down with a gulp of wine. He was startled by loud banging on the door, and when he opened the door, Pierfrancesco stormed past him.

"Che fai? What are you doing? Pierfrancesco barked as he scanned the room. "Where is your father?"

"I believe he's gone to witness a contract signing, why?"

"And your wife?" Pierfrancesco asked angrily, though he knew the answer.

"She went to visit your parents."

"When will your father be back?"

"Soon, I think. My mother is in the back now, preparing our pranzo." Jacopo was always unnerved by his bullying brother-in-law.

Pierfrancesco started to leave. He opened the door himself and was halfway out before Jacopo added, "How is your father?"

"Dying," Pierfrancesco answered without stopping.

VI

One guard propped Lorenzo up while the other unlocked the dark, wooden, arch-topped door. The lock took a moment to open, and Lorenzo's anxiousness grew. At last the door swung back, and bright sunlight smacked him hard in the face. His eyes immediately squinted shut. The air was cool and damp. He could make out a crowd of people, but no one cheered; he just heard the murmur of multiple simultaneous conversations.

"I'll take him from here," a voice said as someone grabbed Lorenzo's arm. The man with the voice shook hands with the guard, and Lorenzo thought he saw him give the guard a small purse, hand to hand, very discreetly.

He could not yet open his eyes fully and did not recognize the man.

"Lorenzo, do you remember me? I am Giovanni Coraggiosi."

"Sì, certo, of course, but why...what...?"

"Where should I take you?"

"San Felice, per favore."

The walk to San Felice was slow and agonizing. Coraggiosi did not speak, and Lorenzo was confused. He could not process what had just happened. He was free; no one was following them, but why?

In the small Piazza San Felice, the two stopped, and Coraggiosi turned and faced Lorenzo. After a pause, he looked Lorenzo in the eye and held the gaze for a few seconds. He looked as if he were about to say something, but then didn't.

"Addio," he said softly, and he turned and walked away.

Now Lorenzo was really confused, but he did not dwell on the matter. He went quickly to Father Vincenzo's door and knocked eagerly. He could not wait to tell the priest what he had been through and to hear his thoughts on the subject. Surely, Father Vincenzo could make sense of the situation. Carla opened the door and smiled, though her eyes remained sad.

Seated at the table was Matteo. He rose and went to Lorenzo and hugged him. He held the embrace for a while. Lorenzo was happy to see the friar.

"Where is Padre Vincenzo?" he asked.

Matteo stepped back. His eyes watered up. Lorenzo looked from Matteo to Carla, who was also crying.

"He went to Rome, to petition the pope for our release." Matteo paused, looked at the floor, and added, "He hasn't returned."

Lorenzo's heart dropped. He felt exactly the way he had felt when Vincenzo had told him his father was in danger before setting off on horseback to try and save him. It was a massive weight of worry, lightened only by the faintest of hopes that he was still alive.

"I am setting out for Rome in the morning. I *will* find him," said Matteo with certainty.

"I'll go with you," Lorenzo replied, eager to find the man he had come to love as a father.

Matteo shook his head. "No, you must stay here. I will be able to move around the Vatican, but not with you. I can sneak around more freely alone."

"But then what can I do?"

"The papal seal…I'll need it if I'm to do anything. The Chilli boy took it. You have to help me get it back tonight!"

Lorenzo was a little startled at the thought of confronting Pierfrancesco that night. He was not sure how he could get near him, and how would he get the seal back if he did?

Carla brought out some bread and a bowl of hot, thick lentil soup. She set it down and pulled out a chair for Lorenzo. She went over to the cupboard and returned with a small bottle of olive oil and sprinkled some on top of the soup and then added a pinch of salt from a small bowl on the table. The smell hit Lorenzo, and his stomach churned with deep, empty hunger.

He looked Carla in the eye. "Grazie," he said wholeheartedly as he sat and tore a piece of bread. He shoveled up a scoop of hot lentils with the bread and jammed it into his mouth. He chewed a couple of times and swallowed hard. It was the best meal of his life. Carla placed a cup of wine in front of him, and he alternated between swigs of wine and healthy scoops of lentils.

When he had finished eating, he lay down on a bed upstairs and slept deeply. It was dark when he was awakened by the sound of voices downstairs. The darkness confused his sense of morning and night, and he needed to think for a moment. Had he been dreaming? Had he really been in prison? Was Father Vincenzo missing? Was Claudia really married to Jacopo? The voices downstairs sounded familiar, and his senses returned. It was evening. He had slept all afternoon. He got out of bed and slipped his shoes back on, heading downstairs toward the voices.

As he descended the stairs, the crowd around the table came into view. Matteo sat in Vincenzo's seat, and opposite him was Adélaïde, who stood immediately as he reached the lower steps. On one side sat Jacopo, and Lorenzo felt a quiver of nervous anger in his stomach. Opposite Jacopo sat Claudia. When Lorenzo saw her, his heart beat faster; his eyes met her watering brown ones and he held her gaze while Adélaïde ran to him and embraced him fully. She openly wept as she hugged Lorenzo. She wept for the joy of his safe return, and she wept for the son she could not hold. Lorenzo was her son now.

Lorenzo looked over her shoulder at Claudia, who stood. He noticed her pregnant belly and was hit with the reminder that she belonged to Jacopo. He stared at Jacopo, saying nothing. He felt numb.

Claudia approached and kissed his cheek. She held his hand in hers.

"I am so happy to see you," she said softly.

Lorenzo nodded, still numb.

"Jacopo knows where the seal is," Matteo announced. "He says he can get it for us."

"Where is it?" Lorenzo asked as he sat on the stairs. Claudia and Adélaïde returned to their seats. Carla brought a pitcher of wine in from the kitchen and set it on the table.

"Coraggiosi has it; Pierfrancesco sold it to him," Jacopo answered.

"And *you* can get it back!" Lorenzo shot back sarcastically.

"We need it to help Padre Vincenzo." Jacopo was defensive.

"Help...help him, you say? Is that what you do now? Help your friends?" Lorenzo did not mask his anger.

"Lorenzo, mon cher," Adélaïde broke in, "it was Jacopo who arranged for your release."

Lorenzo was startled. "È vero?" he asked Jacopo, still angry.

Jacopo nodded.

"Perché?"

Jacopo, slightly annoyed at being questioned for his actions instead of thanked, took his time to speak.

"It was Coraggiosi," he said at last, "who killed your father. He killed him for the bezant. He collects things from famous people. That is why he bought the papal seal.

When I confronted him with what I knew, he said he would get you out of the Stinche. Maybe he thought I would denounce him; maybe he feels guilty, I don't know."

"It was Coraggiosi who asked Domenico to send my father to Fiesole," said Lorenzo, still not looking at Jacopo.

"I do remember that," added Adélaïde.

"But why would he kill him? He was to get the coin anyway?" Lorenzo asked almost rhetorically.

"What do you mean?" asked Matteo.

Now Lorenzo looked Jacopo dead in the eye and said, "I was to be his apprentice. The bezant was to be part of the payment. My father was to meet him that day to give it to him."

Jacopo shot to his feet, and his chair slid back loudly. He stared at Lorenzo. Then, he stormed out of the house, slamming the door behind him.

"I never knew that," said Adélaïde as she fought back tears. She stood and caressed her daughter's shoulder before carrying some cups from the table into the kitchen.

"Mi scusate," said Matteo as he left to find a chamber pot.

Claudia went to Lorenzo and pulled him to his feet. She again began to cry. "I never wanted this, I swear it, never," she sobbed as she hugged him.

"Lo so, I know it," he answered in a whisper as he held her in his arms and smelled her soft hair.

VII

Jacopo raised the iron ring and knocked on the heavy wooden door. After a moment, a servant answered.

"Tell il Maestro that I await him in his study," Jacopo said curtly as he brushed past the servant without invitation.

Jacopo stood in front of the tall shelf and stared at the bezant. He heard footsteps from behind and the door closing.

"Who do you think you are? Io sono il maestro," Coraggiosi stated forcefully. "You don't just barge into my house and demand to see me!"

"Was Lorenzo Simoni supposed to be your apprentice instead of me?" Jacopo asked without turning to face his master.

"Basta, enough. I got the boy out of prison, but I won't be held prisoner myself, by you or him...I have done enough! Capisci?"

"Was he to be your apprentice?" Jacopo turned and looked Coraggiosi dead in the eye, angry and irreverent.

"I owe you no explanation. In fact, it is *you* who owe me, and if you're not careful all of your work will have been in vain. I would not hesitate to denounce you to the guild."

"Nor I to denounce you," Jacopo shot back.

Coraggiosi grabbed him by the throat and pushed him back against the wall, choking him hard. Instinctively, Jacopo threw a solid punch, landing it square on his master's nose, which instantly gushed blood. Coraggiosi's eyes watered up to the point of blocking his vision, and he felt his way over to his desk and sat. He opened a drawer and found some rags and held them to his nose. He sat back in the chair and tilted his head back. The blow had drained him of his anger.

"I need the papal seal," said Jacopo unapologetically.

"Che?" Coraggiosi replied from behind the bloody rag.

"The papal seal, the one that Pierfrancesco Chilli sold to you...I need it!"

Coraggiosi let out a small laugh. "Vaffanculo!" he answered smugly.

Jacopo grabbed him by the shirt and pulled him forward. For a moment, the elder feared another blow from the younger, stronger man. But Jacopo shoved him back and opened the desk drawers. He shuffled through quickly looking for the seal. It was not there. He surveyed the shelves and saw a small wooden case. Inside was the seal, and he put it in the small purse tied to his belt.

Coraggiosi leaned forward, lowered the rag, and with blood still running from his nose said, "Go ask your father about Lorenzo's apprenticeship!"

"What does that mean?" asked Jacopo impatiently.

Coraggiosi smiled and repeated, "Go ask your father!"

Jacopo turned to leave and noticed the bezant on the shelf. He grabbed it, shot Coraggiosi a nasty look, and walked straight out the front door without seeing the servant again. He was certain his days in the Calimala guild were finished.

* *

Coraggiosi remained seated behind his desk, holding the rag to his nose. After a few moments, a servant knocked on the study door.

"Entra," he yelled.

The servant pulled the door back and stood in the doorway. He saw his master bleeding and was speechless.

"What is it?" asked Coraggiosi impatiently.

"Il Signor Chilli is here to see you, Signore."

"Send him in."

Pierfrancesco entered the study and was surprised by Coraggiosi's bloody face. He sat opposite the desk. "Ch'è successo, what happened?" he asked.

"Your brother-in-law needs a lesson in humility," answered the Calimala master in a heavy, nasal voice. "He will get it very soon."

"Our deal with the English wool vendor is far too important for you to jeopardize over some petty grievance," Pierfrancesco countered condescendingly. "We're having a hard enough time with the consuls of both guilds as it is. Don't go bringing them into your private affairs with an apprentice. And don't take matters into your own hand. I will handle my sister's husband when the time is right."

"And I'm to swallow my pride?"

"This deal will make you one of the wealthiest men in Florence. You will have all the pride you need. As for the Giotti boy, let him be for now. Soon my father will be dead, and I will be paterfamilias. If my sister were to become a widow, I could certainly arrange a more beneficial marriage for her than the one my father did."

Coraggiosi sat back and lowered the rag; his nose had stopped bleeding, and all that remained was a dry crust under his nostrils. Once again he was being lured into a murderous plot. He did not relish the idea, but this plan had the added benefit of removing one of the few people with knowledge of the first murder. There were others out there, he knew. There was Lodovico, for one, and also the mysterious witness in the Campanile. He knew he would likely never be free of his past crimes, but he also felt powerless to stop now.

"He stole from me…He took the papal seal and il Magnifico's gold bezant!"

"You'll get them back," the Chilli heir answered confidently, "but tell me…why would you go to the Stinche and arrange to have the Simoni boy released?"

"I had my reasons."

"Certainly you are aware that it was I who put him there!"

"Sì, to stop him from running off with your sister. But your sister is now married, so this should no longer be an issue."

"I will decide when he is no longer an issue."

Coraggiosi did not answer; he just looked Pierfrancesco in the eye and awaited his next sentence.

"Where did you take him?"

"To San Felice," Coraggiosi replied, any guilt he had felt for being involved in Simone's murder having been overshadowed by Jacopo's actions.

Pierfrancesco stood. "Buona sera," he said as he turned and went out.

"Sera!" answered Coraggiosi as he nodded his head. He sat back and stared at the place on the shelf where the bezant had been.

VIII

Matteo called himself Matteo di Napoli, in the tradition of orphans taking the name of the city they were born in. He knew nothing of his father and little of his mother; only that at the age of five she had dropped him off at the monastery of Santa Chiara in Naples. He was raised by the monks, and when he was old enough, he became a novice, training to take the monastic oaths himself.

He, of course, had sexual urges as an adolescent, but did not dwell often on sexuality. There was very little contact with the world outside of the monastery walls, and the convent for nuns was a completely separate complex. He saw the nuns at church services only, from across the aisle. Sexuality was never discussed among the friars, though occasionally some did engage in sexual affairs either with another friar, or with a woman from outside the walls. These instances were few, and secret, and they were never discussed. If discovered, the guilty were punished, usually with food deprivation or whipping. Most friars, however, lived a celibate life of prayer and work, and struggled with their own sexuality in private.

Matteo made it to his twentieth birthday anticipating nothing more in his future than the life of a monk. He was bright and excelled in his studies. Perhaps in a few years he could rise to a higher position, such as *cellerario* (the official storekeeper), prior, or maybe even abbot. He gave little thought to much else for his life, until he met a twenty-five-year-old priest's apprentice named Vincenzo.

He loved Vincenzo and felt truly alive for the first time in his life when he gave all of himself, physically and emotionally, to him. The guilt he felt because of this forbidden love bothered him, but not in the same way that it bothered Vincenzo. Vincenzo was truly torn between the love he felt for God and the Church and the love he felt for Matteo. The two loves were incompatible, and the conflict troubled Vincenzo greatly. Matteo, on the other hand, had been less spiritual in his apprehensions. Despite the love he felt for Vincenzo, he thought it to be an impractical long-term relationship, given the dangers. Being summoned by Cardinal della Rovere to tutor his illegitimate daughter had made the decision to break off the relationship with Vincenzo easier, although he would regret it later.

In the year 1499, in a palatial villa in Ostia, on the coast outside of Rome, a sixteen-year-old girl sat at a desk in her father's study. Her hair was a dark chestnut, her skin deep olive, and the whites of her eyes contrasted the profound brownness of their center. She was beautiful and smart and eager to learn all that her tutor could teach.

"Gloria Pater et Filius et Spiritus Sanctus est?" she said hesitantly.

"Felice," Matteo responded kindly, "I want you to think about what we said yesterday...Are you saying that glory *is* the Father and Son and the Holy Spirit?"

She laughed, recognizing her mistake. After a moment she said, "Gloria Patri?"

"Sì, glory to the Father...go on." He was pleased. He leaned on the desk and pointed to notes she had written the day before.

"...et Filio... et Spiritui... Sanctui," she said, slightly more confident.

"Sancto!" he corrected her.

"Spiritui Sancto," she repeated, "...sunt?"

"Tell me why you used *sunt*."

"Because there are three, the Father, the Son, and the Holy Spirit."

"But they are not the subject; glory is the subject," he answered.

"Gloria Patri et Filio et Spiritui Sancto est," she said triumphantly.

"Brava," Matteo responded, "but you forgot one thing. We are saying 'glory *be* to the Father,' not glory *is*; it is subjunctive."

Being used to her tutor's thoroughness, Felice corrected herself, "Gloria Patri et Filio et Spiritui Sancto sit!"

"Giusto, right," he replied, "and usually in Church, we leave off the *sit*, as it is implied in the sentence."

Felice laughed. "Then it is a good thing I used the subjunctive; I wouldn't want to imply just any verb," she jested.

Matteo laughed. He was not a very stern tutor. He believed that learning was best fostered when the student was relaxed instead of afraid.

"As it was in the beginning..." he added.

"Sicut erat in principio..." she responded.

Matteo smiled and nodded. "...is now and will be always..."

"...et nunc et semper..."

"Brava!...and in the century of centuries...amen."

"...et in saecula saeculorum...amen."

"Excellent," he said. "Soon you will hardly need me anymore."

Felice's expression became gloomy.

"I was joking, I'll still tutor you for as long as you wish," Matteo said.

"It's not that," she said. "Do you think it's true? Will there always be glory to God, forever and ever?"

"For as long as man exists, he will give glory to God."

Felice was still somber, "Did my father really cause the French king, Charles the Eighth, to invade Italy?"

"Felice, *cara*, who told you such things?"

"I hear whispers, and gossip. I am much smarter than people think."

"I know you are. Do you know what I think?" Matteo placed a hand on her shoulder, standing over her. "I think you will be the smartest person in Rome. Your father is very powerful and grows more so, but I think it will be you that will keep your family strong, and noble."

This thought made Felice smile, but it soon faded. "He hates Pope Alexander; he does not hide it...But to incite the king of France to invade! I heard at Lucca, thousands were slaughtered in the street. He loves the Church, but does the Church not exist to do God's work? How can slaughter be God's work?"

"The Church is a world of politics; it is up to men to find God's work. Look at me, I joined the Franciscans to live a life of prayer and humility, to help the poor...yet I live in a palace, I eat like a king, and you, cara mia, are certainly not poor."

Felice frowned. "You do not like living here?"

"Quite the contrary, I enjoy it very much...and I do believe it *is* God's work, tutoring you. Knowledge is divine, and sharing it is always God's work. I only mean to say that were it not for the politics of my monastery in Naples and your father's connections, I would not be here. We come to our stations in life in many different ways, and maybe it is all part of God's plan, but I believe it is what we do in our stations that determines if we are doing God's work. Remember that one day when you are in a position of power."

Felice looked up at her tutor and smiled. He always showed such faith in her. He was not like any of the other servants at the villa. She had grown into quite a beautiful young woman, and she often felt the male servants leering at her, though they kept their distance out of fear for her father. Matteo, on the other hand, did not leer at all. He spoke to her as an intellectual equal (which was extraordinary for any female in those times) and was always patient and kind. He was also exceedingly handsome. Felice dreamed about kissing him. And she respected him for taking his vows so seriously, for never once did he try to seduce her.

* *

Matteo stood at the guard tower of the Castel Sant'Angelo in Rome. The castle was a huge, rounded fortification built over the tomb of the Emperor Hadrian. Matteo's brown Franciscan robe was freshly clean and sewn; Adélaïde had had the household servants at the Palazzo Chilli see to it. He handed a letter to a tall Swiss guard, replete in blue and gold striped pantaloons.

"Che cos'è, what is it?" asked the guard with a German accent.

Matteo shrugged his shoulders. "I don't know. I was told to report to you and to escort a prisoner."

"Escort him where?"

"That, Messere, is not within my charge to divulge." Matteo kept a stern face.

The guard took the letter and examined the wax seal that crossed the folded flap. It was the seal of the pope. The guard's demeanor changed. He looked up at the friar and nodded; he then broke the seal and unfolded the letter. The letter commanded the release of the prisoner Vincenzo de Marco to the custody of the letter's bearer. At the bottom, in large, blotted script letters, was the signature "Iulius II, Pont. Max." The guard had seen the pope's signature before, on many warrants, and he knew it to be true. He showed the letter to his commander inside the guard tower, who in turn sent two men to retrieve the prisoner.

Matteo waited in the yard between the guard tower and the gate of the castle itself. After what seemed to him to be a very long time, the massive gate swung in, and out stepped an emaciated Vincenzo, thinner and ragged looking. He stepped slowly and kept an unfocused expression on his face. The two made eye contact, and both knew to keep their emotions in check. When Vincenzo arrived at Matteo's side, the two walked side by side past the guards. A couple of hundred feet down the road, they turned down a small alley. Once out of sight, the two hugged tightly.

Vincenzo tried in vain to find words. Tears ran down his cheeks. Matteo was elated to hold Vincenzo in his arms; he was the first to speak.

"I'm glad to see you alive. My time in the Stinche almost killed me!"

"How did you get out?" Vincenzo was barely able to respond.

"It was Giuliano de' Medici; he released all political prisoners."

"And Lorenzo?"

"He is out as well, though we had to hide him. Pierfrancesco Chilli came looking for him at your house the night he was released. He is safe."

Vincenzo was again reminded of his disdain for Pierfrancesco. "How did you find me? How did you get me out?"

"With the help of an old friend."

"Well, I must be sure to thank him!"

"You'll get your chance. Come, we must hurry. At some point, the castle guards will send their daily dispatch to the Vatican. They are sure to report that your release order has been executed. Il Papa guerriero will not take the news well."

"Where are we going?"

Matteo peeked his head around the corner of the building and surveyed the bustling via. "Palazzo Orsini," he whispered.

IX

Jacopo had spent over a week thinking of what he was going to say to his father. He knew he had to confront him, but the idea made him nervous. At suppers throughout the week, Claudia and Maria had both been present, which he used as an excuse to avoid the matter. But still it hung over his head.

To Jacopo's surprise, Coraggiosi had been acting as if nothing had happened. Jacopo had returned to work at the bottega, expecting to be told to go home but Coraggiosi said nothing. He spoke only of business; they were preparing space to store the shipment of English wool. But Jacopo suspected that something would come of the recent events between him and his master sometime in the future, and he felt also that confronting his father might give him some insight on what to expect.

He knew that Maria and Claudia would be at the market and had heard his father say that he would be home in the morning, so

Jacopo left the Bottega Coraggiosi and returned home. Lodovico sat at the table. Even the workmen were gone, awaiting their next payment before finishing the construction. Jacopo entered and saw his father shuffling through some papers. He reached into his purse and took out the bezant. He placed it on the table and sat opposite Lodovico. Lodovico looked at the coin and then returned to his papers.

"Che cos'è?" he asked.

"I took it from Coraggiosi's study."

Lodovico placed the papers down and sat back looking at his son. "You stole from him?"

"It wasn't his to begin with, and *you* know it."

"Does he know that you took it?"

"He was there."

"And you will throw away your apprenticeship for this Simoni boy?"

"*My* apprenticeship! Was it really mine?"

"What do you mean?" Lodovico was growing agitated.

"Was it promised to Lorenzo?"

Lodovico sat back in silence. He looked at his son and remembered how he himself had once been young and idealistic. "You think it is unjust that you were apprenticed instead of him?"

Jacopo did not answer.

"I was once like you...I believed in justice. I gave honest service to our city and for it I was punished...*you* were punished! Through no fault of your own, you were excluded from the judges and notaries guild. You would have been left little choice but a life of servitude or joining the clergy to feed yourself. You pity this boy...but it would have been you in his place. Instead I gave you what I could never have, a profitable business and a bride from a wealthy family, whose name raises our name!"

"Who killed Lorenzo's father?" asked Jacopo in a shaky voice.

After a long pause, in calm deliberate words, Lodovico answered, "It was Coraggiosi. He planned the murder to get the coin. He came to me after it was carried through and asked if I still wanted to apprentice you to him, so I did."

Jacopo sighed with relief. He knew his father to be at times unscrupulous, but did not want to believe he was a murderer.

"Figlio mio," he went on, "I know you are upset with me, that I would make a deal with a murderer. But it was for you. All I have done, I did for you." Lodovico had tears in his eyes. "He could not have been the apprentice, not with his father dead. So why should that have stopped you from getting it? He could not have married Claudia; her father would never have allowed it, so why should you not have married her? I understand your empathy for him; he is your friend, and that is admirable. But throwing away your own future will not help him. It will only cast you down with him."

Jacopo was still torn. He agreed with his father; why should he not have those things? But he also felt responsible for Lorenzo's misery, and he did not like the feeling. If only he could be a Calimala master and have Claudia for a wife and not feel guilty.

"Fortune has smiled upon you, figlio mio. Do not waste it." Lodovico was encouraging in his tone.

It occurred to Jacopo that he *could* have those things without the guilt; he need only choose to stop feeling guilty. He had not caused Simone's death, nor prevented Lorenzo from being Coraggiosi's apprentice, and he had not prevented Lorenzo from marrying Claudia. He rose, put the bezant pack in his purse, and placed a hand on his father's shoulder as he walked out.

Lodovico smirked and returned to his papers.

X

Matteo and Vincenzo sat at a long dining table in the Palazzo Orsini in Rome. They waited for the lady of the house. Vincenzo looked around nervously; he did not know why they were there. Matteo had been too rushed to explain on the way over. The two moved quickly around the city and constantly looked over their shoulders for papal guards.

A beautiful, well-dressed woman entered. She had long, dark hair and olive skin. She was about thirty years old and moved confidently across the grand hall. Matteo and Vincenzo both rose to their feet.

Matteo spoke. "Signora Felice della Rovere, wife of Gian Giordano Orsini, I present to you Padre Vincenzo de Marco of Florence."

"Della Rovere!" repeated Vincenzo quietly but audibly. He looked toward Matteo nervously.

"It was Signora Felice who arranged for your release," Matteo assured.

"My hand to be precise," Felice corrected the friar, "and its ability to forge my father's signature!" She stood in front of Vincenzo and held her hand up.

Vincenzo bowed forward and kissed her hand. "Vi ringrazio, Signora, I thank you," he said kindly.

"Your tongue betrays you, Padre; you are about as Florentine as the Tiber."

"Sì, Signora, Neapolitan by birth," he answered.

"Just like Fra Matteo," she added and smiled. She sat and the two men returned to their seats. "Dimmi, Padre," she said, "did you really choke my father?"

Suddenly there was tension in the room. For a moment, no one spoke. Vincenzo was mortified. Matteo looked back and forth between the two, trying to read the situation. Then, Felice began to laugh. Matteo laughed also. Vincenzo released the breath he had been holding and smiled.

"I'll bet that was the only time in his life when he was scared for his life. It must have infuriated him." She was amused by the thought. "Well, one thing is certain. Were it not for your friend here, you would have certainly died in that cell."

Vincenzo looked over at Matteo, who smiled back.

"Fra Matteo and I go back a long way," Felice continued. "He came to me two days ago and told me your story and expressed his fears for you. I looked into the matter and learned that my father had thrown you in the Castel Sant'Angelo. It was quite easy to arrange your release, actually. I wrote the letter and signed it. I learned his signature well writing his dispatches. And the frate here stamped the wax with his seal. The guards had no reason to doubt the order."

"Brillante come sempre—brilliant as always," said Matteo.

Felice smiled at her former teacher. "My father will send men after you," she said looking at Vincenzo. "Where will you go?"

"I must return to Florence, Signora," answered the priest.

Matteo was horrified. "You cannot! He will look for you there! He knows you came from San Felice, right? That is the first place the guards will go."

"I must go. Lorenzo is in danger; you said so yourself. I cannot escape until I know he is safe." Vincenzo was calm and resolute. "Signora, I know you have risked much to help me, but I cannot abandon the boy; he is very dear to me."

"I know he is," answered Felice kindly. "Fra Matteo has told me everything. I know how much the boy means to you…and I know how much you mean to Matteo."

Vincenzo was startled; he had not expected to hear that. He had never told anyone about his relationship with Matteo, and it felt strange hearing it out loud. He became quiet.

"I must confess, Padre, Fra Matteo is dear to my heart also." Felice was soothing in her tone. "I want to see him and his loved ones safe and happy. I have given this matter much thought, and I have an idea for your future. My family has a villa south of Naples in Ravello. It is peaceful and quiet. It is cared for by the nearby monastery of Santa Chiara."

"Un segno da Dio," interrupted Matteo, referring to the shared name of his former monastery in Naples. "A sign from God."

"Indeed," agreed Felice. "There is a small chapel at the villa. I would be happy to write to the prior of Santa Chiara and inform him of my wish to see you placed as chapel priest at the villa. Matteo will accompany you and assist you with the upkeep of the villa. The two of you may live at the villa for as long as you wish. There is no one else there."

Matteo was ecstatic; he placed his hand over Vincenzo's and shook it excitedly. "It would be just like we always dreamed about," he said, looking Vincenzo in the eye and smiling warmly.

Vincenzo, too, was excited by the idea, but he was apprehensive. "And no one will look for us there?"

"There would be no record of your assignment here in Rome; I would see to it. My family has not used the villa in years. You can live a quiet life together and grow all the food you need in the garden. The monks at Santa Chiara are kind and very appreciative of my family's support over the years. They would welcome you as neighbors."

"Your generosity overwhelms me, Signora. I will happily accept your offer. But first, I must return to Florence. I must find Lorenzo and see to his well-being. Perhaps he will even accompany us to Ravello. And there is Carla, my housemaid…She depends on me also; I must find her as well." Vincenzo was looking at Matteo as he addressed Felice.

"Your concern for others is moving," she answered, "but the trip to Florence would be too dangerous for you. I would be happy to send for the others and have them follow you south to Ravello."

"Once again, your generosity humbles me, Signora," said Vincenzo.

"So you accept?" she asked.

Vincenzo was quiet. He was clearly torn.

"Vincenzo," Matteo appealed, "I know you are worried about him…but you do him no good by getting yourself captured or killed. We can send for him."

"Ci aggia penzà," he answered in Neapolitan. "I need to think about it."

XI

Lorenzo sat on the room's one chair, his book resting on the ornate table. In the little stove, some small scraps of wood burned. He looked around at the room, the mattress on the floor in the corner, the small window that was shuttered closed, and he felt sad. It had been the place of so many happy memories. Looking back, it hurt to think of how he had taken those happy days for granted. The peaceful routine of waking with his father and walking him to the Palazzo Chilli, the lunches down by the river, the evenings sitting in front of the warm stove talking with Simone—all were memories of a time when all he knew was happiness. He sat in the small, one-room shack on the Via del Corso and yearned for those happy days.

The room looked exactly as it had the last time Lorenzo had seen it, with the exception of two empty dye barrels stacked against the wall that had been stored there early on and forgotten about. Domenico had forgotten he had even purchased the tiny shack. It meant nothing to him. Adélaïde had brought Lorenzo there to hide him from Pierfrancesco. It hurt her to see what her son had become. She had lost Giambattista. Her husband was next, dead of pneumonia. Now, she made it her mission to protect Lorenzo.

He hated hiding out. He wanted to go to Rome with Matteo, to help Vincenzo, to feel useful. When Pierfrancesco had shown up banging on the door of Vincenzo's house, the others had hidden him under the cupboard. Pierfrancesco entered, looked around the house, yelled at his mother and sister, and stormed off. They agreed that they should hide Lorenzo. They had talked him into it, but now he regretted the decision. He was lonely. It was almost as if he were in prison again, never leaving the tiny shack. The only difference was that Adélaïde visited him every day. She brought him food, and she sat and talked with him for as long as she could. Even on the day of her husband's funeral, she managed to find the time to visit Lorenzo.

Alone in his childhood home, there was nothing for Lorenzo to do but wait for Adélaïde and to read his copy of the *Commedia* that Carla had let him take from Father Vincenzo's.

* *

Though Pierfrancesco had been a master of the wool guild for a number of years, he had hardly acted like a serious-minded man of commerce. He usually wore a tunic and thigh-high leather riding boots more fashioned toward a hunt than a day of business. He liked to visit the various botteghe and subsidiary guildsmen in his father's employ and exert his authority. He would show up, yell at the workers, and then leave before conducting any kind of meaningful supervision to rectify whatever it was he had been yelling about.

But now things were different. His father was dead, and he controlled one of the most lucrative wool businesses in the city. He now wore a long black robe with pleated ruffles in the front, and a floppy black beret-style hat, in the tradition of the guild masters.

Just north of the duomo, on the Via Larga, stood the colossal Palazzo Medici. Its tall brown stone walls, high-arched windows, gigantic iron hitching rings, and massive wooden doors gave the palazzo a castle-like feel on the city street. The high, over-leaning cornice crowned the palace in Renaissance glory. But the hallways and bedrooms had scarcely seen a visitor over the past eighteen years. The walls had been stripped clean of any art by ransacking looters, and the beautiful statues in the garden had been hauled away, the family treasure, gold, and jewels stolen. The massive library, with its priceless, ancient texts, had been confiscated. All remnants of Lorenzo il Magnifico's golden age had been torn down.

Pierfrancesco walked the halls of the palazzo with Giuliano de' Medici, youngest son of Lorenzo il Magnifico, and newly placed ruler of Florence. Cardinal Giovanni de' Medici had returned to Rome shortly after taking control of the city and left his brother in charge. Throughout the palace men worked to restore its former grandeur.

"I would not worry, Signor Chilli. I have a good relationship with the consuls of all the guilds. If I make it known that I favor this new venture of yours with the English wool, they will go along." Giuliano de' Medici spoke kindly.

"I would welcome such a favor, Vostra Eccellenza. I have not had the easiest time at the guild since my father's death. The masters were not pleased with this deal to begin with, but were perhaps inclined to accept it out of respect for my father's service to the guild. With him gone, they have become openly hostile to me." Even as he spoke seriously, Pierfrancesco seemed like an immature pretender. With social inferiors, he could rely on his temper to get his point across. With the ruler of Florence, however, he was forced to rely on his wanting rhetorical skills.

Despite this, Giuliano smiled warmly. "Well *I* will not forget your family's service to mine. Besides, I hope to assuage all hostility in this city and welcome a new age of shared prosperity."

Pierfrancesco did not know how to respond and so didn't.

"It is a shame, what happened here. Such treasure lost. The things my father valued most: the paintings, the statues, the manuscripts…all gone."

"Lo so, I know," answered Pierfrancesco. "I, too, think it terrible."

"So much is lost forever, but what I wouldn't give to have something…anything of my father's treasure."

It occurred to Pierfrancesco that he had recently seen an ancient gold coin that had belonged to Giuliano's father. Where was it now? And more importantly, how could he, Pierfrancesco, go about being the one who returned it to Giuliano?

* *

Vincenzo crept softly down the stairs. The palazzo was dark and quiet. His cloak was draped over his arm, and he carried his shoes. He sat on the last step to put on his shoes, and from the kitchen, into the entrance hall, came Felice. She was carrying a candle and wearing a long, silky nightgown.

"Se ne va? You're going?" she asked.

Vincenzo finished lacing his shoes and looked up. "Signora, you have been very kind to me. Without seeming ungrateful, may I ask why? I know you care about Matteo and wish to help him, but I was, in fact, insolent toward your father."

"You answer your own question, Padre. I care for Matteo greatly. As for my father…of course, I love him, as any daughter does. But I also know him. He is ambitious and quick-tempered, and at times cruel. I was a pawn to him…to be traded for the support of the Orsini family. His health is waning now, and much of the family's business is handled by me. I cannot undo every injustice he has committed, but I can help you."

"Your help is greatly appreciated, Signora, but I must see to my loved ones first. Will you tell Matteo in the morning that I will meet him in Ravello? He would never let me go to Florence alone, and I've no wish to endanger him also."

"I will give him your message, but how will you go to Florence?"

"I'll walk, I guess. I'll do whatever I have to do."

Felice shook her head. "Assolutamente no. You will take one of our horses. I will wake one of the servants and have him help you out the courtyard gate. Do not wake the stabler. He cannot be trusted to keep a secret, and I will not tell my husband the truth. I trust you can saddle a horse?"

"Sì, certo."

"Good. Take the gray horse on the end."

Felice left the hall for a moment, going to a dark room behind the stairs. She returned shortly with a small leather purse. "Here, take this," she said.

Vincenzo took the purse, filled with gold florins. He was deeply moved at Felice's generosity. "Non posso, I cannot," he said, offering it back.

"Take it. You will need it to get around. And stay off the main roads and out of the osterie as much as possible; the guards will certainly be looking for you."

"Grazie, Signora, from the bottom of my heart."

"You are welcome, Padre. God be with you!"

XII

It was hazy and difficult to make out, but it was definitely the small apartment on Via del Corso. The room, however, had features of his quarters at the Palazzo Chilli. And the door, the door was larger, and intimidating. Light shone in from around its edges, just like the door to his prison cell in the Stinche. He stayed away from the door. Nothing seemed out of place in this conglomerate of rooms. He was sitting on the floor, with his legs folded in front of him and his elbows on his knees, the way he had done as a boy. He was, however, in his grown body. Then he heard the voice, soothing and reassuring.

"So I decided instead to come straight home," Simone said while chewing a sliced apple.

Lorenzo looked up at his father sitting in his chair next to the stove. His eyes teared and he tried to speak, but couldn't. He could not find his voice. He had so much to say, but the more he tried to speak, the weaker his voice became.

Simone looked down at his son and smiled. It was that beautiful, confident smile that had never failed to calm Lorenzo the thousands of times he had seen it in his mind. Simone held his hand up and rubbed his son's cheek.

"I know," Simone said as he nodded his head, his eyes full of compassion, "I know."

There was a knock at the door, but Lorenzo ignored it. The room started to fade, and Lorenzo's heart dropped. There was another knock, and he woke up. He sat up quickly and looked around the room. It was the same dusty shack he had fallen asleep in. There was another knock, and he went to the door. The sun had just come up, and Adélaïde did not usually visit this early, but he opened the door anyway expecting to see her. He was wrong.

* *

Lodovico put the cup to his lips and pretended to sip; he did not want to seem as if he were refusing the hospitality of a cup of wine. It was early in the morning, the sun barely risen. The room was dark and the face of the other man obscured by shadow. Lodovico had done business with him before. He looked down to his belt and pulled a handful of gold florins out of his money purse. He counted them and then placed them, stacked on the table.

"Half now...half when it is finished," he exclaimed.

The shadowy man picked up the coins and counted. He put them in his own purse, saying nothing.

"Also," Lodovico held up a folded piece of paper, "I want you to pin this to his chest."

The man took the paper, unfolded and looked at it, then folded it again. He looked Lodovico in the eye and nodded.

* *

Lorenzo stood at the door in shock, speechless.

"Can I come in?" asked Claudia.

"Certo, of course," he squeaked out over the lump in his throat. "Come in."

Claudia entered and looked around the dusty room. Lorenzo helped her with her cloak and offered her a seat.

"This is where you grew up?" she asked without sitting. Her belly was fully swollen by now. Her hair was tied in a bun behind her head, and she looked very mature. She was not the girl who knelt on the floor and played chess with Lorenzo; she was a woman, a wife, and soon…a mother. All of these things combined made her all the more desirable to Lorenzo, for they were all the things he wanted.

Lorenzo did not answer her question; he just stared at her neck. Her soft skin tapered smoothly up to her tight hairline. He looked at her cheek, rosy from the cool air, and her eyes, misty. They were deep and brown and held his gaze. After a moment he stepped forward and put the palms of his hands on her cheeks and pulled her close to him. He kissed her hard and passionately.

At first she just let it happen, but then she kissed him back with every drop of emotion in her body. They each wrapped their arms around the other and pulled each other tight. He put all of the pain, all of the heartache, all of the loss, and all of the love he had ever had into that kiss. It lasted a long while.

When they had finished, he pulled his head back to see that she was crying.

"What is it?" he asked, caressing her hair.

"I love you," she blurted out, almost sobbing, "I've always loved you."

"Io ti amerò sempre," he replied as he kissed her wet cheek. "I will love you always."

He motioned her to the chair, and she sat. He poured two cups of wine and sliced off a couple of pieces of bread. Thanks to Adélaïde, the little apartment was well stocked with food and wine for the first time in Lorenzo's life. He picked up the bucket from the corner and went outside and dumped it. When he returned, he flipped it over and sat on it, across from Claudia at the table, slightly lower than she. The two broke their fast on bread and wine.

"What are you reading?" she asked, noticing the book on the table.

"*La Commedia* di Dante," he answered.

"Will you read some to me?"

The tender look in her eyes filled him with the desire to please her, however he could. He opened the book and placed it on his lap while he turned the pages looking for the right caption. He remembered the fifth canto of the *Inferno*, and the tale of the doomed lovers, Francesca and Paolo, killed by Francesca's husband (Paolo's brother) for adultery.

> Amor, ch'al cor gentil ratto s'aprende,
> prese costui de la bella persona
> chi mi fu tolta; e 'l modo ancor m'offende.

> *Love, which swiftly takes the gentle heart,*
> *took him, of the beautiful person*
> *taken from me, and the manner still offends me.*

Lorenzo spoke clearly and kept the poem's rhythm perfectly. Claudia listened intently.

> Amor, ch'a nullo amato amar perdona,
> mi prese del costui piacer sì forte,
> che, come vedi, ancor non m'abbandona.

> *Love, which gives no loved person pardon from loving,*
> *took me with such strength of pleasure in him,*
> *that, as you see, does not abandon me yet.*

"Francesca da Rimini," she said and smiled sadly. "Nessun maggior dolore che ricordarsi del tempo felice ne la miseria—there's no greater pain than remembering happy times while in misery." She became somber. "Maman used to read it to me. She loved the part about Arnaut Daniel, where he recites his poem to Dante in Provençal. I loved the story of Francesca, however. While reading the tale of Lancelot and Guinevere with Paolo, the two gave in to their love...and they died for it."

"It reminds me of us," Lorenzo said. "That is why I chose this part."

"You are Paolo and I am Francesca."

"I guess that makes Jacopo Gianciotto Malatesta. We should be careful he doesn't kill us," he said wryly.

Claudia was quiet for a moment, then answered thoughtfully, "I hated him for a long time. I know that I will never love him, but I do not hate him anymore. If it were not for Jacopo, you would still be in prison. If it were not for him, we would not have gotten the papal seal back to help Fra Matteo try to free Padre Vincenzo."

Lorenzo's first impulse was to jump up and scream. *He* was supposed to be the Calimala apprentice, but instead it went to Jacopo. *He* wanted to marry Claudia, but instead she was married to him. It was Jacopo who always seemed to benefit from Lorenzo's misfortune, and it angered him. The impulse quickly faded, however, and Lorenzo did not want to become angry in front of Claudia.

"You know, the happiest time of my life was the day we planned to run off to France together," she said.

"Mine, too."

"I think of that day all of the time," she added.

"Nessun maggior dolore," he answered. "No greater pain."

XIII

Father Vincenzo rode slowly along an unpaved, winding road. He was pretty sure that this road led in the direction of Florence. It would take him longer, going this way, but he knew the main road would be teaming with papal guards. Just north of the Lake of Bracciano, he entered a small town named Vetralla. Overlooking the town was a steep hill with a walled castle built on the summit. A tall tower sprang up from between the walls, and a small patchwork of houses dotted the countryside in its shadows. He dismounted at a well and drew some water, drinking from his hand. Townspeople moved about without giving him much attention. He scanned the road for signs of an osteria or *locanda*, boardinghouse, but saw none.

He was approached by a child, a boy of about six years of age.

"Aiuto, Padre, help!" pleaded the boy in a timid voice. He wore a baggy woolen blouse and torn pants. He had no cloak or overcoat on and seemed cold.

"What is it, child?" asked the priest kindly.

"My mother, Padre." The child held his little hand up, and Vincenzo took it. The boy turned and pulled the priest toward a small alley.

Vincenzo looped the horse's reigns around a post on top of the well and followed him. A few steps down the alley was a narrow, old, wooden door, and the boy pushed it open and pulled Vincenzo into the tiny apartment. In the corner was a mattress on the floor. A woman lay with her dress pulled up above her hips, her legs spread. She was sweating profusely. In her arms was a tiny, wet, newborn baby, wrapped in a blanket and crying. The woman had tears running down her cheeks and was in great pain. At her feet sat an older woman, with her sleeves rolled up above her elbows.

"Mannaggia, damn it," said the older woman. "Child, I sent you to get Padre Michele! Ahh, never mind that now, there's no time. Padre," she said to Vincenzo, "her bleeding won't stop. She needs her last rites."

Dazed for a second, Vincenzo quickly came to and removed his cloak, draping it over a chair. He slipped the wooden cross, which hung from a thin rope around his neck, over his head and held it in his hand. He did not have a Bible or any sacrament books with him, but knew the rite by heart. He approached the mattress and knelt at the woman's side. Blood hemorrhaged out and covered the dirty padding. The older woman leaned forward and placed her palms on the woman's stomach, rolling both hands upward in a forceful, massaging motion. The new mother cried out in agony.

"Are you trying to kill her, woman?" spat the priest.

The older woman was undaunted by the rebuke. "You do your work, Padre, and I'll do mine." She rolled her palms up the woman's midsection again, slowly and methodically.

Vincenzo signed the cross on himself and held the small wooden crucifix up in front of the bed. He looked around at the floor and saw a bowl of water. He slid the bowl closer to himself and with his right hand signed the cross above the bowl. "In nomine Patris et Filii et Spiritus Sancti," he whispered. Many priests would have refused to perform the rite without anointed oil, white linen, candles, and the small bell. Vincenzo, however, had little reverence for what he believed to be pageantry and felt it perfectly acceptable to God to substitute this ad hoc holy water for the oil and forgo the rest. To Vincenzo, all that mattered was God's mercy toward the dying.

He dipped his thumb in the water and reached for the woman's face. For the first time, he made eye contact with her. The suffering in her eyes, which spoke of more than just bodily pain, filled him with a overwhelming awareness of their shared humanity. He put his thumb up to her eyes, and she shut them. On her eyelids he signed a small cross with his wet thumb and began his repetitive chant.

"Per istam Sanctam Unctionem et suam piisimam misericordiam, indulgeat tibi Dominus quidquid per visum."

He dipped his thumb again and signed a cross on each ear.

"Per istam Sanctam Unctionem et suam piisimam misericordiam, indulgeat tibi Dominus quidquid per audiotum."

He dipped again and moved to the nostrils, repeating his prayer. Then, the lips, hands, and feet. Praying for forgiveness of sins committed by *odoratum, gustum, et locutionem, tactum,* and *gressum deliquisti,* all the human senses and abilities.

The woman kept her eyes closed, and her breathing slowed. Her moans became quieter, and she moved less. The older woman continued pressing on her stomach.

"Benedicat te omnipotens Deus, Pater et Filius et Spiritus Sanctus." Vincenzo looked over at the older woman, then at the child, who stood in the corner silently with tears running down his cheeks, then back at the woman lying back with her eyes closed. "Amen," he added quietly.

"The bleeding has stopped," said the other woman. "We can only wait now and hope she did not lose too much blood." She stood, wiped her hands on a rag, and walked over to the child. He hugged her legs and began sobbing. She caressed his head. "There now, my child, don't despair. Your mother is strong. We were lucky to find the Padre here in time, but your mother is full of surprises. I wouldn't be surprised if she's singing you that song you love at bedtime tonight."

The boy wiped his eyes with his hands and looked up at the woman.

"Can you be a helper to us?" she asked.

The boy sniffled and nodded yes.

"Good, run to my place and fetch the jug of wine on my table. Your mother will need it to get her strength back, and I think the good Padre here could use a cup in the meantime."

The boy smiled sadly and went out. Vincenzo rose and sat in the chair he had hung his cloak on. He looked over at the mattress. The woman slept, her head propped up with a pillow. The baby was bundled tightly and was now sleeping, nestled in its mother's bosom. The older woman pulled a blanket over both of them and checked the baby and then the mother, holding her palm to each forehead. She stood upright and wiped her forehead with a rag and sat opposite Vincenzo.

"Grazie, Padre," she said. "I did not get your name."

"Vincenzo…and there is no need to thank me."

She bowed her head. "Maddalena."

The boy returned with the jug of wine, and Maddalena brought two cups to the table and poured. She slid a cup to the priest and returned to her seat. The boy sat on the mattress at his mother's feet.

"On a pilgrimage to Rome, Padre Vincenzo?" she asked as she sipped her wine.

Vincenzo sipped also; the wine was sharper than the Tuscan wine he was used to. He held it in his cheeks a moment, and his gums tingled. He swallowed and was left with a fruity aftertaste. The wine calmed him as it slid down his dry throat.

"Just returning from one," he answered. "Are you family to them?" he asked as he nodded toward the mattress.

"No. I live up the via there. I've been helping women in town give birth for years, just something I've gotten good at."

"Where is the father?" he asked in a low voice.

"Morto, dead," she answered shaking her head. "Died this past summer."

"Ch'è successo? What happened?"

"A long time ago, a pope gave the lords of Vetralla the rights over the woodlands near Monte Fogliano. Ever since, the lords of Viterbo have claimed the woods belong to them. Her husband, Marco, was walking along the woodland's edge, returning from his work. Four horsemen, nobles from Viterbo, rode up on him and killed him. They hacked him down with swords for poaching in *their* forest."

"What happened to the horsemen?"

Maddalena shrugged her shoulders. "Padre Michele and some of the leaders in town here sent a letter to the pope. Nothing happened."

"What will become of them?" He nodded again toward the mother and children.

"I don't know. Marco left nothing. Marco's brother owns this place; they paid him rent. After his brother's death, the bastardo demanded that she pay him rent. Some of us in town made a collection and paid the last two months, but there is nothing left to give. We all have hungry families."

The newborn began to cry, and Maddalena went and picked the baby up. She unwrapped the blanket and wiped the crying baby off with wet rags. After rewrapping the baby in a blanket, she leaned down to check on the mother. The young woman opened her eyes.

"Some wine, Padre," said Maddalena.

Vincenzo brought a cup, and Maddalena fed the woman sips.

"Now sit up some more, cara; the baby is hungry," instructed the older woman.

The mother leaned forward, and Maddalena propped a pillow behind her. The young woman pulled her dress up and exposed a breast. Maddalena laid the baby on the mother's bosom, and the infant latched on. The mother smiled. She looked down at the bed's edge. Her son was lying at her feet, sleeping. He had his arms wrapped around his mother's foot. She closed her eyes again.

Maddalena rose and turned to see Vincenzo standing and wearing his cloak.

"Where can I find your Padre Michele?" he asked.

"Across the piazza, at San Francesco. Perché?"

"I trust he will be kind enough to lodge a traveling priest for the night."

"He is a good man."

"Grazie for the wine. I will pray for her health and for the future of the family," he offered with a smile.

Maddalena grabbed his hand and kissed it. He was uneasy with what he felt to be undue gratitude. He turned and went out.

As the door closed behind him, Maddalena spun and gazed over the darkening room. The baby sucked peacefully and all was at ease. On the table she noticed a small leather purse. She picked it up and looked inside. It was filled with gold florins.

XIV

The chef entered the dining hall carrying a large platter of roasted wild boar. The meat was coated with olive oil, salt and herbs, and the aroma filled the room. He set the platter in the center of the table and cleared away the pasta bowls from each place setting.

Pierfrancesco sat at the table's head, symbolically and literally taking his father's place. Adélaïde sat to his right, in her usual place, Claudia and Jacopo next to her. Across the table sat Lodovico and Maria.

The chef removed the pasta bowl from in front of Pierfrancesco, who then leaned forward and stabbed a big slab of boar meat with his knife. He cut a piece off, picked it up with his fingers, and shoved it into his mouth, chewing loudly. He swallowed and wiped his mouth on his sleeve.

"So who will take over Coraggiosi's bottega?" he asked Jacopo.

"His son is on his way back to Florence. I guess it will be him," Jacopo answered.

"Well, I'm sure he will recommend your admittance as a master to the consuls." Pierfrancesco added, "Have you been to the guild hall lately?"

"No," Jacopo answered.

"I was wondering if you had heard any whisperings," said Pierfrancesco.

"What kind of whisperings, Signore?" asked Lodovico.

Pierfrancesco turned his head and addressed the father. "About the murder! Have you not heard? It was the Calimala masters who killed Coraggiosi."

"This is the first I am hearing of it," retorted Lodovico with a shocked tone. "How do they know it was them?"

"There was a piece of paper pinned to his chest with a drawing on it…an eagle with his wings outstretched, clinging a bale of cloth in his talons, the symbol of the Calimala guild!" Pierfrancesco was excited by the gossip, but his eyes did betray a hint of nervousness. If the members of the Calimala could do this, presumably over the English deal, what would the members of the wool guild do to him?

"I heard the general and special councils were preparing a statement of delinquency to post in the Calimala hall," Pierfrancesco continued. "They would have petitioned the consuls to have Coraggiosi's membership privileges withdrawn."

Jacopo listened intently; this was all news to him. Lodovico listened as well, considerably more informed.

"Meno male per Jacopo! Lucky!" added Pierfrancesco. "If they had, they would have seized Coraggiosi's property and closed his bottega. Jacopo would have never been admitted. Good thing somebody took matters into their own hands!"

"Meno male!" repeated Lodovico as he sipped wine.

Maria looked down at her plate, wishing her husband had not just rejoiced in a man's death. Claudia picked on her food, her thoughts elsewhere. Adélaïde, however, followed the conversation with vigor, though she said nothing.

"Now more than ever it is important to stay in the good graces of the Medicis. The consuls of the wool guild would not move against me without Giuliano's blessing," Pierfrancesco said.

"What more can we do?" asked Lodovico.

"He is a nostalgic man, Giuliano. He mourns the loss of his father's art and treasure…But I know a way we can give some of it back to him."

All eyes in the room focused on Pierfrancesco.

"We will give him back his father's coin!"

Jacopo's heart sank; he looked at his brother-in-law, saying nothing.

"The gold Greek one you were looking at!" he said to Jacopo. "Didn't Coraggiosi say it belonged to il Magnifico? And it's really old, isn't it? I know you took it from Coraggiosi's study. Where is it?"

Now all eyes focused on Jacopo. Though he wasn't sure why, he felt he should not admit to having the bezant. He thought of Lorenzo and, knowing he was hidden, decided to buy some time. "I gave it back to Lorenzo."

"Why would you do such a thing?" asked Lodovico angrily.

"It was his father's. I thought he should have it."

"That's fine," said Pierfrancesco. "We'll find him and get back the coin."

Claudia's heart sank, and she stared angrily at her brother. Adélaïde, not wanting another episode between her children, stood and pulled her daughter to her feet.

"Look at your face, ma chère; the baby is making you ill again. Come with me, and we will rinse your face with cool water." She pulled Claudia toward the kitchen. "Excusez-nous," she said to their guests.

The conversation went on without them. "Perhaps, Signore, if Jacopo was to accompany you when you return the coin to Giuliano, he would allow Jacopo to take over Coraggiosi's end of the English deal," said Lodovico.

Maria looked up from her plate and stared at her husband. She hated the idea, but felt powerless.

"He can persuade the Calimala consuls to accept Jacopo now as a full master, and to allow Jacopo to step into this deal instead of Coraggiosi's son. I'm sure intervention from Signor de' Medici would quell any future rumblings from the other members. After all, their vengeance has been taken out already on poor Giovanni Coraggiosi." Lodovico articulated the whole plan.

Knowing that without the alliance of a Calimala master, the English deal would be dead, Pierfrancesco was willing to share the credit for returning the coin to Giuliano. "Jacopo will come with me, just as soon as we find the Simoni boy," he declared.

Jacopo felt like a ship being pushed by a great wind, bringing him farther and farther away from his port. He wanted to be a full master, but not in this way. The other masters would hate him, and he knew it. This was not the future he wanted.

XV

Felice della Rovere, wife of Gian Giordano Orsini, was one of the most powerful people in Rome. She had been raised to aid her father's ambitions and educated accordingly. As a cardinal trying to secure the papacy, her father had traveled through much of her childhood, and so she was raised by household aids and tutors. Her mother, Lucrezia Normanni, was from a powerful Roman family as well, and her father, Giuliano della Rovere, took care to marry his mistress off to a della Rovere family associate, Bernardo de Cupis. Cardinal Giuliano kept his daughter as his own prize, however, and eventually used her to solidify his Roman power base with a marriage to the Orsini family.

By late 1512 Pope Julius's health was waning. He was bedbound most days, a far cry from the Warrior Pope of just a few years earlier. Felice, through familial bonds and her own cunning, had gradually become the key link between her father and the outside world, and thus a very powerful person in her own right.

Seeing Friar Matteo for the first time in years had filled her with a deep nostalgia for the childhood that had been so long ago bargained away. Quite simply, she loved the man. The flames of her girlish crush had smoldered out, and she was left with a deep admiration for the man who had showed her only patience and kindness, and whose wisdom still shone in on her own thinking. She now understood more about his nature than she had ever known then, and it did not at all diminish her affection. She had helped him free Father Vincenzo because he was important to Matteo. She had offered them the villa in Ravello because she genuinely wanted to see Matteo at peace in the world.

She used her power wisely, with less ambition than her father, and was genuinely concerned with the effects of her actions. What she did inherit from her father, however, was a keen political astuteness and the ability to stay one step ahead of problems. When, shortly after Vincenzo left, Cardinal Giovanni de' Medici approached her with news of new alliances amongst the College of Cardinals, she was quick to formulate a plan.

It was no secret that Julius was dying and the jockeying for election had already begun. Cardinal Jaime Serra i Cau, known as Alborense, was leading a fairly potent anti–della Rovere contingent, and looked like an early front-runner. Felice was determined to keep the papacy away from anyone who might undermine her own power base. The Medici family was now firmly allied with Julius, and Cardinal Giovanni was a natural choice as successor. She knew, however, that the vote would be close.

As a cardinal, Giuliano della Rovere had railed loudly against simony, particularly after the bought election of the Borgia pope, Alexander VI. It was one of the few issues of Pope Julius's tenure that he clung to on strictly spiritual terms. He had even prepared a papal bull denouncing simony to be read after his death to the College of Cardinals upon commencing their conclave. There would be no way of securing an election by buying votes.

Conversely, Julius had no moral issues with simply giving offices away to friends and family. Many of his nephews were now cardinals and bishops. Alliances were built in such ways, and Felice now needed to secure a new alliance. It was times like this when Felice was most like her father.

Matteo was not exactly sure why Felice had wanted him to accompany her to meet the pope. He would just as soon not go. He regretted not having gone after Vincenzo. He had wanted to go, but Felice had argued successfully that the priest would be impossible to find without knowing which backcountry road he would take. Matteo was looking forward to Vincenzo's return and a quiet life in Ravello.

As Felice and Matteo entered Pope Julius's bedchamber, two papal guards were waiting. The pope coughed forcefully into a handkerchief and yelled to them from his bed, "I want him found, capite? Found!"

The guards turned, bowed, and exited. Felice and Matteo were now alone in front of the pope's bed.

"Papà, look who it is," said Felice.

Julius coughed again and then leaned forward, straining his eyes. He leaned back and said nonchalantly, "Bentornato, servus meius— welcome back, my servant," in combined Italian and Latin.

Matteo bowed his head respectfully.

"I understand you were imprisoned for your service to us," said Julius.

"È vero, Vostra Santità, it's true."

Julius nodded to his daughter, and she called outside the door for an aide to come in. The servant entered with a scrolled document and brought it with a small inkbottle and stylus to the pope. Julius took the stylus and dipped it, then signed the document the servant held open. The servant left the room.

"It will be announced to the College of Cardinals this morning that I have appointed a new cardinal," said the pope weakly, fighting off another coughing fit.

The servant returned and draped a crimson red shawl over Matteo's shoulders. Matteo was dumbfounded. Next, a round, red cap was held up in front of him. "Vostra Eminenza," said the servant politely.

Matteo looked to Felice, who smiled and nodded. Without being able to process a thought, he knelt and the servant placed the cap on his head. Matteo remained kneeling, with his head down.

"In nomine Patris et Filii et Spiritus Sancti," mouthed Julius as he signed a cross in the air. "Felice will find an archbishopric to bestow upon you," he added and then lay back against his pillow and began a violent coughing fit.

"Grazie, Papà," said Felice as she led the new cardinal out of the room by the hand. Matteo was speechless.

Out in the antechamber, Felice spoke. "I have a nice archbishopric in mind for you." Her tone showed her excitement.

"Archbishopric…Felice, cara, I don't want to be an archbishop." Matteo was regretful, but sure.

"Non ti preoccupare, don't worry," she answered, "you don't have to go to your diocese if you don't want to. They all have deacons who run the day-to-day things; my father held multiple bishoprics at the same time. You can still go to Ravello."

"Not quietly I can't. I was hoping to stay away from the politics of Rome; now I *am* the politics," he said lowly to himself.

With a sense of guilt for having put her own ambition ahead of Matteo's, Felice became emotional. "Maestro," she said in a choked-up voice. "Cardinale," she corrected herself, "you, above all others, have shown me nothing but kindness in my life. I wanted to thank you. You always told me how many things you wish you could change in the Church, and in Italy…This is your chance."

Matteo was silent. He had no response. There were a thousand things he wished he could change in the world, and being a cardinal did give him a unique opportunity to make a difference. But at that moment, the only thing he could think about was Vincenzo. What would Vincenzo say?

XVI

The library of the Palazzo Medici was in particularly bad shape. The shelves had been loaded with ancient manuscripts and all the leading modern texts, the sum of a millennium and a half of Western thought. But the volumes had all been looted and either burnt or stolen. Shelves had been torn down, the writing table and padded chairs—all gone.

Workers cleared away the broken shelves; the room would be completely cleared out and rebuilt from scratch. As a workman pulled down a vertical shelf board, a brick from the wall behind it fell to the floor. The surrounding bricks were loose as well, and he pulled them down to reveal a sizeable cavity in the wall. The space was filled with dusty ledger books. The workman pulled one down and opened it. It was filled with double-column account entries, thousands of them. He pulled out another, and a folded scroll of paper fell to the ground from between the two ledger books. He picked it up and opened it. It was a fairly long legal document with the large-print heading:

"Testamentum Laurentii Medicis."

The Last Will and Testament of Lorenzo de' Medici.

* *

Lorenzo opened the door for Adélaïde and was surprised to see Claudia at his door with her mother. The two entered. Adélaïde motioned her pregnant daughter to the chair and set a basket on the table, filled with a loaf of bread, a wedge of cheese, and a corked carafe of red wine.

He noticed a worried look on both of their faces. "Che c'è, what is it?" he asked.

"It's Pierfrancesco," answered Adélaïde. "He is after your father's coin."

"The bezant?" he answered.

"Sì," answered the two women simultaneously.

"Perché?"

"Because it was owned by Lorenzo il Magnifico. Apparently Giuliano would like it back," answered Adélaïde.

"So much trouble has come from that coin," Lorenzo stated without showing much concern.

"You must be careful. You have hidden here and Pierfrancesco has stopped looking for you, but with this coin in mind he will never stop," Claudia pleaded.

"Why would he come after me for it? I thought Coraggiosi had the coin." Lorenzo's surprise surprised the mother and daughter.

"Coraggiosi is dead!" answered Adélaïde. "He was murdered by his own guildsmen."

Though he did not doubt the news, Lorenzo looked to Claudia for verification.

Her eyes answered yes, and she added, "Jacopo took the coin the night he went to get Fra Matteo's papal seal back. He told Pierfrancesco and Lodovico that he gave the coin back to you."

Lorenzo was silent. None of the three knew why Jacopo would keep the coin.

"Well regardless," said Adélaïde, "my son thinks you have it." Her eyes watered at the thought of what her son had become. "There's no telling what he may do. We must find someplace else for you to go."

"I can stay here," he protested.

"No, mon cher, it is too dangerous. Pierfrancesco will eventually find you here. He has that Lodovico working with him; it is only a matter of time."

"Where can I go?" Lorenzo asked in resignation.

"You should go to Provence, like we talked about before. My family will take care of you. You can live on our property, and you will be safe."

Lorenzo knew what this would mean; he would be separated from Claudia forever. It pressed a sunken weight on his chest to hear the words. He knew that he and Claudia were separated by the bonds of matrimony, but this would complete the separation by adding hundreds of miles between them. He looked to Claudia. She was crying and did not look at him. She sat with her hands resting on her belly, looking at the wall, tears running down her cheeks.

* *

"Archbishop of Ravenna?" asked the notary.

"Sì," answered Cardinal Matteo.

"I was there last month, to see Arcivescovo Roverella. I was not aware he had died."

"I don't believe he has. He's been recalled here to Rome; I am not sure why. Perhaps il Santo Padre wishes to exert more influence in the city now that the Venetians are gone. Arcivescovo Roverella has led the archdiocese for thirty-five years; I'd imagine he has become fairly autonomous in his power. I, on the other hand, owe my position to the pope." In no mood to hide his feelings, Matteo was candid with the notary.

"Well, Cardinale, you will have your work cut out for you!"

"Come? How?" Matteo asked.

"The city is devastated. The battle was over six months ago, but nothing has been repaired. The death toll, already staggering, keeps rising from famine and disease. Imagine being one of the lucky few to not fall under the French sword, only to starve or fall to illness. It is a terrible thing, war, and this battle, so meaningless in the course of events, was particularly cruel."

"Lo so, I know," answered the cardinal. "I was there. It was the only battle I've ever seen, but it was terribly frightful. I was nearly trampled by horsemen. I even met the French condottiere, Gaston de Foix, moments before his death."

"Ahh, sì," said the notary, "the death of de Foix, a true tragedy. From what I know, he was noble and brave…and above all, honorable. His death signaled the true tragedy of that battle, for his successor Jacques de la Palice, a lesser man in every way, knew not how to follow up on victory. He instead turned his troops, reeling with the savage ecstasy of Spanish blood dripping from their lances and swords, loose on the poor citizens of Ravenna. The women were raped, the men killed, houses burned. Not a coin of wealth was left in the city. And now, half a year later, the suffering continues." The notary was saddened to recount his experience in Ravenna. He was in his sixties, though he looked younger. His sharp mind and jovial nature took years off of his appearance. His tale of the suffering he had seen, however, put him in a somber disposition. He bundled up the documents he had been stamping and tied a cloth ribbon around them.

The notary slid the documents across the counter to the cardinal, and a younger notary entered the studio. Upon seeing the cardinal, the young man swiftly removed his black *notaio* cap, bowed his head, and said, "Buon giorno, Vostra Eminenza."

"The cardinale here is setting out for his new archbishopric in Ravenna!" announced the older notary. The younger nodded in acknowledgement.

"Actually, I'm off for Florence. I do not plan on going to Ravenna," answered Matteo.

"Oh, scusa, Cardinale," said the elder.

"It's quite all right. I must confess, I do not plan on being a very hands-on archbishop. There is a priest in Florence I must find; I have important business with him."

"I am from Florence," said the younger notary. "In what church is the priest you are looking for?"

Matteo was looking through the documents in front of him and answered before thinking. "San Felice, he's on his way back there now and I hope to catch up with him." The second Matteo said this, he regretted it. Vincenzo, after all, was now a fugitive from the papal guards. It would be best to share as little as possible with anyone he encountered. He noted this to himself, but was not very worried. This notary studio was not connected to the Vatican.

"That's across the Arno; I never spent much time over there," answered the young notary.

"Cardinale," said the elder *notaio*, "may I speak frankly? I have a question, and I would later regret not putting it to you."

Matteo rested the documents on the counter and gave the man his full attention. "Certo, dai! Of course, go on," he said.

"Who will shepherd the poor flock? The miserable, suffering people of Ravenna, Signore, who will look to them?" He looked Matteo square in the eye.

"There is a deacon. There are priests. The Church has many hands available for the people," Matteo answered feebly.

"Followers of the Church, sì, there are many in every diocese. But now, Cardinale, at this moment, the poor people need a leader. There are not many leaders anywhere." The old man grinned with an air of melancholy. He did not wait for an answer. He shuffled through some papers behind the counter.

Matteo felt as if he had just received a blow to the stomach. He had no answer to give. He thought for a moment. "Vi ringrazio, Signori, I thank you," he said as he gathered his documents and left the studio.

The younger notary watched him leave, pensively. He then turned to the elder. "Anything for me?"

The older man picked up a wooden box that lay on a shelf along the back wall. It was filled with folded letters and documents. He placed it on the counter in front of the young man. On the front of the wooden box was painted a name: Dottor Giovanni de Angelis.

XVII

Pierfrancesco paid little attention to either his mother or his sister on a daily basis. Since taking over for his father, he spent most of his time either at the guildhall or preparing the new bottega in anticipation of the shipments of raw English wool. He had put his mind to finding Lorenzo and returning the gold bezant to Giuliano de' Medici, but did not know where to find the Simoni boy. Lodovico had said he would investigate the matter, but Pierfrancesco had not heard anything from him yet.

He had hardly noticed when Adélaïde started going out every morning, taking a basket with her. As time went by, however, he became suspicious. He said nothing, but watched her go out every day. So, being in the kitchen earlier than usual, it seemed totally strange to him to see, out in the courtyard, the stable doors open and saddled horses being led out. He saw a man atop one horse, holding the reins of the other. Adélaïde spoke with the man and then helped him out the rear gate, closing the gate and stable doors before crossing the courtyard to come back in the house.

Pierfrancesco shoved a piece of cheese in his mouth, ripped a piece of bread from the loaf he had been working on, and swiftly left the kitchen and went upstairs. He clumsily swallowed his food as he listened at the top of the stairs. When he heard Adélaïde fumbling in the kitchen, he came back down and walked in on her. She had filled the basket and covered it with a cloth.

"Buon giorno, Mamma," he said casually, "going out?"

"Oui, mon cher," she answered nervously; she hardly ever addressed her son this way anymore, "I like to go out and do some of the shopping myself. Since Giambattista…and your father…I like to walk. It gives me peace."

"Che cos'è? What's that?" he asked, nodding his head toward the basket.

Adélaïde picked up the basket quickly and said, "Just some old bread for the beggars alongside the Ponte Vecchio."

Pierfrancesco pretended not to care and picked up another piece of cheese from a plate on the small worktable. He left the kitchen chewing, saying nothing.

* *

Lorenzo sat at the table anxiously. He had packed the few possessions he had in a small leather case to be tied to the horse's saddle. In his satchel he put Father Vincenzo's copy of Dante's *Commedia*. He planned on stopping by San Felice before setting off for Pisa, where he would board a ship to France. It was out of the way, and it increased his chances of being spotted by Pierfrancesco, but he had to go back there. He wanted to return the *Commedia* to Carla and see if there was any news about Vincenzo. Perhaps, by some miracle, the priest would even be back at San Felice already. Either way, Lorenzo needed to leave word with Carla on where Father Vincenzo could write to him.

His initial reluctance aside, Lorenzo had decided to go to Adélaïde's family estate in Provençe. He could have just continued hiding in Florence, but for how long? Pierfrancesco seemed to possess an inherent hatred for Lorenzo that defied understanding. Even when they had had contact growing up, Pierfrancesco had been mean. After Lorenzo started working for the Chillis, he became even meaner. Hearing that his sister and Lorenzo were lovers sent him into a rage. And now, he was coming after Lorenzo for a coin he didn't even have. It seemed to Lorenzo that it would never end. Pierfrancesco would always hunt him down. And even then, Lorenzo would have endured such a fate if it had meant being with Claudia, but that was not possible; she was married.

He could have just gone to another city in Italy, but where? How would he work? Cities and towns at this time where not at all welcoming to strangers. Adélaïde, who had always looked out for Lorenzo, was offering him a fresh start. He would miss Father Vincenzo, though. He sat at the table and hoped the priest would make it back to San Felice in time to see him off. There was a knock at the door.

Lorenzo opened the door. Claudia stood alone, bundled under a thick woolen cloak, her pregnant belly barely visible under the heavy clothes. She entered.

"Maman is not here yet?" she asked.

Lorenzo just shook his head. He offered her the chair. Seeing her had two contradictory effects. It both weakened his heart to leave and fortified in his mind the need to get away.

The fire in the stove made the shack comfortable, and Claudia removed her cloak. Lorenzo took it and hung it on a hook. As he turned back to face her, he realized she had moved closer to him. They looked each other in the eye and moved closer still. Lorenzo thought he should step back, but could not. The morning chill had reddened Claudia's cheeks and her shining, deep brown eyes shone brilliantly. Lorenzo leaned in and kissed her passionately. The two held this kiss, their last kiss, a long time. They were only disrupted by another knock at the door. As they stepped apart, Claudia smiled, an almost melancholic grin, and sat. Lorenzo answered the door; it was Adélaïde.

Adélaïde set the basket upon the table. There was a small, round loaf of bread and some cheese wrapped in cloth. There was also bottle of wine and a small, leather purse of gold florins.

"I brought you these for the trip, and also this." She handed him a folded and sealed letter. "I have sent word to my cousin Jean to expect your arrival at the villa in Salon-de-Provençe, but messengers are so unreliable. If my message does not reach him, at least you can present him with this letter."

"Grazie," said Lorenzo. "Why are you so good to me?"

Adélaïde put her hands on Lorenzo's shoulders and kissed his cheek. "I promised your father I would look after you!" she said in a low voice.

There was a knock at the door. The three looked at each other in silent apprehension. There was another knock, louder and more forceful. Lorenzo looked at the door latch; he had not locked it when Adélaïde arrived. He lunged forward to flip the latch, but was too late. The door swung in. Pierfrancesco stood in the doorway. The sight of his mother and sister with Lorenzo enraged him.

Pierfrancesco had planned on hunting Lorenzo down with a couple of hired hands, then killing Lorenzo and taking the bezant. The hired hands would dispose of the body; it would be no problem, with no family to report Lorenzo missing. Now, finding Lorenzo in the presence of Adélaïde and Claudia meant he obviously could not kill him. And the lack of any hired hands meant the odds would be much more even, but the surprise of the discovery and the rush of anger made Pierfrancesco forget any prior thought.

"Hand over the coin!" he shouted.

Lorenzo stood his ground firm and answered coolly, "I don't have it." He had long been intimidated by the eldest Chilli son, but Adélaïde's kindness and his love for Claudia filled him with courage.

Pierfrancesco sprang forward and grabbed Lorenzo by the throat, pushing him back all the way against the far wall. Lorenzo reached up to grab Pierfrancesco's throat, but could not get a firm grip with Pierfrancesco's arms in front of him. He swung feebly at his attacker's head while his own face began to turn blue. Adélaïde and Claudia both yelled out, and at the same time grabbed Pierfrancesco by the hair, ears, and face and ripped him back hard. He peeled away from Lorenzo, who gasped violently for air.

Pierfrancesco pushed Claudia back and in one spinning motion slapped Adélaïde hard across the face with the back of his hand. She fell back in both pain and disbelief, landing on the floor in a seated position, holding her face and crying. Pierfrancesco stopped. He saw his mother crying on the floor and felt an instant surge of self-loathing. All his anger and courage were drained. He could not even open his mouth to speak, afraid his quivering lips might start blubbering. In a split second, he felt his mother's immense grief and wanted to pick her up and hug her.

Lorenzo caught his breath and took advantage of Pierfrancesco's pause. He crashed his fist down hard on the side of Pierfrancesco's head, in the temple. Pierfrancesco was completely stunned by the blow. Lorenzo rained down another blow, then another. Pierfrancesco lost his feet and hit the ground in a lump where he stood. Lorenzo towered over him, delivering punch after devastating punch, until Pierfrancesco stopped moving.

Claudia stopped the last punch from landing, catching Lorenzo's fist. She hugged him, and they both cried.

They helped Adélaïde to her feet. She dried her eyes with a handkerchief, in apparent embarrassment.

"I'm sorry," said Lorenzo.

Adélaïde sniffled. "It is I who am sorry, mon cher. I know who my son is, and I know what he has done to you."

Without saying it, all three were aware of a new reality. Lorenzo's leaving Florence was no longer a matter of convenience, but of survival. Pierfrancesco would now hunt Lorenzo down for as long as he lived.

Adélaïde handed the basket to Claudia. "Vas avec lui à la porte, les chevaux seront là, ma chère!" She hugged Lorenzo and kissed both of his cheeks. "Adieu, mon cher," she said. She then took her handkerchief, dipped it in the water bowl on the table, and wrung it. She knelt down next to Pierfrancesco and straightened his body out, placing the wet cloth on his forehead.

Claudia handed Lorenzo his satchel and travel bag. "Vieni," she said, "come."

"Your mother is staying here?" he asked, dumbfounded.

"Oui!"

XVIII

The gray horse clopped steadily along the unpaved road. The air was crisp and cold, but there was no wind, and the overhead sun felt warm on Vincenzo's face. He was in an isolated wooded area between Siena and Poggibonsi. The road was little more than a footpath in the forest. Vincenzo thought he could make out a contingent of papal guards returning to Siena along the main road between the two cities and had opted for the more secluded path.

It turned out he was being overcautious. The captain of the papal guards, an astute and mostly loyal Swiss career soldier had, in fact, sent a group of guards after the priest as Julius had ordered. It was four men on horseback riding hard to Florence along the main roads. They would look for him at San Felice, as instructed, and then return to Rome, with or without Vincenzo. The captain knew these orders were the ramblings of a bitter, dying, old man, and he was determined to commit the least amount of resources possible to honestly carry out the pope's order. Felice, who effectively controlled the Vatican, seemed little interested in recapturing this priest, so the captain did not feel it was a priority. The captain was much more interested in devoting his manpower to shoring up his own power base in Rome. The Papal Guard, after all, was a new institution, started by Julius, and might not survive the succession of a new pope.

For these reasons, Vincenzo need not have feared the guards he had spotted on the road. They were simply traversing Florentine territory on their way back to Rome from the Romagna region. Vincenzo, of course, did not know this and imagined a countrywide manhunt out for him. He stayed along the small country roads, daydreaming as he rode. He had not eaten much on his trip, just some bread that he had begged from churches he had stopped at along the way. He had no money to stay in osterie but was fortunate to find a priest who let him water and feed his horse in the stable behind the rectory house. He slept on a bench in the church. Nobody asked questions about his journey. Priests traveled back and forth to Rome all the time. If Vincenzo had been worth knowing, he'd have had money and traveled in a carriage. He, however, was poor, and not worth interrogating.

His thoughts were interrupted when a short, stout man jumped out of the woods and into his path. The man was brutish and would have been fat, had he been well fed. His cheeks were sunken, however, drooping where the fat once had been; his hair was long and unkempt, and he had a poorly trimmed beard. His clothes were ragged but bundled on thick to fight the cold.

"Buon giorno, Padre," announced the man, seeing the cross around Vincenzo's neck underneath the travel cloak.

The gray horse stopped and showed his displeasure at the interruption with a deep, snorty exhale. Vincenzo sized the man up and saw another come out of the woods behind him. This man was the physical opposite of the first; he was tall and bony, had little hair on his head, and wore only a few stubbly whiskers on his chin. He said nothing. Vincenzo knew he was being robbed by brigands.

The first man had wrapped his hand around the horse's reins and pulled the animal's head low in submission, keeping him still.

"If you're looking for money, you're out of luck. I have none," said Vincenzo with contempt.

"Non c'è problema, Padre…we'll just have your horse." The short man spoke with sinister politeness, which angered Vincenzo all the more.

Vincenzo was always generous with beggars and even forgiving of thieves. He saw the world as inherently unfair and tried not to judge a man reduced to stealing in order to eat. These two men were different, however. Vincenzo knew the type—highway brigands without pity, ready to kill for a few coins. They did not want Vincenzo's horse because they were starving. They wanted it because it was not theirs. What was worse, as far as Vincenzo was concerned, was their willingness to use violence, to prey on the weak to get their way.

He was sure of two things: first, these two thieves would not be talked out of robbing him, and second, they would surely kill him in the act. Robbing a priest was considered especially heinous, and these two would not chance letting the priest go to the next town to describe what had happened. No, for sure they would kill Vincenzo and hide his body in the woods to cover their crime.

Vincenzo's hunch was confirmed when the short, hairy, man in front of him drew a dagger out of his cloak.

"Scendete, get down, per favore," he said with an evil little smile. His eyes twinkled in the cold air, and his tongue could be seen behind a missing tooth.

* *

Lodovico read the letter attentively and then crumpled it and tossed it into the fire. It had arrived that very morning by an express courier from Rome. He sat back and pondered the news. He had thought all loose ends were tied up regarding the Simone Simoni affair, but now he was not sure. If what the priest said were true, and he had witnessed the conversation in the Campanile, then he could be a danger to Lodovico. He thought the matter had been resolved with Coraggiosi dead and the priest rotting away in the Castel Sant'Angelo, but apparently not. The priest was heading back to Florence. What to do next?

Lodovico had worked hard and plotted carefully to ensure his son's future. He felt that now, with Jacopo married well and about to become a Calimala master, his future was secured. He could not let a scandal from the past jeopardize the strides he had made. He would not let the family name be once again dishonored.

He thought about how to move forward. The priest must be neutralized. It would not be as easy as it had been with Coraggiosi. Few hired killers would agree to murder a priest. Bringing harm to a man of God, for some reason, put fear in the hearts of those who otherwise gave little thought to their souls. Still, the priest had knowledge and must be dealt with. He was probably heading back to San Felice. Lodovico determined himself to spy on him there and gain some knowledge of his own.

* *

San Felice was still a long way off for Vincenzo at that moment. He looked down upon these two cretins holding him up and could feel his own pulse in his temples as he gritted his teeth hard and squinted his eyes. On top of the injustice of the robbery, and the survival instinct, what angered Vincenzo the most was the obstacle these two posed to him finding his way back to Lorenzo. These two were not going to prevent that from happening.

War repulsed Vincenzo, and he hated violence, but only unjust violence. At that moment, he knew he was in a fight for survival, and the last thought in his mind was to turn the other cheek. The fact that these two brigands had driven him to violence made him even angrier. It was a fury the priest had no hope of controlling.

"Avit sbaglàt kèsta vota, bastardi," he said in thick Neapolitan. "You've made a mistake this time, you bastards."

Neither man fully understood the sentence, except for the word "bastards." It sounded strange coming from a priest, but there was little time to dwell on it before Vincenzo kicked the short man square in the nose, knocking him off his feet and causing him to drop the dagger. His nose gushed blood, but the man could not fall all the way to the ground, as his hand was wrapped in one of the reins. Vincenzo kicked the horse into a rear, and the man was jerked violently up by his arm. His hand slipped out of the reins, and he fell to the ground hard.

The tall, bald man behind the horse attempted to grab Vincenzo by the cloak and drag him off, but failed. Vincenzo was able to get the horse clear of the man, and a few feet separated the two while they stared each other down.

There was enough space for Vincenzo to ride off. He could get away without a scratch and never see the two brigands again. But

Vincenzo's temper was controlling his actions at this moment, and he wanted to teach these men a lesson. Instead of turning the horse and riding off down the road, he charged the tall man. He might have trampled him had the man not spun aside. Vincenzo grabbed hold of his cloak and dragged him down the road. After the man's feet went limp, Vincenzo threw him down. He stopped the horse and dismounted. He spun the man over and raised a fist to strike him hard in the face, but hesitated.

In a split second, the whole chain of events ran anew through Vincenzo's mind. Throwing the man to the ground had cooled his temper, and as he cooled down he was starkly aware of his vows as a priest, his vow to live like Christ. He lowered his raised hand. The man relaxed his tensed face and lay back against the ground, accepting defeat. Vincenzo stood, looked down at the man, and said nothing. He decided to simply remount his gray horse and ride away.

As he looked down at the bald man on the floor, he noticed his eyes turn from Vincenzo to something off behind him. In a flash, Vincenzo spun quickly. As he did, the short, hairy man swung the dagger down swiftly with both arms. Vincenzo happened to have spun the right way to avoid the worst of the thrust, and the dagger tore through his cloak, above his right elbow, without scratching the priest.

Vincenzo took advantage of the missed blow to follow the man's momentum to the ground, landing on top of him. The two began a life-and-death wrestling match over possession of the dagger. The advantage switched sides several times as the two rolled along the dirt path. At one point, the brigand had the point of the blade at Vincenzo's throat but lacked the leverage to drive it in. Vincenzo used all of his strength to push back. The two rolled again, then again. Finally, as he let out a guttural scream, Vincenzo turn the dagger and drove it into the man's chest with the man's own hands still holding the handle. He fell back limp, dead.

Vincenzo fell off the man and quickly turned his attention to the other, who was now standing. He took three steps backward, awkwardly, staring at the priest, clearly frightened. He then turned and ran off into the woods. Vincenzo caught his breath and looked around, scared. He got on his horse and rode at a gallop to get clear of the woods.

After a while he slowed the horse and rode at a steady trot. He now started to think. His hands were still shaking. It was the first time he had killed a man. He had always been strong and occasionally fought as a child. He had fought off the men who had tried to kidnap Lorenzo. But this was different. He had taken the life out of this man. Vincenzo was deeply ashamed of himself. He knew that the brigands had initiated the confrontation, and he did not blame himself for initially fighting them off. What he hated was what came next. He knew he could have ridden off; he could have gotten away, but his temper made him stay. His temper made it necessary for him to kill. Once again his temper had gotten the better of him. He had spent his life trying to overcome this flaw, by reading, meditating, and praying. It had all failed. He knew he sometimes lived his life outside of the expectations of the Church, but now, at that moment, he truly felt like a sinner. He was depressed and full of self-loathing. He talked out loud as he rode, with tears in his eyes. The horse trotted in silence, without answers, without judgment.

XIX

Lorenzo and Claudia slowly crossed the small piazza in front of San Felice. It was not easy for her to walk without stopping to catch her breath every so often. She did not want Lorenzo to return to San Felice; she would have preferred they go straight to the gate and meet the man waiting with the two horses. Lorenzo, however, insisted on going to San Felice first. He was holding Claudia's hand to steady her. Despite the cold, she was sweating and breathing heavily. Finally, she stopped walking all together and sat on the ground, not ten steps from the rectory house door.

"What is it?" he asked, kneeling beside her to keep her hand in his.

She breathed heavier, looked Lorenzo in the eye, and fainted.

Lorenzo didn't know what to do. He called out to her several times. He laid her back flat on the ground and went to pound on the rectory door. He then returned to her side and leaned over her, caressing her head.

Carla came out and rushed over. "Ch'è successo?" she asked.

"I don't know, we were walking…and then she sat down, and then she fainted."

"Let's get her inside and in a bed!" said Carla.

They lifted her up and carried her upstairs. Carla brought a bowl of water and some clean rags and left them on a small table next to the bed. They had laid her in Vincenzo's room.

"Stay with her. Keep a damp rag on her forehead, and let her drink if she wakes. I will go and get some help," Carla told Lorenzo. She left.

Lorenzo sat at her side, holding Claudia's hand, praying for her to be well.

The better part of an hour passed with no change in Claudia before Carla returned with a doctor and Adélaïde. Carla had run to the Palazzo Chilli, only to be told that Signora Chilli was out. Fortunately she ran into Adélaïde and a bruised Pierfrancesco on the street as she was leaving. She told Adélaïde what had happened, and they went to get a doctor and returned to San Felice together.

It was a quick run across the Via degli Speziali to the Mercato Vecchio, where many of the doctors shared shop space with apothecaries in an effort to maximize the customer base. Dottor Palmieri, great-great grandson of one of the preeminent doctors of the age, was the Chilli family doctor. They found him standing in front of his shop, donning a long, flowing robe with baggy, pleated, sleeves. The robe was richly ornamented in scarlet sashes and had a big fur hood in the style of the Capuchin monk hoods. The robe was buttoned up to his neck, with a thin collar band. On his head was a round, small velvet cap, with his long gray hair mushrooming out the sides. He also wore matching velvet gloves and stood center of the doorway with his hands on his hips. He was in his fifties and of medium height. He stood sternly as if trying to project a regal air. He noticed Adélaïde and another woman approaching and smiled politely.

"Buon giorno, Signora," he said as he dipped his head without appearing in the slightest way deferential.

"Dottore," said Adélaïde without greeting, "my daughter is ill; she fainted. I fear there is a problem with the baby."

"Then I shall come with you to your home, Signora Adélaïde."

"She is at San Felice!"

"In that case…palafreniere, groom!" he shouted to a boy behind the shop. "Bring my horse around."

"Dottore, it is not far, and we can cross the Ponte Vecchio quicker on foot," appealed Adélaïde.

"We have our customs, Signora; besides, my instruments are kept in my saddlebags."

The groom brought the horse around to the front of the shop, requiring a number of pedestrians in the *mercato* to squeeze around.

The doctor made sure all of the surrounding people caught the full spectacle of him mounting his horse and made a show of being led out of the *mercato* by the groom.

At the house, the doctor felt Claudia's pulse on her wrists and had her (now responsive to speech) stick out her tongue. "Had the girl eaten this morning?" he asked, to no one in particular.

"I'm not sure," answered Adélaïde.

"I've seen this before, especially with the servants and poorer women…They don't eat, and then they faint. The baby needs food." He felt her belly for movement and took a pair of spectacles out of his bag, placing them on the tip of his nose. He used his thumb to open Claudia's eyes wide, one at a time. Then he stood and faced Adélaïde, Carla, and Lorenzo. "Give her some water, and when she wakes fully, give her some bread. Be sure she has a proper lunch." He took a small sheet of paper and an inkbottle and stylus out of his bag. He scribbled some notes on the paper and handed it to Adélaïde. "If you give this to the apothecary in my shop, he will give you some herbs to mix with warm water. It will help keep her strength up. Be sure to go to my apothecary; the others are not dependable! And rest…she needs rest. Until the baby comes, she must stay off of her feet."

Adélaïde took a gold florin out of her purse and handed it to the doctor. "Grazie, Dottore," she said.

"Prego, Signora," he answered and left the room.

Adélaïde sat on the bed beside her daughter and caressed her head. "Carla, ma chère," she asked.

"Sì, Signora Adélaïde."

"Would you do me the favor of going to the Bottega Coraggiosi on the Via Calimala and telling my son-in-law the news of his wife? Bring him here; he should be with her."

Lorenzo's heart dropped.

"Sì, certo, Signora," answered Carla as she went out.

"Lorenzo, mon cher," Adélaïde added as she stood and faced him, "merci for taking such good care of her." She pulled Lorenzo to herself and hugged him tightly. To Lorenzo it was reminiscent of the hug Adélaïde had given him downstairs, right after his father had been killed. "Mon cher, you must go. The courier is waiting for you at the gate with the horses. He will escort you to Pisa. You must go to Salon-de-Provençe; you will be safe there."

"I want to stay. I need to see her get well!"

"You heard the dottore; she will be fine. It is you I am worried about; you know we will not be able to stop my son from looking for you. You know what he's capable of." She spoke with a heavy heart.

"I don't care about that."

"Figlio mio," she said gently, "she has a husband now. Her child has a father. I know it did not turn out the way you wanted it to. It is not what I wanted either. But take it from me; you do not want to torture yourself. Seeing the one you love married to another will be a knife in your heart every day. Get away! Start a new life in a new place, away from your torture, away from all of the reminders of the terrible things that have happened to you."

Lorenzo reflected quietly on Adélaïde's words. He looked over at Claudia, resting peacefully on Vincenzo's bed. Her eyes were closed again, and she was sleeping. She breathed rhythmically in a soft-pitched, musical snore that was simply beautiful to Lorenzo. It hurt his heart to think of leaving her, but he knew that Adélaïde was right.

"Would it be all right if I said goodbye to her?" he asked.

"Of course, mon cher, I need to go down to the kitchen anyway." She took the water bowl and left the room.

Lorenzo sat beside Claudia on the bed and kissed her on the cheek. He brushed her hair back with his fingers and whispered, "Arrivederci, amore mio."

XX

Vincenzo rode wearily through the streets of Florence. He saw no papal guards at the city gate and was at the point of not caring all that much if he did. His cloak was dusty and torn. He had not eaten a proper meal in days. The last leg of the trip had taken the longest; the horse was underfed and underwatered as well. The priest was physically rundown from the journey. But worse, he was emotionally and spiritually rundown. He could not forgive himself.

He dismounted in the small piazza in front of San Felice; the rectory house had no stable. He lashed the reins around an iron ring on the wall, gave the worn, gray horse a pat on the neck, and opened the front door, which had not been locked. He was surprised to see a house full of people.

Carla was the first to run over to him. She picked up his hand and kissed it with tears running down her cheeks. "Bentornato,

Padre, welcome back," she cried. She helped him remove his dirty, shredded cloak. He was bewildered.

Adélaïde approached and kissed his cheek. Jacopo, Lodovico, and Maria were there as well. All seemed surprised to see Vincenzo and were shocked at his appearance. At the table sat Claudia, who struggled to her feet and waddled slowly to greet the priest. Vincenzo could not believe how large her belly was. He scanned the room for Lorenzo, but instead his eyes were caught by a scarlet red shoulder shawl over a silky white gown, worn by a man just exiting the kitchen. He wore a rounded red cap. It was Matteo.

He stopped in the doorway in disbelief. After a moment's pause he ran to Vincenzo and embraced him. He hugged him tightly and held it for a while. Vincenzo was too weary and confused to hug back; he just stood with his arms at his side.

Lodovico looked on from across the room.

"Where is Lorenzo?" asked Vincenzo worriedly.

"He is far away, in a safe place," answered Adélaïde.

Vincenzo knew this to mean that Adélaïde would not like to disclose Lorenzo's location in front of everyone and let the matter rest for the time being. Matteo released him, and Vincenzo rubbed some of the scarlet shawl between his fingers. "What's this?"

Matteo grinned with embarrassment, and Adélaïde answered for him. "You are looking at Cardinale Matteo di Napoli, Archbishop of Ravenna," she announced.

"Non ci credo! I don't believe it," answered Vincenzo, shocked. "But how?"

"It was Felice; she somehow convinced her father to name me a cardinal," answered Matteo.

"But why?" Vincenzo was still shocked.

"Most likely to vote for Giovanni de' Medici in the next conclave."

"Conclave?" Vincenzo was more confused.

"Sì, Julius is not expected to survive the winter. His cough has gotten worse, and most days he cannot get out of bed. I guess that is good news for you, my friend."

Vincenzo nodded silently.

"What has happened to you? You look terrible," Matteo asked.

"It was a long journey," mumbled Vincenzo, barely audibly. "When did you get here?"

"I left three days after you, and I arrived this morning," answered the cardinal.

"I hope you don't mind, Padre, but my daughter here was forced to use your home to rest in the past few days," said Adélaïde. "She collapsed just outside, and Carla was good enough to take her in. The doctor said to let her rest. We all came today to bring her home."

Vincenzo, still subdued from the trip and the surprise crowd, answered softly, "Of course, I don't mind at all." He looked at Claudia. "Are you feeling better, cara mia?"

"Sì, Padre, grazie," answered Claudia with a warm smile from the chair she had returned to.

"If you will all excuse me," said Vincenzo, "I have had a long trip and would like to clean myself up and rest a bit. Signora Adélaïde, perhaps I may call on you this evening to discuss Lorenzo; he is quite dear to me, as you know."

Adélaïde took Vincenzo's hand and kissed it. "Reposez-vouz, le Père Vincent. We will leave you in peace. I look forward to your visit later."

All but Vincenzo, Matteo, and Carla left. The group walked slowly, escorting Claudia to the Giotti house, except for Lodovico, who went off on an errand.

Upstairs in Vincenzo's house, Matteo sat on the bed while Vincenzo undressed. He piled his dirty clothes in the corner and wore only a thin white dressing gown. He dipped his face in the bowl of water resting on a small table and wiped himself off with the hand towel Carla had laid out. He closed the door and sat next to Matteo, leaning and resting his head on Matteo's shoulder.

Matteo swung an arm around Vincenzo and kissed the top of his head, "Che c'è? What is it?" he asked.

"I killed a man."

The sentence hung on the air for a moment before a stunned Matteo could respond. "What do you mean?"

"Two brigands attacked me on a wooded path outside Siena. I fought them off. But I was angry. I wanted to teach them a lesson, so I stayed...and when one of them tried to stab me, I used his knife to kill him."

Matteo turned and faced Vincenzo, placing both hands on his shoulders and looking over Vincenzo's body. "Are you hurt?" he asked.

"I was not injured."

"Grazie a Dio, there was nothing you could have done; you were attacked!"

"I could have ridden away after I fought them off; there was a moment when I could have gotten away."

"You cannot be sure of that…Besides, what good would that have done? You would have left them to attack the next traveler."

"God's judgment is not mine to give out!"

"You are being too hard on yourself."

"Why should I not be? I have given myself over to God, I have prayed, I have contemplated, I have spent my life trying to control my temper, and I have failed."

"You are Nnapulitan! Fire runs through your blood. You see the bad side, but I look at the good you have done. You saw the injustice of Lorenzo's danger, and you fought to save him. You sacrificed yourself to save Lorenzo and me from prison. That fire in your blood fuels a big heart. You need to see the good in you!"

* *

Outside, in the small piazza that faced San Felice and the rectory house, Lodovico crept along the paving stones and looked around for other souls on the street. It was the late afternoon, after *pranzo*, when most people rested before going back to work for a couple of hours. The streets were deserted. Clouds shaded the piazza, and a cold wind whipped up the narrow via from the Arno.

Lodovico approached the rectory house and peered into the ground-floor window, expecting to see Vincenzo and Matteo at the table. He planned on knocking on the door and offering some excuse for returning. He wanted to speak with Vincenzo, to size up the priest before formulating a plan. The ground floor was unoccupied, however, and Lodovico noticed the gray horse that stood lashed to the iron ring next to the entrance door. Vincenzo had forgotten to have Carla walk the horse over to the stable at the nearby convent. He looked up at the shuttered windows above and then over his shoulder again to ensure he was alone. He climbed up the saddle of the horse, and then stood on the saddle, steadying himself by holding the wall. His ear was now close to the closed wooden shutter; he listened.

"I need to earn God's forgiveness. I need to serve Him humbly, as I swore to do in my oaths." Vincenzo was sad but resolute.

"There may be a way," Matteo answered. "I am going to Ravenna. The city was devastated by the war. The people are dying in the streets. They need help. You can come with me. Together, we can do God's work."

"So you are not going to Ravello?"

"I did not want to be an archbishop or a cardinal, but when I heard about the condition of the people, I resolved to help them. I want to help them in the way we always talked about…in the way that the Church should act, as a simple shepherd instead of a greedy lord."

"You should."

"And you?"

"I will stay here at San Felice. As you said, we are called upon by God to be shepherds. I am needed here. The people of this parish need me. Carla needs me. And someday, Lorenzo may once again need me. It is all I can do; it is my humble service. I owe it to God for what I have done.

Matteo's voice became shaky. "You're really not coming with me?"

"No."

"But what about our plans. We were to spend the rest of our lives together. I love you. It is a true love. It is a love I am not ashamed of."

"You know that the world sees it differently," Vincenzo answered.

"That is what the Church has always told us, but is it really what God says?"

Vincenzo held the scarlet shawl in his hand again. "Now, *you* are the Church. It is up to you to tell us what God says. As for me, I think God wants me to spend the rest of my days in His service." Vincenzo stood and opened the door. "Carla," he yelled down the stairs. After a moment he followed with, "I forgot that the horse was lashed out front; will you walk it over to the stable for me?"

At hearing this through the shutter, Lodovico quickly and nimbly jumped down from the shivering gray horse and ran off down the via.

LIBER QUINTUS

Et ne nos inducas in tentationem

I

SPRING 1513

Salon-de-Provençe sits on the southern coast of France. It had been a trading post since pre-Roman times. Within the old city walls was a villa, halfway between the Chateau de l'Emperi and the Chapel Saint Michel. It had been in the Laroche family for generations, and the caretaker, Jean, was Adélaïde's cousin. Lorenzo had been staying there for the past few months and was settling into life in Provençe. Adélaïde had given him money for the voyage, and did not charge him rent for staying at the villa. In return, Lorenzo was helping Jean with the upkeep of the estate.

In Rome, Pope Julius II had died that February. By April, word reached Salon-de-Provençe that a new pope had been elected and consecrated. It was Giovanni de' Medici, who was now known as Pope Leo X. Lorenzo received this news with indifference. He knew Father Vincenzo was safe, and that was all that mattered.

It was a beautifully sun-filled afternoon. The soft breeze had finally shed all hints of winter coolness, and few clouds passed overhead. That morning, Lorenzo had helped Jean milk the three cows they kept in the large courtyard. He carried the buckets of milk to the market near the town's center, where Jean sold the milk to one of the shop owners and used the money to buy provisions for the villa. Later, Lorenzo walked the three cows, together, outside the city gate to a small hill just before the forest, to allow them to graze. Once the cows were back inside their penned-in area in the courtyard, Lorenzo had some time to kill before lunch.

He sat under a tree in the courtyard. On his lap was his one and only book, Dante's *Commedia*. Lorenzo had done a few odd jobs for the people in town, saved his money, and purchased the book. Lucien des Livres, the bookseller in town, had to order it from Venice. Reading Dante reminded Lorenzo of Father Vincenzo and of Florence, and he read the *Commedia* every chance he could. He flipped through the *Paradiso* to the canto he had recently found, the one that spoke to him at that moment of his life:

> Tu lascerai ogne cosa diletta
> più caramente; e questo è quello strale
> che l'arco de lo essilio pria saetta.
> Tu proverai sì come sa di sale
> lo pane altrui, e come è duro calle
> lo scendere e 'l salir per l'altrui scale.

> *You will leave everything loved*
> *most dearly, and this is that arrow*
> *which the bow of your exile first shoots.*
> *You will learn how salty*
> *is the bread of others, and how hard it is*
> *to descend and climb the stairs of others.*

Lorenzo especially liked the double meaning Dante hid in the passage "come sa di sale lo pane altrui," how salty is the bread of others. He was speaking, of course, of the figurative bitterness of begging for one's meal, but true to Dante's style, he was also being literal: the typical bread baked in Florence was unsalted, so the bread of others would therefore taste salty to a Florentine.

Lorenzo thought of his own exile and how he had been forced to leave everything he loved most dearly. It was comforting to know that the great Dante had felt the same emotions himself. But he was also reminded of the fact that Dante never did return to Florence and that he was only reunited with his beloved Beatrice in the afterlife. Nevertheless, Lorenzo was grateful to Father Vincenzo for giving him the gift of reading, the gift of poetry, and most of all the gift of Dante. To Lorenzo, this poem was a letter through time in which the poet could speak to him across the centuries. Dante wrote of the politics of his time in the framework of God's universe as he knew it, but the emotions he expressed and the humanity he portrayed shone as a beacon for the people of any time, regardless of their political system or religion. Dante guided the reader through a vision, his vision, beautifully described and fundamental to the question of what it means to be human.

Lorenzo sat back against the tree trunk and closed his eyes. The soft breeze blew his hair up gently, and he could feel the sunlight on his eyelids. He was about to doze off when he heard a voice from a man standing over him. He opened his eyes to see the shadow of a large man he could have sworn to be his father. The light of the sun beamed around the man's figure, obscuring him. In a split second Lorenzo's mind sharpened, and he realized it was Jean standing over him. He did, after all, resemble Simone, except Jean wore no beard.

"Un courier vous a apportè cela, a courier brought you this," said Jean as he handed Lorenzo a letter.

Lorenzo's French was improving rapidly, and he had no problem understanding the caretaker's news. "Merci," he replied as he took the letter.

As Jean turned and walked away, Lorenzo recognized the seal. It was oval in shape with a round shield in the center, representing the shield of Achilles—the seal of the Chilli family. It was pressed hard into the thick red wax. Lorenzo was excited, as he thought it would be a letter from Adélaïde. He cracked the seal and opened the letter, which was several pages long.

Mio carissimo Lorenzo, it began.

I hope that this letter finds you well and that you have been safe and happy. So much has happened in the months since you have gone. I sit here at my father's desk to write to you and send my dearest wishes for your quick return. Pierfrancesco is dead. He was killed in the street as he returned home late one evening from the new bottega. On his body was left a paper with a drawing of the shield of the wool guild. It is said that members of the guild killed him because of a deal with Englishmen. Maman fell once again into despair. She is sad all of the time. Jacopo and I visit her almost every day, but her sadness persists. She says little. I think seeing you again would raise her spirits. Besides, there is no longer any danger in your returning.

There is also another reason why you should return. Giuliano de' Medici discovered a Last Will and Testament of his father, Lorenzo il Magnifico. He presented it to the Signoria as proof of his inheritance in some banking interest. However, the Signoria also discovered a line in which il Magnifico left to your father and to my father each five thousand florins, in gratitude for having saved his life. The heirs of both men were designated as recipients. Pierfrancesco was to receive my father's share, but he was killed shortly after it was announced, so the money came to Jacopo and I. Your father's share has been set aside for you. You are rich, and I could not be happier for you.

In February I gave birth to a son, Lodovico Domenico di Jacopo Giotti. We at first called him Lodovichino, but now we call him Chino. He is a beautiful boy with dark brown hair and eyes.

I am sorry to write of some misfortune that has befallen on Padre Vincenzo. He was denounced in a letter to the archbishop as a sodomite. Maman interceded on his behalf to the archbishop, who said the matter would be closed if Padre Vincenzo swore such allegations to be false. Padre Vincenzo, however, said that he could not swear falsely and affirmed the charge. He would not say with whom such acts were committed, which infuriated the archbishop. Padre Vincenzo was removed from San Felice and was sentenced to serve his penance in the dungeon of a monastery. Maman was able to convince the archbishop to allow him to repent in our private chapel here in our palazzo. He has been staying at the palazzo, along with his maid Carla, who now works for Maman.

Maman instructs you to ask Jean for money to sail from Provençe to Pisa. Padre Vincenzo will meet you in Pisa and escort you home to Florence. I look forward to your safe return, as you are always in my heart.

Con Amore,
Claudia

Lorenzo held the letter and stared and the salutation for a long while: "with love, Claudia." He knew she sent her love, the same love a sister or dear friend would send. But he knew that between the lines was a deeper love, the same love he had for her. He had so many conflicting emotions: love for Claudia, empathy for Vincenzo, relief at being free from Pierfrancesco's wrath, sympathy for Adélaïde, a pang in his chest at learning Claudia had had Jacopo's child, and elation at the inheritance. What would he do? Pierfrancesco had not been the only reason he left Florence. Adélaïde had been right; seeing Claudia married to Jacopo was a slow torture to him, and he did better to be far away from it. Life was peaceful in Salon-de-Provençe. He, of course, still loved Claudia, but he could be happy in Provençe. Jean was a kind and decent man. He could work for him indefinitely. Perhaps he would find a French girl to marry and have a family of his own.

He knew, however, that he had to go back. For one thing, five thousand florins was a huge sum of money to him. It was not greed but survival. If he were ever to have a future, the type of future he wanted, that money would be his only means of rising above the poverty he had been born into. He knew he had to go back for Father Vincenzo as well. Vincenzo had been the rock of Lorenzo's life. He was his savior and his friend. If Vincenzo was going through a hard time now, then Lorenzo would be by his side.

And then there was Adélaïde, poor Adélaïde. She was so kind, and forced to deal with so much loss. She had seemed to come back to life, after the death of Giambattista, when Lorenzo needed her help. He wanted to console her somehow. But most of all, there was Claudia. He missed Claudia more than anything. He knew in his head that Adélaïde had been right about the situation, but in his heart he needed to see her again.

He had made up his mind. He was going back to Florence.

II

Francesco Chilli, the younger brother of Domenico, was by this time around fifty years of age. Being the eldest, Domenico was naturally the heir to the family business and fortune. This left their father, the senior Francesco, with two choices for his younger son: the clergy or the military. He chose the latter. At seventeen Francesco was sent to the camp of the *condottiere* Federico Gonzaga in the duchy of Milan. Francesco participated in several skirmishes with the Milanese army against the Venetians, in which he failed to distinguish himself to Gonzaga. Falling out of favor with the *condottiere*, he was sent back to Florence. The episode was a minor embarrassment to the Chilli name, and Francesco senior then apprenticed his son to the wool guild at the late age of seventeen.

Being the son of a Chilli quickened the apprenticeship greatly and the father set his sights on a marriage arrangement. A betrothal was made with the daughter of another wool merchant, who later broke the engagement in favor of a more distinguished groom. It was not too long after that that the elder Francesco died. Domenico took over the business, and Francesco Junior settled in as his brother's right hand. He was apparently happy to not marry and to split his time between a room at the Palazzo Chilli and a small apartment on the Via dei Calzaiuoli. He was some times seen in the osteria near the apartment, drinking and playing cards, and other than that he kept mostly to himself.

With Pierfrancesco dead, it was now left to Francesco to run the Chilli wool enterprise. It officially belong to Adélaïde, who had no interest in running the business and who, besides, would not have been permitted to participate in the day-to-day dealings because she was not a guild member, and would not have been permitted to be a guild member because she was a woman. So Francesco carried on as his nephew had before, and in some ways the business was doing better. He was more affable than Pierfrancesco had been and did not have as many enemies at the guildhall. Nobody knew who had killed Pierfrancesco, despite Giuliano de' Medici's inquiries. It was thought to be guildsmen on account of the drawing of the guild seal found with the body. It is true that the English deal with the Coraggiosi foreign wool bottega had rubbed the other guildsmen the wrong way, but the venture seemed to have had the Medicis' blessing, and nobody was vocally against it any longer.

The deal had, in fact, proved lucrative. The new bottega was churning out ever more rolls of wool, and the increased profit margin was a windfall for the Chilli family. Francesco dutifully set the profits away for his sister-in-law. Normally, a son-in-law would be a perfect candidate to step into a situation such as this, but Jacopo was strictly forbidden from working in a wool merchant's bottega; he was a *Calimala* merchant and could only act as such. Jacopo had finished his term of service for Coraggiosi's son and was now a full Calimala master, building up his own trade. Whatever Domenico may have intended, Jacopo no longer had anything to do with the deal his former master had made. He was on his own.

Fortune had worked in his favor, for just as he was renting his own space for his own bottega and struggling to put together the funds needed to lay out for raw material, Claudia had inherited the five thousand florins meant for Pierfrancesco. Things were good at home since the baby came. Claudia beamed with joy at the sight of her son, and she had warmed up to Jacopo a great deal as a result. Maria was quite the loving grandmother, and even Lodovico seemed to dote on his little grandson. Adélaïde showed brief moments of happiness with the baby in her arms, but then would soon slide back into depression. Pierfrancesco's death had been a shock, but the birth of Lodovichino served as a distraction for the family.

* *

At the port of Pisa, a midsize cargo ship docked. It brought mostly dry goods from southern France and a few passengers. Down the plank walked Lorenzo. He searched the dock for Father Vincenzo but did not see him. Ship voyages were unpredictable, and it had not been possible to give Vincenzo an exact arrival time, although the boat had arrived on that day as planned.

Lorenzo had written to Claudia that he would disembark and wait at the closest osteria. As he headed for a small, single-windowed inn with a faded wooden shingle over the door, he saw a man exit. The man wore a white blouse, baggy and tucked into tight wool pants. Over his arm was a black robe. Around his neck was a wooden cross on a thin rope. It was Vincenzo. From a distance Lorenzo did not recognize him, never having seen him in public without his black robe.

The two saw each other and ran quickly to embrace. Vincenzo let out a heavy, audible sigh in obvious relief at finding Lorenzo, who hugged him tightly. A lot had happened since the last time he had seen his priest, mentor, and friend.

"Ti trovo bene, I find you well," said Vincenzo, happy to see Lorenzo in good health.

"Sì, sì, I am good, and yourself?"

"I am fine, grazie," answered Vincenzo with his words, though his eyes said otherwise.

"I heard what happened."

Vincenzo nodded. "I know, but never mind that now. We've got to get you back home!"

Lorenzo did not know what to say. He assumed that whatever allegations were made involved Matteo as well. He was confused. Vincenzo was a parental figure in his life, and so seemed completely asexual to him. He was also conditioned to believe that priests were immune from bodily urges. The idea that two men could truly love each other was foreign to all except the men who did, in fact, love other men. These ideas went through Lorenzo's head, but still he did not know what to say. He closed his eyes for a second and then said the first thing that came into his mind.

"You've been like a father to me," he said kindly.

Vincenzo looked him in the eye and smiled thinly.

"Let's go home," added Lorenzo as he put his hand on Vincenzo's shoulder.

The two turned and went back to the osteria, where Vincenzo had stabled two horses. Though he hid it, Vincenzo's eyes were wet.

III

The rain fell hard outside, and thunder crashed through the heavy air. It was a nice day to stay indoors. Adélaïde sat in the sitting room off the main entrance hall in the Palazzo Chilli. She sipped on a warm cup of red wine and honey. Father Vincenzo sat opposite her and drank his wine unhoneyed. Lorenzo sat on a padded sofa in front of the unlit fireplace. Both he and Vincenzo were staying at the Palazzo Chilli for the time being. Having Lorenzo home did, in fact, raise Adélaïde's spirits somewhat, but she was still not her old self.

In the kitchen, the chef prepared a grand *pranzo* of a roasted pork saddle, called *arista*, with numerous roasted vegetables and pies baked with herbs as side courses. The knocker could be heard falling on the front door, and the servant Paolo hurried down the hall to answer.

In a moment, the entrance hall was flooded with visitors. Claudia, with baby in arms, Jacopo, Lodovico, and Maria had arrived. They were all to spend the Sunday meal together.

The party stood in the hall for some time, shedding wet outer layers of clothing. Jacopo and Lodovico had held a small tarp over Claudia's head to keep the baby dry. They, in turn, were soaked. Paolo and Carla helped them out of their wet cloaks and boots and handed each a small towel to dry their heads. It was raining quite hard, and had the Giotti house not been so close, they would not have ventured out. While the door had been open, a booming thunder had filled the first floor of the palazzo.

At last, they all made their way into the sitting room, and everyone exchanged greetings and kisses. Claudia continued to hold the baby while she hugged Lorenzo with the other arm and kissed him on the cheek. It was hardly noticeable to anyone else, but she held the kiss a fraction of a second longer than a friendly greeting would have called for. It was not lost on Lorenzo. He moved the blanket to expose the sleeping infant.

"Veramente bello, truly beautiful," he said.

Claudia smiled and moved over to Father Vincenzo, while Jacopo stepped in front of Lorenzo. For a moment there was an awkward silence, which Jacopo broke by offering his hand. The whole room seemed to stop and watch.

Lorenzo looked down at the hand and stood perfectly still for a second. He then grabbed it fully and pulled Jacopo in, kissing him on each cheek. "Congratulazioni, Papà," he said.

Jacopo smiled. "Grazie," he returned quickly. The whole room smiled.

"I have something for you," added Jacopo. He reached into the purse tied around his decorative belt and pulled out a gold coin. It was the bezant. He held it up in front of Lorenzo and handed it to him. "It belonged to your father; you should have it!"

Lorenzo had not expected this and was truly moved. He held the coin in his hand and looked down at it intently. He thought of the first time he had held it in his hand, the last time he saw his father. He was filled with peace. Jacopo had given him his peace. He would always carry a sadness in his soul for Claudia's marriage, but he now felt at peace with the situation. He looked Jacopo in the eye and said, "Ti ringrazio, I thank you," in the familiar tense.

Claudia and Adélaïde both smiled with tears in their eyes, and Father Vincenzo was happy, too. Only Lodovico was unmoved. In fact, the elder Giotti was quite angered by his son's magnanimous gesture. He kept his emotions in check, but he was furious at the loss of the bezant. He had believed his son had already returned the coin, prior to Pierfrancesco's plan to offer it back to Giuliano de' Medici. Now here it was, a golden opportunity to gain great favor with the ruler of Florence, and his son had just given it away.

As thunder once again crashed outside, Lodovico angrily stared on at the scene before him. No one else noticed, however, and Carla soon came to call everyone to the dining hall.

The topic of conversation around the dinner table centered around Lorenzo's five-thousand-florin inheritance. He recounted the story Simone had told him, about the day Domenico and Simone had saved the life of Lorenzo il Magnifico. Jacopo told of his confrontation with Coraggiosi, and all reviled the man for his role in Simone's death.

Lodovico sat silently, uneasy, at the table. He waited for Vincenzo to accuse him, not knowing his fears were ungrounded. Vincenzo had overheard the conversation in the Campanile and had come to know that one of the men was Coraggiosi only after Jacopo had seen the bezant in his house. He did not suspect that the other voice he had heard in the bell tower was Lodovico's. Lodovico did not know this, of course, and had taken steps to discredit the priest preemptively. He had written an anonymous denouncement to the archbishop, which had the desired effect. He had not counted on Adélaïde's intervention keeping Vincenzo out of a cell. He watched nervously while the stories were told, but Vincenzo seemed to pay him no mind. Perhaps he didn't know.

Lodovico used a lull in the conversation to pose a question. "Have you decided which banking house you'll use?" he asked Lorenzo.

"Mi scusa?" asked Lorenzo in turn.

"Banking house! Surely you won't keep five thousand gold florins under your pillow."

All eyes turned on Lorenzo in agreement.

"I hadn't really thought about it," he answered.

"I would use either Perotti or Barzo; they are the biggest and most reputable," offered Lodovico.

"We've used Barzo ever since the Medici bank closed, mon cher; they are honest," added Adélaïde.

"Sì, and they keep a banco under the canopy in the Mercato Nuovo; you can go straight there after claiming the money in the morning," said Lodovico with a smile.

"Grazie," answered Lorenzo.

Father Vincenzo ate his meal quietly. He was happy Lorenzo was back. His removal from San Felice angered him, but it was not the disgrace but his newfound idleness that bothered him most. Since the episode with the brigands, he had resolved to humbly do his duty as a priest. He could not do that without a congregation to serve. He was used to serving the working people of his parish daily, with everything from spiritual guidance to loaves of bread. Now he felt useless. Having Lorenzo back helped alleviate this feeling, but Lorenzo was grown now; he did not need him in the same way. Still, he needed to find some way of feeling useful. "I will go with you," he told Lorenzo.

Lorenzo smiled.

"What will you do with your money?" asked Claudia, who had just returned to the dining hall from checking on the sleeping baby.

"I'm not sure," he answered.

"Tu vas commencer ta vie, mon cher," said Adélaïde softly. "You will begin your life."

* *

The heavy rains had stopped, and only the occasional drizzle fell outside. The streets were now quiet after the barrage of thunder, and although it was still light out, few people were on the streets. Claudia carried the baby, and Maria and Jacopo walked at her side. Lodovico had parted ways to go confirm an appointment for the next day.

* *

Later that night, in his bed in the Palazzo Chilli, Lorenzo lay awake staring at the ceiling. For some reason, he kept thinking of the dream he had had one night while in the Stinche, the vision of Claudia, as Beatrice, reciting the words of Dante.

> Dante, perché Virgilio se ne vada,
> non pianger anco, non piangere ancora;
> ché pianger ti conven per altra spada.

> *Dante, just because Virgil goes away,*
> *do not cry yet, do not cry yet;*
> *for crying will come to you through another sword.*

Why had he dreamed this particular passage, what did it mean? To Dante, the pilgrim of the *Commedia*, Virgil's departure would have been a sad event. Virgil was Dante's poetic inspiration and his spiritual guide. In short, he was his conscience. He had guided Dante through the horrors of hell and the trials of purgatory. But just as Moses could only guide his people through the desert but not enter the Promised Land himself, Virgil could only deliver Dante to Beatrice; he could not himself enter Paradise. And so, Dante would have cried at Virgil's leaving him. But Beatrice tells him not to, for crying will come "per altra spada." For Dante, this other sword could signify his exile from his beloved city.

Lorenzo stared at the ceiling and contemplated his own life. Would he cry through means of another sword?

IV

The following morning Lorenzo awoke early, only to find that Father Vincenzo and Adélaïde were already downstairs, eating bread and fruit at the table. They were all excited about the day. Even Adélaïde seemed in high spirits. She had been correct; five thousand florins would be the start of a new life for Lorenzo. He woke in a wonderfully happy mood. He had Father Vincenzo near him again, and he was at peace with Jacopo and Claudia. The love for her that he knew would always be there in his heart no longer seemed like a burden. In fact, he felt as if a weight had been lifted from his shoulders.

While Vincenzo and Lorenzo were preparing to leave, Adélaïde stopped him in the hall.

"Je suis tellement heureuse pour toi, mon cher. I'm so happy for you," she said while kissing him on the cheek.

"Et je te suis éternellemente reconnaissant—I am eternally grateful to you," answered Lorenzo, slowly with a Italian accent.

Adélaïde smiled and hugged him.

Lorenzo and Vincenzo headed out for the Palazzo Vecchio, the seat of Florentine government. The Signoria had been weakened by the installation of Giuliano de' Medici, but still performed many important functions of civil administration.

Having no business with the Signoria himself, Father Vincenzo had been barred from entering the palazzo with Lorenzo. He instead waited outside. In the piazza right in front of the entrance stood Michelangelo's *David*. He gazed up at the muscular youth. The determination in the future king's eyes to do his duty gave the priest comfort. Honor to a sense of duty knew no social class.

After quite some time, Lorenzo exited the imposing palazzo with a heavy wooden crate on his shoulder. He joined Vincenzo in front of *David*.

"I see Lodovico was right. I had thought they might give you a Lettera di Cambio, but they gave you the florins directly," said Vincenzo. He looked around suspiciously; nobody else in the piazza seemed to notice Lorenzo and his crate. "He was also right about depositing it right away; come, let's go to the Mercato Nuovo and find the Barzo banco."

The two crossed the Piazza della Signoria and walked down the tight Via Calimaruzza toward the Mercato Nuovo, the banking center of the city. The via was narrow, a long, straight walk with no turnoffs. It was still quite early in the morning, but merchants, moneychangers, and bankers were starting to make their way to the *mercato*. The via, however, was not yet crowded.

A white-haired, frail man walked toward them from the other end of the alley. He carried a wooden crate with handles on either side. The man needed both hands to carry the crate in front of himself, but did not seem weighed down by it. He wore leather sandals on his feet over green *calze*, or stockings. His outer garment was a mix between a robe and a tunic, with long sleeves, and was cut just above the knee. It was pleated and cinched around the waist with a leather belt. Three buttons closed the neckline high. His hat was the same color as the garment, dark crimson, and it flopped over the band to cover much of his white hair. It looked more like a wig of cloth than a hat. He appeared to be in his sixties, but healthy. He walked quickly and seemed to notice Father Vincenzo from the opposite end of the via. He made eye contact with the priest and walked toward him and Lorenzo. As he drew closer, Vincenzo noticed that the man had tears in his eyes.

"Padre," started the man from a short distance, "can you help me?"

"Sì, what is it, my friend?"

The man walked up close and rested his crate on the ground. It contained a balancing scale made of a wooden balance rod and two bronze plates, all connected by ropes and made to hang from a hook. Lorenzo, too, rested his small crate on the ground at his feet.

"It is my wife…She has been sick. I just received word that she will not live out the day. I am on my way home. She will need unctio infirmorum, last rites," he said.

"I will come at once. Where is your wife?" asked the priest earnestly.

"At my house. I am Andrea Alamanni, a banker in the Barzo house. I live in an apartment on the Borgo dei Greci."

"Barzo house, you say. We were on our way to the Barzo banco in the Mercato Nuovo," answered Vincenzo.

"Mi dispiace, but I just closed it. I left an apprentice to watch the banco while I return to the Palazzo Barzo to tell them I need to attend to my wife. Signor Barzo will probably send somebody to reopen the banco this afternoon."

Father Vincenzo looked at Lorenzo. "That is not ideal; we would have preferred to take care of this now."

Lorenzo nodded in agreement.

"I'm afraid I can't help you. Withdrawals are only made from the palazzo. We only accept deposits and Lettere di Cambio at the banco," said the banker regretfully.

"We were only making a deposit," answered Vincenzo.

"I see. Well...I could take care of that for you. Are you the depositor, Padre?"

"No, the boy," answered Vincenzo instinctively, forgetting that Lorenzo was now a man.

"Peccato, pity," said the banker. "We make transactions for clergy members sine arbitrio, without witness, but the boy will need...Oh, well I guess you could act as his witness!"

"Certo," said the priest.

The man shuffled through the crate at his feet and pulled out a leather portfolio. He opened it and removed two printed sheets. The top part of the page was preprinted, and underneath were thin ledger lines. He turned the crate on its side to use as a desk and laid out the two papers. He opened a small inkbottle and with a stylus from his pocket began to write.

"Nome?" he asked without looking up.

Vincenzo looked to Lorenzo, who had not been listening.

"Lorenzo Simoni," Lorenzo hurriedly answered.

"Figlio di?"

"Simone Simoni."

"Residenza?"

"Palazzo Chilli."

At hearing the address, the banker stopped writing and looked up. He made a surprised look and then returned to his writing. He was writing the same information on each identical form.

"Cifra, sum?" he continued.

"Five thousand florins."

The banker stopped writing again and looked at Lorenzo. He nodded his head and continued.

"Sign here," he said to Lorenzo as he handed him the stylus and pointed to a spot on the page. He then indicated to Lorenzo to sign the second sheet as well.

"Testimonio, witness!" he said as he then handed the stylus to Vincenzo, repeating the process. When the signatures were finished, he asked, "And the money?"

Lorenzo opened the crate at his feet to reveal row after row of perfectly stacked gold coins.

The banker fluttered his hand over the stacks, seemingly counting the rows. He then added the figure of 5,000 to the ledger line of each sheet and signed the bottom of each page. He handed one of the sheets to Lorenzo and then closed Lorenzo's crate. He put the other copy back in the portfolio and righted his crate. He laid the portfolio and Lorenzo's crate on top of the balancing scale and stood.

"I will deliver these to the Palazzo Barzo. I trust you know where the Borgo dei Greci is, Padre?" said the banker as he lifted the crate.

"Can I carry that for you?" asked Vincenzo.

"I would rather you not waste any time in retrieving your prayer book and oils. My house is next to San Fiorenzo."

"I know the street. I will see you there shortly," the priest answered. Vincenzo was, of course, saddened by the man's wife's illness, but he was also a little excited to be needed as a priest again, to tend to his flock.

The banker's eyes watered again. "Grazie," he said softly, looking Vincenzo dead in the eye. He then continued down the Via Calimaruzza, straining to hold the heavy load out in front of himself, at a quick pace.

"I'm off to give the poor woman her last rites. What will you do?" Vincenzo asked Lorenzo.

"Not sure. I'll probably walk around a bit." Lorenzo folded the sheet of paper twice and stuffed it inside the fold of his trousers, behind his belt.

"Ci vediamo a pranzo; we'll see each other at supper," Vincenzo said as he grabbed the top of Lorenzo's arm and squeezed. He, too, walked off down the via, but in the other direction, toward the Mercato Nuovo, so he could turn up the Via Calimala and return to the Palazzo Chilli to retrieve his prayer book and anointing oils.

Lorenzo headed back toward the Piazza della Signoria, feeling totally free for the first time in his life. The sun was now shining brightly in the morning sky. Spring was in the air. He felt happy.

* *

Father Vincenzo reached the end of the Via Calimaruzza and made a right turn; as he followed the building line to go up the Via Calimala, the Mercato Nuovo was on his left. This "new market" was now centuries old, but retained its name. For decades it had been the only banking center in Florence, before the consuls of the bankers and moneychangers guild decided to allow its members to also conduct business in their residences. Most banking was now done in the bankers' houses or in studios rented for such purposes. The older banking families, however, still kept a *banco*, or wooden table, in the Mercato Nuovo.

Vincenzo walked along, looking at each *banco* he passed. At the height of Florence's banking days, there would have been as many as eighty *banchi* crammed in the small piazza. Now, due to the failure of many of the ancient banking families and the dispersal of many others to houses and studios, there remained scarcely two dozen *banchi*. Vincenzo regarded each table he passed, all now busy with clients. As he reached the end of the *mercato*, something struck him as odd. There were no empty tables.

The banker had told them he had closed up his *banco* and left only an apprentice to stand guard, but now every *banco* was teeming with activity. He approached the last table and caught the attention of a man seated behind it, dressed much like the old banker in the via had been.

"Scusa...la casa di Barzo?" he asked.

The banker pointed to a *banco* adjacent from his. "Over there," he answered.

Vincenzo approached the *banco*, busy with clients queued up in front. He walked past the line of people and spoke without greeting, "Was Messer Alamanni here this morning?"

"Chi? Who?" asked the banker. The client he had been helping turned angrily to face the interrupter, before biting his tongue at seeing it was a priest.

"Alamanni...Andrea Alamanni, he is a banker for the Barzo house, no?" Vincenzo was impatient.

"No," answered the banker coolly, "I've never heard of him."

Vincenzo's blood ran cold. His face turned white, and he slowly backpedaled away from the *banco*. What had he done? In an instant he was petrified. This could not be happening! If it were true, if he had stood by and watched Lorenzo get hustled, he would never forgive himself. In his eagerness to be a priest again, to help a dying woman, he had let his guard down. It seemed so obvious now. The man had a balancing scale, yet he did not weigh the coins, as was the custom. He barely counted the stacks. How could he, Vincenzo, let this happen? This feeling was entirely new to him. Throughout his life, his first instinct had always been anger. Fear was different, and much worse.

LIBER SEXTUS

Libera nos a malo

I

Jacopo had woken early that morning. Claudia had just returned to bed from nursing the baby. They might have been able to afford a wet nurse, like most wealthy families had, but chose to use the money instead for Jacopo's business. Besides, Claudia preferred nursing the baby herself. She had spent most of her life having household tasks done for her by others and now took pride in doing them herself. She also loved the bond it gave her with the child.

When Claudia returned to bed, it woke Jacopo and he could not fall asleep again. Shortly after sunrise, he heard some shuffling in the kitchen and, soon after, the front door closing. He knew by the weight of the footsteps that it had been his father going out. Lodovico usually left the house much later, after having breakfast with the family. Why was he out so early? Where had he gone the night before?

He had grown accustomed to his father's peculiar and often secretive ways. As a child, it was all he had known of the man. But Lodovico had been different of late. He was now a loving grandfather, showing more tenderness around the child than he had ever shown to his own son. Jacopo, too, had opened up to his father recently. Their last confrontation had set his mind much at ease. All of his father's machinations, the apprenticeship and the marriage, had worked out for the best—he was a Calimala master, he was married to Claudia, he had a son. Claudia had even warmed up to her husband and all was going well.

But his father's secretive excursion the night before and his sneaking out early that morning combined to whisk Jacopo back instantly to suspicion. He was not sure why; he had no desire to change anything in his life, but something in his soul yearned for truth at any cost. He sat up quickly and slipped his shoes on. He stood and pulled his robe over the gown he had slept in. Claudia had fallen back asleep and he leaned over and kissed her gently on the cheek. Lodovichino slept in a bassinet opposite the bed. Jacopo walked over to it and looked down with pride and love at his son. He kissed his hand and touched the sleeping child's forehead. The baby opened his eyes and looked up at his father. Father and son, man and infant, held a common stare, eye to eye, for a few seconds, before the child closed his eyes again and fell back asleep.

Jacopo ran out of the house in time to see his father at the far end of the via, just before he turned off. He ran in that direction. As he approached the corner, he stopped and peeked his head around the building to see Lodovico at the end of that via, turning again. Jacopo once again ran up and peeked around the corner. This continued several times, until Jacopo watched Lodovico enter a small door on a tiny side alley. The door had a shingle hung next to it with "Notaio" written on it. It was a notary studio, but it was not Lodovico's. Jacopo remained hidden around a corner. He watched the small door, wondering what was going on inside. He stayed there an hour. A servant girl walked by with two empty water buckets; she paid no attention to Jacopo, and other than her the street was deserted.

Finally, a frail-looking, white-haired man wearing a short, crimson robe, a hat the same color, and green *calze* came down the alley from the opposite direction. He struggled with a crate that he carried out in front, and he kicked the door with one foot, so as not to let go. The door opened, and Lodovico pulled man and crate into the doorway. Lodovico looked up the alley. Jacopo took this opportunity to pull his head back around the corner, knowing his father would look down his direction also. After a moment, Jacopo peeked around the corner again. The door was closed. Jacopo stared at the door, wondering what he should do next.

He did not know what was going on inside, but he was pretty sure that if he asked his father about it later, he would not get the truth. He decided to act boldly. He was not a boy anymore. He was a man, he was a father, he was a Calimala master and saw no reason why he should be intimidated by his father anymore. He turned the corner and approached the small door. He knocked. Nobody answered, no one came to the door. He knocked again.

"Papà…sono io," he called out. "It's me."

After a few seconds, the door creaked open very slightly. Lodovico peaked out with one eye from behind the door.

"Jacopo! Che fai? What are you doing?"

"It's all right. Let me in. I'm here to help."

"Help?"

"Sì…help! I know what you're doing, and it's time I did my share to help our family also."

Lodovico opened the door fully and pulled his son in quickly. He again looked each way down the alley and then shut the door and latched it. The room was small and lit by just one candle sitting on a square table. At each side of the table was a grouping of perfectly stacked gold florins, thousands of them. The elderly man in banker's clothes sat silently. He looked up at the father and son, clearly nervous about the intrusion.

"What is this place?" asked Jacopo.

"It belonged to a notary who died last year. He had given me a key while I was drawing up some documents for him."

"Is that what I think it is?" Jacopo asked as he nodded his head toward the money on the table.

Lodovico thought for a second and then spoke clearly: "Sì."

Jacopo shook his head in amazement. "Genius."

Until then, Lodovico had not been sure how his son would react. He now relaxed and sat down.

"Ma…come? Jacopo asked. "But how?"

"Quite easily, it turns out. I had the cap and robe from my days at the Palazzo Vecchio. Our friend here had the calze. I drew up some phony Lettere di Cambio, and we put a scale in a crate. That was enough to convince your friends that he was a banker. They handed the money right over, without a thought."

"And now?"

"And now, half goes to our friend here and half goes to us."

"Genius," Jacopo responded. "How do you know such talented men?"

Lodovico looked down at the white-haired man, who was staring back at him intently. "It is useful to know such men. You should not associate with such men in public, of course, as their reputation is usually well established among men who know about these things. But when there is a need, I sneak off to the Osteria del Gallo and find who I am looking for."

The man shot Lodovico a deadly look. He did not want any details about him shared with this boy he did not know. "That's enough. I think we are through here," he said as he slid the florins on his end of the table into a large leather purse. "You have my cloak?"

Lodovico gave him the long brown cloak that he had brought for the man. The man slipped the crimson robe off and left it on the table with the hat. He draped the purse over his shoulder and then put the cloak on over it to conceal it.

"Addio," said the man as he left, closing the door hard behind him.

Lodovico said nothing as the man left. He thought that perhaps the man was right; he, in his satisfaction at having hatched such a brilliant plan and his pride in having impressed his son, probably did say too much.

Jacopo sat down in the chair the man had just abandoned. He felt like perhaps the situation had progressed beyond his control. He did not want to let the man leave, but could not think quickly enough to make him somehow stay. He was not happy at all. He now knew what he had at times suspected in the past. He knew that which he had chosen not to believe, that which he had fooled himself about. His father was a wretch.

It had been a self-defense mechanism. By choosing not to believe that his father was evil, then he, Jacopo, could be happy about the life his father had carved out for him. He now questioned everything his father had told him. Was he really innocent in Lorenzo's father's death? How had he convinced Domenico Chilli to allow Claudia to marry him? And there was more. Coraggiosi had accused his father, and now he was dead. Pierfrancesco had inherited five thousand florins, and he died just in time to have them go to Jacopo and Claudia. His father admitted to knowing some unsavory individuals. What were these men capable of? In that moment, in that small dark room, Jacopo struggled with the most important decision of his life. Would he go along with his father and have the life he always wanted, or would he do what was right?

"We're giving the money back," Jacopo began, his mask of acquiescence gone, his face was now determined and serious.

Lodovico was again surprised and snapped instantly to the defensive. "To the Simoni boy? Absolutely not. I thought you had grown up, but now I see you're still a child. Go home. I will do what needs to be done for this family."

"What family? The web of lies you have woven! You have not made a family; you have made a sham. I will take care of *my* family! We don't need you anymore."

"And where would you be without me? Not in a guild! Not married to a Chilli! Not with any money to start your business! I gave you those things. Don't you forget it."

"You stole those things. You lied, you stole, you killed! You wanted to restore honor to our name. You have forever dishonored it!" Jacopo was worked up, and shouting.

Lodovico laughed. "It is only dishonored if you don't keep your mouth shut. You'll get over your self-righteous indignation and see that I am right. You will go home and know that you have no choice but to keep silent. Do you want to be expelled from the guild? Do you want to lose our house? Do you want your wife to leave you? And how about the rent on your bottega and the rolls of wool you've already purchased…Do you want to go to debtor's prison? Your son will grow up with the same disgraced name."

Jacopo was getting angrier. His father's smug arrogance and condescending tone unleashed a lifetime's worth of resentment in his psyche.

Lodovico read his son's face and changed tactics. "Figlio mio," he started gently, "I know you are a better man than me. You prefer honesty. You can afford such pretensions because of the position I was able to attain for you. It is always easier to stand tall at the top of the ladder, but while climbing you are forced to cling on every rung anyway you can. Take this gift and build on it. Build a fortune your son can use to be a good and honest man! And don't look back."

The words sank in, and Jacopo thought about letting it happen, about keeping silent. He loved his life now. He did not want to lose it. But soon other thoughts crept in. He stood quickly and grabbed the crate the florins had been in from the floor. He slid the piles of coins off the edge of the table and into the crate and closed the lid.

"Che farai? What will you do?" Lodovico asked mockingly.

"What is right," Jacopo answered as he headed out the door.

"Then I shall do what is necessary," said Lodovico calmly.

Jacopo left without looking back.

II

Father Vincenzo had run back down the Via Calimaruzza and into the Piazza della Signoria, knowing he would not find the thief there but needing to try. He asked a few people if they had seen anyone in banker's clothes carrying a crate; nobody had remembered seeing such a man. He was sure the thief didn't really live on the Borgo dei Greci, but out of desperation Vincenzo checked there anyway. He looked for Lorenzo but did not see him either. He did not know what he would say to him. After a while, he decided to go back to the Palazzo Chilli; perhaps Lorenzo was there. The short walk back felt very long.

On the Via dei Calzaiuoli, not far from the Palazzo Chilli, Vincenzo saw Jacopo. His face was sullen, and his eyes looked as if he had been crying. In his hands was a small crate. Vincenzo recognized it. The priest's spirits instantly rose from the pits of hellish despair. The crate contained hope.

"Jacopo, che fai?"

"I need to see Lorenzo," Jacopo said gravely.

"What happened?"

"It was my father. It was all my father. He helped Coraggiosi kill Lorenzo's father, to get me the apprenticeship. He stole Lorenzo's money…It was all him."

Vincenzo was shocked, but at that moment, he had only one thought. "Is that Lorenzo's money?"

"It is half. An old crook from the Osteria del Gallo took the other half."

Father Vincenzo breathed the biggest sigh of relief he had ever exhaled in his life. Half the money was returned. They had a clue to find the other half. Lorenzo would have money to build his future on. The heavy crush of weight on Vincenzo's conscience eased.

"Grazie mille, a thousand thanks, Jacopo!"

Jacopo was worn. He had wandered the streets for some time in despair, and for a few moments contemplated returning to the notary shop and going along with his father's plan. But in the end, he chose to go the Palazzo Chilli. Now his eyes watered up. "Padre," he began and then paused. After a moment he went on, "I am so sorry. I didn't know what my father was doing. I don't deserve any of this…my guild membership, my wife, none of this."

Vincenzo grabbed Jacopo by the shoulders and looked him in the eye. "Figlio mio, God does not punish or reward us in this life. You are not your father. You are your own man. Your wife loves you; I can see that she does. You have a beautiful son. Do not think of these things as reward or punishment. Accept them as a gift from God, and show your gratitude by being a good man."

Jacopo sniffled and nodded.

"Come, let's find Lorenzo."

* *

Once inside the Palazzo Chilli, they learned that Lorenzo had returned, only to go out again shortly after. They recounted the morning's events to Adélaïde, whose heart swelled with sadness for Lorenzo. She was happy that half the money was returned, and she was proud of her son-in-law.

"Did he say where he was going?" Vincenzo asked her.

"Oui, he said he was going to visit his father. He was in such a happy mood."

"I will go to the Osteria del Gallo to look for this thief," Vincenzo told Jacopo, knowing there was precious little time to intercept the bandit. "You wait here for Lorenzo."

"Should we not report the theft to the Signoria or the constables?" asked Adélaïde.

"I would prefer to get the money back on our own. Denouncing Lodovico to the Signoria could only hurt Jacopo and Claudia and the baby. I don't think this man will return to the osteria anytime soon, but the *oste* may know who he is and where to find him."

"Then take this," Adélaïde said as she opened the cupboard and took out a small purse. She handed fifty florins to Father Vincenzo. "Osti tend to remember names and faces better when they have a florin or two in their hand."

"Grazie," said the priest, "a più tardi." He went out.

Adélaïde rubbed Jacopo's shoulder, "Are you all right, mon cher?"

"I still can't believe my father would do such a thing."

"Oui, it is hard to accept. He was very friendly this morning; I would have never thought."

"This morning?" asked Jacopo confounded.

"Oui, this morning, not long before you and Père Vincenzo arrived. Your father was here. He asked if I had seen you; then he asked for Lorenzo."

"Did he say why?"

"No, he just said he needed to see you and thought, for some reason, the two of you would be together."

"What did you tell him?"

"La vérité, that I had not seen you and that Lorenzo had gone to the cemetery to visit his father."

Jacopo remembered what his father had said before: "Then I shall do what is necessary." He was filled with dread. "Lorenzo is in danger," he said.

"O mon Dieu! I should not have said where Lorenzo was," cried Adélaïde.

"You could not have known that something was wrong. I need to take a horse!"

"Of course, take whichever one you want. Paolo will help you with the saddle."

III

The Osteria del Gallo was a small, one-room inn with two square tables and a fireplace. Any cooking was done over that fire, and there were two rooms above that were hardly ever occupied for more than an hour at a time. The only marking out front was a wooden shingle with a faded red *gallo*, or rooster, painted on it. The front door opened onto a narrow, unnamed alley off a small side via, and unless one knew it was there, it was difficult to find. Father Vincenzo knew where it was. One cannot tend to sinners for long without becoming familiar with the places they frequent.

It was still quite early in the day, and there were only two people in the osteria when Vincenzo entered. A thin, forty-something man knelt in front of the fireplace and scooped ashes into a bucket. He was balding, with just patches of long dark hair sprouting from his temples. At a table sat a woman in her early twenties. Her hair was long and brown, and she had it tied back in a ponytail. She wore a pleated light brown dress, cut low on her chest. Her face was youthful, but her eyes showed an age greater than their years. She ate a piece of bread and had a cup of wine in front of her. They both stared up in silence at the priest standing in the doorway. Vincenzo addressed the man.

"I am looking for an old man, white hair, the same height as me...quite frail looking. He's been known to hang around here."

The kneeling man stood and walked his bucket of ashes over to the door, leaving it on floor near the doorway. "Doesn't sound like anyone who comes here much. I get mostly boys...young tradesmen, looking to lose a few coins to wine and women."

Vincenzo knew the man was lying and he could feel himself getting angry, but for the moment, he kept his anger in check. "Could I get a cup of wine?" he asked as he sat down at the empty table, across the room from the woman.

The man brought him a cup, filled it, and then left the carafe on the table. Vincenzo took out ten florins and placed them on the table. He slid the pile of coins across, closer to the man.

The man picked up the coins and spoke with some hesitation, "Now that I think about it, there was an old man in here last night, not that I know his name, of course, but he looked something like the one you described. Is the man a friend of yours?"

"Sì, that is why I must find him."

"Well, as his friend, you should know he left without paying. I will speak no more of this man; it upsets my pride, as an honest businessman!"

Understanding perfectly, Vincenzo took ten more florins out and laid them on the table. "Per il suo conto, for his bill," he said.

"Un buon amico, indeed," the man said with a smile. "You must really need to find him."

"Sì."

"He went out early this morning...said he was leaving town. Lucca, I think, isn't that right, Giuseppina?"

The woman sat at her table, listening but saying nothing. The *oste* did not wait for an answer. "Sì, sì, it was definitely Lucca!"

"Lucca!" Vincenzo repeated.

"That's right. He set out on foot. If you are riding, you should be able to catch up with him." The man returned to the fireplace and began scooping ashes into another bucket.

The woman at the other table, Giuseppina, was looking intently at Father Vincenzo. The *oste* was looking at the ashes, and Vincenzo turned his gaze from him to her. When they made eye contact, the woman pointed both of her eyes in the direction of the upstairs, without making a sound, without moving her head.

"*Oste*, since I am here, I think I will use a room for a while," Vincenzo said to the man while looking at the woman.

"Wouldn't be the first priest to see the inside of a room here! Twenty lire for the room, twenty lire for the girl. Pay me before you go up," he answered without stopping his shoveling.

Vincenzo took out one florin and placed it on the table. It was about one hundred lire too much. "You can give me the change when I come down," he said dryly, annoyed that the man would even ask for money after the twenty florins he had just received, and for lies, no less. Vincenzo and Giuseppina went upstairs and closed the door.

Giuseppina sat on the bed. Vincenzo stood near the closed door.

"Tu o' saje ca' isso nun è a Luccà," she whispered in Neapolitan. "You know he is not in Lucca."

"Sì, o' so, I know," he answered in dialect as well.

"He was here, just a little while ago."

"Do you know his name?"

"I know they call him Pepe; that is all."

"Do you know where he went?"

"No. But he asked the *oste* where he could go to change florins to ducats."

"Venezia, Venice," said Vincenzo.

"Perhaps. The *oste* told him to go to the Mercato Nuovo, but he said he would rather not. I did not hear where the *oste* sent him to."

"Killu maledètt buciardo! Damned liar!" cursed the priest in hushed Neapolitan, a tongue much better suited for a raised voice.

"He is protecting him! Pepe comes here often and cuts him in on whatever he steals. The oste lets him hide out up here sometimes."

"Is there anything else?" he asked.

Giuseppina looked Vincenzo softly in the eye. She was actually quite beautiful, and sad. It was easy to see that she would soon look aged. Her life was not the kind to keep her looking young. "You tell me!" she answered as she patted the mattress beside her.

"Grazie for the information, but that is all I need."

Her face became serious. "You cannot go down yet!"

"I am in a hurry."

She jumped up on her feet a couple of inches, letting her backside slam down on the mattress. She then rocked her body to and fro, shaking the bed with her hands at the same time. She did this for half a minute or so, while Vincenzo watched saying nothing. At last, she stopped.

"What would happen if he thought we hadn't done it?" asked the priest kindly.

"He wouldn't feed my daughter. He says that my work pays for her food. She is three years old and stays at his house while I am here."

"Can't you leave?"

"I still owe him; the lodging and feeding of my baby costs two hundred lire a month. He pays me a hundred and eighty. I am behind by a couple of months. And where would I go? There is no honest work for a lupa!"

Vincenzo reached into his pocket and pulled out the remaining florins, twenty-nine of them. He placed them in her hand. "Pay your debts to him and take your daughter. Stay at another osteria for a few days. On the third Thursday of every month, *this* Thursday, an emissary from Rome visits the archbishop and then continues to Bologna and Ravenna. Take three or four florins and go to the Via Calimala; buy some new clothes. Thursday morning, go to see the archbishop. Tell him that your husband, a lawyer, has just written to you from Ravenna and asks that you and the child join him there. Make a twenty-florin donation to the Church and ask if you may accompany the emissary to Ravenna. When you arrive in Ravenna, go straight to the archbishop, Cardinale di Napoli. Tell him that Padre Vincenzo from Florence said that you could be *his* Carla. Use those words exactly. He will take you in as a housekeeper, with your child; I am sure of it."

Giuseppina had tears running down her cheeks; she could not speak for fear of blubbering too loudly and being heard downstairs. She tried to open her mouth but only cried harder. Between sobs she managed to whisper, "O' mie salvatore vienè ra Napule—my savior comes from Naples."

"Comm ognì cosà buona!" he said softly, with a smile. "Like all good things!"

* *

Having returned downstairs, Vincenzo now looked upon the *oste* with complete contempt, barely hidden. The man had finished sweeping out the fireplace and was wiping off the tables. The florin Vincenzo had left on the table was gone; no change was there. This angered the priest further, but he spoke in even tone.

"Grazie, Signor l'oste, that was what I needed."

"Prego, Padre, we are always at your disposal…There are prettier girls here at night!"

"And the hundred-lire change?"

"Sì, sì, the change. I was meaning to talk to you about that. You have caught me early in the day, and I do not have any change on hand. For a man of your obvious means, would it be a burden to you if I give you the hundred lire upon your next visit?"

This boiled Vincenzo's blood. This vulture of men, this liar, this thief. As he was about to lay a trap, Vincenzo fought the urge to wring the man's neck. "Certainly! After all, you have earned a loyal customer. It is a pity, of course, that I was not in time to catch my friend. Will you do me a favor?"

"Certo."

"If you should see him in the future, relay to him that his cousin has left five hundred florins in my care, an inheritance from his dead uncle."

"Assolutamente, Padre." The *oste* was shocked, but feebly tried to regain his composure. "Such a sad thing in life to lose the ones dear to us!"

"Indeed."

Giuseppina descended the stairs and entered the room, straightening her dress as if it had just been off. Her eyes were dry, but had the *oste* looked closely, signs of recent tears were there. He noticed nothing.

Vincenzo stepped to the door and then turned. "A presto, Signor l'oste…Monna Giuseppina, addio!"

"Buon giorno, Padre," said the *oste*. Giuseppina said nothing.

* *

Father Vincenzo waited around the corner, hidden behind the stanchion of a second-story overhang. The tiny alley where the Osteria del Gallo stood was a dead end, and Vincenzo knew the *oste* could only come this way. It was not even a quarter of an hour before the balding innkeeper stole down the via like a cat in the night. Vincenzo waited till he was a safe distance and then followed the man, via by via, corner by corner. He did not walk very far before knocking on a workshop door. It was a narrow, two-story building, and the front only had the stable doors leading to the shop. One-half of the door swung out, and Vincenzo could see the white haired man ushering in the *oste*.

If the man were really planning on going to Venice, this would be the only chance to get him. Moreover, there was now not much time—as soon as the *oste* told him about the phony inheritance, he would know someone was on his tail. There was no time to go and get help; Vincenzo needed to act now. He stared at the door, contemplating his course of action.

In his mind came the memory of his last confrontation with two thieves. He had come away from that unscathed, but he had turned into something he did not want to be. Was this situation different? The last time, his pride and his anger had led him to a fight to the death. He did not want such a thing to happen again. Nobody's life was yet in danger, only Lorenzo's money. True, the money represented a whole new life for Lorenzo, but he did have half of it back already. Twenty-five hundred florins would be a new life for him indeed. Still, Vincenzo was not about to just let them steal it. He decided to go in, but not as an enforcer of justice. He would go in as a priest.

Vincenzo approached the door and stood in front of it for a few moments. He decided not to knock. There might have been a back door or some other way of escaping, and he did not want to give them the opportunity to sneak away while he knocked on the front door. He could see from the space between the doors that they were latched on the inside. If he had had some kind of tool, he could have slipped it in and raised the latch. He decided to step aside and wait.

He stood next to the doorway with his back to the wall. It was not long before the latch sprung up. Out of the doorway stepped the white-haired man and the *oste*. The white-haired man had a large leather purse slung over his shoulder. They stepped out quickly without seeing the priest next to their door. As the *oste* pushed the door closed, Vincenzo was revealed standing behind it, and the priest put his hand on the door and pushed it all the way shut.

"Padre!" said the *oste*, surprised.

"Buon giorno, amici," replied Vincenzo, staring with contempt at the two thieves. He knew he could take them. He could strike the white-haired, elderly man and knock him out before the *oste* had a chance to do anything. Then, Vincenzo would only have to fight one man, a man he knew he could beat, even if he had a knife. But then what? Another fight to the death? And over money, no less! This was not the path he wanted. This was not the man, the priest, he wanted to be.

The two stood there, saying nothing, sizing Vincenzo up.

"Going somewhere, eh, *Signor Alamanni*?" Vincenzo snarled.

"What's it to you, Padre? Who is this boy to you?" answered the white-haired man.

"He is a boy who has already suffered too greatly in this life. He has lost his family. He has lost his home. He has even lost the woman who would be his bride. And now, thanks to you, he will lose his future...the only future his father was able to give him!"

"So you came to preach to us?"

"Sì, esatto. I've come to see if there is any good, any humanity left in your decrepit bones."

"Good! Huh," said the *oste*, "listen to him! Not half an hour ago he was praying to a puttana, and now he comes here to pray for our mercy!"

"Step aside, Padre," said the white-haired man.

"Non lo farò. I will not do it," the priest answered resolutely.

"I know who you are." The white-haired man squinted his eyes and spoke threateningly. "Giotti told me all about you. The archbishop removed you from San Felice...You are a sodomite! You defile your body in the worst of ways against God's laws, and you come here to preach to us. Step aside, or we will beat you down and tell the constables you attacked us. Who will they believe? The reputable owner of an osteria or a disgraced priest who tried to steal the *oste*'s money? For all we know, you sin with the young man! That is why you come for the money, to get it for him."

Vincenzo's anger grew. He hated being looked down upon, most of all by these two. All of his life he had fought an internal battle. There was always a struggle between what he was taught to be right and the feelings he had inside, the feelings for Matteo. At times he defended his love to Matteo, telling him that he could not believe God would make him this way only to tell him he was wrong. But underneath this self-justification was always the feeling that he was a sinner and the guilt of living outside of God's law. That was why he had been hesitant to go off with Matteo when he had first returned to Florence. Vincenzo had forgotten it at times, but the guilt was always there. Now he stood and took this recrimination from a thief; he no longer cared about the guilt. He was better than these men, and for the first time in his life, he truly believed it. His anger, for once, led to resolution instead of violence; it lead to self-confidence.

Vincenzo lunged forward and swiped the strap of the purse from the white-haired man's shoulder. He yanked it clear and turned to walk away. The old man lacked the strength to keep Vincenzo from tearing the purse from his grasp, and the priest was a few steps away with his back to the men before they could react.

The *oste* reached to his belt and drew a short dagger from his back. "Not so fast, Padre," he shouted menacingly.

Vincenzo turned his head and saw the knife. He then turned fully and looked the man dead in the eye. It was the time in the woods all over again. He knew he could take these two. He had no doubt. He also knew he would probably kill one or both of them in the process. The anger was there, again, but it was not his master. He had a greater master. He was sure of himself. He was sure he was right, and he feared nothing. He stared into the *oste*'s eyes with such intense ferocity that the man looked away, turning to the white-haired man as if to see if he would make the first move. Vincenzo knew he had him beat. He turned and walked away. They did not follow him.

* *

Father Vincenzo returned to the Palazzo Chilli with Lorenzo's money. He was happy to have gotten it back and pleased with himself for how he had handled the situation. Inside he found Adélaïde in the sitting room off of the entrance hall with Claudia. He entered and placed the purse on the floor.

"All of the money is returned," he said triumphantly. He looked at the two women, each wearing a gloomy and worried expression. "Che c'è, what is it?" he asked.

"Jacopo went out before I awoke this morning. I went to see him at the bottega, but he was not there. I was worried so I came here," said Claudia.

"Do not worry, he is here." Vincenzo looked around; he looked to Adélaïde and asked, "Dove andò? Where'd he go?"

"He went to warn Lorenzo," answered Adélaïde.

"Warn him from what?"

"Lodovico was here this morning. He knows Lorenzo went to the cemetery. Jacopo thinks something might happen to him." Adélaïde's voice and hands were shaky.

"I'll be right back." Vincenzo left the purse at the women's feet and ran out of the house. The triumph of just a few minutes before had fled and given way to new panic, and new rage. In his desperation to find Lorenzo's money, he had yet to fully digest Jacopo's confession. It had been Lodovico all along. It all made sense now. Vincenzo was angry with himself for not making the connection sooner. Lorenzo had told him that he was in line for the apprenticeship. Why hadn't he suspected Lodovico sooner?

He ran straight to the Giotti house and barged through the unlocked door. Lodovico was seated at the table. Maria stood in the corner of the room, holding the crying Lodovichino in her arms. Vincenzo charged the stunned Lodovico and tackled him off his chair. The two crashed to the ground. Maria screamed. The baby screamed louder.

Vincenzo punched Lodovico three times, hard in the face.

He had controlled his temper, before with the two thieves. He did not turn to violence to protect money. This was different. He was protecting Lorenzo. He landed all his punches cleanly, as he was kneeling on Lodovico's arms.

"Che feci tu?" he yelled. "What'd you do?"

Lodovico gurgled blood. Vincenzo stopped punching and grabbed Lodovico by the collar and lifted his head up. "Che feci?" he repeated.

There was no answer. Maria cried; Chino screamed in the same high, shrieking pitch, over and over again. Vincenzo stood, hovering over the bloody-faced Lodovico.

"Is it to happen at the cemetery?" he grunted down as he nudged the motionless body with his foot. After a few seconds, he kicked harder. "*Is it?*"

Lodovico nodded affirmatively as he coughed up more blood.

"Can it be called off?"

Lodovico shook his head no.

Vincenzo stepped back. Lodovichino cried. Maria looked down at her husband; she hugged her grandson and wept. Vincenzo was not happy with what he had just done, but he did not waste a moment dwelling on it. He ran back to the Palazzo Chilli.

Vincenzo was out of breath as he entered the sitting room again. "I need to take a horse," he announced, before stopping short. A young novice monk stood in the center of the room. Adélaïde and Claudia were crying.

"Ch'è successo?" he asked.

Adélaïde spoke through her tears. "We need to go to the Convent of San Marco."

"Perché?" asked the priest.

The novice monk turned to Vincenzo and spoke reverently. "Padre, I was told only to come and ask that a family representative accompany me for an urgent matter."

IV

It was a beautifully sunny April day. The sun was shining, not a cloud in the sky. The softest of breezes blew every so often, but the air was mild, and the streets of Florence were full of activity as people went about their business, hurrying to finish up before the midday break. Some shops had already begun to close up. The tall, brick bell tower of San Marco's cast a short shadow underneath the high sun, and the church's light stone soaked in the rays.

Across the courtyard, the tall, arched, timber doors of the cloister house swung in. Slowly, an old man made his way out, dragging a handcart behind. He walked hunched over, and his long, stringy, white hair obscured his face, with the exception of a hooked, protruding nose. His body creaked as he moved like a rusty iron gate. He seemed to hunch down lower under the bright sun as if repelling the light as he crossed the courtyard.

From the Via Larga, Father Vincenzo, Adélaïde, Claudia, and the novice monk crossed the Piazza San Marco. They approached the gate to the courtyard and had to step aside to allow the old man with the cart to pass. The man did not look up as he pulled his handcart through the gate, but Vincenzo felt a hint of familiarity. It took a second, but then he placed him: stringy hair, hooked nose, and handcart.

"Vi conosco! I know you!" said the priest.

Lucio did not look up; he just spoke under his breath in a mixture of Bolognese and Tuscan, "They all know me."

"What are you doing here?" asked Vincenzo.

Lucio let go of the handles and stood up straight; that is to say, he hunched less. He looked Father Vincenzo in the eye and said, "This is where I bring them."

"Bring whom?" Vincenzo was confused. The women just looked on.

"I morti fiorentini," the old man answered with a cryptic smirk. "The dead Florentines."

A chill went down Vincenzo's spine. He looked to Adélaïde and Claudia and saw the fear in their eyes. They spoke no more to the old man; all of them sidestepped the handcart and followed the novice to the door of the cloister house.

They stood in the hall and were soon met by the abbot. It was indeed the same abbot who had ushered the dead Simone back into his city of birth nine years earlier. His hair was completely gone now, and so were many of his teeth. He bowed his head before Adélaïde and kissed her hand.

"Signora Chilli, my apologies for the intrusion, but I felt this matter needed your immediate attention. I did not realize that you would come yourself; I expected a servant or a…oh I see you brought your priest! Buon giorno, Padre…"

"Vincenzo," answered Vincenzo.

"What is the urgent matter, Abate?" asked Adélaïde politely.

The abbot's expression turned grim. "You'd better follow me," he replied. He led them to the room with Fra Angelico's *Annunciation* fresco. Vincenzo was first struck by the beauty of the Archangel Gabriel and the Virgin Mary, and the serenity and surprise, two opposing emotions, brilliantly captured in the Virgin's face. He then noticed the table in the center of the room. On it a body lay face up, covered by a blanket.

"He had this folded in his pocket," said the abbot, holding the Lettera di Cambio up for them to see. "It has the Palazzo Chilli listed as his residence, so I sent the novice to your house. Do you know him?" he said as he pulled back the blanket to reveal the face.

Claudia was the first to let out a cry of despair. She put her hands over her face and wept. Adélaïde put her arms around her daughter and cried as well. Father Vincenzo stood stoically. He made no move and said nothing, a single tear running down his cheek.

The novice monk had remained in the hall and was about to return to his cell when he heard a horse gallop right up to the cloister door, followed by frantic banging. He opened the door to see a young man, bridle in hand, looking right past him.

"Are they here?" he asked hurriedly.

"La Signora Chilli, sì, they are in the *Annunciation* room," answered the novice. He led the young man into the dark, frescoed room.

Claudia was the first to notice him in the doorway, and she cried out as she ran across the room to embrace him.

"Lorenzo!" she cried. "Grazie a Dio, you are safe!"

Lorenzo hugged her tight, reveling in the embrace and not yet understanding the gravity of the moment. His eye then caught Jacopo's body lying on the table, and he began to weep. He hugged Claudia tighter and sobbed into her shoulder.

Adélaïde came over and kissed Lorenzo's cheeks. When Lorenzo was clear, Father Vincenzo gave him a hug.

"Ch'è successo?" asked the priest.

Lorenzo wiped his eyes on his sleeve and sniffled in deeply before speaking. "I went to the cemetery outside of the Porta San Gallo, to visit my father's grave. I was feeling happy and I wanted to tell my father I would be all right from now on. While I was there, Jacopo rode in on a horse and told me I was in grave danger. He said that his father had stolen my money, and now he was sending someone to kill me. He said that his father had helped Coraggiosi kill my father, and that he was sorry for what his father had done to me. I could not believe what I was hearing. I even showed him the Lettera di Cambio!" Lorenzo saw the abbot holding the lettera. "He forgot to give it back to me. He told me I should take the horse and get away quickly. I wanted him to get on the horse with me, but he said the horse would ride much faster carrying one. He told me to ride around to the east gate, as anyone following me would be coming from the Porta San Gallo. He said we would meet back at the palazzo."

Lorenzo walked over to the body. Jacopo's throat had been slit, and the front of his reddish-brown Calimala robe was wet with blood. He had marks on his nose and mouth. Someone had come up on him from behind, held his mouth, and slit his throat.

"Where was he found?" Lorenzo asked.

"In the cemetery," the abbot replied. "A drifter found him and brought him to us."

"Did he mention where in the cemetery?" pressed Lorenzo.

"Signore?" asked the abbot, confused.

"Did he mention a grave marker? Anything?"

"He did. He said the grave marker said Simoni," the abbot answered.

Lorenzo thought about Jacopo standing in front of Simone's grave, being mistaken for Lorenzo and massacred, and his heart was filled with sorrow for his friend's fate. Any heartache he had felt over the past year due to Jacopo melted away. Jacopo had saved his life.

He reached into the small pocket sewn to the waist of his trousers and pulled out his gold bezant. He looked down at the coin his father had preserved to secure his future. It was an award from il Magnifico, Simone had won it and then saved it for his son. Jacopo had returned it to Lorenzo, at great risk to himself. The worn yet shiny symbol of a lost empire represented the two men lost, the two men who had given their lives for him. He turned to Claudia, once again crying in her mother's arms, and felt deep sympathy for her and her child. He did not feel worthy of Jacopo's sacrifice.

Father Vincenzo put his arms around Lorenzo. A day so beautiful, which had started with such happiness, was now terribly sad.

V

Three weeks later, Lorenzo stood in the courtyard of the Palazzo Chilli. He and Claudia had accompanied Father Vincenzo to the stable to wish him farewell. The horse was packed with the few supplies Vincenzo was bringing.

"How long will it take?" Lorenzo asked.

"Two days, maybe three." Vincenzo strapped the last bag to the saddle and faced them. He looked at Lorenzo, at the man he had become, and felt proud. For the first time, he was confident of Lorenzo's future. He put his hand on Lorenzo's cheek. "Cresciuto!" he said. "Grown up!"

Lorenzo smiled. Vincenzo was his one constant in life. He felt grateful. "I wish you would stay!" he said.

Vincenzo shook his head gently, "Non posso, I cannot," he said tenderly. "I must be a priest again, and that door is closed to me here in Florence."

"You can stay with us," pleaded Lorenzo.

"You do not need me anymore. You have a new life. It is your time to live it. It is my time to move on."

Lorenzo leaned forward and hugged Vincenzo tightly. Many years of gratitude went into that hug. They held it for a while and then broke.

Vincenzo then kissed Claudia's hand.

"Buon viaggio, Padre, write to us from Ravenna!" she said sweetly.

Vincenzo mounted the horse and gave Lorenzo a final smile. He turned the horse around and trotted out the back gate. Horse and rider clopped down the via and faded.

"Addio, Virgilio, addio!" said Lorenzo softly as he watched his friend and mentor, his rock, fade away.

He turned around to face Claudia. The sunlight was arching up behind her, and the brilliant rays shining around her wavy hair looked like a halo. Lorenzo squinted to see her smile, and she held out her hand to him. He took it in his and moved closer. The shadows playing off the light behind her highlighted every beautiful curve of her face. He brought her into his arms and met his lips softly to hers.

Epilogus

"…Claudia Chilli, the daughter of a rich wool merchant. This painting was commissioned shortly after their marriage in the year…" she paused to remember how to say the year in German, "eintausendfünfhundert und zwölf, one thousand five hundred and twelve."

On their own, the tour group moved forward to the Michelangelo section. The tour guide was disappointed, as she had more to tell of this, one of her favorite paintings. A teenaged boy of the group remained, fixated on Granacci's portrait.

"Was waren ihre Namen, schon wieder?" he asked.

"Their names were Jacopo Giotti and his wife, Claudia Chilli," answered the guide, basking in the interest. "They were not married for very long, as Jacopo died young. Their son, Chino Giotti, became the heir to the Chilli fortune and grew to become one of the richest and most powerful men in Florence in the mid fifteen hundreds."

"It is sad he died so young," answered the boy.

"Ja, very sad. Claudia, however, remarried. I forget her second husband's name, but they lived together for many years at the Palazzo Chilli. The palazzo is a museum now, with a beautiful statue garden in the courtyard. She had three daughters with her second husband."

"Her eyes are very interesting," added the boy. "I cannot tell if she is sad here."

"They, to me, are the most interesting part of the painting. It is not believed that her first marriage was a happy marriage. There was actually quite a scandal after the death of Jacopo. His own father was implicated in the murder and was put on trial for that and other crimes. He was executed six months after his son's death."

"Ich liebe die italienische Renaissance—I love the Italian Renaissance," said the boy sarcastically.

The tour guide again wiped the sweat off of her forehead with the back of her hand. Tourists jostled around her to get to

Michelangelo, but she stared up into Claudia's eyes. Without noticing that the boy had walked away, she went on. "To me, her eyes tell a story. A story of love, of pain, and of rebirth. It is a timeless love. Here it is five hundred years later, and she is just as beautiful."